THE LAND
BEYOND
THE RIVER

BOOKS BY JESSE STUART

Man with a Bull-tongue Plow
Head O' W-Hollow
Trees of Heaven
Men of the Mountains
Taps for Private Tussie
Mongrel Mettle
Album of Destiny
Foretaste of Glory
Tales from the Plum Grove Hills
The Thread That Runs So True
Hie to the Hunters
Clearing in the Sky
Kentucky Is My Land
The Good Spirit of Laurel Ridge
The Year of My Rebirth
Plowshare in Heaven
God's Oddling
Hold April
A Jesse Stuart Reader
Save Every Lamb
Daughter of the Legend
My Land Has a Voice
Mr. Gallion's School
Come Gentle Spring
Come Back to the Farm
Dawn of Remembered Spring
Beyond Dark Hills

For Boys and Girls
Penny's Worth of Character
The Beatinest Boy
Red Mule
The Rightful Owner
Andy Finds a Way
Old Ben

THE LAND BEYOND THE RIVER

by

JESSE STUART

MCGRAW-HILL BOOK COMPANY
New York   St. Louis   San Francisco
Düsseldorf   London   Mexico   Sydney   Toronto

This book is dedicated to Erik,
our grandson

123456789BPBP79876543

Library of Congress Cataloging in Publication Data
Stuart, Jesse, date
The land beyond the river.
I. Title.
PZ3.S9306Lan   813'.5'2   72-7287
ISBN 0-07-062241-8

We waited for Poppie to return from Ohio where he had gone to find fame and fortune. Not so much fame as fortune. And fortune didn't mean big riches for us as much as it meant that for a lot of people. Fortune for us meant making a better living.

"I have to give up here in my native state of Kentucky," Poppie had said. "I think we'd better cross that Ohio River like so many others have done. Look at them now! Many of them own their own farms. They don't rent any longer like we've had to rent here on Lower Bruin. We've gone from farm to farm—eight farms since we've been married—and I can hardly keep the starvation dog from our door. So, I'm off to Ohio to look around for a farm. I want Social Security or welfare and old-age pensions which are all better in that wonderful state, so Uncle Dick told me. You know he's been in Ohio many, many years now. He said Ohio was not only a nice place for young couples who wanted to work, to find work, but it was a good place for old people to live in their twilight years and to receive the proper benefits that mankind deserves—right up until their death—with all this free medicine and free hospitalization." But Poppie said, last thing before he went to Ohio, his Old Family Cemetery, the Perkins' Cemetery on Lower Bruin, was where he wanted to be buried when his life's trials and tribulations were over.

My Poppie is about six feet tall with broad shoulders, big strong arms and thick hands. He can sink a double-butted ax up to the handle of a green oak every time he strikes a lick. Poppie has a nice pair of blue eyes, a nose not much bigger than his thumb in the middle of his face, which is as round as a plate. He has heavy hair as brown as October oak leaves, which he parts on the side when he bothers to comb it. He wears overalls, a blue workshirt, a jumper and brogan shoes six days a week. But when he fixes up on Sundays for the Freewill Baptist Church, he can, as Mommie says, get real "doody" and look real sharp. He's got one blue serge double-breasted suit and a pair of Sunday shoes. He's got a half-dozen neckties and a change of white shirts.

Now let me tell you about my mother. Mommie is a little woman and every time I think of her I think about a piece I read in my schoolbook about a wee elf sitting under a toadstool. Only my mother is a woman wee-elf. She's about half the size of Poppie. Maybe she's not half as large. Because Poppie is about two hundred twenty pounds. Soaking wet with her clothes on, Mommie won't weigh over a hundred pounds. But to see her and hear her talk you'd think she weighed a thousand pounds! My little Mommie runs the place. Her real name is Sylvia. Poppie calls her Sil. Poppie's real name is Gilbert—Gilbert Perkins, but Mommie calls him Gil. So we hear Gil and Sil all the time around our house. The two names rhyme, don't they?

Mommie and Poppie never have had a quarrel. They get along fine. Poppie leaves a lot of our bringing up to Mommie. As small as she is, when she says "scat," we jump. Mommie might be small but she's out of what everybody on Lower Bruin says "rough stuff." This means both her pappy's and mammy's families.

Mommie was a Simpson. Her mother was a Cornett. Talk about two family names! When they met and mingled they produced something that Ohio needed. A woman with the stuff in her, like a good bluetick fox hound's leaving Kentucky, was Ohio's gain. Her people were more rugged than Poppie's people. Our great-grandparents, Ike and Ethel Simpson, at eighty-eight and eighty-six were living on relief grub and old-age pensions, but Grandaddy could outrun his grandsons and great-grandsons to the hilltops three nights a week with his six hounds when we went fox hunting. Fox hunting and listening to his hounds, I've heard him say many a time, was the sweetest music under Heaven. He said that he and his good wife Ethel would die on Lower

Bruin and be planted there to rest eternally. He'd never approve of my mother's and father's going to Ohio to find something better. This was not his nature. He was a stay-putter and not a venturesome man. He'd never cross the Ohio River and go North regardless of how much bigger the "commodities" were in Ohio and how much bigger the old-age pensions. As he said, they'd take smaller ones and live on Lower Bruin where they were born, had lived all their lives and raised a family of twelve.

Grandpa Solomon (Sol) Perkins and Grandma Aremitha had once talked of leaving Lower Bruin, after the timber was all cut and the topsoil too worn to produce as it had once done. But their children were now the ones leaving, mostly to Ohio, but to Indiana and Michigan too. Mary had even gone to California. When Poppie went to Ohio, he was going straight to Uncle Richard Perkins' place to get his help to find a farm for us to rent.

Poppie's people, too, lived on Lower Bruin. They had been born there for generations, farmed the steep hills, fox hunted for their pleasure and gone to the same little Free-will Baptist Church. They were all Freewillers! And when they departed this world, they were joined in the end for all eternity in the Perkins' Family Cemetery.

Grandpa Perkins had been considered a very nervous and strange man who believed in ghosts and the spirits of his dead returning from the Perkins' Family Cemetery and warning the living Perkinses about things to come. Grandpa Sol had told us about different ones of our ancestors coming back—how they looked and what they told him. And I'm telling you if you ever heard Grandpa Solomon talk, he was so convincing you might even believe him.

But it was Grandma Aremitha Perkins, who was a Floyd, that brought the nervousness to the Perkinses, so Poppie said—I never knew her. Her grandchildren called her Grandma Rim. She always carried a little rag in her hand which she squeezed. It was a little dirty rag but it was always in Grandma Rim's hands. She went about among her children and her neighbors squeezing this little rag.

And Grandma Rim had a green oak stump in her yard which was hollowed out, and sap from the green stump flowed into it. Grandma Rim thought this "oak-ooze," which she called it, had healing properties, and she took a swallow of this three times a day before her meals. But his mother was the one, so Poppie said, who gave him and members of his family their nervousness.

I won't tell you about all of their eleven children—my uncles and aunts. If I did, it would be a book. And I can't tell a book story. But I will tell you about three of this family, two of my uncles and one aunt.

Aunt Martha was really something. As a young woman, when Grandpa Solomon Perkins had a little country store and the post office, Aunt Martha got jealous of some of the girls on Lower Bruin. So she watched the letters going through the post office. She saw to it that the young men she would have liked to have dated, who wrote letters to young women she didn't·like, never got their letters delivered. She almost got into some serious trouble. But she missed it. She took all these letters and hid them under a stump in the corn field. Later in the spring when William Crump was plowing, his plow hit the stump where all these love letters were hidden, and imagine what young William thought when all these love letters came out. He spent a couple of days reading letters. He didn't know how they got there. And he didn't tell anybody about reading all these love letters from the young men of Lower Bruin to the young women of Lower Bruin until nearly a year later. I've heard a lot about them letters. But to try to explain them and tell about them would be another book.

Well, Aunt Martha settled down when she married my Great-uncle Red Doore. But Aunt Martha and Uncle Red were always very nervous, like Poppie. Aunt Martha and Uncle Red had seven children, and they were all nervous and Poppie had little to do with these first cousins. As Poppie always said, he had too many relatives to keep up with and the only ones of his or Mommie's relatives he paid any mind to had to be of extreme closeness and special choosing. And I remember when his and Mommie's cousins, nieces and nephews went to Ohio, Indiana and Michigan by the dozens, Poppie always said: "Let them be lost from the Tribes forever! Who cares? There are plenty left."

Poppie's Uncle Beckham Perkins, my great-uncle, had two sons, Poppie's first cousins, Melbourne (we called him Mel) and Claybourne (we called him Clay). All the other nine children had flown Uncle Beck's and Aunt Parsie's nest —most had gone to Ohio but Mel and Clay had never married—well, Poppie said both were married to the bottle. They'd work a few days for a farmer—long enough to get money to buy moonshine hooch—and they'd go back home and beat their father and mother, Great-uncle Beck and Great-aunt Parsie. The law would arrest and jail them until they got sobered again. Poppie hired them to help us with the tobacco a few times. Then they tried that drinking on Poppie. And in the night, Cousin Mel tried to open Sister Cassie-Belle's window from the outside and get into her room. Poppie shot out of the bed like a bullet and he was on him in a minute and nearly beat him to death.

Poppie had me walk that night from Lower Bruin to Townold, to the first phone where I could call the sheriff to come and get both his cousins. He had Clay and Mel put in the cooler for four months. By the time they got out, they were good and sober and knew how to act. But Poppie never let them work for him again. He said they were his people, his own flesh-and-blood first cousins, but they were dangerous. He often wished they'd go to Ohio so his Uncle Beck and Aunt Parsie would have some peace.

Now I'll say this for Uncle Dick and Aunt Susie Perkins. Uncle Dick had the good sense to leave for Ohio thirty years ago. And he owns a big farm, a big truck and automobile, and all kinds of farm equipment. We know he has amounted to much in his lifetime. All the Perkinses were Republicans and Uncle Dick is one of them red-hot Republicans. I mean he's a hot one. When he first moved over in Ohio near Agrillo, county seat of Landsdowne County, which is a red-hot Republican county, he stepped right into getting a truck-driving job on the Ohio State Highway. And since Great-uncle Dick and Great-aunt Susie didn't have any children—they're the only ones that didn't breed —they've come up in the world. He has money in Agrillo's First National Bank. Yes, Uncle Dick and Aunt Susie has got along fine in Ohio, and Poppie hoped Uncle Dick and Aunt

Susie might help him to get to Ohio where he could be more successful.

Now, I had better tell you a little about myself. I am Poppie's and Mommie's number-two boy. I am Pedike Perkins. I am not a big square-shouldered young man like Poppie. But I do take more after Poppie's people. I'm a big surprise when it comes to work. You should see me getting around. I am fast on foot. I move. And I can work. I can be everywhere at one time. If Ohio needed a young man to do farm chores, I could do them.

About Mommie's and Poppie's number-one boy. This is sad. He is no longer with us. He is planted in the Perkins' Family Graveyard here on Lower Bruin. We take flowers there on each Decoration Day but we've not got the sprouts cut among the graves. Poppie said if we didn't get it done real soon, we'd leave a young forest in the Perkins' Family Graveyard. I'd say it would be a small forest, though—not more than an acre.

My number-one brother was named Percival Perkins. I don't know where they got the name but this doesn't matter. There's not another name like it in Mommie's or Poppie's families. Mommie and Poppie called their number-one boy "Little Pearse." He left this world at six and is planted in the Lower Bruin earth but he is very much alive to Poppie and Mommie and to all my brothers and sisters. And there are ten of us living. But "Little Pearse" is gone. And Mommie is expecting her eleventh. She hopes this one will be born in Ohio. And just as soon as this one is born, her first born in Ohio, either Baby Brother's or Baby Sister's name will change and go back to Dickie, or Faith, the names Poppie and Mommie gave them. And the new baby, a him or a her, if he or she lives, will be called Baby Brother or Baby Sister. This is the way it works in our family.

I can remember when Timmie was called Little Baby Brother and Maryann was called Little Baby Sister. I was pretty small myself then but I remember. You'd be surprised how well I remember. I'm number-two boy but I've really had to take the place of number-one boy—"Little Pearse"—who sleeps under the sprouts at the Perkins' Family Graveyard with a flat fieldstone at his head with his name, dates of birth and death and *At Rest In Heaven* cut on the stone by Poppie with a coal chisel and hatchet. I was with Poppie when he chiseled his name and dates. "Only six years alive," Poppie sighed. And he broke down and cried more then than Baby Sister or Baby Brother had ever cried at one spell.

Sister Cassie-Belle is the number-one girl in our family. She's a year older than I am and awfully good in high school. She and I ride a school bus to Wonder High School and she leads her class. She is seventeen and I am sixteen.

Sister Tishie, next to me and only eleven months younger, was Mommie's and Poppie's number-two girl. And brother Timmie was a full year younger than Sister Tishie.

Maryann was Mommie's and Poppie's number-three girl. She was eighteen months younger than brother Timmie. Mommie always called on numbers one, two and three girls and numbers two and three boys to help her in a pinch. This was the way it was in our family. The older ones all the way down the line looked out for the younger ones.

"It will give you, Cassie-Belle, and Tishie, good training when you marry and have a home some day and replenish the earth," I heard Mommie once say to my sisters. "It is good training for you to diaper and feed babies. You will know about them when you grow up."

But that was once when Cassie-Belle talked back to Mommie.

"Since books come easy for me and since I like to go to school, I may go on and finish high school and college and be a teacher. Mommie, I may never marry. And if I do, I think I'll wait to be older so I won't replenish the earth!"

This was some different thinking coming from one of Poppie's and Mommie's children.

"You could do a lot worse than not marry and replenish the earth as The Word tells you," Mommie told Cassie-Belle very quickly.

Mommie wouldn't take any back-sass from any of us. As I have told you, when she said "scatt" to us, we jumped. And this was one time Mommie didn't like what Cassie-Belle had said to her.

Poppie and Mommie believed in The Word and the Free-will Baptist Church. They followed The Word. They believed they should have children and more children and replenish the earth. Mommie even kept a list of our names, beginning with "Little Pearse" at the top—all the way down to Baby Brother Dickie and Baby Sister Faith, written in her own handwriting and tacked on the wall by the cookstove in our kitchen in Lower Bruin:

1. "Little Pearse," First Son
2. Cassie-Belle, First Daughter
3. Pedike, Second Son
4. Tishie, Second Daughter
5. Timmie, Third Son
6. Maryann, Third Daughter

Then she listed the Little Ones:

7. Martha
8. Edward, Little Eddie
9. Susie, Little Susie
10. Richard, Little Dickie, Baby Brother
11. Faith, Little Faith, Baby Sister

When our neighbors and kinfolks on Lower Bruin asked Mommie why she kept this list she would always say: "I've got too many names to remember. I forget their names. I want to be able to call out my youngins' names at one time, know where they are, and what they're doing. I want to be the boss. And I am the boss!"

And Mommie was the boss on Lower Bruin as she would be the boss in Ohio. She would be the boss wherever we went. As a lot of people have said—I've heard them talk—you really know a mountain woman from Appalachia. Mommie might be that little woman-elf under the toadstool, but she was powerful when she said "scat." She could almost make big, powerful Poppie jump!

When the big farm truck pulled up to our house at about six o'clock on that May evening, all ten of us ran outside with Mommie to meet it. It was Uncle Dick Perkins' big farm truck. But Poppie's Uncle Dick and my Great-uncle Dick wasn't at the wheel. Boswell (and Poppie called him Cousin Bos) Auxier was at the wheel.

"What's the news, Gil?" Mommie asked.

"It's great news, Sil," he said. "I believe Ohio belongs to us. And we are headed for that Promised Land. Just as much as the Hebrew Children of Egypt were headed for the Promised Land when God parted the Red Sea and Moses led them to the Promised Land. This truck is here to take us to the Promised Land. Sil, I've got the contract here in my pocket! You will be surprised! Wait until you hear the many bargains we got. Thanks to Uncle Dick!"

I think Uncle Dick got an eyeful of Mommie's and Poppie's children. He looked at all ten of us. Two were in Mommie's arms. And "Little Pearse" was not with us. When poor old Great-uncle Dick and Great-aunt Susie wanted offspring, they were never fortunate to have them. I'd heard Mommie and Poppie talk evenings how wonderful the Baptist Lord had been with them to let them have offspring to replenish the earth, and how unfortunate Uncle Dick and Aunt Susie were not to have them. They wondered if Uncle Dick and Aunt Susie had been visited by the sins of the fathers of the tenth generation. This can happen, you know, if you believe The Word as Poppie and Mommie believe it. Each evening in our home they read and studied

The Word and talked about it—and one thing was to marry and replenish the earth. We were Freewiller Baptists and The Word was always with us in our home. We lived by The Word and by our textbooks, which were furnished free by the state. These were the only books we had in our house. Poppie and Mommie had warned us many times about sinful books. They warned us about novels, which were to them sinful books, but they had never read one.

"Sil, can you find beds for Uncle Dick and Cousin Bos tonight?" Poppie asked.

"Yes, I can, Gil, if it means that you and I sleep on the floor," Mommie said. "It is such great news that we are going to Ohio—the way so many of our people have gone—to that Promised Land beyond the Ohio River to the North!"

When Poppie got out of the big truck, we swarmed around him. This time it wasn't like honeybees swarm around the Queen Bee—we swarmed around Poppie the King Bee. Mommie, our Queen Bee, put her arms around his neck and kissed and hugged him. Three days and nights she'd been away from Poppie and she was really glad to see him. She hugged him in close—I'd say tummy to tummy—while Uncle Dick and Cousin Bos Auxier looked on.

Poppie's Cousin Bos Auxier and his wife Faith who lived in Ohio had only one son, Boswell, Jr., better known as Buster Boy. We had heard "Buster Boy" Auxier, our second cousin, was not exactly a prominent citizen of Ohio. He had been married and divorced three times before he was twenty-nine. He really liked drinking more than girls. But one nice thing was all our people in Ohio, especially in Landsdowne County, voted the Republican ticket. We had voted it in Kentucky and we didn't change in Ohio. It was as much a part of us as our Freewiller Baptist religion. I wondered if we would find our church and our faith in Ohio.

When Poppie and Mommie finally got parted from kissing, hugging and squeezing as if they'd not seen each other in over a year, they held hands. While Mommie still held one baby in her arms and Cassie-Belle held another, Poppie said: "Uncle Dick and Cousin Bos, come in our home. As humble as it is you are welcomed to our grub and our roof. And after yesterday and today, how I love both of you! How can I ever thank you enough!"

"You really mean we're going to Ohio, Gil?" Mommie said.

"Yes, I mean we're going tomorrow, Sil," Poppie said.

"I helped arrange the contract," Uncle Dick Perkins said.

Great-uncle Dick Perkins was a big two-hundred-forty-pound man, a little nervous, like all the Perkinses. As Poppie and Mommie had so often said, it was a shame that the stock of such a big fine-looking man as Uncle Dick would die and be wasted on the Ohio wind. If Uncle Dick had married some other woman and Aunt Susie had married some other man, they could have replenished the earth in accordance with The Word.

All fourteen of us went into our little house. Not all walked. Two toddled in and two had to be carried.

And when we went inside the house we had rented from Fred Thombs, which had once been the old Lower Bruin school with two rooms—now with two lean-tos built on—I watched Uncle Dick's and Cousin Bos' eyes when they looked at our walls that Mommie had papered with newspapers. We were really poor people on Lower Bruin in Greenwood County, Kentucky, and in America.

"Welcome, Uncle Dick and Cousin Bos," Poppie said. "Cousin Bos has fetched Uncle Dick's big truck to haul all our house plunder and every member of this family but "Little Pearse" to Ohio tomorrow. We have to get packed tonight. Our house is waiting. Sil, after we have a little supper, Uncle Dick and I will explain this contract I have here in my pocket."

"Then I'll get us a dab of supper," Mommie said. "I want to hear this new contract."

"I'll tell you before you put a bite on the table for us: Uncle Dick, Cousin Bos and I are hungry men," Poppie said. "It's been a long time since we had a bite at noontime with Uncle Dick."

"Now, the reason I've come along, Sil, is to help load and drive the truck," Poppie's Cousin Bos said. "You know your Uncle Dick has had trouble with his ticker! He's worked like a mule in Ohio, has voted for our party and he has prospered. You ought to see the house, barns and farm machinery Uncle Dick has. He has plenty. I don't know how much. But he has prospered."

"Yes, they used to call me a Kentucky Briar when I first went to Landsdowne County," Uncle Dick said. "But now when I walk into First National Bank, Jake Eversole, banker there, tips his hat to me. I'll say this for myself. Ohio people like money. When a man works hard, votes right and prospers, he becomes a part. I'm really a citizen in Landsdowne County. Nephew Gil, you'll find this out when you move there. You and Sil will be proud of your uncle. You'll never hear me called a Kentucky Briar any more. I'm called Mr. Richard Perkins. People respect me too much to call me Dick. You know that's the name I went by on Lower Bruin."

"I say your Uncle Dick Perkins has done well," Poppie's Cousin Bos Auxier said. "I wish I could say I'd done half as well as he has! But we've not been in Ohio but twelve years. And Faith and I are still hoping for fortune. We work hard and we vote right! I know one thing, to look at this sorry land on Lower Bruin makes me sick. It's no place here for a man! I wish we had left here long ago! We missed a fortune by not leaving earlier."

"But you have to manage well and you've got to know the right people, Bos, I keep telling you," Uncle Dick said. "You got to play it smart!"

"Cassie-Belle, you can help me put a little bite on the table," Mommie said. "Tishie, you take care of Baby Brother. Maryann, take care of Baby Sister. Timmie, you fire the cookstove!"

Timmie, the number-three boy in our family, took off running to fire the stove. And why shouldn't he? I, Pedike, number-two boy, had cut dry dead poles upon the hill and dragged them in and chopped them into stovewood with a double-butted ax.

Great-uncle Dick pulled a long cigar from his inside coat pocket.

"Maybe not good for my ticker but Old Doc Zimmerman lets me smoke about a half dozen per day," he said. "Old

Doc said he didn't want to take all my enjoys from me. He said no more a box of cigars a day for me. He said if I's a tempted man, he'd rather I'd lean a little heavier on the bottle. But I'm afraid of that stuff a-gettin' a hold on me— whether White Mul in Lower Bruin like I ust to drink here, or that good store-bought kind in Ohio. I'll say it shore will get a holt on a man. But I do like my nip before bedtime."

"Yep, I'm afraid of it too," Cousin Bos said as he took a pack of Honest John scrap-chewing tobacco from his coat pocket and crammed about a third of the sack into his mouth. "When I was a young man here on Lower Bruin I got on a few rip-snorters. But to see what that stuff's done to Buster Boy is enough for me! After all, Buster Boy is our only one. He's our only chance to carry our name to re-plenish the earth and because of that damned drinking he never begot a baby with one of his three wives. I don't know why. Nothing like that ever happened in my family before. The men are all good studs! And our women take good to stud men and in a short time they have them tamed!"

"Yes, Cousin Bos, I've heard a lot about your Buster Boy, who is my blood-kin second cousin," Poppie said in his slow voice.

Now Poppie really didn't say more because he couldn't say what he thought when Cousin Bos, the little driver of a big truck, had come to take us to Ohio. But I'd heard Poppie and Mommie discuss Cousin Buster Boy. They said Cousins Faith and Bos didn't make him jump when he was a little boy because they had only one and they let him get out of control. Poppie and Mommie also said one bird in the nest was better than an egg that wouldn't hatch. They talked this before us in front of the fire on winter evenings. They wanted us to hear. They said twelve birds or even more in the nest was better than one bird or twelve rotten eggs in the nest. And they wondered, I heard them almost whisper, if their Cousins Bos and Faith had wanted more than Buster Boy. They wondered if they had tried and failed to replen-ish the earth as the Master had intended or if they had done a lot of sinning.

"Our Buster Boy weighs exactly one hundred pounds

more than I do," Cousin Bos said. "He's a big fine-looking man. And I think he has been a good stud among women—but he can't beget and he can't get along with people. He's got us worried. He's back home with us now. His spirit is low!"

"You mean, Cousin Bos, you weigh one hundred and twenty pounds?" Poppie said.

"That's right," Cousin Bos said. "And I can work with any man. I don't care who he is! I can use about any kind of machinery made for a farm and I can repair it!"

"Yes, Bos, you're the workingest handiest man I know," Uncle Dick said. "Your loss to Lower Bruin and Kentucky is Landsdowne County, Ohio's, gain."

"I don't mean to be bragging for I love my wife Faith, but I don't know how many older big women have taken to me," Cousin Bos said. "So many it's made my old lady Faith a little jealous. I just about have to push them off with a stick about the size of a broomhandle, only I don't carry that stick. I'm just talking."

Well, I never heard anybody laugh like Poppie! He went over double in his chair laughing.

"Funniest thing I ever heard in my life, Cousin Bos," Poppie said. "I didn't know you was such a great lover among the wimmen folks!"

And Poppie began to laugh again. And I laughed too! And Uncle Dick looked up at our newspapered ceiling and blew a blue cloud of strong-smelling cigar smoke.

"I'm not a great lover, Cousin Gil," Cousin Bos said. "It's in The Word a man shall take unto himself one wife until death they do part. I took Faith and she took me. And she is my wife. I want no other. I've had no other. I've just said big women over there in Landsdowne County, Ohio—women Faith's and my age, no young things, and married with families and husbands—I'd say about a half dozen have got after me. It's hard to dodge 'em! And here our big two-hundred-twenty-pound Buster Boy has all kinds of trouble! It's hard to figure out!"

Poppie had never been more tickled in his life. He began laughing again, while Cousin Bos, who had been holding his big chew of tobacco in his mouth, got up and went to the door, opened it and spat out into the yard. There were no spittoons in our house. Poppie doesn't chew. He smokes cigarettes. And Mommie doesn't smoke at all. She has always said she's been too busy with us to smoke. But Uncle Dick used Poppie's ashtray, which was half of a gourd we raised in the garden, to dump the ashes in from his cigar.

"I'll say this, Gil," Uncle Dick said. "Your Cousin Bos is telling you the truth about women flocking after him. They're all big women. He didn't tell all, either. He's got a dozen or so real mushy love letters from some of the gals but they've never signed their names. Bos and Faith know who they are. At least they think they do."

This time Poppie let out a big whoop when he laughed, and slapped his knees and thighs with his big hands.

"Letters, huh?" Poppie shouted until Mommie came to the door, opened it and looked in. Then Mommie laughed because Poppie was laughing so and closed the door and went back into the kitchen. Mommie was getting the vittals cooked and put on the table. Every time we had company we had to have two sittings: first for guests and parents—and a few older children, and second for the little ones and the babies, with my sisters' and Mommie's help.

After hearing all this about old women's taking to Little Cousin Bos, honest, I had to wonder why. He was a little man as compared to Poppie and Uncle Dick, who were big, broad-shouldered, over two hundred pounders. He had the color of the good corn field earth in his face. Not too dark—his earthy-colored skin—but a rich color. Maybe his face coloring was made by the sun and wind. His nose was a little long and hooked like a hawk's beak. And he had glassy-blue eyes bright as a polished silver dollar that were as keen and sharp as briar points. He looked at everybody and everything in front of him at the same time.

3 Mommie came, opened the door and stood before us.

"The little bite is ready," she said.

"I'm ready for it, Sil," Poppie said as he got up to go. "Uncle Dick and Cousin Bos are ready for it, too. I'm sure they are mighty hungry."

"Yes, it's been a long time since I've eaten grub from Lower Bruin," Uncle Dick said. "I grew to rugged manhood strong as a young bull on the grub raised from this valley and its hillslopes."

"Well, I have to say I come up on it too," Cousin Bos said. "And it's been a long time since I had any of this old Lower Bruin grub under my belt."

When we walked into the kitchen, Mommie showed Uncle Dick where his place was. She put him at the head of the table. Poppie sat at his place at the other end of the table. Mommie and Cassie-Belle sat on the side of the table, next to the kitchen stove where they could get up and run to bring more vittals to the three hungry men.

Cousin Bos and I sat on the other side of the table opposite the stove. And between us was a plate, a knife, fork and spoon. And no one sat there. I knew there would be questions about this, for Cousin Bos' eagle eyes looked it over.

"We don't say Grace to the Lord but we are thankful Freewill Baptists for what we have," Poppie said. "Now you begin to fight your face! You see what is before you!"

"Yes, a mighty full table," Cousin Bos said. "I'll help myself to some of this beef. Did you kill a beef this year, Gil?"

"No, we didn't, Bos, not this year," Poppie spoke softly.

Now Poppie squared around at his end of the table and sat the way he always sat. It took a little more space for Poppie at the table than it did two others. Mommie had always talked to him about his eating manners. She always said that was the reason she hated to have guests.

"This is awful good pork," Uncle Dick said. "And I never tasted better taters! Good old taters out of the Lower Bruin earth! I remember how Pap used to raise them—and I did too before I left here. In the wintertime we buried our taters with oak leaves all around them. We buried them too deep to freeze. In spring when we opened the last hole they'd be sprouted and honest they'd taste like young taters! These couldn't be young taters, could they? Last of May, you know, and with this large family you could be opening the last hole of taters!"

"But I'm not," Poppie said softly. Poppie acted like he was taken aback. Maybe he couldn't come out and tell Uncle Dick where we got the potatoes. He didn't tell Cousin Bos where we'd got the beef either.

"About this pork," Uncle Dick said. "It's about the best I've tasted. Good old cornfed hogs fed from corn raised in the valley bottoms and on the slopes of Lower Bruin!"

Again, Poppie didn't say anything. He seemed more taken aback than ever and he dropped more vittals on the floor than usual. This was Poppie's big fault, so Mommie thought. It was the only fault he had, so I had heard her tell him— he shouldn't eat real fast like a hungry animal and do everything but growl over his food. And everybody who knows us knows we are poor, but Mommie and my sisters are the cleanest housekeepers on Lower Bruin. It's just Poppie! He got these manners from some place far back! We don't know where or how he got them, for Poppie might have strong long arms and walk like a gorilla, but he is no animal. In Wonder High School I liked Geography best. And I read about countries, people and animals. This is how I know about the gorillas.

"Say, I don't like to be inquisitive," Cousin Bos said, "but I would like to know what this empty plate is doing here? Have you failed to call someone else to supper?"

"No, Cousin Bos, if we could call him we would," Poppie said. "He can't be called back. That empty plate is always set at our table for our oldest child, our first boy, Percival—"Little Pearse" we call him—we lost him when he was six. He is planted over there in the Perkins' Family Cemetery!"

Well, I noticed that Cousin Bos had a strange look on his face. I couldn't tell what his hawk eyes were taking in at this minute. He looked at the food on the table and everyone sitting at the table. Great-uncle Dick looked a little strange, too, but he didn't say anything.

"Yes, Sil, I do like this corndodger bread," Uncle Dick said. "It takes good meal to make cornbread like this! I don't know when I've had better! I'll say we never taste cornbread like this in Ohio! I remember when I was a boy, Pap'd shell a stiff coffee sack full of the best corn we raised and he'd lay it across the back of Old Doc, a horse that weighed a ton if he weighed a pound. Then he'd lift me upon his back behind the sack and I'd take it to Red Callihan's grist mill and have it ground. Old Red would lift the sack down and then he'd lift me down. I liked so much to go to the grist mill on Saturday and watch him grind the meal. It was a great trip for me. After it was ground into meal, he'd balance a sack of ground meal in each end of the coffee sack, lay it over Doc's broad back, lift me up and lift me down behind the sack on his bareback and I'd rein him home. We'd have the best cornbread ever baked for a week until I went to the mill again."

Poppie didn't say anything about the cornbread. And I wondered when he would break our story.

"Well, I have to tell you," Poppie said, "that we don't raise hogs any more and we don't raise corn. We don't have to raise them! And we don't raise our beef and kill it as we used to do on Lower Bruin. We don't even raise our potatoes and bury them in holes with oak leaves wrapped around them in winter as our people used to do! I hate to tell you that this grub is not from Lower Bruin!"

Uncle Dick didn't say anything. But Cousin Bos looked us over with his hawk eyes. He waited for Poppie to tell us about the good grub we were eating.

"What you have been eating this evening, which is the best grub that money don't buy—is commodities grub."

When Poppie said this Uncle Dick again didn't say anything, but Cousin Bos looked strangely at us.

"Yes, what you've eaten—this good grub—my number-two boy Pedike and my number-three boy Timmie walked to Blakesburg to get. We walked to Blakesburg—and we walked five miles home with loads in sacks on our backs!"

"Yes, we got it all there," Mommie said. "We are poor people. We can no longer raise it here on Lower Bruin. That is why we want to go to Ohio, because Lower Bruin can no longer provide!"

Uncle Dick and Cousin Bos looked at us and they looked at each other. There was silence at our table. Sister Cassie-Belle and I didn't speak a word.

"This is the only way we have to live," Poppie said. "We have to leave Appalachia and get out of here. Ohio is the best place for us to go. Kentuckians have gone to Ohio and they have made good. Look at you, Uncle Dick! Look at Cousin Bos!"

"I can't say I've got rich in Ohio," Cousin Bos said. "But I can say I've worked and I have made a living! I've grown corn for my bread. I've raised hogs! And I've grown beef cattle. I've never taken any gifts from the Government!"

There was "Little Pearse's" empty plate. I looked at it. There was Mommie with her head bowed. There were Cassie-Belle and I who said nothing. But I could tell right now Cousin Bos was against our way of life. Uncle Dick had finished his supper and he had lighted a new cigar.

"I'm sorry to disappoint you," Poppie said. "We are poor people. We know we are. We have been told so many times we are."

"Well, I'll say you have better potatoes, beef, pork, chicken, turkey and cheese than we have," Cousin Bos said. "How in the world did you get these?"

"I don't know," Poppie said. "Don't ask me!"

"I've never tasted better grub in my life," Cousin Bos said. "Faith and I don't have better grub in Ohio! But what we have is our own grub! We kill a beef of our own! We kill our hogs—and we grind corn that I have grown but it won't equal this!"

"Well, I really didn't know this grub was so good," Poppie said. "We take our sacks and we walk five miles to get it. And we carry it five miles home. They hand it out to us!"

"You don't have food stamps?" Uncle Dick said.

"No, we don't," Poppie said.

"We have food stamps in Ohio," Uncle Dick said.

"I've heard of food stamps," Poppie said, "but we don't have them here. We've got a number of the Greenwood County's Fiscal Court who are against food stamps!"

"But food stamps are accepted all over this nation," Uncle Dick said. "How backward can you be? Over in Landsdowne County, Ohio, we have food stamps! What about this Hamlin Curtis of your Fiscal Court? He's a relative of ours!"

"He is a Fiscal Court member of Greenwood County and he controls the Fiscal Court," Poppie said. "He's not of our party, Uncle Dick. He's got a lot of his friends and relations who hands out our grub to us—and this is their jobs. They get paid for doing this. He's not about to change. But God Almighty is on our side. He's on the side of the poor people. Old Hamlin has got cancer and he can't live much longer. He's running again to be re-elected. But it won't matter. He can't live. All the merchants in Blakesburg want food stamps."

"Don't you worry about this, my nephew Gil," Uncle Dick said. "When you move to Landsdowne County, Ohio, you won't need food stamps. You won't have to worry. I will see to it you don't have to worry. You don't know Ohio. Ohio is one of the most progressive states in the United States. Ohio will help the poor people. Why do you think so many people have gone from Appalachia to Ohio?"

"About these food stamps—" Poppie said.

"Well, you pay a little for them and you get a lot of grub," Uncle Dick said. "But you will be able to buy your grub in Ohio."

"But I can't pay for them," Poppie said. "I can't pay for anything! Not now!"

"But I will help you," Uncle Dick said. "You will really be surprised! You will buy at the store like other people. No more of these handouts like you have in Greenwood County."

"It sounds mighty good to me," Poppie said. "Getting grub at the store and the contract I have on the farm where I am to move. I believe we can make it much better than we are making it here!"

"I'll say you can," Uncle Dick said.

"We have a second sitting of the Little Ones at this table," Mommie said. "And they are hungry, too. If we are through, I think you should go to the living room and let them come to the table."

"I'm willing," Cousin Bos said. "I've had a real good meal and my stomach is as tight as a banjer head."

Cousin Bos was the first to get up and go. Uncle Dick, Mommie and Poppie followed and sister Cassie-Belle and I followed them. There were eight more to eat at our house and they were eager to get to the second table.

4 Mommie, I want you, Pedike and Cassie-Belle to hear this contract while the Little Ones are at the table," Poppie said. "You can't believe what a bargain we have here!"

Then Mommie went to the living-room door and she told second-sister Tishie and third-brother Timmie to scat with all our little brothers and sisters and get them around the table. This was going to be a big night at our house on Lower Bruin. This was going to be our last night. Mommie came back and got in a chair up close to Poppie.

"Now does either one of you want to read this contract, Cousin Bos, you or Uncle Dick?" Poppie asked them. "Since you know about it, I thought maybe you'd like to read!"

"I can't read it," Cousin Bos said. "I'm a good worker and I know how to handle any machine on a farm—even to a bulldozer—but I had a time learning to read a few words and write my name. All the education I got was right in this house where you live, Cousin Gil. I can read figures on gauges on machines, and I can tell the time on my watch and read stop signs along the road. You know about me, Cousin Gil, how I used to slip off from the Lower Bruin school. I ought to have had my hide busted! I never knowed you'd be living in this schoolhouse some day and I'd be moving you to Ohio."

Well, I had to smile. I didn't know this about Cousin Bos. Sister Cassie-Belle, not given much to laughter, had to put her hand over her mouth. Mommie smiled, too, for she had gone to the fourth grade at the Lower Bruin school where we now lived and many of us had been born.

"They didn't have much school on Lower Bruin when I went here," Uncle Dick said. "I went to school in this house when it didn't look as old as now. I got some good horse sense, I think, and know what is right and fair and I can deal with men. But I say it in words. I don't put anything in writings. I let a friend or my lawyer do this. My manager's from the old country—down in these parts—and he's a Republican. So, I will sit here and do more thinking as you read the contract, Gil! I'll try to help you with some of the shades of meaning!"

"Before I start to read this I will say to you, I might get a little nervous to read in front of Cassie-Bell and Pedike," Poppie said in his slow soft voice. "Cassie-Belle and Pedike that are in big Wonder High School. I went to school in this house but only to the third grade."

"Talk about schools," Uncle Dick interrupted Poppie, "Ohio has the schools! If your youngins are good in books they will go places in Ohio. I mean, if they take to learning and they like to go to school!"

"They do," Mommie said.

"Now, I'll do my best," Poppie said. "I think this should be read by a man—not one in school and not by my wife. I think a man understands it better. You help me, Uncle Dick, on the explaining of this important paper."

"I'll help you all I can," Uncle Dick said as he puffed on a cigar and blew more clouds of blue smoke up to the news-papered ceiling. "Go on with your reading."

"Here is where I begin," Poppie said. "It says in this contract, 'Party of the first part, Joshua Herbert—' "

I could tell Poppie was getting nervous, for he stumbled over his words. But Uncle Dick broke in, in time to save him and give Poppie a rest from his reading.

"He's better known as Old Josh Herbert, and the hardest man with the hardest working family in Landsdowne County, Ohio," Uncle Dick said, letting his cigar rest. In the front pocket of his double-breasted blue-serge suit was a fountain pen and two pencils, which made him look important and educated. "And Old Josh is not from Greenwood County, but from some county farther back in the mountains. He's from Appalachia and he's done well in Ohio—as he has said, if he had only known about Ohio as a young man, he'd just about own all of Landsdowne County now! He owns eighteen farms and they all jive. He's got plenty in The First National Bank in Argillo—enough until they call him Mr. Herbert when he walks in. Some people have called him a big tycoon. Often I can't get the word for I always think of cyclone—and cyclone is a word that fits him. He's older than I am but what a working man he is! He drives a hard bargain, but I told him Gil Perkins, who had a big family and was from a good family, was my nephew, would be a good man for him—and, of course, that he had several children that would do some work too. He's got a farm for nearly everything. One is for tobacco. One is filled with coal mines. On one he raises strawberries and he needs berry pickers in season! He raises corn, hay and has whitefaced cattle. And he sells paper wood! Anything there's money in, he's into it. He buys a farm and cuts the saw timber and paper wood and these pay for his farm. Then he converts slopes where he's stripped the timber into pastures for more and more cattle. He owns his own bull-dozers and bogharrow to do this. He's a man of means. And he's a big Republican wheel in our Party. Big state men come and consult him about state politics!"

Now Uncle Dick struck a match to his cigar, for the fire had gone out.

"As I was saying, 'Josh Herbert, party of the first part and Gilbert Perkins, party of the second part—' " Poppie looked up and said, "You know that's me—'agree to enter on this agreement, binding between said parties for one year.

" 'Party of the first part agrees to furnish party of the second part with house of six rooms—' "

"How wonderful," Mommie said. "That will give us two more rooms! What about water, Gil?"

"I'm glad you asked me about the water," Poppie said. "Mommie, we got a pitcher pump from a drilled well right in the kitchen. You won't have to go to the well and draw water! Of course, we will have a big open well in the yard!"

Now Cousin Bos was smiling all over. He wanted to say something.

"Water and electric lights," Cousin Bos said. "I have to tell you, Faith and I got rid of the outside wells about six years ago! We've got water and electricity in the house. We've got sinks and a bathroom. No outside water wells and privies for us! Everything takes place in our house! And no more lamps. We've got electric lights in our barn too."

Mommie looked strangely at Poppie and I looked at Cassie-Belle, and Uncle Dick looked up at the ceiling and blew a cloud of smoke. I don't believe what Cousin Bos said set very well with Uncle Dick.

"I just had to tell you about our house. Faith, Buster Boy and I are proud of it. First time we ever lived in a house with a bathroom. I'll tell you I've rented from a real man— Essej Trants, a German fellow over there. This is what Ohio has done for us. No more of this Lower Bruin living. I wouldn't return to it for anything on earth!"

Well, I thought, Cousin Bos was already slurring Poppie and Mommie about the house we had rented.

"But a man has to get his feet planted in Ohio," Uncle Dick said. "He has to get in, and the way to get his feet planted and to get into Ohio is to take the best contract he can get. See, when I went to Ohio, I rented land. Now, I rent from no one! And when you went to Ohio, Bos, did you get a house on the farm with indoor water, sinks, basin and a bathroom?"

"No, I didn't, Dick, you know what I rented, but I was such a good man for Essej Trants that you know he went all out to build us a new twenty-thousand dollar home," Cousin Bos said. "And I'm proud of our house where we will live for life. And it's rent free too! Yes, this is what Ohio has done for us! Could you ever get a bargain like that here on Lower Bruin or any place else in this county?"

"No, not in our old county," Uncle Dick said. "But as I have said, you've got to work in and up and expand!"

Poppie, who was a little red in the face and nervous, went back to his contract: "With the house, we get a cellar, smokehouse, barn, hoglot and piggery, chicken house and pasture for six cows!"

"But, Gil, we don't have a cow or a hog on the place," Mommie said. "And we don't have chickens!"

"Now, I don't understand this," Uncle Dick said. "You won't be able to stay with Old Josh very long with a family like you have unless you get them. He's a man working for a living and he expects all the people who live on his farm to live and work, too!"

" 'Party of second part, Gilbert Perkins,' " Poppie went on reading, " 'agrees to work one day a week for these considerations, or fifty-two days in the year'!"

"Then we don't get free house rent," Mommie said.

"No, Sil, we don't," Poppie said. "But wait until I read you this part of the contract which beats the old three dollars a day around here. And we've had to pay ten dollars a month for this old Lower Bruin schoolhouse with four rooms. I told Mr. Herbert I couldn't drive a car or use any kind of machinery but I was good with a hoe, mattock, pitchfork and shovel! And that I had worked with terbacker all my life! This is what pleased him. I'll be working on his terbacker farm."

"How much does he pay you a day, Gil?" Mommie asked. "I can't wait!"

"Just a minute, Mommie, until I read on," Poppie said.

" 'Party of the first part, Joshua Herbert, agrees to pay party of second part, Gilbert Perkins, one dollar per hour for every hour he works and give him all the work he wants—' "

"It can't be, Gil," Mommie said.

"But it can be, Sil," Uncle Dick said. "I bargained with him for this!"

"Who ever heard of such farm wages in this day and time?" Mommie said. "I never heard of such wages. He must be a rich man!"

"He's not only a rich man who made it from scratch in Ohio, but he is a Republican," Uncle Dick said. "One thing the Ohioans have found out, when they get Republicans from our county, they are not wishy-washy. We'll never switch over to vote the other ticket like a lot of the Ohioans. We are stand-patters. The old party is as close to us as our Baptist religion—we won't let either one of them down!"

I was glad Uncle Dick said these words for Cousin Bos was wanting to talk again. He wanted to say something but

Poppie wouldn't let him. Poppie got back on the contract again.

"Now look what it says here about our children," Poppie said. " 'Party of first part, Joshua Herbert, agrees to pay the children of party of second part, Gilbert Perkins, children from twelve to sixteen, and wife of said Gilbert Perkins, if she has the time, fifty cents per hour to pick strawberries, red and black raspberries in their seasons.' "

"It's a great contract, Gil," Mommie said. "Pedike, Timmie, Cassie-Belle, Tishie—four of our youngins will qualify —that will be two more dollars an hour in the summer when they're not in school. I'm afraid I can't qualify for we'll have another Baby Brother or Baby Sister at our house. Our first Ohio born!"

Uncle Dick blew more blue clouds of smoke toward the ceiling and looked up at the swirling clouds when Mommie talked.

"This is the most important part of the contract," Poppie said. "There is some more but I won't go on and read it. It's about taking care of the house and other properties and to be careful about putting out fires. And you know we have always done these things every place we have rented and lived."

"Gil, this means you will work," Cousin Bos said. "It means you'll work like your Cousin Bos and Faith Auxier— it means you'll work for what you get and you'll feel like a man when you do it! You won't be a-gettin' this give-away grub which I think is a-goin' to be the ruination of this country! Although I'll admit the Government gives you better than what we can raise!"

"Yes, I'd rather earn it myself," Poppie said. "I don't feel exactly right taking Pedike and Timmie and walking to Blakesburg on Relief Day and walking five miles home a-carryin' loaded sacks. I carry a stiff coffee sack across my shoulder—must weigh about eighty pounds. Pedike totes about forty and Timmie about thirty."

"I won't say anything to Old Josh about this free grub," Uncle Dick said. "You mustn't either, Bos! Because this will hurt my nephew Gil with Old Josh!"

"Yes, it will be hard for a big Ohio farmer like Old Josh

Herbert or Essej Trants to understand if you move from a farm onto one of their farms without a chicken, a cow, hog, horses or mules," Cousin Bos said.

"We'll just have to tell them we are poor people," Poppie said.

"I think it's time to turn in," Uncle Dick said. "I like to get my seven hours' rest and we're going to have a big day tomorrow!"

"Uncle Dick," Poppie said, "you and Cousin Bos will have to sleep together in the bed in the living room. You don't mind, do you?"

"Neither of us will have to keep his eyes on the other one to watch his pocketbook," Cousin Bos said. Then he laughed wildly at his own joke.

"Come on, Bos, let's turn in," Uncle Dick said.

I knew what Poppie and Mommie had done. They had given their bed to Uncle Dick and Cousin Bos—we only had four beds. Mommie and Poppie always slept in their bed with Baby Brother and Baby Sister. I slept with Timmie. Cassie-Belle and Tishie slept together. And third-daughter Maryann and the three Little Ones—boys and girls—slept in a bed together near Poppie and Mommie so if one cried in the night Mommie could jump up and be at the bedside. Tonight Mommie and Poppie would sleep in our bed and Brother Timmie and I would have to sleep on the floor. We'd be a little crowded but just for tonight. Tomorrow night in Ohio we would get our fourth bed back.

5 When the alarm clock went off Mommie shot out of the bed and lit the lamp. She dressed in a jiffy and left Poppie in the bed with Baby Brother and Baby Sister until Maryann could go get in bed with them and relieve Poppie.

The alarm clock woke Timmie and he got up and dressed in a hurry and then went to fire the cookstove. Cassie-Belle jumped up and dressed fast to help Mommie.

"Pedike, you wake your Uncle Dick and Cousin Bos," Mommie said. "All of you, after we get to the dabblin' pan, soap your hands and faces!"

Mommie didn't have to tell us to do this. Mommie kept the cleanest house on Lower Bruin. And if you'd talk to the people on Lower Bruin, she kept her children the cleanest of any mother. Our clothes were not the best but they were always clean.

"We went to bed at nine and it's now four," Mommie said. "Uncle Dick has had his seven hours' sleep. It doesn't matter whether Cousin Bos has had four, five, six or seven hours of sleep! He brags too much! Someday, over in Ohio, your father and I will surpass our cousins!"

Mommie and Cassie-Belle were running circles. And I went to the living-room door and knocked loud enough to wake Uncle Dick and Cousin Bos.

Believe me, Timmie knew his jobs around the place. He knew how to build a fire. It didn't take him three minutes to fire the stove. In five minutes coffee and water were boiling and Mommie was putting in a big bread pan of biscuits to bake. Everyone helped at our house. I set the table while Mommie and Cassie-Belle cooked. Mommie made a pitcher of powdered milk. She put plenty of butter on the table. She cooked rice, prunes and she served grapefruit we had carried from Blakesburg in coffee sacks for five miles. Grapefruits can get heavy when a body carries a dozen or so on his back along with other things. Mommie scrambled a skillet of powdered eggs. She had breakfast on the table before Poppie had soaped his face and hands and dried on one of Mommie's coarse feed-sack towels. Next came Cousin Bos. Uncle Dick was last.

I had set the table as it was set last night: seven places. When Cousin Bos sat down he looked the table over with his eagle eyes.

"It's a full table, Sil," Cousin Bos said. "What an industrious little woman you are! I've never seen a faster one! I'd hate to tell my old lady Faith you're faster than she is! And she's mighty fast!"

Mommie was pleased with Cousin Bos' words. But Cousin Bos kept looking at "Little Pearse's" empty plate.

"First time I've had biscuits in a long time," Uncle Dick said. "And I'll say this one melts in my mouth with this good butter melted on it!"

"Glad you like them, Uncle Dick," Mommie said.

"Faith never takes time to make biscuits any more," Bos said. "You live in Ohio awhile, you get to the place you live in a hurry! Ain't that right, Dick?"

"It sure is," Uncle Dick said.

Poppie wasn't saying a word. He looked very sad the way I had often seen him look.

"Won't you be glad to be leaving Lower Bruin, Gil?" Uncle Dick asked. "You seemed to be so sad this morning."

"I'm looking at our number-one boy "Little Pearse's" empty plate," Poppie said. "Maybe it will never be set on a table again on Lower Bruin, the land of our people in the old country! We have to leave him, his little six-year-old body—a handsome little boy he was—almost returned to dust under the broomsedge and sprouts in our family graveyard. Thank God, I made a marker for him from a field stone with a coal chisel and a hatchet."

"Nephew Gil, look what a fine family you have," Uncle

Dick said. "Forget the dead and worry about the living is the way I see it. You've got ten young mouths to feed—and you and your wife make a dozen!"

"I know, but look where he would have been now," Poppie said. "Our oldest child, almost a man grown by now!"

"But look at your Pedike," Cousin Bos said. "He'll soon be a man. Cassie-Belle is might nigh a woman! Don't worry, you've got men and women coming on here!"

But this didn't satisfy Poppie, and really it didn't satisfy Mommie. With all of us that had been born since "Little Pearse," and all that would be born, they would never get over losing their first born. And they would not let us forget he was number-one son and he was our brother.

"Yes, 'Little Pears' will be riding in the truck with us to Ohio this morning," Poppie said. "You won't see him but his spirit will be with us."

I could tell Cousin Bos didn't care about the way my father talked. Maybe Cousin Bos had been in Ohio and away from his native Appalachian hills long enough to change him. Cousin Bos actually acted like he wanted to laugh. But I knew he had better not. This would have made Poppie and Mommie furious.

"I'll have some cream for my coffee," Cousin Bos said.

Well, Mommie used the powdered milk we had carried from Blakesburg on Commodities Day. Mommie had put the powdered milk in a cream pitcher and Cousin Bos used a lot of milk in his coffee. After he poured it in, he took a big swallow and tasted a few times. I could tell Cousin Bos was used to real cream skimmed from the milk. Mommie noticed too.

But Cousin Bos helped himself to the scrambled eggs and rice and he ate some cooked prunes from a side dish.

Uncle Dick ate scrambled eggs and cooked rice and he drank his coffee black, just the way Poppie and Mommie did. Sister Cassie-Belle and I drank our powdered milk. Poppie and Mommie said we were not ready for coffee yet.

"Sil, it's a good breakfast," Uncle Dick said.

Now Uncle Dick was very kind to us and he didn't look down on us like I had thought Cousin Bos did.

"Bos, what is your Buster Boy doing now?" Poppie asked.

"Well, our Buster Boy finished Landsdowne County High School," Cousin Bos said. "He wasn't very good in school. He didn't take to books much. But since he was a high-school graduate, Essej Trants recommended him to DuPont's. He got a wonderful pay check—but as I say he took to hooch and then a bad marriage. He had a lot of fights with other men over his wife anyway. And Buster Boy can give more than a two-hundred-pound punch—maybe this don't interest my relatives!"

"Oh, yes, it does," Mommie said. "We want to know more."

"Well, it's the old story: he lost wife number one, married again and he had a lot of fights over his second wife. Faith just wondered where he got these wives. Met them in bars or beer parlors. While married to his second wife he quit his job at DuPont's and moved to Detroit. Well, his second marriage ended there! We had to go bring him home!"

Cousin Bos took another drink of coffee with powdered milk, which surprised me.

"Yes, we brought our only child home," Bos said. "Faith cried herself sick. She said if we didn't stand by him, who would? And in no time he married that third wife. And if she wasn't a floosie, we never saw one! All wild women I'd say—well, this third one didn't last. I went to his home and when I got there he was fighting with some man over his wife and when he struck at him he hit me and laid me out! That's why I said he could hit more than a two-hundred-pound lick! Well, Buster Boy divorced her. He had to. There's not a better automobile mechanic in Ohio than our son!" Cousin Bos talked on. "And right up there at the end of the table, Richard Perkins—your Uncle Dick who recommended him to an Ohio State Department of Highways garage where he works now. If he can't fix a car, no one can. His hobby is taking parts of old cars, putting them together, making cars and selling them. He does this on the side! And he lives with us!"

"You say he had no little ones by any of his three wives?" Poppie said.

"No, he didn't," Bos said. "And growing up an only child I've never seen a big grown-up man like little children more than he does!"

"How long has he been married to his wives?" Mommie asked.

"Married when he was nineteen," Cousin Bos said. "He went from one marriage right into another! Now he's divorced the third wife at twenty-nine. That would make ten years of marriage."

"And no children to replenish the earth?" Poppie said.

"That's right," Cousin Bos said.

"It's too bad," Mommie said. "Maybe if he'd had little ones by his first wife, his second wife or his third, he'd have been happy!"

"We don't know. Faith and I wonder about the situation," Cousin Bos said.

"We don't have any trouble about replenishing the earth, do we, Mommie?" Poppie said. "When I married Sil, a little tiny woman, many people wondered if she could conceive and bear! But look at our crop!"

"You're lucky, Gil," Uncle Dick said. "A nice big family many people would like to have! I wish we could have had children! Look what we could have done for them! We've got the money to do it but we don't have the children."

"I'll say this, that it causes frustrations when a young man likes children and can't beget," Bos said. "Faith and I think Buster Boy is frustrated—maybe because he can't beget. This is something I don't like to talk about."

"Well, since he doesn't have a wife now," Uncle Dick said, "if he can find a widow with a houseful of youngins —divorced or husband dead—marry her and adopt the children, he'll be a happy man. And Bos, you and your Faith will be Grandma and Grandpa."

"Well, as you know," Cousin Bos said, "he's a-goin' with Widow Ollie Mayhew now. She's twenty-seven, a widow with five little ones, nine, seven, six, four and two. I think he's more in love with her youngins than he is with her!

Her man, a no good, just walked right off and left her. Buster Boy has been bringing her and her little ones out to see us. But we want him to be sure this time. We want him to date Ollie and to be with her enough to know he loves her and her children. Then, when he is sure he loves her we want him to take her for his lawfully wedded wife."

6 With breakfast finished for the first sitting, Timmie, Tishie and Maryann helped with our brothers and sisters. And Mommie began directing the packing and the loading. My little mother was always there. She was the spark that struck the fire. Big Poppie was slow and nervous—but not little Mommie! She was the woman wee-elf under the toadstool. Only she didn't stay under it. She could give ten orders in one minute.

Now, while the Little Ones were at the second table, she gave us orders to put our four beds in the truck—and all of our chairs. And one thing Mommie didn't leave out were the sacks of commodities we had carried from Blakesburg day before yesterday in boxes which we put onto the truck. We would have something to eat when we got to Ohio.

We didn't have a cow, a hog, a mule or a chicken—not any livestock, swine or fowl of any kind to move, and we lived on a farm. We had lived from commodities and Poppie had worked enough days for farmers on Lower Bruin, three dollars a day, to pay our rent. He'd made most of this money working for tobacco farmers on Lower Bruin in tobacco season—hoeing, suckering, cutting and grading to pay our rent and have a few extra dollars. Tobacco is the money crop of the people on Lower Bruin. But we no longer raised tobacco, we no longer farmed. Really we stopped raising a garden when we started carrying the give-away rations home on our backs. Poppie worked enough to pay our rent and buy our clothes.

Now, I saw Cousin Bos in action, and I'll have to say he

was a worker. Uncle Dick wasn't much because of his heart. He smoked long cigars and looked on while we loaded by lantern light, for we wanted an early start.

By daylight all my younger brothers and sisters had been fed. Mommie and sisters Cassie-Belle and Tishie had dressed them in their best clothes. With all the furniture out of the house we were ready.

"We don't have to tell Frank Blair, who owns the school-house, we are leaving," Poppie said. "Our rent is paid for two more weeks. He'll find out in that time we are gone. He never liked us too well nohow and we've not liked him. He doesn't need even to know where we are going. Let him find out the best way he can where we have gone."

"That's all right with me," Cousin Bos said. "I don't care whether you pay your rent or not. What I'm interested in is getting you to Ohio in your Uncle Dick's big truck!"

Well, I was ready for the trip. Sister Cassie-Belle and Brother Timmie and I wanted to see Ohio, but Mommie, who was so clean and persnickerty, had to sweep all four rooms of the Lower Bruin schoolhouse where thousands over the past seventy-five years had gone to school.

"I can't leave it dirty," Mommie said. "It's not my nature."

Now, when we left this house, we older ones all waved goodby to it.

"Ohio bound," I said.

"Ohio bound," Cassie-Belle said.

"Good-by, Lower Bruin," Mommie said.

"Good-by, 'Little Pearse,' " Poppie said. "We will never forget you in Ohio although we have to leave you planted here. If we had you, we would be taking eleven of our children to Ohio—and one to be born in Ohio!"

Now, Uncle Dick got up in the front seat of his truck. Little Cousin Bos was at the wheel. And Poppie got up in the front seat with them. But Mommie got in the back of the truck with all of her children and all the possessions we had on earth. We sat in our chairs in the back of the truck. The truckbed was high and broke the wind. If we wanted to see out we had to stand on our tiptoes to look over the truckbed. But when Cousin Bos started the motor and rolled away from Lower Bruin we knew we were on our way. Mommie and Cassie-Belle looked after the Little Ones but Timmie and I stretched on our tiptoes and looked over the truckbed at the scenery.

7 The high truckbed was a solid wall—no cracks where the wind could get into us. Uncle Dick told us he had another truckbed, one with slats and opened places he used when he hauled cattle in this truck. We were riding in a cattle truck. Cousin Bos was really driving us fast.

"It is so early in the morning and because of the mists—" I said, "I can't see very much!"

But Brother Timmie had to crawl up on our kitchen cookstove so he could look out. Sister Maryann got up beside him.

"Now, you children be careful," Mommie said. "Don't lean too far over and cause a calamity on this greatest day in our lives."

I was standing close by Brother Timmie and Sister Maryann. I had my eyes on them.

"We're on the road to Auckland," I said.

Timmie and Maryann were looking with wild eyes at everything along the road. I'd walked up this road with Poppie twice when he'd gone to the stock market. But this was something for people who had lived on Lower Bruin who didn't own a car and had never gone any place—not even to the stock market. We passed houses and more houses.

"It's something to see so many houses," Brother Timmie said.

"We're coming to the Ohio-River Bridge," I said.

But I didn't more than say this until Cousin Bos blew the horn.

"Mommie, I want to see the Ohio River," Cassie-Belle said.

"I do, too," Tishie said.

"Well, I really do, too," Mommie said.

Timmie jumped down from the stove. Mommie put Baby Sister and Baby Brother down in the big rocking chair. Timmie and I helped her up on the stove so she could see the big river below and the rugged Ohio land on the other end of the bridge, where the big rock cliffs went almost straight up to a patch of blue sky. Sisters Cassie-Belle and Tishie got up in chairs, held on to the top of the truckbed and looked down at the Ohio River.

"What a big bridge and a big river," Mommie said.

Of course, I'd seen the river before, but we had never crossed this bridge into Ohio. When Cousin Bos reached the Ohio end of the bridge he bore down on the horn so much a man in front pulled over, stuck his head from the window and cursed Cousin Bos. But he still bore down on his horn and moved on. Cousin Bos with his crooked hawk-bill nose and hawk eyes was in many ways a feisty, briggity and mean little man. But he wanted us to know we had reached Ohio—the Promised Land.

"It's like Moses leading God's Children out of Egypt," Mommie said. "Only God parted the waters of the Red Sea for them so they could walk over—and we have had it so much easier leaving poor Appalachia for the Promised Land. We are riding in a cattle truck and having everything we have on a truck to haul us. Think what a time they must have had walking and carrying all they had. We ought to be thankful to God!

"Pedike, you and Timmie help me down from this stove."

Timmie and I helped Mommie down. She went back to the big rocker and picked up Baby Brother.

"Cassie-Belle," Mommie said, "pull out that top dresser drawer and look in the right-hand corner to see if I didn't put your school report cards in there! Ohio, we are ready for your schools!"

Cassie-Belle looked in the dresser drawer.

"Yes, Mommie, our report cards are here with a ribbon

tied around them," Cassie-Belle said. "You remember tying a ribbon around them?"

"Yes, I do," Mommie said. "I'm proud of my children's learning. I'm proud of your grades, Cassie-Belle. No one could go above the grades you made last year! Wonder if you will do as well in Ohio as you did in Kentucky?"

"I don't know, Mommie!"

I didn't make grades in school that made her proud as Cassie-Belle's, Tishie's and Timmie's. I made average grades and as I have told you, I am the silent one. But I record our story. I like to tell our story. Each one to his own talents, and I like to tell of my family, what we have done and what we are doing now.

"Gee, four lanes of highway," Timmie said. "What a road! Did you ever see anything like this, Pedike?"

"You know I've not," I told him. "Where have I ever been to see anything like this? We've walked about every place we've ever been!"

"I just can't believe it," Mommie said. "I feel already like we've been delivered!"

Speaking of that word delivered, I didn't know too much about the meaning of words, but I knew that word had meaning. I would hear it again, and again and again. It had a special meaning for Mommie. After a Baby Brother or a Baby Sister was born Mommie would have delivered again.

"Look at two lines of cars moving in both directions," Timmie said. "Look how they're passing our truck! Gee, I'd like to know how fast they're going! I'll bet they're going fifty miles an hour!"

"Cousin Bos is driving Uncle Dick's big truck fifty miles an hour—maybe faster," I said. "Look at the road signs! Trucks sixty miles an hour! You know Cousin Bos is taking us sixty if Uncle Dick's truck will go that fast! And I believe Cousin Bos will go faster if Uncle Dick doesn't watch his speed! Cousin Bos can't stand for anybody to get ahead of him!"

"Cousin Bos is bad to brag," Mommie said. "When I am in his presence and hear him talk, I think I hear the wind blow! He's changed since he went to Ohio. His voice ain't the same. I remember how he used to talk on Lower Bruin."

"Mommie, do you believe that man he rents from built him a twenty-thousand-dollar house?" Cassie-Belle asked.

"I told you I heard the wind blow when he talked," Mommie said. "He's not the same man he used to be. I wonder if Cousin Faith has changed too? But it won't be much longer until we'll be living closer to them! And we'll know the truth!"

"Passenger cars, seventy miles an hour!" Timmie said. "Gee-whilligens! Think of that, seventy miles an hour!"

"I think they must be going faster than that," I said. "They pass this truck like it is standing still! They pass like big bullets fired from a big gun!"

Speed of the cars and highway signs excited my brother Timmie, while Mommie was thinking about other things.

"Now, I wonder if Gil and I will get so we talk like Ohioans," Mommie said. "And I'm sure if our children live and grow up in Ohio you will talk like Ohioans! Cousin Bos and Cousin Faith talked slow on Lower Bruin. Then they moved to Ohio and stayed four or five years and when they returned for family reunions or the death of relatives left behind, they came back a-talkin' so fast it was hard to understand them!"

Cousin Bos slowed the truck and came to a stop. He waited until there was a chance for him to drive across the other two lanes where cars had been zipping westward toward the sunset. But it wasn't high noon yet. And when Cousin Bos got the truck over onto a two-way road—where car met car—Rural Route No. 5 was on a sign. Cousin Bos bore down on the horn again to let us know we were on our way to Landsdowne County, Ohio.

"Pretty white houses on these farms," Timmie said. "I'll bet nobody in Ohio lives in an old schoolhouse like we did on Lower Bruin!"

"Don't be smarty pants already, Timmie," Mommie said. "Don't start talking above your raisin'."

"Look what big barns the farmers have here," I said. "They're nearly all red barns! I believe they're prettier than the houses!"

Mommie sat in Poppie's big rocker with two children in her lap and eight around her. Our house plunder was stacked up near the cab. Our cookstove was placed on the side and Timmie and Maryann were up on it seeing the wonderful sights as we drove along.

Cousin Bos was driving slower over this road because there were curves in it. I'd never seen houses and barns such as I was seeing—but I'd never been any place. My brothers, sisters and mother had never been out of Greenwood County. Only Poppie had been in Ohio and he had been there just once and stayed overnight. I'll tell you, this was a big, beautiful world we were having in Uncle Dick's cattle truck going from Appalachia, a land filled with poor people, to the Promised Land of Ohio. And right now, from where I was looking on my side of the truck, it looked like what everybody who had come back, but only for a visit—never to live on Lower Bruin again—had said about it. They called Ohio the Land of Milk and Honey.

"Pedike, what are you seeing from your side?" Cassie-Belle asked me.

I turned to look around and she was up in one chair and Tishie was in one looking over the truckbed from the other side.

"I never saw anything so pretty as the houses, barns, green fields, plowed fields and cattle and sheep on my side," I said.

"It's the same way over here," Cassie-Belle said. "I never saw a land so clean and beautiful!"

"How pretty it is, Mommie," Tishie said. "Maryann and I will hold Baby Brother and Baby Sister and let you look out. Come down from the stove, Maryann. You've looked out more than anybody but Pedike and Timmie!"

Maryann jumped down off the stove and got Baby Brother and Tishie got Baby Sister. The rocker was so big they could both sit there and hold them. I walked over and steadied Mommie across the floor of the moving truck. I didn't want Mommie to fall, not now—we didn't want her hurt. We needed our Little Mother more than Poppie or anybody on earth. How could we ever do without her? I'd often thought, and it was a sad thought, if something happened to Mommie, what would happen to all of us?

Here we were in this truckbed, ten of us, all around her. She was the little Queen Bee of our growing hive. I helped her up in the chair.

"No wonder my children are excited," she said. "What a pretty country! Look at these pretty houses and the painted barns! Look at the milkcows, cattle, sheep—and even hogs out on pasture. Children, I've never seen anything as pretty at this!"

Now Cousin Bos bore down on the horn again. He was leaving Rural Route No. 5 for a one-lane road. And this meant we would soon be there. But now there were not the pretty barns, houses, plowed fields, green fields, sheep, cattle and hogs that we had been seeing. The landscape was changing. The ride on the truck was rougher.

Cousin Bos took us down this road about ten minutes when he blew the horn again. And he began to slow the truck. Something was about to happen. He brought the truck to a stop in front of a six-room house—and it was pretty, too—but not as pretty as most of the houses we had seen along the way. But it was a painted house. It was the first painted house we would have ever lived in. Out in front of the house there was a man standing alone.

It was hustling little Cousin Bos who got around to the rear of the truck first and lifted the truckbed so we could get out. I, Pedike, my father's second son, was the first to jump down from the truck and plant both feet on Ohio soil. Of course, Timmie followed me.

"All right, Pedike, help me to help your mother down," Cousin Bos said.

By the time Poppie and Uncle Dick got to the back of the truck we had Mommie's feet planted on Ohio soil. We had lifted Sisters Cassie-Belle and Tishie down. And Maryann carried sleeping Baby Brother from the rocking chair and reached him down to Cassie-Belle. Then she fetched sleeping Baby Sister over and reached her down to Tishie. We kept Mommie free to be with Poppie. And one by one Timmie and I helped our brothers and sisters down from the truck. We were fast. We'd not been over a minute unloading.

"It's Joshua Herbert in the yard," Uncle Dick said. "I'll want you to meet my old friend, Josh. He's come to meet his new tenants!"

Joshua Herbert was older than Uncle Dick. He wasn't as tall as Uncle Dick but his shoulders were broader. His hair was gray. He was wearing overalls and a blue work-shirt.

When we walked through the gate, all eight of us with Tishie and Cassie-Belle each carrying a little sleeping one, I wondered what Mr. Herbert thought. But when we walked up he had a smile on his face.

"I've been looking for you," Mr. Herbert said. "I know my friend Dick Perkins and his friend Bos Auxier are men who move. I figured you'd get here before noon. My old turnip says," he looked down at the watch on his wrist, "ten until eleven. When did you leave this morning?"

"About daylight," Cousin Bos said.

"Just a little bit later than that, Bos," Poppie corrected Cousin Bos, with his soft-spoken Lower Bruin words.

"Well, it doesn't matter a lot," Cousin Bos said, "about the time we started. You got here in a hurry! And you're now in Ohio at your new home!"

"It looks so nice," Mommie said. "It's so pretty!"

"Let's go inside," Brother Timmie said. "I want to see that pump in the kitchen! Boy, think of a pump in the kitchen where we can pump water right in the house!"

"Right here is your key, Mr. Perkins," Joshua Herbert said as he gave Poppie the key. "Take the family in and look the house over."

Poppie's hand was shaking a little when he put the key in the hole. I could tell Poppie was a little nervous. But he opened the door and Timmie rushed in first and made for the kitchen and the water pump.

"Look, Mommie, at the wallpaper on the walls! How pretty it is!"

"It's a little stained and some places a little dirty," Mr. Herbert said. "People I bought this farm from let the farm run down and his women folks didn't take much care of the house!"

Brother Timmie ran back into the front room where we stood looking at the wallpaper on the walls.

"It works, it works!" Timmie shouted. "It will pump water! I've tried it and I know!"

"Leave the pump alone, Timmie," Mommie said. "We'll get to it later!"

And when little Mommie said "scat" to brother Timmie, he left the pump alone and he behaved like a little man. Just a few words from Mommie and one look at him were enough to calm his excitement.

"You've got a big family, Mr. Perkins," Joshua Herbert said. "I hope this house will be big enough!"

"It's got two more rooms than where we lived on Lower Bruin," Sister Maryann spoke out of turn.

And don't you think Mommie didn't make a face at her.

"Mr. Herbert, if you don't mind, just call me Gil," Poppie said in his slow voice. "We're going to get to know each other mighty well. There will be plenty of room in this house for us."

I was looking at the fireplace in this big front room which would be our living room.

"Now, about new wallpaper for this house, Mrs. Perkins, just go to Herns Quality House in Agrillo, pick out the wallpaper you want for the rooms in this house and I'll pay for it," Mr. Herbert said. "But you put the paper on! That is the rule here!"

"Sil, I'll tell you," Cousin Bos said, "my old lady Faith is a expert when it comes to papering. You do as Josh Herbert tells. Go get the paper and charge it to him. Faith will come over and help you paper. You don't need to be standing up in chairs and climbing up on ladders right now. And you don't need to be putting your hands up over your head!"

Maybe I'd misunderstood Cousin Bos. Maybe he was kinder than I thought.

"Yes, I'll get the wallpaper as soon as we can and have Cousin Faith to come and help me paper these rooms," Mommie said. "Mr. Herbert, you are so nice to give us a chance like this. We've never had one like this!"

"I'm pleased you feel this way, Mrs. Perkins," he said. "You know, I'm from the old country and I like giving my people a chance! You've probably heard if I'd come to Landsdowne County, Ohio, when I was a young man, I'd have owned the county."

"Yes, I have," Mommie said.

"My friend Dick Perkins or Bos Auxier told you," Mr. Herbert said.

"That's right," Mommie admitted. "When we went over Gil's contract with you last night this was explained!"

"Now about your livestock, will your Uncle Dick and Cousin Bos Auxier go back and fetch them?" Joshua Herbert asked Poppie.

"We don't have any," Poppie said. "Not a living thing!"

"Not a cow with all this family?" he asked Poppie.

"No, not one," Poppie said.

"You have to have cows, chickens and hogs," Joshua Herbert said. "Did you sell all your livestock?"

"Yes, we did before moving to Ohio," Poppie said.

I could have said something here. We sold our livestock long before we moved to Ohio. We sold our last cow when we could get powdered milk. We never bought any more pigs to raise to hogs and fatten, when we could get free pork. I could remember when my Grandmother Perkins made cheese. My mother could make cheese. But why keep cows and make cheese when we could get cheese given to us? And we used to have apple, peach, pear and apricot orchards on Lower Bruin—but not any more. We got better fruit given to us. Even grapefruit from Florida! No need to raise tomatoes, as we had once done when we made our own tomato juice, put it in glass jars and in our cellars. Now we got it given to us. No use to raise cattle and fatten a beef to kill as our ancestors had done when we could get all these things free. This is the way Poppie and Mommie looked at the situation after that woman, who worked for the poor people in Blakesburg, drove up to our home and persuaded Poppie to get our family on commodities. She said she'd heard we were very poor people. And she explained about the free rations there would be for us if we'd only sign and come and get them. She said there was plenty of food for poor people and it was free.

"Now," Mr. Herbert said, "since you don't have cows, I'm sending you two of the best from my herd of ninety-six up here for you to milk," he said. "They will be free. If two good ones are not enough, I'll send you two more."

"Do you have a churn?" Mommie asked him.

"What a beautiful word," he said. "The word 'churn' brings back memories of my dear old mother in Pike County, Kentucky. I think we have a churn. If we don't have, I'll get you one!"

"Mr. Herbert—I mean Josh—we are poor people," Poppie said.

"I understand," Mr. Herbert said. "Now about chickens. One of my farms is all chickens. I'll bring you sixty hens and two roosters! For this big family you will need them!"

"I'm afraid we can't pay for all of these things," Poppie said. "We are poor people!"

"I know you are poor but these won't cost you," Mr. Herbert said. "I want to see you raise these nice looking children. I'm out to help you fine people because you're poor people. You are my people. And you're in Ohio—the state that gives poor people (even like me when I came here)—a chance. And I want you to have hogs for your pork so I'm sending about six pigs to you," Mr. Herbert said. "I won't charge you much for these—six dollars apiece, let us say—and you can work these out. Say, when do you want to start work?"

"This is Sunday, so how about tomorrow?" Poppie said. "I want to get started, and since Pedike and Timmie are out of school, do you have something for them to do?"

"I sure do," he said. "I've got plenty to do for men and their children who are willing to work."

"I am willing to work," Poppie said slowly. "I've got children who are willing to work. We need to work. We need money to live. We have to work. We've got grub for one week!"

"Don't you worry, Gil Perkins," Mr. Herbert said. "I'll see to it you don't starve! Gil, walk down to my house in the morning. You bring your ax. Bring your two sons if they want to work and you want them to work. I need all three of you right now! And I'll go away now and let you move your furniture into the house."

Mr. Herbert said good-by to us and he walked out and down the road.

"You can't miss his house, Gil," Uncle Dick said. "It's a big white house on the right side of the road about a half-mile down."

"Don't worry," Poppie said. "I'll find it early in the morning. I need ten dollars a day. I need that much every day, besides what my sons make, for a spell."

Now Poppie and Bos unloaded the truck with Timmie's and my help. Uncle Dick helped us some. Sister Tishie and Cassie-Belle used brooms and Mommie directed where our furniture, such as we had, would go.

"Cassie-Belle, you and Tishie will have a room all of your own," Mommie said. "For the first time in your lives you will have some privacy! And when we select wallpaper for the rooms, I'll want you to go and select the wallpaper you will like!"

"Thank you, Mommie," Cassie-Belle said. "This is really something!"

"And just to think," Mommie said, "Mr. Herbert said next year we'll have electric lights and a telephone! A telephone where we can speak to our neighbors over a wire."

"And call long distance," Cousin Bos said as he and Poppie came in carrying a bed. "We can call all over Ohio. We can call Kentucky. We can call all over the United States! You think of this! Think of what it means!"

"I can't believe it," Mommie said.

"This is not Lower Bruin," Cousin Bos said. "This is Ohio. This is the state I've been telling you about. It's a poor man's dream. There was never a greater state in these United States of America than Ohio!"

Cousin Bos and Poppie went back for another load. Timmie and I followed them. They told us what to bring and we brought a load—each one of us carried a box—of the most important things. We carried the commodities we had once carried before in coffee sacks from Blakesburg to Lower Bruin. We had about a week's supply ahead. And this would give Poppie a chance. In five days he would have fifty dollars. In six days he would have sixty. And if brother Timmie and I worked, we would earn together as much as Poppie. So we would really be making money at our house and from the stores in Agrillo we could buy what we wanted. And I believed this would be better than commodities. It would be better to work for what we got than to have it given to us. I had long been tired, a fifteen-, nearly sixteen-year-old boy, carrying a stiff coffee sack full of commodities for five miles. This was too much. I would rather work for it.

We kept on carrying loads from the truck. But the big load was our kitchen stove. We brought it into the kitchen and we set it down. Our stove pipes reached the flue. They were a perfect fit. And leave it to my little Mommie. She didn't leave anything out. She had a bushel basket of coal and one of kindling. So now we had a stove in our kitchen where we could build our first fire in Ohio. Brother Timmie put a fire in the stove. And Mommie started getting our first lunch in Ohio. I know Uncle Dick and Cousin Bos must have been getting hungry. Cousin Bos had sweat streaming down all over his face. I'd never seen such a worker. I knew he bragged, boasted, and, maybe, lied but he was the best worker I'd ever seen. And, I thought, maybe that man Essej Trants, that German farmer, really had built him a twenty-thousand-dollar home to hold him and Cousin Faith and their son, Buster Boy.

Cousin Bos never stopped working for us until everything we had was unloaded from Uncle Dick's truck. He and Uncle Dick didn't wait for lunch as we thought they would surely do.

When they had finished Uncle Dick said: "I will see you again soon."

Cousin Bos said: "If you need anything, see me later! I'm not far from you. Everybody around here knows where Faith, Buster Boy and Bos live. And call on us and we will be at your service!"

Well, how could you beat this Cousin Bos?

Cousin Bos got into the big truck again with Uncle Dick beside him. And they drove away. Here we were in our Ohio home with what furniture we had in all the rooms. We were in Ohio and ready to go to work tomorrow. Our Little Mommie was cooking our lunch and she would soon, with the help of my sisters, have our vittals on the table. This would be our first meal in Ohio. This would be our first day and night in a painted house.

8 While we were at the table eating our noonday meal, Mommie said, "Gil, we've got grub enough for a week."

"I know, but we'll have money by then," Poppie said. "We can go to the store and buy. We'll have Bos or Uncle Dick to take us to the store and haul us in a supply!"

"For the first time in three years we'll be working for it," Mommie said.

Poppie didn't say that he was glad to be working for it. I think he dreaded to go back to work for day after day, week after week, and maybe, month after month, except on Sundays. Poppie had never liked to work on Sunday. He liked to get us to the Freewill Baptist Church on time. People from the old country had established this church on Lower Bruin. Cousin Bos and Faith, Uncle Dick and Aunt Susie went to the Freewill Baptist Church. Joshua Herbert, his wife, children and grandchildren were members of this church too.

As Poppie had said so many times, we were poor people. But never once had he, Mommie, or anyone else told us why we were poor people. I'd never understand what separated poor and other classes of people, but maybe there was a bigger separation than I had ever known.

We had left the old country that had not been too kind to us—and we had joined Ohio. What would Ohio do for us? What more could Ohio do than the old country had done? Well, Ohio was a new country. And I did believe everybody would be on our side. In Ohio, that great state north of Appalachia, the Land of Milk and Honey, how could we fail? Mr. Herbert, who was from the old country and who had worked up in Ohio until he owned eighteen big farms, would not let us fail. We were not about to fail. We were in a new country and we must have courage.

After we had finished our lunch, Mommie put the list of her children's names on the kitchen wall, just as it was in Lower Bruin. She was a mountain mother. She was from Appalachia and now she was in Ohio. She wanted to know what all of us was doing at the same time. She was working for us. She was willing to fight for us! But she wanted to be boss at all times.

In the afternoon, Poppie, Timmie and I carried beds from the living room to other parts of the house where Mommie wanted them. Mommie let Cassie-Belle and Tishie select their room. This pleased them. We put a bed and dresser in this room. And in this new home, we didn't have to put a bed in the living room. We put Poppie's big rocking chair and a sofa there and some chairs. We arranged what furniture we had in our home on Lower Bruin and it didn't look like we had very much scattered over this big six-room house.

Just as we had got our furniture placed over the house, two men came up, each one leading a cow. They were as fine a-lookin' cows as we had ever seen.

"I'm Jim, son of Josh Herbert," said a big square-shouldered man, nearly as old as Poppie. "Pap said for brother Al and me to lead these cows to you for milking."

Al Herbert was a big rough-looking man, too. His face was already tanned brown from the wind and sun and both men wore overalls and blue workshirts.

"Pap said put the cows in the barn at night and let them out on pasture during the day," Al Herbert said. "They'll be on a good forty-acre pasture that will furnish grass for a half-dozen cows. He said you had a big family and if these cows didn't give enough milk, he'd send two more. He's bringing feed to feed the cows night and morning, a milk churn and other utensils such as milk buckets, strainers and crocks. He said you might not have these things!"

"No, we're poor people," Poppie said slowly. "We didn't fetch any from the old country."

"You won't be poor long if you'll stay with old Josh Herbert," Al Herbert said with a smile. "We're real Ohioans now. Ohio gives you a chance if you'll work. I was a boy of ten when we moved here. I'm forty now, with a family of six! Brother Jim has six, too! We're workers, we're Ohioans, Freewill Baptists and Republicans!"

"We're Freewillers and Republicans, too," Poppie said. "And I suppose from this day forward we'll be Ohioans too! And we'll plant the seed of our people in this wonderful state! Rich to overflowing and the Land of Milk and Honey, so everybody tells us."

Jim and Al Herbert didn't pay too much attention to Poppie's remarks about the Land of Milk and Honey. I wondered just how religious they were, even though they went to our church.

"We'll put the cows in the barn," he said. "I've got to get home to my feeding and milking."

"I'll have to get back, too," Jim said.

They acted for the world like Cousin Bos and a lot like Uncle Dick. They were Ohioans, always with something ahead to do—always in a hurry. We went to the barn with them. It was a nice barn with many stalls for cattle, but here we would only have two cows if they gave enough milk for us. If they didn't, we would have four. They showed us the corncrib inside the barn where we would keep feed for the cows. They left with their ropes, after they put each cow in a stall.

They had not more than walked away when Josh Herbert drove into the barnlot in a little truck.

"Dairy feed for the cows," he said. "I grind my own feed at my mill. It's a good mixture, good feed for milk cows, and it makes them give milk!"

Poppie and Mr. Herbert carried a half-dozen hundred-pound sacks to the corncrib. He was white-headed and very old, I thought, but he picked up a hundred pounds like he would have lifted a bucket of milk. I carried a sack of feed into the crib, too. But Timmie wasn't quite able to carry a hundred pounds yet. He went to the cellar with milk buckets, crocks, strainers and buckets. I'd seen people on Lower Bruin living in houses not as nice as this cellar and barn. All the barn needed was a floor to make a big fine home. It was painted red—and we'd never even lived in a painted house until now.

"Your Uncle Dick told me you couldn't use a tractor," Mr. Herbert said. "But you can harness a mule team and use cutter and turning plows on slopes too steep for a tractor, can't you, Gil?"

"Yes, I can do that all right," Poppie said slowly but proudly.

"Buying this last new farm, I'm clearing up fields with bulldozers, where we set tobacco and some of the land we plant in corn, which we will later sow in grass for pasture land," Mr. Herbert said. "There are places where we can't use tractors to plow around the slopes. Now we can push the trees over on these slopes with our bulldozers. My sons go up the hill straight and they come down straight with our bulldozers. But when we plow, you know we have to plow around these slopes and here is where we use a muleteam!"

"Yes, I understand," Poppie said. "I've done a lot of this plowing on Lower Bruin."

"Your Uncle Dick said you belonged to the old school: the muleteam, wagon, hillside plows, hoes, mattocks, shovels —not the machine—and I'll tell you, we've got a place right here for a man like you." Then Mr. Herbert spat amber, for he chewed tobacco like Cousin Bos. "And I've got more to tell you! I'll have six pigs in that hoglot for you tomorrow night. These will cost you six dollars each and you can work these out and pay me later. I'll suggest you feed them skimmed milk you don't use. And I'll bring you some free feed. It will be in your corncrib. Also, Gil, I'll have truck patches free for you where you can raise your potatoes, your garden things—you can have my team and as soon as you can, get your potatoes in the ground. It's late now. No one ever lived on my land and went hungry. I give people a chance! You'll get all the work you want here! And you'll have a chance!"

"Josh Herbert, I've never had a better chance," Poppie said. "You're wonderful to us. We're poor people, you know!"

"But don't say you're poor people," Mr. Herbert said. "If you keep on saying that you'll start believing it. Somebody must have been telling you you're poor people. I think you're a rich man with all that nice looking family you've got. You're a lot richer than your Uncle Dick or your Cousin Bos!"

Now a smile spread over Poppie's face.

"Take this from me, a man old enough to be your father, a man who has worked all his life like a mule and who still works like one," Mr. Herbert said. "It's time for you to stop thinking poor and start thinking rich. As I say, you are rich with the family you have if you teach them industry —teach them to work. See that they work and send them to school! You know we have great things in Ohio. I hear we've got the best schools in all the United States. If we didn't have, why would we be getting the best teachers the old country ever produced coming here to teach school? Why would families just move across the Ohio River to educate their children? And we've got the best old-age pensions, too! They move across the border and live long enough to establish residence to get them, then they move back to the old country to live in comfort in their last days."

"Repeat what you said about the old-age pension in Ohio," Poppie said.

"I said it was about double to what people get in the old country," Mr. Herbert said.

"I didn't know that," Poppie said.

"We'll talk more, Gil," Mr. Herbert said. "Bring your ax and come at six in the morning. Come down the lane to the big white house on the right side of the road. If your boys can come and pile brush on the slopes, bring them too!"

"We'll be there," Poppie said. "Don't you worry."

"It's best to bring your lunch if you want a ten-hour day," Mr. Herbert said.

"We'll do that, for we need some ten-hour days," Poppie said.

Josh Herbert got back inside his little farm truck and he was on his way.

"He's a working man and he's all business," Poppie said. "Think of the wages he pays on a farm for this day and time! Three times and over as much as I got on Lower Bruin."

9 After we had had our suppers, Cassie-Bell, Tishie and Timmie and I went to the barn to watch Poppie and Mommie milk.

"It's been so long since I milked a cow my hands might be a little stiff," Poppie said.

"It's a long time for me, too," Mommie said. "But we want all four of you to learn to milk cows. It's not hard. When I was a little girl I sat on a stool and milked a cow! It's one of the first things we learned to do."

"And as big and as old as we are not one of us can milk a cow," Timmie said. "We've not had to learn how to."

Well, Mommie gave Timmie a look that made him get quiet. Now what if he'd have said this in front of Mr. Herbert? And what if Mr. Herbert had asked him why? Timmie would have said, "We don't have to own cows and milk them for we get powdered milk free." And this would have hurt us with a man like Mr. Herbert after Uncle Dick had done all this talking for us with Mr. Herbert to get us such a fine bargain.

We watched Poppie and Mommie put feed in the boxes for the cows so they would stand patiently while they milked them.

"Go back to the house, Timmie," Mommie said. "Fetch us a couple of stools—chairs without backs. Hurry!"

Timmie took off like a bullet from a pistol. He wasn't gone longer than two shakes of a calf's tail until he was back with the stools. When Poppie and Mommie began to milk, we saw the white streams hit into their milk buckets. Each one milked with both hands. But before Poppie had filled his first bucket, he stopped. "I'll tell you my big hands ain't done this in a long time. And they're so tired now they ache, I'll have to rest!"

Mommie laughed at Poppie and she went on milking with her little hands. And we all laughed at Poppie for getting tired as we watched Mommie fill her big bucket.

"I'm not near through," Mommie said. "Her sack has plenty of milk yet. This is some cow, Gil! Take this bucket to the cellar, Pedike, and fetch two more!"

I took Mommie's full bucket of milk to the cellar in a hurry and when I got back to the barn with the two empty buckets, Timmie was laughing at Poppie because little Mommie's hands had beaten his big hands.

"Timmie, quit laughing at your father," Mommie scolded him.

"I'll tell you what we'll do with Timmie, Pedike, Cassie-Belle and Tishie," Poppie said. "We're goin' to learn all four of them to milk cows! Then Timmie will stop laughing at this hard work. It's harder than swinging the ax for me."

Poppie had rested his hands and started milking again. Mommie was milking with both hands into her second bucket.

"Yes, in my confinement with a Little Brother or Sister soon to be born, some of you are going to have to learn how to milk a cow and help your father," Mommie said. "It will be too much for Gil! When he uses the ax all day his hands will be stiff."

"I want to learn how to milk a cow and I'll be the first one to learn how," Timmie said.

This was my brother Timmie. He never stopped talking. I was the quiet one. Timmie did enough talking for both of us.

Mommie finished and had half of the second bucket filled. Then she took over on Poppie's second bucket. And Poppie's cow gave more milk than Mommie's and all of us laughed real hard as we stood watching them.

After they had milked the cows, we went to the cellar with them. We watched Mommie strain the milk into crocks.

"Gil, have you ever seen two cows that give this much

milk?" Mommie said. "We must have ten gallons of milk here!"

"Must be the two best cows in his dairy herd," Poppie said.

"Poppie, is real milk better than powdered milk?" Timmie asked.

"There Timmie goes again," I thought.

"You'll just have to wait and see, son," Poppie said. "You children will have real milk for your breakfast!"

Mommie didn't make a face at Timmie this time. I thought Poppie had answered his question all right.

"After all the excitement of moving to Ohio in one day, getting our furniture set up and getting two cows, don't forget, my sons, we will have to get up at four in the morning so I can help Mommie milk these cows," Poppie said. "We will have a day's work before us tomorrow!"

"Gil, to help you on your first day, I'll milk both cows in the morning," Mommie said. "And we'll get up at five. This will give you more time for rest. I think you might need it for tomorrow."

10 At five in the morning the alarm went off. Timmie did his old job of firing the cookstove. I went to the cellar and got milk. Mommie and Cassie-Belle got breakfast while Tishie set the table. Mommie made biscuits out of our commodity flour. She cooked eggs, prunes and rice. And she served each of us a half-grapefruit. And while she cooked breakfast, she packed part of our lunch in a bucket for each of us.

We sat down to a hot breakfast. Poppie and Mommie had coffee to drink while my brother and two oldest sisters and I had milk.

"Don't you worry about the cows, Gil," Mommie said. "I'll get them milked."

"I worry about the day ahead of us, Sil," Poppie said. "It's been a long time. I don't know what it will be like. I'm not used to it!"

"Don't worry, Gil," Mommie said. "You're my Gil of old. You'll do it!"

Mommie never said anything to Timmie or me. I wondered if we'd make it. I thought we would. I wasn't afraid. Just to think, if we worked ten hours Poppie would earn ten dollars and Timmie and I five dollars each. That would be twenty dollars for a day. If we were back on Lower Bruin and told this, people wouldn't believe us.

At five-forty, just before the break of dawn, we left home. Poppie with his ax and file, his lunch and a jar of coffee. Tommie and I with our lunch buckets and jars of milk. We walked down the road about fifteen minutes, just as Mr. Herbert had told us to do, and we found his big white house on the right where we stopped and found him out waiting for us.

"Good boys," Mr. Herbert said. "You are here on time! Follow me."

Poppie had a home-rolled cigarette in his mouth, a little bent until it looked like a crow's bill. He had only a dollar in his pocket, an ax on his shoulder, a file in his pocket and lunch in his hand. And it was just getting good daylight as we followed Mr. Herbert up the path, past his house, over a little hill and down into the next hollow.

"Now this farm where we will be working today is part of the farm you live on," Mr. Herbert explained. "See how close it is to the farm where I live! I like to buy all the farms that join mine. I tried to buy old Seth Winters out afore he died. He wouldn't sell. My land surrounded his. I offered him big. I knowed his reckless sons would run through with all he had. So his wife and sons were glad to sell and at my price! I about had to have this farm."

"Yes, if you've got land all around it, I'd think you ought to have it," Poppie said.

"In two years, I'll make it pay for itself," Mr. Herbert said.

He was walking in front of Poppie and getting his breath easy as we climbed the little hill.

"I hear something," Timmie said.

"You hear bulldozers," Mr. Herbert said. "My boys Al and Jim are already at work. They've been up, fed and milked their cows."

When we reached the top we stood on the divide and looked down. We could see well now, for darkness had left and lightness had come to the land, and I saw what I'd never seen in my life before. Two big giant machines would go up the slopes and come back down pushing trees out by the roots. If the helpless tree tried to stand, the big bulldozer would climb upon it and push and over it would go.

"This is the no-good trees we're taking off," Mr. Herbert said. "Before we began clearing this land, we cut the saw timber first and hauled it to my sawmill on this farm. Then we went among the second growth with power saws and cut all that would make paper wood. Forty acres will be cleared this first year. The best acres will be set in tobacco; the rest we'll plant in corn. We do this to get the wildness from the land, such as roots and stumps, and next year, you will see the pasture grass we will have here! We might have to farm it two years to get it ready for grass."

"Just what do you want us to do, Mr. Herbert, so we can be sure," Poppie said in his voice as soft and slow as a soft, sultry summer wind.

"You, a man from the soil of the old hill country, are among the last left to know how to do a job like this— today's Ohio men do everything but this and they don't want to do it or learn how to do it—not even your Cousin Boss does this any more. I want you to use your ax to chop off under the ground tough little white oaks and other trees that wouldn't give up their hold on life to the mighty bulldozers—chop them up so your boys can pile them. Do they know how to pile brush up and down hill so the piles will burn better when we pour the coal oil to them?"

"Yes, I'll show them how to pile," Poppie said. "Don't worry about them! They're young and fast! They get around faster than men!"

And Poppie was right this time. He told us to cover the ground and pick up loose pieces the bulldozers couldn't scrape up from the earth without taking away all the top soil. Mr. Herbert stood there watching while we started work.

Timmie and I started finding plenty to pile. Poppie started finding many little trees that hadn't given up to the big bulldozers. The little tough-butted white oaks had taproots, plus other roots that went deep into the ground. Their roots had held even when the giant heavy blades of the big bulldozers had split the trees up the middle trying to tear them out. While Mr. Herbert stood watching us a few minutes, Timmie and I had made one pile of sticks, tree branches and roots the bulldozers had not pushed out in front of their shining blades.

"See, we try to leave that dark topsoil, Gil," Mr. Herbert said. "The dozers can't clean the land like man. I've always said a man's hands are the best tools on earth. And you can really use an ax! This side of the valley is in good hands. I'll go to my work."

"Where do you work, Josh?" Poppie asked.

"I'm on the other side of the valley working by myself," he said. "I'm doing this kind of work—hard work—but I can use any kind of machine—even a dozer. I can't get men to do this kind of work. You, your boys and I will do this and leave the dozers to younger men and my sons!"

So Joshua Herbert walked down the hill. Poppie went back to chopping. And Timmie and I began our second pile. We picked it up from the ground; we'd not piled anything yet that Poppie had chopped. And the sound of Poppie's ax could hardly be heard for the roar of the bulldozers.

"One of these days, when I grow up to be a man, I won't be picking up brush," Timmie said as he stopped to watch the bulldozers. "I'll be upon one of them big babies pushing over trees. You wait and see!"

"You're a-thinkin' like a young Ohioan right now," Poppie said. "But stop watching the bulldozers and get back to work. Remember you're paid to pick up and pile, and not to watch the bulldozers!"

Poppie's voice was in spurts like starting and stopping winds. He was getting his breath hard! As Poppie had often said, it took a lot of windbreath to swing an ax.

Now I'd glanced up out of the corner of my eye when I picked up something from the ground to see the big dozers in action. As I've said, I like geography in school better than any subject and I remember reading about and seeing pictures of the dinosaurs—largest animals ever on earth that could stand up on two strong hindlegs and eat leaves from the tops of the trees. And now they had disappeared from earth. But our man-made bulldozers climbed up the side of trees without legs on broad steel tracks that carried their wheels but they didn't eat leaves on the trees as the dinosaurs had—they just pushed the trees over—uprooted and destroyed them! I thought, a bulldozer is our mechanical dinosaur that operates on fuel, a substance that comes from deep in the earth. I could understand why Timmie was so in love with the big dozers; I was, too! We'd never seen ground cleared this way.

Back on Lower Bruin, before we went on the "draw" and walked to Blakesburg and got our commodities, I went with Poppie, who cleared ground with his ax, mattock, sprouting hoe and briar scythe. I worked behind him and piled brush. But for the last three years I'd not piled any brush. I had hoed some tobacco with Poppie when he got three dollars a day and I got two. I'd never seen land cleared this way and this fast before. Bulldozers always moving—up the slope empty—down the slope pushing a load to the little valley between the slopes. They had already cleared the other side of the valley. There would be a lot of brush, logs and briars in the little valley below. When it decayed and settled down, this would make a small fertile bottom between the two slopes. Mr. Herbert was a smart man. He knew what he was doing. He was going to add another farm which he would make pay for itself in two years. And if he converted these hills to pasture grass such as those we had seen from Uncle Dick's cattle truck on our way yesterday over Ohio, he would improve this farm until it would be worth ten times as much as when he bought it. We didn't know and didn't ask what he'd paid for it. This was none of our business. I'd made two dollars a day with a hoe on Lower Bruin. Now I was making five, and Timmie was making five and Poppie was making ten dollars a day. I couldn't believe this. This was twenty dollars a day. And we could certainly live on this.

When Mr. Herbert came to our side of this slope with his lunch in a paper sack and a bottle of milk, he looked at what we had done. He just stood there for a minute and looked. We'd piled all Poppie had chopped except a few of the heavier poles. We couldn't carry these. Poppie had to put them on the piles himself instead of chopping them in two again.

"Gil, you're the best man I ever hired for this," Mr. Herbert said. "You know how to do it. And these sons of yours are on eight legs!"

"Timmie takes after his mother," Poppie said. "Just a

spitting-image of her and her people. Pedike is more silent than me. But the boy we lost, our oldest one, I'm sure would have been more like me!"

"But you're a millionaire, Gil," Mr. Herbert said, "Yes, you've lost one—it's regrettable. You can't recall him! You have to go on from here. You've got ten living and one on the way! So talk positive! Don't go back! Let's eat our lunches together!"

I knew why Mr. Herbert had come over. He'd come to see what we had done. And I was so glad to see him pleased. Mr. Herbert seemed to like us so much and he was so nice to us. Maybe Poppie had been right all the time. People in the old country and now in Ohio all seem to like poor people—even when they were well-to-do like Uncle Dick or rich like Mr. Herbert. And to us Mr. Herbert was a very, very rich man—Uncle Dick told Poppie that he had passed the million mark a long time ago. And Cousin Bos, though we regarded him as windy, told Poppie that Uncle Dick was worth millions. Uncle Dick told Poppie if it hadn't been for Buster Boy's troubles and wild spending, Cousin Bos and Cousin Faith would be worth a hundred thousand. If this wasn't big money, I'd never heard tell of it. We had only children in our family, very few clothes, no livestock and all of our furniture, which wouldn't be worth over two hundred dollars.

"You know, Gil, as I said, next year I'll have electricity put in the house where you live," Mr. Herbert said as we sat down on a brush pile together eating our lunches. "I already have an estimation on the cost it will take to run the line. It will cost me twelve hundred for the line to the house. Then I'll have to have the house wired. I figure the rent you pay me by working one day each week—that's ten dollars each week, fifty-two weeks a year, which will be five hundred twenty dollars—will wire the house. And I figure by that time, if you work on for me, it will be a safe investment. I'm a practical man. I'm Ohioan now. I make things pay or I don't fool with them. And while I make things pay off for me, I like to help others."

Well, Timmie and I listened while Mr. Herbert and Poppie talked.

"Did you have radio in your house in the old country?" Mr. Herbert asked.

"No, we've never lived in a house that had electricity in it," Poppie said. "We've never had a radio. But many people on Lower Bruin had radios. I think they had battery sets."

Well, this gave me an idea. I almost said something but I held my speech. I knew what I was going to do with some of my money when I earned enough. I planned to buy a battery-set radio for the living room in our house where we could all gather on evenings after our work was done and listen to music and the news.

"When I put electricity in that house you can have a radio and television, too," Mr. Herbert said. "You can have entertainment right in your home for the family! You won't have to go out places to see plays or movies!"

"We've never done that, Mr. Herbert," Poppie said. "Sil and I and our children have never seen a movie. I just wonder how sinful one is!"

Mr. Herbert looked strangely at Poppie. I thought he was going to tell Poppie that this was Ohio and not Lower Bruin in the old country. But maybe he didn't want to hurt Poppie's feelings as we ate our lunches, and Poppie drank cold coffee while we drank milk. I never tasted better milk. I'd never drink that powdered stuff again unless I had to. No wonder Cousin Bos had asked about it when Mommie had given it to him for cream in his coffee.

After a silence, Mr. Herbert said to Poppie: "We've had TV in our home for years. We get a lot of programs we enjoy. We get the news. And very often we watch a movie. It's all clean entertainment for the family. Next year when I get electricity in the house and a bathroom I hope you will get a radio and TV. These will be good for you and your family for evening hours after your work is done."

Poppie didn't say anything. He had finished his lunch and now he rolled himself a crow-bill cigarette from a little sack of cheap tobacco he carried in his pocket. Mr. Herbert, who had finished his lunch, took a sack of Honest John scrap chewing tobacco from his pocket. He put a big hand-

ful into his mouth until his jaw looked like Cousin Bos'.
Then, Mr. Herbert looked at his watch.

"I must be getting back to my side," he said. "I'll leave
you with yours!"

He walked down the slope and we got up and went to
work. We had begun working at six. We'd quit at eleven-
thirty for lunch. We were back at twelve noon and we
worked until four. At four o'clock you should have seen
what we had done. At four the bulldozers stopped. And
we walked from the field toward home. We were happy.
We had earned twenty dollars.

11 When we got home, Mommie was glad to see us.

"How did your day go, Gil?" she asked. "Remember you've not worked in a long time!"

"Yes, I know," he said. "But I stood it well. Don't forget I packed some stiff sacks of commodities a long distance back in the old country. That was harder than using an ax."

"How did Pedike and Timmie do?" she asked Poppie.

"Wonderful, Mommie," Timmie said before Poppie could answer.

"He's told you right, Sil," Poppie said. "Our boys are good workers. And it is the kind of work they can do!"

"Well, I've got some good news for you," Mommie said. "It won't be long before Cassie-Belle and Tishie can milk the cows. I had them trying this morning and they did well! A few more times and they will be good milkers!"

"This is really good news," Poppie said.

"I've got more good news," Mommie said. "We got six nice pigs in the hoglot. Someone who works for Mr. Herbert brought them here in a truck and he brought feed for them!"

"We've never been treated better," Poppie said. "If we could have found the work on Lower Bruin, it would take us about four days to have earned what we have today!"

"One more thing to tell you," Mommie said. "Cousin Bos drove by to see how we were getting along and he said Cousin Faith asked us to come to dinner Saturday at seven! And you know me, Gil," she said, laughing. "I told Bos dinner was at noon. He said in Ohio it was in the evening!"

Well, Mommie and Poppie both laughed and we laughed too for we had always known in the old country dinner was at noon.

"Bos and Faith must be real Ohioans," Poppie said.

"I told you Bos had changed, Gil," Mommie said. "I told him we didn't have any way to get there and he said he'd come and get us in his truck. I told him we'd like to come. I'd like to see Cousin Faith and Buster Boy. And I'd like to see where they live."

"Well, now, I wonder, boys, if we can work all day Saturday as we had planned," Poppie said. "Grub is going to be running out. We'll have to replenish Saturday. I thought about saying something to Josh Herbert about this. I need me some good store-bought cigarettes instead of these things I roll and smoke."

"Maybe you can work until noon on Saturday," Mommie said.

"But if we work all day on Saturday, we'll have a hundred dollars comin' to us," Timmie said. "If we lose Saturday afternoon we'll just have ninety. It's big money, Mommie!"

Timmie had spoken out of turn again. Poppie should have spoken, but Timmie was like Mommie—he just loved to talk. But he had spoken the truth of what we had planned.

"I'll see Josh Herbert about this and tell him we want to work six days if we can, instead of five-and-a-half, for we need the work," Poppie said. "Maybe he'll know the answer! He's an older man and he likes to give advice."

"Supper is ready, so wash your faces and hands in the dabbling pans, dry them and sit down at the table," Mommie said.

We still had two settings.

"As soon as we can, Gil, we've got to get a bigger table and some high chairs," Mommie said. "All of us need to eat at the same time!"

"We're making money now, Sil, and we'll be able to do this," Poppie said.

Well, we had the same kind of grub we'd been having for three years. There had been very few things added or subtracted.

"Saturday night when we all go see Cousin Bos, Cousin

Faith and Buster Boy we'll get off this old grub," Timmie said. "Mommie, you always said Cousin Faith was a good cook but with all her good grub she couldn't put any pounds on Cousin Bos."

Timmie had said the wrong thing at the wrong time. Mommie made a face at him.

"Always be thankful for the vittals you have in this world," Mommie said. "A lot of people don't have as much as we do."

But two things on our table were big pitchers of milk. One was at each end of the table. And I'll tell you we really went after the sweet milk cooled in our cellar. Poppie and Mommie had fresh buttermilk, which Mommie had churned. There was a dish filled with golden butter on our table. And we sliced hot cornbread Mommie had baked, and spread yellow butter between the slices. Talk about something good! We really had a good supper. We didn't sit long at the table. After we had eaten we had work to do and there was another sitting.

"Cassie-Belle, you and Tishie stay here, help with the second sitting of the little ones and fix Baby Brother and Baby Sister's bottles," Mommie said. "We'll let Timmie and Pedike start learning to milk this evening."

When we walked outside the cellar, we looked up and there stood the cows.

"Josh said if you feed them in the evening they'll come in from the pasture to be fed and milked," Poppie said. "So one of you boys don't have to go hunt the cows. This saves time!"

Now the pigs were running along the lot fence squealing for their feed.

"Pigs or hogs will always let you know when they are hungry and they are hungry most of the time," Poppie said. "So I'll feed them corn!"

"And, Pedike, you and Timmie fetch them the two big buckets of skimmed milk," Mommie said. "Be careful not to spill it when you pour it in their troughs. That's their feed and they're hungry."

By the time Poppie had brought a basket of corn from the crib inside the barn, we had fetched the milk from the cellar. Poppie threw the ears of corn over onto the ground —nice sound yellow ears of corn. Timmie and I opened the gate and went inside where we carefully emptied the milk pails into the troughs. The six pigs, very hungry pigs, didn't know whether to eat the corn first or drink the milk. But they went after the milk. They drank until they were stuffed. They'd not finished all the milk, before they ran for the corn.

We stood a minute watching them pushing and shoving over the corn when there was plenty on the ground for them.

"You see how some people are hoggish and want it all," Mommie said. "Right in this pen is the example!"

"But they're pretty things," Poppie said. "And they're not squealing."

Just then one of the cows looked up toward Mommie and mooed.

"She's telling us she wants her supper and she wants to be milked," Mommie said. "We'd better get feed and milk them, Gil!"

So we left the hoglot and walked toward the barn.

"Put a gallon of dairy feed in each box, Pedike, you and Timmie," Poppie said. "We'll come with the buckets."

Well, it was real nice, so I thought, to feed animals around the barn. This was a new experience for Timmie and me. Mommie and Poppie and all their people before them had lived on farms as far back as they could remember.

We put the feed in the cows' feed boxes. Mommie went to the cellar after buckets. Poppie turned the cows into the barn and the cows already knew their stalls. They had been trained.

"My old hands," Poppie complained when he went into the stall and sat on the stool, "have gripped that ax handle today. They might be a little stiff! I might have to call on Timmie or Pedike."

"I'm ready to try, Poppie," Timmie said quickly. "I believe I can milk a cow!"

"It's easy as can be, son," Poppie said, "but you've just got to know how!"

Mommie never said a word. She sat on her stool and

milked with both of her little hands. Poppie was milking with both hands, too. And milk was really flowing into the buckets as the cows ate contentedly from their feed boxes. Mommie milked until she filled her first bucket.

"Pedike, come down and try," Mommie said.

"I've not finished my bucket yet, but Timmie, I'm a-goin' to give you a chance," Poppie said.

"Wonderful," Timmie said. "I've been wanting to try since I watched you last night."

Timmie hurried into the stall. Working all day hadn't tired him. It hadn't tired me either.

"Just reach up with your hand and squeeze down gently and the milk will come," Poppie told Timmie as he gave him the stool. "Just be gentle and keep trying and your smaller hands will do it better than my big hands!"

Well, I had heard what Poppie said and I was trying. Timmie was the first to bring milk down into the bucket and when he did he shouted: "I've done it! I've done it! Gee-whilligens!"

"Not so loud," Mommie said. "You'll scare the cow!"

"But look, Mommie, I'm milking this cow," Timmie said. "And it's so easy! Tishie and Cassie-Belle won't beat me!"

Well now, I was getting milk into the bucket, but not as fast as Timmie. He had always wanted to milk a cow and now he was doing it. And he had said this morning that one of these times he'd be operating a big bulldozer. And I had the feeling he would. I had learned from a younger brother who, when he was determined to do something strong enough, could do it. And I could, too. After Mommie and Poppie had rested their hands—Poppie had rested longer than Mommie—they went back to finishing milking the cows. Poppie told us to go chop wood for the stove and some for the fireplace. I would do the chopping while Timmie carried the wood in the house. After this we would bathe in the washtub in the smokehouse and go to bed.

"Oh, if I only had that battery radio set," I thought.

12 Very quickly life had taken on a pattern for us. In the morning we went to work early with our lunches. And we worked ten hours a day. We didn't bother about milking the cows and feeding the pigs in the morning. Mommie, Cassie-Belle and Tishie did this. But as soon as we walked home, supper was ready and we ate. Then we got into our work. We boys helped Poppie and Mommie with feeding the pigs, the cows and doing the milking. Then we chopped wood for our stove and some for the fireplace where we sat awhile in evenings before going to bed.

When Mr. Herbert came over from his work to see what we had done and eat lunch with us on the second day, Poppie said: "Josh, we have a close shave on Saturday. We've got to buy groceries and we don't know where to go. We have a way to get there. And Cousin Bos and Faith have asked us to eat with them at seven. My wife didn't know we wanted to work six days this week, so she told them we'd come."

"I'll help you solve your problem," he said. "I believe I know how we can do it. You come to work at five in the morning—early, but it's getting to be daylight at that time. And I'll cut an hour from your day—making it really nine hours—but I'll pay you for ten. So, you'll leave here at two! In a very short time, I'll pick you and your wife up. You can go with me to Agrillo. I'll have your check written out, Gil. Do you want your boys' checks included with your own?"

"Only this one time," Poppie told him. "Our check will be for one hundred ten dollars, since we owe you ten dollars for rent. This will be the biggest check I've ever received in my life. After this time, pay each son his own check."

"I'll have this check made out for you then," Mr. Herbert said. "You can get it cashed at Cantwell's Super Market," he said. "The people know me there and we can buy groceries—plenty of them—all you want. We can get more and the best for the least money."

Then I knew I wouldn't be buying my battery-set radio but this was all right. I would buy it at some later date, if I could keep on working for Mr. Herbert. And I thought I could keep on working, for he had plenty of work to do that could not be done by machines.

On Saturday at two o'clock Mr. Herbert gave Poppie a check for one hundred twenty dollars.

"But this check is too much," Poppie said. "You didn't take out for rent."

"You need money now, Gil," Mr. Herbert said. "I'll take out the rent money later. You need dollars for your fine family more than I need them!"

Poppie smiled his thanks.

When we walked toward home, he showed the check to Timmie and me. This was the biggest check we had ever seen. We couldn't believe we had earned this much in six days, but this was Ohio—the Land Beyond the River.

"Look at this check, Sil," Poppie said. "He didn't take out this week's rent money."

"I can't believe it, Gil," Mommie said. "Come, Cassie-Belle, Tishie and Maryann, and look at this check!"

"When berry season comes, I want to pick berries for Mr. Herbert," Cassie-Belle said. "I want to get me some new clothes. I'll be in a new school where many of the girls will be from rich families and well dressed."

"Mommie, if Cassie-Belle picks berries to buy herself clothes," Tishie said, "I think I should too. I'll need clothes as well as Cassie-Belle."

"Showing this big check, Gil, has spiled all our oldest children," Mommie said. "This gives them idears!"

"Only to get out and work and make money," I said. "What's wrong, Mommie, with our making money?"

"Not anything wrong for you boys," Mommie replied, "but I may be confined at just about any time—maybe right in berry season! I'll need help taking care of the little ones. I won't be able to do it all by myself—prepare the meals, keep the Little Ones bathed and dressed, prepare Baby Brother' and Baby Sister's bottles and very soon another Baby Brother' or Baby Sister's bottles!"

"Well, we'll work out something," Poppie said.

"When is Mr. Herbert coming to get us?" Mommie asked.

"He said in about thirty minutes after we walked home," Poppie said.

"Gil, don't you think we'd better take Pedike and Cassie-Belle with us so they'll know about Cantwell's Super Market?" Mommie said. "I can make out grocery lists for them. They might have to go to the store for us. Young people have to learn!"

"It's a good idear, Sil," Poppie said softly in his slow voice as he went toward the kitchen to dabble.

"I'd like to go, too, Mommie," Timmie said. "I'd like to see Agrillo and Cantwell's Super Market."

"Timmie, your time will come," Mommie said. "The oldest ones have to go first. If we're not back home by five you and Tishie feed the pigs, and feed and milk the cows."

In five minutes Mr. Herbert pulled up in his farm truck. The front seat was broad enough for Mommie, Poppie and Cassie-Belle to sit beside Mr. Herbert. I climbed into the back of the truck where I stood up and held to the cab. I looked over the countryside, nice white farm homes, red barns, plowed fields, green pastures filled with sheep and cattle. From what I had seen in the few days we had lived here, I was in love with this state. We certainly didn't live in one of the best houses I'd seen, but we did have a water pump in our kitchen and a promise of electricity and a bathroom next year.

Now we were really moving fast. My hair was wild and blowing in an Ohio wind. But I stood like a man because I was a wage earner. And I was learning how to do things. We met many cars and many passed us. And then we drove into Agrillo. Mr. Herbert found a place to park, put a nickel in a parking meter—then, Mommie, Poppie, Sister Cassie-Bell and I followed him across the street to the store that was one-half a city block in the center of town.

When we went inside, Mr. Herbert said: "Let me introduce you to Don and Marilyn Cantwell. They own and operate this store. They started with a small one but look what they have now. My word for you with these people will be good."

As sure as I ever met a man, I thought Don Cantwell wouldn't be able to stand on his feet much longer. As Cousin Bos said: "He is a man all lit-up." He looked at us with a glassy stare. He wasn't working. He was watching about two-dozen people work. Now when we met Mrs. Marilyn Cantwell—she was nice and friendly and full of smiles.

Mommie had a list of groceries made out that she wanted. And Mrs. Cantwell was nice enough to go with us. She showed us how to get the grocery carts. Poppie pushed one and I pushed the other. A clerk, a very heavy woman, who knew we were strangers and that Mommie was heavy in the family way, almost ready to birth one, walked with us. Mr. Herbert had his own grocery cart and was buying his own groceries.

Well, I'll tell you when Mommie had got everything on her list, both carts were filled. The lady worker had shown us where different groceries were kept. Then we pushed our carts up where there were four places to pay, where women took groceries from our carts, and checked them on the cash register, while a boy about my age working there put them in sacks and boxes. This was really something. When our two grocery buggies were emptied, the boy who had been placing them in sacks and boxes now loaded one of these with what we had bought. Poppie did what Mr. Herbert had told him. He gave his check to the cashier. She looked at it and said: "Sign here!" Poppie signed the check. Our groceries had come to sixty-three dollars and thirty-three cents. They were the first groceries we had bought in years. Mommie had listed some new groceries she had been wanting for a long time—things we couldn't get from commodities back in Blakesburg.

I figured quickly in my head. We had worked six days, Timmie, Poppie and I, and we'd earned enough to buy groceries for at least two weeks and we had fifty-six dollars and sixty-seven cents left. Poppie had treated himself to a carton of his favorite brand of cigarettes.

I had heard so much about food stamps instead of handing out the commodities, and in Cantwell Super Market in the line next to ours, I saw a woman and three sons pushing four grocery carts up—holding up everybody behind them. And this woman paid for all her groceries with food stamps. She even got a half-dozen roasted hens. I didn't know any grocery store had roasted hens for sale. But I was learning. Three boys about my age pushed our two and Mr. Herbert's loaded grocery carts across the street and unloaded them into Mr. Herbert's truck. Mr. Herbert opened his pocket-book and gave each boy a quarter.

"Don't the store pay them to work there, Josh?" Poppie said.

"Yes, but not enough, Gil," Mr. Herbert said. "I always add a little—and a lot of other people do too—to the small wages they receive. They don't pay their boys to help them as well as I pay boys who help me!"

I climbed up in the back of the truck and rode with the groceries. And Mr. Herbert drove away while I stood up, looked out over the many busy people walking the streets of Agrillo on Saturday afternoon. And a thought went through my mind. Would I ever own a car? When would I ever learn to drive one? I also thought about the battery-set radio so we could have music and news in our house where we didn't have electricity.

When Mr. Herbert got us back home, it was ten past five. Poppie, Cassie-Belle and I carried in the groceries in one big load. Mr. Herbert went in with us.

"I know Bos Auxier will be here for you at six," Mr. Herbert said. "I'm not going to stay a minute!"

I knew why he was going in. He was going in to see how the house looked. He wanted to see how clean Mommie and my sisters kept it. But just as we entered the front door, Timmie met us at the door.

"Mommie, Tishie and I fed the pigs, fed and milked the cows," he almost shouted. "And we've strained the milk just the way you did. We've got the work all done."

"There goes Timmie again," I thought. "He just can't keep his mouth shut."

"Say that again, young man," Mr. Herbert said.

"I said, while Poppie, Mommie, Cassie-Belle and Pedike went to the store with you, Sister Tishie and I fed the pigs, fed and milked the cows, strained the milk and put it away just as Mommie showed us," he repeated. "Tishie and I wanted to go to Agrillo to see the town and to see Cantwell's Super Market, too. But we stayed here and worked. See, we go to Cousin Bos' and Faith Auxier's home for supper!"

"Dinner, Timmie," Mommie said. "It's dinner in Ohio."

I saw Mommie make a face at Timmie, but I saw a smile come over old Josh Herbert's wrinkled face.

"When did you learn to milk a cow?" he asked Timmie.

"Maybe I'd better tell you," Poppie said, as he put his heavy box of groceries on the floor and I put mine down, too. "Four of our children, our oldest girls and oldest sons, learned this week to milk the two best cows we've ever had."

"I told you, Gil, you were a rich man," Mr. Herbert said, as his eyes looked all over the living room. "You've really got a family! They'll work! And you're clean. Your wife is a good housekeeper."

Poppie picked up his box of groceries and I picked up mine, too, and we started for the kitchen. Honest, if Mr. Herbert didn't follow us through all the rooms to the kitchen. And when he saw how clean Mommie and my sisters kept the house where we had been only six days, his old eyes lit up until they were as bright as dim stars on a starry night.

"Yes, a million-dollar family," he said. "One with a great potential."

I didn't exactly know what potential meant. But with more schooling in Ohio I would soon know.

"Say, I must leave you," Mr. Herbert said. "I'd like to stay longer. But I know your Cousin Bos is coming after you. And you won't have long to wait before he comes. Bos is now an Ohio man. He moves. He acts. He does things on time."

13 After Mommie and my sisters had put away the groceries, Mommie saw to it that each little face had been washed clean. And she saw to it that her oldest children were clean—that we were dressed in the best we had. And we had just got ready when Cousin Bos Auxier pulled up in his red farm truck. He had seats across the truck bed for us children, and Mommie and Poppie were to sit up in the front with him.

Cousin Bos lived in Pleasant Valley, five miles on the other side of Agrillo, so we lived about ten miles from Cousin Bos, Faith and Buster Boy. We would be seeing them in their own home in just a few minutes. Instead of sitting on the plank and seats, Brother Timmie, Sister Maryann and I stood up and looked over the plowed fields and pasture land where there were flocks of sheep and fine looking herds of cattle. We also saw hogs, hundreds of them, running on pastures fenced with woven wire. The fresh late May wind blew into our eyes and faces but we didn't mind. Now the truck pulled up and stopped. Cousin Bos came around and let the tailgate down.

"Now get out, all you youngins, our good kinfolks from Lower Bruin," he said, in a rough way. He didn't mean to be rough. This was the way he talked. "I want you to be as welcome here as the flowers in May. Be keerful, girls, with the Babies."

Cousin Faith was on her way to the truck to meet us. I saw their son, Buster Boy, waiting for us on the porch. I could see the smile on his face from the road over to the porch. When Cousin Faith reached us she hugged and kissed Mommie.

"Cousin Sil," she said.

"Cousin Faith," Mommie said. "It's been such a long time since I've seen you."

"Back in the old country on Lower Bruin the last time at a family reunion," Mommie said. "Then, you and Bos stopped coming to the Perkins Family Reunion!"

"I know we did," Cousin Faith said. "When a new world and an old world are so many miles apart to separate us, memories grow dimmer!"

"Now before we go to the house, Gil, I want you to see the barn and toolshed," Cousin Bos said. "That barn will hold one hundred cattle, nine thousand bales of hay—and inside it has a big cornbin—and we have two cornbins down the valley. We filled all three with corn and that big barnloft with hay."

"Don't take too long, Bos," Cousin Faith said. "I know they're hungry and want to eat!"

"Cousin Faith, are you as good a cook as you used to be?" Mommie asked her.

"She's better," Bos said. "I eat until I stretch and I still weigh one hundred twenty pounds!"

Now everybody laughed. Poppie, who seldom laughs, laughed the loudest of all. Here was Cousin Bos, who acted like a banty rooster leading us to the big barn, not more than one hundred feet away. And when he reached the barn, he switched on the electric lights. We didn't need the electric lights to see the barn. It was still good daylight. He just wanted to show us.

"This winter I fed one hundred head of white-face cattle in that barn," he said. "I never bought a one of the cows or the fourteen-thousand-dollar bull that Essej Trants got from Nebraska. He weighs twenty-three hundred pounds and his brisket and his bag nearly touch the ground. He's built right on the ground. Gil, it's too late but I wish I could show him to you. I've always been afraid for this big bull to rear upon a cow—afraid he might break her down! Essej Trants likes a hornless bull but he thinks the horny cows are bigger and finer cows than them without horns. And I go along with Mr. Trants."

"Looks to me, Bos," Poppie said, "like you've got a good chance here!"

"A wonderful chance," Bos said. "I could never ask for a better! Now, I want to show you this toolshed—and later the lot we have for hogs if and when we want to raise them. We're set up for real living here, Gil. This is Ohio."

When we walked from the barn to the toolshed, Bos switched on the electric lights.

"All lighted," he said. "I've even got lights at the hoglot! But right now we don't have hogs. We may get a hundred pigs to feed this year."

"Why don't you have them?" Poppie asked.

"The price hasn't been right," Cousin Bos said. "Faith studies the agriculture magazines. When the price isn't right, why try to raise and sell hogs?"

At this time we were looking into a toolshed that has two ends, a backside and a roof. All the front was opened. I asked Cousin Bos what one of the machines was, for I'd never seen one before.

"It's a bushhog," Cousin Bos said. "You saw all these nice meadows when you left State Route No. 3 and came this way."

"Yes, I did," I said.

"Well, all the green fields you saw are on Essej Trants' farm," Bos said. "And I am the man who sees they are kept green. See, I've been with Essej Trants now twelve years! He trusts me, for he can't do without me and I can't do without him. He owns most of Pleasant Valley. He owns a lot of houses too that I rent for him. I rent the houses and collect the rent. I just about run this thousand-acre farm. I feel that I own a part of it!"

Poppie and Timmie kept looking at the two tractors.

"I use both tractors," Cousin Bos said. "One pulls that big manure spreader and the other tractor has a loader on it. I use it to scoop manure from the barn and load the spreader. This saves the work of two men! I use every piece of machinery you see in this toolshed. Now, step up here and look what a fine hoglot, fenced with woven wire, and hog houses we have. When hogs get the right price you might see one hundred or more in here."

"And don't you raise terbacker too, Bos?" Poppie asked.

"Only a couple of acres," he replied, "since our base has been cut down each year. We have two terbacker barns—one down in Pleasant Valley and one high upon the Ridge which is really good for curing terbacker. See, if I don't grow a ton of light burley to the acre, I consider myself a failure!"

"How much corn do you grow, Bos?" Poppie asked as we left the hoglot and walked toward the house.

"About twenty-five acres," he replied. "I always say about twenty-five hundred bushels. Maybe a little more. That's all we need and we have some to sell!"

"You do all this by yourself?" Poppie asked him. "What about weeds in the corn?"

"I spray for weeds," Bos said. "I fertilize. I plow corn a couple of times—I ride the tractor with plows that take care of four rows at a time. Never have a hoe in it! Remember how we used to plow and hoe corn and slopes on Lower Bruin? Not here! This is Ohio! Oh, but I forget," Bos spoke quickly. "Now, where you're working for Josh you'll have plowing and hoeing to do. He's getting that new ground cleaned by his bulldozers ready for pasture."

"How do you rent here, Bos?" Poppie asked him as Timmie and I followed Poppie and Cousin Bos along a concrete walk bordered by jonquils. On either side of the walk the yard had been mown until it was as beautiful as some picture postcards I'd seen.

"I told you he gave me half the white-face herd when we moved here," Cousin Bos said. "He furnished all the fertilizers, tools—all the expenses—a rent-free house and he takes half the cattle, terbacker and corn!"

"That's great, Bos," Poppie said.

"Wait until you see inside this house," Cousin Bos bragged. "I don't mean to be bragging. And this is not all. He gives me a check each month for the extra things I do!"

"I've never heard of anything like it," Poppie said. "What else does this Mr. Trants do? He just don't do all farming, does he?"

"He deals in real estate," Cousin Bos said. "He does a lot of things I don't know about. He and his wife travel a lot. All I know is he doesn't farm any more. I do the farming. I run this farm. I've even got a key to his house. I run this farm and I look after things."

Now, I knew Cousin Bos had told us the truth when he came to move us from Lower Bruin. He'd not been slurring Poppie and Mommie.

Now Cousin Bos had reached the front door which he opened for Poppie, Timmie and me to enter.

"Essej Trants and Ohio have given Faith and me a chance," he said.

Poppie walked through the door and Timmie and I followed him. Well, I'll tell you, Cousin Faith's living room was nice. It was real fancy, with good chairs and window curtains and nice wallpaper on the walls. When Cousin Faith heard us, she walked in. She was all smiles.

"I've got a big table and a little table in the dining room —with grub such as we have waiting for you," she said. "Any of you need to wash your hands? Here is the bathroom. Do it in a hurry!"

Cousin Bos had said they had running water in the house and a bathroom. We knew now he'd not been lying.

"We washed good and clean before we come, Cousin Faith," Poppie said.

When Poppie got a little disturbed he got a little nervous. Poppie called it getting vexed. When he walked to the barn, toolshed, hoglot and now inside this fine home, I think Poppie was a little vexed.

"Now all the big folks will eat at the big table," Cousin Faith said. "The little folks will eat around the little table."

"I'll eat at the little table, Mom," Buster Boy said. "I'd rather eat with them."

"Suit yourself, Buster Boy," she said.

I'd not seen Buster Boy in years. Not since the last time he'd come back to Lower Bruin for the Perkins Family Reunion. Here he was a big fine-looking man in a suit of clothes, a white shirt and necktie. He was about a two-hundred-twenty-pounder as Cousin Bos had said—almost as large as his mother and father put together.

Baby Brother and Baby Sister had their bottles and they were on a bed in Cousin Faith's and Bos' bedroom. Cousin Buster Boy sat in a small chair at the end of the little table where Cousin Faith had put little dishes, knives, forks and spoons.

"I'll help you, Mother, with the Little Ones," Buster Boy said. "I will really like to do this!"

"Now you be seated here," Cousin Faith said. "Bos has his place at the head of the table! Gil, you eat at that end. Sil, you, Pedike and Timmie on that side. I'll eat on this side closest to the stove. And Cassie-Belle and Tishie can eat on this side with me!"

"They can help you, Cousin Faith," Mommie said.

"No, they can't either," Cousin Faith said. "I've already got it prepared."

Cousin Faith went into the kitchen. She returned with a platter of steaks.

"These are T-bone steaks from our cattle," she said. "We raise the best! I've had these steaks in the deepfreeze in the utility room. And these are especially selected steaks for our people!"

She walked around the table and laid a steak on each plate. Then she walked over to the little table and laid a big steak on Buster Boy's plate. She went back into the kitchen and brought each of us a baked potato on a separate dish. She took one over to Buster Boy.

"We raised these potatoes, too, and I think just as good as any Idaho Bakers we've ever bought from Cantwell's Super Market," she said.

"One more trip to the kitchen and we all go to eating," she said.

Now, she came with a tray load of small dishes.

"This salad will fool you, Sil," Cousin Faith said to Mommie. "We still hole our late cabbage up in holes for the winter. I made this slaw from our cabbage."

"All this meal is from the farm," Cousin Bos said. "Everything but the coffee we'll have later. And this is real butter from our cows for your taters. Spread it over the hot tater and pepper it black if you want something good."

This was the first time in my life I had ever sat down at

a table to eat a steak, baked potato and fresh cabbage slaw. I'll tell you, a baked potato sliced open while it was hot, smeared with butter that melted into the potato, then peppered black, was out of this world. And this steak was better than the canned pork and canned beef we got from the commodities.

Over at the little table there was a lot of laughing. Our little brothers and sisters liked Cousin Buster Boy because he liked them. Now he walked over from the table with Sister Maryann and the little ones.

"Well, Mom, I've finished supper and I want to go," he said. "I'd like to have a little money!"

"How much do you want?" Cousin Faith said.

"About five dollars," he replied.

"You don't want to go out and get suds do you?" Cousin Faith asked him.

"No, Mom," he said.

"Well, I would think you wouldn't," she said. "Don't forget, Buster Boy, you have now come under responsibility with five little ones! You've got to live a good example before those five little youngins! Who do they have to depend on but their mother and you?"

"Mom, I'm not going to drink," he said. "I'm going straight there to see Ollie and the children!"

"But why do you want five dollars, Buster Boy?" she asked him.

"I might just need that much," he said. "And I don't have any money on me. I hate to go to see Ollie without anything."

"All right, Buster Boy," Cousin Faith said. "Here is your five dollars. But you be darned sure how you spend it! Spend it on Ollie and the youngins, all right! But spending it for suds and white lightning to wet your gullet, no! Remember, Buster Boy!"

"Yes, I'll remember, Mom," he said.

Cousin Faith gave him a five-dollar bill from her pocketbook. He took the money, thanked her and rushed to the door. He was off and away.

14 We were still sitting around the table after Buster Boy left.

"Bos and I have fallen in love with Widow Ollie's five little ones!" Cousin Faith said. "Honest, we could take all five children and raise them! We'd love to do it. Widow Ollie has really settled Buster Boy down."

Well, Poppie looked at Mommie and Mommie looked at Poppie.

"I'd better tell you—as you know, Buster Boy is our only child," Cousin Faith said. "And we've had our problems. We've seen him married to three wives and not one of his marriages worked. He didn't beget with a-one of his wives."

Poppie and Mommie got awfully quiet at the table.

"The first little thing he married and lived with longest— three years—she left him or he left her," Cousin Faith went on, "and in a month's time her comb got red and she married again. And in seven months she had a baby. She said she had a seven month's baby—well, our Buster Boy thought she had a nine month's baby boy and he was a-goin' and try to take him. This is what confused him most. Then the next marriage, he married a strollop and in two years this was on the rocks. The third woman he married was a floozy if I ever saw one. His marriage to her was one year. Now he's going with Widow Ollie Mayhew."

"How old is Buster Boy now, Cousin Faith?" Poppie asked.

"Twenty-nine years, one month and three days," she told Poppie. "He wants his fourth wife and to be settled before he's thirty!"

"Buster Boy almost growed up in Ohio didn't he?" Mommie asked.

"Yes, he did," Cousin Bos said. "We brought him here when he was a little shaver. He'd not gone to school a day. We moved from one farm to another until we found this bargain with Essej Trants. And we think this is better than owning our own farm! Yes, our Buster Boy lived right here with us when he went to Landsdowne County High School!"

"See, things can happen to a boy and girl in Ohio same as they can in the old country," Cousin Faith said. "You heard him ask me for money tonight! Well, that's his money. He earned it working in the Ohio State Department of Highway's Garage!"

"He can do anything mechanical," Cousin Bos bragged. "He takes that after me but he gets his size and good looks from his mother and her people."

Then Cousin Bos laughed and all of us around the table laughed or smiled except Cousin Faith.

"Bos, will you let me finish my story about Buster Boy to Gil and Sil and their oldest children," Cousin Faith said. "They live here now. They will find out from other people sooner or later and I'd like to tell it as it is."

"All right, Mother, you just go right on; I'll keep my mouth shet," Cousin Bos said.

Cousin Faith reached over behind her and got herself a pack of cigarettes from which she took one, and when she did, Poppie took one from his pack and struck a match and lit both cigarettes from the same match. Then Cousin Bos took his package of Honest John chewing tobacco from his pocket and crammed a chew bigger than a hen's egg behind his lean sun-and-wind-tanned jaw. His hawk eyes looked over everyone at the table. Then he got up and walked over and fetched himself a spittoon. This was something I'd seen in many of the houses on Lower Bruin. We'd never had one in our home for Poppie had always smoked and never chewed the fragrant weed, which was what we had always called tobacco. Cousin Bos hurried back to his seat at the head of the table as if he thought he might miss some of the talk. He picked up the spittoon and placed it down beside his chair.

"As I was saying about our son, Buster Boy," Cousin Faith continued. "When he gets a check he turns it over to me. And I pay so much each month on the debts he owes. I allow him just a little to spend. And I want his debts paid before he marries—I hope he marries Widow Ollie. She's twenty-seven—just the right age for him.

"Before I finish, I want to tell you what caused the downfall of our boy here in Ohio," Cousin Faith continued as she dubbed the end of her cigarette on the ashtray. "Now everybody talked about hooch, white mule and white lightning in the old country. Well, it was far harder to get than it is to get suds and liquor from the State Stores here. Agrillo don't have a State Whiskey Store, but believe you me—and you may not believe this—I'm the mother of a son who got to that stuff through the bootleggers. We had three big bootlegging jints. So one day I called the Sheriff's Office; I said: 'Sheriff Walmsey, why don't you and your deputies raid some of these bootlegging jints here in Agrillo?' 'Woman, we have no bootlegging jints here,' he said to me. 'Who told you we had them?' 'I don't drink and my husband don't drink,' I told him, 'but we have a son who is sinking to hell because of that stuff.' Then he said to me: 'Woman, what is your name?' And I said: 'This is none of your business what my name is. I'm telling you the truth! Now if you don't do something with these bootlegging jints, I'll tell you what I'm going to do. I'm going to get me a piece of sawed-off pipe and put it in a big pocketbook. I don't want a pistol. I'm too much of a lady to use one. And I might shoot and kill a man that might reform later and get on the Lord's side. But I'll go to his jint and ask with a smile for a pint or quart and open my pocketbook like I'm getting the money to pay him and come with the piece of pipe—hit him over the head and lay the son-of-a-bitch out.'"

Right here when she said that word I thought Poppie and Mommie would rise from their chairs at the table. Timmie was really wanting to say something but he was afraid. Well, I wanted to laugh. Tishie and Cassie-Belle wanted to laugh, too. We had never heard a woman talk like Cousin Faith. And I knew right now it wouldn't have been good for any older or younger woman to chase Cousin Bos. I knew Cousin Faith's people in the old country, the Bentons, were good people, but fighting people when they were stirred.

"And I said to the Sheriff over the phone: 'After I laid him out, I'd walk into your office with the bootleg whiskey he was getting for me—which I'd not paid for—and I'd say your son-of-a-bitch of a bootlegger is laying over there knocked out. Go get him. Send him to the hospital!' 'Woman are you crazy?' he said to me. And he hung up the phone on me. So I called the Federal Alcoholic Beverages in Columbus, Ohio. I told them my story. And, of course, they wanted to know why Sheriff Walmsey and his deputies hadn't acted. I told him there was some kind of a political tie-up—that our county was Republican and my family were all Republican, too. But the situation in Agrillo was terrible!

"Well," Cousin Faith talked on as she lit another cigarette, while Cousin Bos lifted up his spittoon from the floor and poured a full mouth of amber spittle into it, "the next night all three places were raided. I told them where to go. They got two of the bootleggers and all this news was in the *Ohio Gazette*. I wonder if Sheriff Walmsey thought the woman who had called him was so crazy, after all!"

"But what about this third place where they didn't catch them?" Poppie asked. Poppie was real alive and interested. "Why didn't they make arrests there?"

"I'll tell you, Gil," Cousin Faith said. "Our Buster Boy came home from work and he was talking about the raid. And he said: 'Mom, they didn't get my friend Jack Eversole and his brothers. And they'll never get him.' 'Why do you say that, Honey?' I said real sweet to Buster Boy. 'They've got a real place to hide their whiskey,' he said to me. 'I'm not too much interested,' I said to him, 'but I would like to know where they could hide whiskey these raiders couldn't find.' 'Mom, I don't mind telling you,' Buster Boy said. 'They hide it in the wall between the weather-boarding and the boxing. They've got that place loaded.' Well, I couldn't wait for Buster Boy to get off to work that morning and I got on the phone and called Columbus again. And I told them who I was and how I got my information. People, they come down here with some force. They tore that wall off and they took nearly a truckload of whiskey—all brands —and beer, too, from that place. They arrested the brothers, fined and jailed them. And you've never seen such a piece as there was in the *Ohio Gazette* about this one. Biggest raid ever staged in Ohio."

"What did Buster Boy say about it?" Mommie asked.

"He never thought about my calling Columbus," Cousin Faith said. "He never knew or suspected how it happened."

"What about the County Sheriff?" Poppie asked. "Did he know who reported them?"

"I'm glad you asked me, Cousin Gil," Cousin Faith said. "After the reports of these raids were published I picked up the phone and I called Sheriff Walmsey: 'Have you read about the raids on the three bootlegger jints?' I asked him. 'Yes, I have,' he said. 'We aided in these from my office.' 'You are a liar,' I said. 'You wouldn't do anything. I'm the woman who called you and you said there were no bootleggers here and I was a crazy woman. But I had all the dope on them. And I've got influence in a church here and among a lot of people. If you or any of your deputies ever run for a public office again, then you'll find out who this crazy woman is!' I hung up the phone."

Well, I was getting tired of sitting at the table. I got to fidgeting around. So did Timmie. Maybe, Cousin Faith suspicioned what was wrong.

"Pedike, come, I'll show you where the bathroom is," Cousin Faith said.

Brother Timmie got up, too, and as we followed her I saw a telephone on a table. We had never lived in a house with a telephone. "Think about her calling Columbus, Ohio, and reporting bootleggers in Agrillo," I thought as I followed her. And I knew I'd never want her after me. Women after Cousin Bos, if he told us the truth, had better be on the look-out too. She'd take care of them—maybe with a piece of pipe.

"Go right in there, boys," she said.

She went back. I opened the door and Timmie followed me in.

"What about this, Pedike," Timmie said. "Cousin Bos didn't lie about this place! What about this—right in the house! Can you believe it?"

Well, it was hard for me to believe. But I had used the boys' room in Wonder High School. I knew how to do it. Timmie had used the bathroom in the Wonder Junior High School. But we had never before used a bathroom in a home. Cousin Bos and Cousin Faith had really made good in Ohio.

When Timmie and I went back to the table, everybody was up.

"I'll rid the table, Sil," Cousin Faith said. "You and the girls won't need to stay and help. Your little ones need to be home in their beds."

Poppie went to the bed and lifted Baby Brother and Cassie-Belle got Baby Sister in her arms.

"Now, Sil, Bos can take you, Cassie-Belle and Tishie to Agrillo and get your wallpaper. I'll come and your girls can help me paper your house. I think we can paper a room a day."

"But Cousin Faith, we're having trouble now making both ends meet and I am expecting confinement and we'll have little or no money ahead and can't pay you to help me," Mommie said.

Then, Cousin Faith laughed and laughed and hugged little Mommie close to her.

"Pay from you, our people, I wouldn't think about," she said, with a happy smile. "Bos and I will help you all we can!"

"You know, I almost forgot something very important," Cousin Faith went on. "There will be a church bus at your home to get you and take you to our Freewill Baptist Church. You'll get to meet a lot of people from the old country."

"A church bus!" Mommie said.

Mommie and Poppie looked at each other. They couldn't believe, and I couldn't either, what people were doing for us.

"But my children's clothes for a Freewill Baptist Church in Agrillo, Ohio—" Mommie said. "So many will come in fancy Sunday clothes!"

"Don't worry about that," Cousin Faith said. "You've

got a fine-looking family and you always keep them clean! And your children are so well behaved. They let their elders talk first. And they come when you call them!"

"Church in the morning," I said to Timmie in a low voice. "We'll have to get up and stir and feed the pigs, milk the cows and I'll have to chop wood ahead to fire the cookstove!"

"Attaboy, church," Timmie almost whispered. "Going to church in a bus! Ever hear of anything like it! Church in a bus seeing all them people!"

Timmie was so excited I thought he'd say something before we got out of the house. Cassie-Belle and Tishie were excited too but they were like I was—they held their tongues and listened.

Cousin Bos was waiting at the front door. He was ready to take us home. Now we were moving—moving slowly out of the house—through the front door—along the walk between the rows of flowers on either side—and we could see our way just as if we walked in good daylight. Cousin Bos had flipped a switch by his front door and turned the lights on all the way to the road, barn, and toolshed where his truck was parked.

After we were all in the truck, little banty-rooster Cousin Bos hopped up like a rooster sparrow behind the wheel. He started the engine with a quick jerk that nearly threw us from our plank seats. In a jiffy he had us home.

"Don't forget to be ready for the church bus at nine-thirty," he told us as we unloaded from his truck. "Be ready at nine-thirty! The bus might not be here until nine-forty-five, but you got to be ready. See, we go on the minute in Ohio!"

15 Now in our house, as soon as the lamps had been lighted and the Babies and Little Ones put to bed, we met in the living room where Poppie dropped in his big rocking chair and lit himself another cigarette.

"I tell you, Cousin Bos didn't lie when he come over to Lower Bruin to move us," he said. "I thought he was slurring us or lying. But we know better now. I never saw anything like it! Look at his barn, toolshed and tools and that wonderful hoglot made of woven wire with all the hog houses and not even a hog there! Oh, what a chance he had!"

"And look at their home," Mommie said. "What if there was one house like it on Lower Bruin! All the people would be coming in to see it! What about renters on a farm having a chance like they have! I've never heard of anything like it! Honest, I could be so jealous but I won't. Look how Cousin Bos helped move us here. Look how he comes to see about us! And look how nice Cousin Faith was tonight! Look what a good time we had. And we never had a better supper."

"Well, Mother, I wonder if we will ever do so well," Poppie said. "Electric lights in a barn, a toolshed and even a hogpen!"

"And a house," Cassie-Belle said. "Look at the beautiful bathrooms! I tell you, the way we have lived on Lower Bruin—and still with lamps—but next year the promise of electricity and a bathroom."

"It's because we're so poor," Poppie said. "But Mr. Herbert said we were millionaires with this family!"

"But we don't show it with oil lamps in Ohio same as we had in the old country," Cassie-Belle said. "We lived in that old schoolhouse with two rooms added. The schoolhouse was nearly a hundred years old. We've always been on the tail-end of hard times!"

"Listen!" Mommie said.

She looked pretty hard at Cassie-Belle. Back on Lower Bruin, Cassie-Belle would have been considered marriageable age, for the girls married from fourteen to twenty; older than twenty, if one wasn't married, people wondered. She was considered an "old maid." But my sister Cassie-Belle took to school, to books, and she had a head of her own. I knew what Cassie-Belle was thinking. Why couldn't we have electricity in our house, electric lights, and everything like electric stove, refrigerator, bathroom—even television like other people had—even like the others on Mr. Herbert's many farms. We were the only family that didn't have this.

"But we have to crawl before we can walk," Poppie said.

"I've crawled long enough," Cassie-Belle said. "Look what we saw tonight!"

"And I feel the same way," Tishie said. "I'd like to have electric lights in our room and a little radio beside our bed, Cassie-Belle!"

"I didn't know this visit would make our youngins so dissatisfied, Gil," Mommie said.

Well, I didn't say anything. I didn't tell Poppie and Mommie that I planned to take some of my money I earned working for Mr. Herbert and buy us a radio set. I thought Sister Cassie-Belle was right in what she said.

"But look at the good things that have happened to us," Poppie said. "Now take a little time and think! And look how fast good things have happened. As The Word says, earn your living by the sweat of your brow. We are now doing this. We live in a six-room house. And it's never been a schoolhouse. Ain't I right?"

"Yes, Gil, you are," Mommie said as Poppie blew two

thin pale gray streams of cigarette smoke from his nostrils. "I want you to talk on. You're talking right. We ought to be thankful to the Lord for what has happened to us!"

"Yes, we're in Ohio," Poppie said. "We're in that blessed land beyond the river—a land where we've got a chance. And we've got a promise of better things to come. First time in my life I ever was paid a dollar an hour! And Timmie and Pedike earn together another dollar an hour! How can we beat this? What if we'd stayed on on Lower Bruin? What chance did we have there?"

"We could have been carrying commodities five miles on our backs," I said. "I want us to get away from that forever! I want us to forget it."

"But will we ever live in as nice a home as Cousin Faith and Bos?" Cassie-Belle asked. "Look what they have! Look at the way they live!"

"Yes, I expect we will catch up with them some day," Poppie said in his soft slow voice. "We might even go past them! But I've never even thought about passing them. I'm a humble man myself—a humble poor man. I'm a meek man and, according to The Word, the meek will inherit the earth. And this is the reason I say we will rise up in this beautiful land."

"I don't believe it, Poppie," Cassie-Belle said.

"Cassie-Belle," Mommie said.

"I know, Mommie, but I don't believe that," she said.

"Never talk back to your father," Mommie said. "Time might prove him right and then you will be ashamed of yourself!"

"I don't think time will prove him right," Mommie," she said.

"My daughter, you will see it pays to be poor," Poppie said. "You will see that living according to The Word will pay off in the days to come."

"I could say a lot more, but I won't," Cassie-Belle said.

Cassie-Belle was almost crying.

"Well, I know Cousin Bos and Faith left the old country —as poor a people as we had on Lower Bruin—and they've made good," Mommie said. "They have a nice home. And they have good vittals. But don't forget they left Lower

Bruin a long time ago and they have worked for everything they've got!"

"It's up early in the morning to do our work before we go to church. So, I think all of us had better get to bed and have good dreams," Poppie said. "Mommie, don't forget to set the alarm clock."

16 When the alarm clock went off, Timmie and I rolled out. I'd cut a big pile of stovewood for Timmie to carry in when he came outside and told me breakfast was ready. I'll tell you, to swing a double-butted ax before breakfast is good exercise and it will give you an appetite, too. I was hungry when I went to breakfast.

"We've got store-bought vittals," Mommie said. "But I can't cook like your Cousin Faith."

One thing about this breakfast, we didn't have grapefruit, cooked prunes and rice. We didn't have one thing in the commodities we'd lived on for three years in Lower Bruin. And we didn't have powdered eggs. We had real fresh country eggs—Mommie was told at Cantwell's Super Market by the clerk that they were. And we had real bacon and cinnamon rolls and coffee cake. And we had milk from our cows and fresh butter from our churn. But we had boiled coffee in a pot on the stove—Poppie always said when coffee was boiled it was strong enough to "bear up an iron wedge."

Timmie stood up at the table and each freckle on his face got browner as he stretched his body, so he could eat some more.

"My tummy feels as tight as a banjer head," Timmie said, patting his stomach as he sat back down in his chair and began to eat some more.

"Mind your manners, Timmie, and no more outbursts at the table like that," Mommie said.

My brother Timmie, all talk and all movement like my

mother—everywhere at once—freckle faced with light blue eyes and brown hair. Just about everybody liked Timmie, too. Now, I'm more like Poppie, slower to speak with broader shoulders. I have black hair and blue eyes and anyone who knows me will tell you I'm shy and hold my tongue. I think and wait before I ever speak. I liked my breakfast, too. I liked a change of food as well as Timmie. But I never said I did at our breakfast table.

When Poppie lit his cigarette at the end of the table he was through eating. All were through eating and this meant that Cassie-Belle, Tishie and Maryann would help Mommie wash dishes and put away the little food left. Then they would help Mommie dress the Little Ones for church. After they'd done these chores, they'd have to dress themselves.

"This morning, Timmie, I'll carry in the stovewood and let you and Pedike feed the pigs, feed and milk the cows and put the milk away," Poppie said.

This was the way it was in our home. Each one had work to do. And if we hadn't worked we could never have got it done. When we had done our Sunday-morning work, we would go in and dress in our Sunday best—which was not really good—to ride in a Freewill Baptist Bus to the Freewill Baptist Church in Agrillo, Ohio.

17 When the bus arrived, all of us were ready.

"I'm Jimmie Artner," said the driver.

He was a young man of about thirty. He was not more than five feet six with blue eyes, a long nose and a pimpled face.

"We're the Gilbert Perkins Family," Poppie said. "I'm Gil and my wife is Sil and if you haul us back and forth to church you'll get acquainted with our youngins!"

Poppie was dressed in his old blue-serge double-breasted coat suit with a couple of pencils up in the front pocket. He had on a stiff collar that fastened to his shirt with a collar button and a black bowtie. Little Mommie was dressed in a loose mother-hubbard dress. Mommie was little, yet so big she had to wear loose clothes. She had Baby Sister in her arms.

"What a fine looking family you have," Jimmie Artner said with a big toothy grin. "Just about enough to fill my bus."

There was a little seat up front for Jimmie Artner. Behind him was the first seat which was taken by Mommie and Poppie. In the seat behind them Cassie-Belle and Tishie sat with one of the Little Ones on each lap and one on the seat between them. Maryann, Timmie and I sat on the third and last seat. We filled the little bus which had a big sign up front, Freewill Baptist Church Bus.

"We've just moved from the old country south of the River," Poppie said.

"Yes, your Uncle Dick Perkins told me," Jimmie Artner

said. "Today you'll meet a lot of people from south of the River. They brought their religion with them and your Uncle Dick just about built our church."

"Yes, Freewillers believe in The Word," Poppie said. "We show the signs of our belief. Marry and replenish the earth."

"Now as your family grows—and it shows signs—I'll have to get a bigger bus!" Jimmie said.

A big smile was on Mommie's face as she turned around to look at us, to see if we were in order—sitting up straight with our faces to the front. Mommie often reminded me of a hen with her little chickens when they first come out of the eggs and she is looking them over and clucking to them.

"Everybody ready?" Jimmie asked. "All the babies safe?"

"All in good careful hands," Poppie said in his slow soft voice.

Jimmie started the engine and we were off.

"It's wonderful to ride to church in a car for the first time," Mommie said. "I can't believe it!"

"What?" exclaimed Jimmie Artner looking back. "Never rode in a car to church?"

"No, we've never owned a car," Poppie said. "I can't even drive one. We're poor people. Back on Lower Bruin we always walked to church and Mother and I toted the babies while the older children had to tote some of the Little Ones when they tired out on our two-mile walk. But we got to the House of the Lord, which was to us the Freewill Baptist Church."

"You can say that again," Jimmie said as we rolled pleasantly along, "the House of the Lord is a Freewill Baptist Church! We've got a lot of Freewillers in and around Agrillo, Ohio. And wait until you see what a nice churchhouse we have!"

"Ours was not much of a house back on Lower Bruin but the Spirit of the Lord was in it with us on every Sabbath," Poppie said. "And the Lord was present. Not one saw him but everybody felt His presence in our great revivals! I know I felt his touch on many occasions!"

"How did Poppie know He was there if he didn't see Him?" Timmie whispered in my ear.

"Shh—be quiet," I whispered to Timmie.

Mommie had heard the noise behind and she turned and looked straight at Timmie. She knew where to look, where the talk always started. Timmie just wouldn't keep his mouth shut. Some day if he kept on I knew his tongue would cut his throat. Mommie always said if a baby could talk before it could walk it's tongue would cut its throat. Well, Timmie had been the only baby in our family who talked before he could walk.

I could tell Jimmie Artner was happy to be handling a big family like ours to the Freewill Baptist Church! I wondered who else was hauled free. There was just something about a big family and being poor that made everybody take to us and want to help us—especially here in Ohio.

"We're getting close," Jimmie Artner said as he looked at his wrist watch. "We'll be a little early but our minister will want to meet you. And I think you've got kinfolks in our church!"

"Oh yes," Mommie said. "Uncle Dick and Aunt Susie. Cousins Bos and Faith Auxier—and their son Buster Boy! I don't know whether he goes to church or not!"

"Yes, sometimes," Jimmie Artner said. "But he's more on the Devil's side. But we know, no man gets so far away he can't be reached and cleansed of his sins! Buster Boy is a big fine-looking man. His looks, I've often thought, might have gone to his head—all his marriages—and the trouble he's given his parents!"

"Mr. Artner, I think you're wrong about his good looks among women being his downfall," Poppie said. "He's an only child. He growed up a lonely boy. And he said when he married wife number one they'd have more than one child. Well, they couldn't have any. He married wife two and they couldn't have any. He married wife three and it was the same. He really loves little children. And he's frustrated—tormented and troubled because he can't beget. The Lord said marry and replenish the earth, but some won't do it and some want to and can't. I've often thought about this!"

"Well, I'd never known Buster Boy felt that way about

children," Jimmie Artner said. "This will make me feel kinder toward him! He is faced with a problem only the Lord can solve."

"I see it!" Timmie called out. "I've been looking for a church all the way. I know it's a church! Look at that tall thing going up toward that white cloud!"

"It's a spire, Timmie," I said.

Mommie gave Timmie a look.

"What a smart boy he is to pick out our church in the distance," Jimmie Artner said with a big smile. He was pleased even if Mommie wasn't.

When our bus pulled up in front of the church, there were several people gathered on the front steps. They were there, perhaps, to meet us. Well, I'll never forget how wonderful we were treated—never anything like this that I could remember for us—when Poppie went up the steps carrying Baby Brother, and there was Little Mommie big and ready to have another.

Sisters Tishie and Cassie-Belle were caring for the Little Ones—then, Maryann, Timmie and I followed. And here we met Brother Cashew Boggs, from the old country, Pastor of the Freewill Baptist Church. He was a tall stooped man, wearing a gray suit, white shirt, black string necktie, with a Bible in his hand. I looked down to his feet. I never saw bigger shoes. They looked like runners on a sled.

"What a wonderful family," he said with a smile.

And he shook hands with all of us but the Little Ones and the Babies. And we told him our names. Here were Uncle Dick and Aunt Susie! Uncle Dick was all smiles when he introduced Poppie and Mommie as his niece and nephew. And here were Cousins Bos and Faith Auxier—and believe it or not, Second-cousin Buster Boy with Widow Ollie Mayhew and her five children. Buster Boy was all dressed up. He had Widow Ollie's baby in one arm and with a hand he held the next youngest child. He acted like a father with a family of five children.

And here were Mr. and Mrs. Joshua Herbert, who were as kind to us as kinfolks—and their two sons who ran the bulldozers.

Well, we met many people before Sunday School began. Then Timmie, Maryann, Cassie-Belle and I were sent into Sunday-school classes. Poppie and Mommie had the Babies and the Little Ones. There was a nursery at the Freewill Baptist Church that took care of the babies and the little children. This allowed Poppie and Mommie to go into the Bible class taught by Brother Cashew Boggs. I'd never heard tell of a church having this. Well, you should have seen this church. If there was one person here, there were three hundred.

After Sunday-school classes we assembled in the church to hear Brother Boggs preach what Poppie called a powerful sermon. The title of his sermon was *You Must Be Born Again.* I remember he made it plain that to be born again, people had to confess their sins, and when they were baptized, no sprinkling—they had to be put under the water. And it was better to put them under in a running stream, like the Jordan, where our Savior was baptized.

When the last hymn was sung and the last prayer was said and church was over, Poppie and Mommie made for the nursery to get Baby Brother and Baby Sister. My sisters, Cassie-Belle, Tishie and Maryann got the Little Ones.

And when we left the big Freewill Baptist Church— biggest building I'd ever been in—people seemed to follow us. We were dressed old-fashioned compared to them. But they liked us. They could tell Poppie was a family-loving man. And they could tell Mommie was a good mother. So many people met us and shook our hands in fellowship I couldn't begin to remember all of them.

I'll tell you when we got in our seats in the church bus, sitting up straight and facing the front, away from all the people who admired and loved us, I was glad. I was glad to be on our way home, to our cows and our pigs. And Jimmie Artner had us home in thirty minutes.

"Thank you, Mr. Artner," Poppie said.

"Just call me Jimmie," he said. "I'll be hauling you to church every Sunday. This is a pleasure to haul a family like yours to our Freewill Baptist Church."

When we got out of the bus and went into our home,

Poppie said, "I tell you it pays to have a big family and to be poor! Look how the people took to us! They loved us."

"I've never seen anything like it," Mommie said. "People just couldn't be nice enough to us! And what about Buster Boy being there with Widow Ollie Mayhew and her five youngins!"

"And he's not divorced," Poppie said. "That third wife won't give him a divorce. I know it's sin. But he's disturbed with a troubled mind. And we don't want to talk about him. It's up to Buster Boy and Widow Ollie and their Lord!"

But I had heard Poppie tell Mommie he was glad he didn't have a son like that Buster Boy. "Sil," Poppie said to her, "we'd have squared off and fit it out long ago. All them marriages and all that boozing! I'd have pounded some common sense and decency into his frustrated head."

18 Monday morning early, Timmie and I went by lantern light and fed the pigs, fed and milked the cows, turned them out for the day on pasture. We did our chores while Poppie filed his ax. We were ready now to begin another week's work.

"I look to be called home any time," Poppie said as he walked down the lane road toward Mr. Herbert's with his ax on his shoulder. "I'm looking for your mother to give us a Baby Brother or Baby Sister any time."

"Cousins Bos and Faith are coming today," I said, "to take her, Cassie-Belle and, maybe, Tishie to Agrillo to select wallpaper for our house."

"I know that," Poppie said. "It makes me worry. And when I worry I get so nervous! Mommie is the greatest person in my life. I know she runs things. What would I ever do without her?"

"Poppie, there's something I want to ask you," I said. "I won't do it without your fatherly consent! But I want to take some of my money and buy a battery-set radio for our living room so we can hear music and get news!"

"Poppie, I'd like to help him," Timmie shouted.

"If we get all week's work this week, we'll have one hundred dollars, for Mr. Herbert will take twenty dollars for two weeks' rent," Poppie said. "And we should be getting some dollars ahead. But there will be a doctor bill for your mother. Still we need music and we need news. This is Ohio. It is different here!"

A stream of cigarette smoke came back over Poppie's shoulder and thinned on the sweet-smelling wind of morning just as dawn was breaking and there was light enough to see our path.

"Pedike, I'm all for your getting that battery-set radio," Poppie said. "I think it would be wonderful!"

"Why not go Saturday after work?" I said. "I'll check the prices! If I don't have the money, I'll tell the merchant I work for Mr. Herbert and I'll make a down payment and finish paying for it by the week."

"We're strangers in Ohio but we won't be for long," Poppie said. "Maybe the merchant might let you get it on tick. Ohio is a good state but it makes youngins want more of the world's goods and finer things than the old country did. Seems like we're always moving and doing here, and on Lower Bruin we just stood still. Same old things day after day there."

"The reason I like Ohio, Poppie, the people don't stand still," Timmie said. "I don't like to stand still and I don't like to be still!"

"There goes Timmie popping off when Mommie's not around to make a face at him," I thought. "Poppie is easier on Timmie when he pops off."

We heard the bulldozers before we reached the field. And when we got there we knew exactly what to do. We were to do the same work we did last week.

When we went home, a little tired after our day, we got some surprise. And I thought to myself, people as good to us and had helped us as much as Cousins Bos and Faith, we should never say a word against them or Buster Boy.

"Well, what do you think about it, men?" Cousin Faith said. "We've just finished papering this room!"

"I've never seen anything so pretty in my life," Mommie said.

"It's too pretty for us," Poppie said.

There stood Cousin Faith in overalls and a blouse, a stocky big-bosomed woman, relaxing now and smoking a cigarette.

"It's nicer than newspapered walls on that old Lower Bruin schoolhouse," Tishie said.

"I love this room now," Cassie-Belle said. "It's nicer than

anything we've ever had. Think of this—the first wallpa-pered room we've ever had."

"Gil, I've had good helpers," Cousin Faith said. "Cassie-Belle and Tishie have good hands and they've learned quickly. They can really get up on the ladders! And they'll work!"

"Yes, Sil has learned them to work," Poppie said.

Brother Timmie wanted to whisper to me Poppie had made a mistake. Timmie made the same mistake once at the Wonder Junior High School and his teacher corrected him. Poppie should have said taught them instead of learned them.

"You know, Gil, who selected the paper for this room?" Cousin Faith said.

"I've no idear," Poppie said.

"You ought to know, Gil," Mommie said. "I selected it."

"Oh, that's why it has roses," Poppie said. He almost cried. "When we were sparking back in the springtime on Lower Bruin we walked the paths over the hills and searched for wild roses. We've never lived anywhere we didn't have rose bushes in the yard—from one to a dozen. So why not rose wallpaper in our living room! Oh, Sil, it's so pretty. It's just too nice for us!"

"If you feel like that in Ohio you'll never get any place, Gil," Cousin Faith said. "There's not anything too nice for you and this fine family. Beauty in a home for your children is great. Come Saturday at about noon, all these rooms will be papered! And we don't let Sil do a thing but stir the paste."

"I just can't believe it," Poppie said. "Everybody has been so kind!"

Cousin Faith lit up another cigarette and so did Poppie.

"Something else happened here," Mommie said. "I won-der if you noticed what has happened!"

"No, I didn't," Poppie said.

"All I saw as I was looking around on our way home was some fresh-plowed creek bottoms," Timmie said.

I'd seen them, too, but I didn't speak up. I've always been the most silent one among my brothers and sisters.

"That's just it, Timmie," Mommie said. This time she didn't make a face. He'd not spoken out of turn. "Mr. Herbert sent one of his workers here with a tractor, harrows and laying-off plows. All the plowed ground is what he's given you rent free for our garden and truck patches! Think, he wasn't a day doing all this with a tractor and it's more than what we used to farm on Lower Bruin with a mule and turning plow! And," Mommie said with a smile, "he sent seed potatoes, all kinds of garden seed, sugar corn and field corn seed and said you could plant your garden in the evenings after you and the boys had worked for him. The man—I didn't get his name—maybe he was one of Mr. Herbert's sons, said Josh Herbert needed you so much in the work you were doing and that you were one of the last earth men who knowed how to stack roots and burn, to plow mules on steep hills to set terbacker plants and the like!"

"What about that," Poppie said. "Garden and truck patches plowed free and free seed to plant 'em! I wonder if I'm dreaming all this! It's so hard to believe. So many good gifts are coming to us free. No, I can't believe it! It's because we're poor and we have a big family!"

"That might be it," Cousin Faith said.

At this moment Cousin Bos pulled up in the drive in his red farm truck. He came into the living room where we were all standing. He never spoke to anyone. He looked up and all around at the paper.

"A nice job, Mother," he said to Cousin Faith. "Were the ladders all right?"

"That's Cousin Bos," I thought. "Always the doer, the mover, the practical man."

"Yes, Bos, the ladders are okay," Cousin Faith said. "And I've had good help with Cassie-Belle and Tishie. They'll work. They've got good hands!"

"They'll make some men good wives one of these days," Cousin Bos said.

"I'm not eager," Cassie-Belle said. "I'm not so sure I would! I've got ideas beyond marriage!"

"What did you say?" Mommie asked her. "Talk like that! Marriage and children is part of The Word, Cassie-

Belle. Sometimes you talk so strange. I can hardly understand you, my own blood and flesh."

"I can't help it, Mommie," she said. "I speak from my
head. It is also in my heart!"

"Ohio and eddication will change our youngins," Mommie said.

"I hope so," Cassie-Belle said.

Tishie and I didn't say anything. And for once Timmie
kept real still.

Cousin Bos thought he might have stirred up a hornets'
nest in our family.

"Come on, Mother, we've got to get home," Cousin
Bos spoke softer.

Cousin Bos had a big chew of tobacco behind his sun-
and-wind-tanned jaw.

"My kinfolks, I'll be here early in the morning to paper
the second room," Cousin Faith said. "As I've said, Saturday at noon, the Lord willing and barring accidents, we'll
have this house papered."

And Cousins Bos and Faith walked out of the room toward the red farm truck. They were on their way, while
our family stood in the living room looking at our first
wallpapered room—a wallpaper of roses, Poppie's and
Mommie's favorite flower. Very soon Timmie and I would
do our evening chores.

"But if this house is wallpapered by Saturday afternoon,
late Saturday evening we might have music and news in
here with a battery-set radio," I thought.

This battery-set radio was on my mind. It would not
escape. I had to have it. I thought our family would love
music and news—and we had never had anything like this.
We'd never even taken a newspaper in the old country.
And I wanted a change. I agreed with Cassie-Belle on a lot
of things—only I was silent. I knew we ought to have
things other people had. And now we were getting our
house wallpapered—this was great. I'd be glad to see the
paper Cassie-Belle and Tishie had selected for their room.
And what they had selected for our room since we were
working and couldn't be there to help select it.

19 This was one of the greatest and busiest weeks in our lives. Poppie, Timmie and I finished chopping, piling and burning all the bulldozer clearings. We were ready for Poppie's plowing the steep places and our planting the corn and setting the tobacco plants on the best acres Mr. Herbert had selected to take the new ground wildness from the land, before he sowed it in fescue grass for pasture. Fescue was a wonderful grass, so Mr. Herbert told us, a grass that would hold topsoil—found in the old country on a mountain top. Now it was the rage all over America. Something really good had come from the old country. I didn't realize now that something more good had come from the old country to Ohio—and this would be our family.

This week Cousin Faith and Cassie-Belle and Tishie papered all of our house. Cassie-Belle and Tishie had selected a wallpaper of a little red and black design. Poppie and Mommie said they didn't understand it—I know I didn't. I think it was modern.

"Why did they select this kind of paper?" Mommie asked. "I don't understand my daughters!"

Well, our sisters had selected for us a wallpaper with model cars—and a car we had never owned. I wondered why they hadn't selected one with radios or televisions. But Timmie and I loved the wallpaper in our room. All other selections in our house, Mommie, with Cousin Faith's help, had selected. And here we lived in a six-room house with new fresh wallpaper on the walls of each room. I must say, I liked the paper on my sisters' and our walls better than the other rooms. I didn't care for the old-fashioned roses on our living room that caused Poppie and Mommie to shed tears.

On evenings after our ten hours' work was done, Poppie, Timmie and I planted first our potatoes—we were so late. Potatoes should have been planted in late March in the old country. Now we planted them in late May in Ohio. And we planted our sweet corn and our field corn. In our garden, Poppie, a good gardener, took charge and we planted everything from beets and radishes to butter beans. I couldn't believe Mr. Herbert had left out any garden seeds. He'd even sent us a peck of onion sets to plant in rows.

"One seed he left out and I'll have Cousin Bos to fetch me," Poppie said. "He didn't bring any pumpkin and cushaw seeds. I want to put them down everyplace in this fertile ground. Come falltime when we harvest the crops we'll have big pumpkins everywhere and we'll have the long-necked cushaws laying over the ground! Oh, how I'll like to see this again. I'll put the pumpkins and cushaws back in the fodder shocks and let them ripen. This will give Josh Herbert something to see!"

And this is what Poppie did. He planted pumpkins and cushaws in our garden and in all of our truck patches. And as Poppie said, our garden and our truck patches on Josh Herbert's farm were bigger than all our farming on Lower Bruin. In one week we had got our truck patches and garden planted and our house papered.

I'd asked Cousin Bos if he'd come and get me on Saturday at four o'clock and take me to Agrillo and help me find a battery-set radio. And he promised to come and get me.

On Saturday when Mr. Herbert came to the field with our checks I received my first pay check for thirty dollars. Timmie received the same and Poppie received as much as both of us together.

"But, Josh, this is too much," Poppie said. "You didn't take out for two weeks' rent."

"I'm breaking my contract with you, Gil," Mr. Herbert said.

"What?" Poppie asked.

Poppie was really vexed.

"But don't worry, Gil, it's all in your favor," Mr. Herbert said. "I'm not going to take any rent from you for the house. You and your family will work. Your wife is a real mother. And you've got a million-dollar family. And as I've said, you need dollars more than I do. I've been a slave to make dollars, but what are they? I like your big family and your children."

"I don't know what to say," Poppie said. "I can't believe all this is true! You've been too good to us already! Now, to give us free rent!"

"I'm an old man and I can't take it with me," Mr. Herbert said. "I'd rather give you dollars than take them.

When we went home, Cousin Bos was there waiting for me. He'd already taken Cousin Faith home at noon for she had papered our house—all six rooms—as she had planned. Saturday at noon. What a woman! What a worker! But Mommie was sure Ohio had changed Cousin Faith. Mommie thought she was as rough as a cob with all the cuss words she used.

"Well, I'm here, Pedike, to take you where I think you can get that battery-set radio," Cousin Bos said. "We'll go to Smith's Television and Radio Appliance Company. I know Bert Smith who runs the place. I know him well."

Poppie had let Timmie and me keep our checks.

So I got in the truck with Cousin Bos and we were off. Cousin Bos was nice. Maybe he bragged a little too much. But that was his way.

"You'll want radio today, but it will be television tomorrow," he said. "Right now, to be up-to-date, it's television in Ohio!"

Well, we were in Agrillo in a few minutes. And Cousin Bob parked in front of Smith's Television and Radio Appliance Company.

When we walked in, Cousin Bos did the talking as usual.

"We want to look at a battery-set radio," he said.

"We don't have one," a young clerk said.

"If you don't have it where do you think we could find one?" Cousin Bos asked.

"Maybe at Prater's Secondhand Store, Main 103," he said.

"Thank you," Cousin Bos said. "Come on, Pedike."

The clerk laughed. I think he laughed at my name.

We left Cousin Bos' truck parked here. We walked only a block. There was no one in this secondhand store except an old man. He was much older than Cousin Bos and Poppie.

"Do you have a battery-set radio?" Cousin Bos asked.

"We've a beautiful radio cabinet piece," he said. "One of the finest! Really a nice piece of furniture! But, of course, we don't have batteries for it!"

"Forget the batteries," Cousin Bos said. "What's the price of the radio?"

"Ten dollars," he said.

"Will you take eight?"

"Yes, I will."

"Sold," Cousin Bos said.

"Will you take my check?" I said.

"Who's on it, Sonny?" asked the older man.

"Joshua Herbert," I said.

"I sure will," he said. "You bet I'll take a check on him. He's a hard-working old millionaire. He came to Ohio with nothing. He's made it with hard work and good management. And he's a Republican."

I endorsed my check. I paid him eight dollars and he gave me twenty-two dollars. Cousin Bos had gone to get his truck. We loaded the radio cabinet into his truck.

"Now we'll get batteries," Cousin Bos said. "And I'll set it up for you. You'll have music and news this Saturday night."

Well, Cousin Bos knew where to go to get the batteries. I paid for them with my cash. Batteries cost only six more dollars. I had fourteen dollars in my battery-set radio. And when we drove home, Mommie and Poppie thought my radio was a pretty thing. So did my sisters.

Cousin Bos put the batteries in. He turned the dial. He got music from Nashville, Tennessee. He got a man named Johnny Cash. I'd never heard of him. It was a wonderful program.

"Just turn that dial and you can get stations, music and news from all over," Cousin Bos said. "You've got a radio now! And it plays. If it ever stops, let me know. I'll fix it for you."

Cousin Bos, always in a hurry, left us as fast as he had come. All our family gathered in our living room. And we had music now that we loved. We sat and listened to the Nashville music until it was over. Then I turned the dial. I picked up stations in Louisiana; Atlanta, Georgia; Denver, Colorado; San Francisco, California; Chicago, Illinois; New York City and Boston, Massachusetts. We stayed up until eleven o'clock listening. This was the longest we'd ever all sat up together. What a great joy this radio had brought us. And this had been my idea. It was a great evening, and to think I had only to work less than a half week for it.

"Ain't it sweet music?" Poppie said. "Think of it a-comin' into our new wallpapered room from all over America! The Lord has sure been good to me! I say it pays to trust and obey and live by The Word. Two firsts here tonight! We're living in our first wallpapered house and we've got a nice radio bringing in the good music!"

As I say, I never remembered a week in our lives that would equal this week.

20 Monday morning we were in the field at the break of dawn. Mr. Herbert had the muleteam fed, harnessed and waiting when we arrived at his barn. He drove the team and Poppie carried the roto-cutter plow on his shoulder while I carried the single-shovel plow used for laying off rows to plant on the hillslopes. Timmie carried a basket of tobacco plants Mr. Herbert had pulled from the tobacco bed last night. The large tobacco bed and a water hole was down in the valley between the two slopes of our clearings. Mr. Herbert was a wise old farmer. He put them close to the tobacco ground so we could get plants and water in a hurry.

Now the very first thing that Poppie did was to take one of the big mules and hitch him to the laying-off shovel plow. Mr. Herbert stood by watching Poppie lay off the rows as straight around the slope as if each had been surveyed. While Poppie laid off ground, Timmie went down to the water hole and came back up the slope with a full bucket of water. He carried the plants in a coffee sack shaped like a hammock, which he swung on one shoulder, and the bucket with a dipper on the side in his hand. Timmie was prepared to drop the plants and pour the water, too. This was the way we used to set tobacco on Lower Bruin before Poppie went on to commodities. After we went on to the commodities, we just did enough day's work to pay house rent and buy a few secondhand clothes to wear.

Mr. Herbert, who liked to see how we began each new piece of work, stood by and watched Timmie drop plants, pour water and wet the ground where he set tobacco. I looked up and Mr. Herbert smiled at me and shook his big old roundish face in a friendly way. There was a half-moon smile on his lips.

"Only boys and men from the old country know how to set terbacker on a hillside," he said.

I didn't say anything. I kept on setting, with Timmie dropping the plants and pouring the water, and around the hillside in a long row we moved while Poppie went up the hillside, row after row, using one mule, until he had laid off rows for this tobacco patch. It was in the most fertile ground on this big hillslope—a half-mile long, a fourth of a mile high—cleared by bulldozers and by Poppie's ax chopping poles, big roots, and stumps and Timmie's and my carrying them to piles where we burned them with the help of cans of kerosene.

Poppie came down the hill leading the big mule, whose name was Dick, to where Mr. Herbert was standing. "Gil," he said, "I've never seen a man who can plow a straighter furrow!"

At this time, Timmie and I were back to the end where Poppie and Mr. Herbert were standing. This made two rows we'd set and we'd have to pull more tobacco plants and get more water. Poppie had furrowed about two acres of ground in the center of this slope which had the best topsoil.

"Well, I've plowed many a furrow on the hillslope but not many in level land," Poppie said. "All we had to farm on Lower Bruin were the steep slopes. More well-to-do farmers had the bottoms. Now, Josh, I'll hitch the team up together again and use the root cutter on the places where the bulldozers couldn't plow the ground with bogharrow. I've got enough ground laid off here for my boys for a couple of days at least!"

"They can't pull plants, water and set this patch in two days," Josh Herbert said. "If they can, I'll raise their wages to seventy-five cents an hour. As I've told my wife and sons, you and your boys are the last of the earth men. You're just what I need on this farm."

"We'll set this piece in two days," Timmie whispered. "Seventy-five cents an hour! Think of it, Pedike! Nearly as much as Poppie!"

"Shh—" I whispered for Timmie to shut up. He was nearly beside himself to make seventy-five cents an hour.

I knew that a man couldn't drop plants any faster or pour more water than Timmie. And I knew Poppie with his big hands, his big block-body couldn't bend over as well and couldn't set as many plants as I could. As heavy as he was, he couldn't hold his footing on a slope as well as I, either. I could move so much faster. Timmie and I were doing the work of two fast men. And Mr. Herbert, who knew how to work, knew in a few minutes what we were doing. Poppie as doing something with a big muleteam—Dick and Dutch —holding the handles of a shovel plow and a big root cutter. Timmie couldn't do this. But I thought I might be able to.

Poppie had his team hitched to the root cutter and was plowing one of the steep slopes. We used up our plants and were going to the tobacco bed to get more.

"Can Pedike select the right plants?" Mr. Herbert asked Poppie.

"Have no worry about Pedike," Poppie said. "Timmie can do it too. They've helped from the time they were little boys!"

"Oh, something else before I leave you and go back to my work," Mr. Herbert said. Timmie and I were taking the canvas up from the tobacco bed. But we were close to Poppie and Mr. Herbert and we could hear them talk as we pulled the larger, nice tobacco plants and stacked them closely and neatly—better than Mr. Herbert had done—in the sack.

"Can Pedike use an old-fashioned corn planter!"

"Yes, he can follow me like a grown-up man with one," Poppie said. "But do you have a corndrill?"

"Yes, I have," Mr. Herbert said. "Do you suppose you could use a muleteam corndrill on these steep slopes?"

"Yes, I'm sure I can," Poppie said. "I've drilled corn on steeper slopes than these back on Lower Bruin. This is a good muleteam. I can pace them real slow for the steep places. And while I drill this slope, which will be ready soon as I get this steep bluff plowed—I can do it today—I'll be ready to start drilling the corn into this slope tomorrow! I'll work on this while the boys finish a-settin' the terbacker here tomorrow. See, if I drill, this will free both boys, one to drop and water and one to set!"

"Great management, Gil," Mr. Herbert said. "I thought I'd be able to do my picking up roots, poles, stumps and burning over on the other slope by the time you and your boys finished this one. But I've not. It's been said I used to be able to do the work of three men!"

"Yes, but when you get to be a Grandpa—" Poppie said.

"Seventeen times," Mr. Herbert had broken into what Poppie was saying with a big smile.

"And the hair changes color—" Poppie started to say.

"Yes, from black to snow white," Mr. Herbert interrupted Poppie again.

"It's time for you to slow down," Poppie said. "And you can't take all your land, money, livestock, houses, farm machinery, sawmill and feedmill to Heaven with you!"

"That's a fact," he said. "I know that but I've enjoyed making it. I've liked to work. Don't know what I'll do when I can't work any longer. I was hungry as a boy. And, after I crossed the River to Ohio, I foresaw great wealth. I've enjoyed matching my trading ability, my work and management against others. I've got a family that will work, just as you have. This has helped me. You have to work for it! This is the only way! So, I'd better get back to my slope and get it finished!"

"Yes, you had," Poppie said in a voice slower than this morning wind down in this valley. "We'll soon be over on that side! How much will you set in terbacker over there?"

"About four acres," he said. "I've got it staked off. It's better around on my side—north hillside is always better ground. I don't know why it is—but it's the truth!"

"Yes, but that good old sunshine on south hillslopes of a morning helps grow terbacker," Poppie told him. "I think of the old worn-out hillslopes of Lower Bruin! What good terbacker the sun helped us grow! This far North in Ohio, I don't know!"

"We can still grow it here," Mr. Herbert said. "And the timber we've taken from these slopes, the paper wood, and now the terbacker and corn crops will pay for this farm. And look what pasture land I'll have when I sow this in the wonder fescue grass. Fescue for my dairy herd or my white-faced beef cattle! And another thing, Gil, I've got a breed of cattle going! I breed the black Angus bull to my short horn—you know, roan-colored cattle—and I get a silver breed. Such pretty things—for both beef and milk. Have you heard of my new breed?"

"No, I've not," Poppie said. "You know I don't care too much about this mixing. The Lord put everything on this earth—and for a purpose. And the birds of the fields don't mix. Owls don't mix with hawks. Hawks don't mix with chickens. Sparrows don't mix with redbirds. The black-snakes and copperheads and rattlesnakes don't mix. The rabbits, possums and squirrels don't mix. So I've allus believed with The Word—everything to its own kind. I've watched all living life around me all my life and this is the way its been."

"Poppie's said the wrong thing," Timmie whispered.

"Shh—" I whispered for him to keep his mouth shut.

This was what Poppie believed. Let him say it. I didn't know of any mixtures in wildlife I'd known. I'd read where there were twenty-eight kinds of sparrows and each to its own kind had kept its identity.

But Mr. Herbert just stood there. He didn't know what to say to Poppie. So he turned and walked up the slope to finish his gathering of poles, stumps and roots torn up by the big blades of the bulldozers.

Now, it was something to see mighty Poppie, strong as a bull, with a big muleteam in front of him, holding the handles of the root cutter around the steep slope.

When Mr. Herbert returned to eat his lunch with us, his eyes got big and he smiled.

"Work is moving here," Mr. Herbert said. "And this is man and mule work. Machinery can't do this."

"Have the seed corn and drill ready for me tomorrow," Poppie said. "I'll be ready to plant this big slope."

"Look at what Pedike and Timmie are doing," Mr. Herbert said. "I wouldn't have thought it! About one-fourth done!"

"Seventy-five cents an hour," Timmie blurted out.

Poppie was plagued and I wish I could have put my hand over Timmie's mouth. Timmie was letting his tongue cut his throat. This tongue was helping cut Poppie's and my throats, too.

At the end of this week, Poppie had plowed the bluff and he had drilled the corn into this slope. On Monday and Tuesday, Timmie and I had finished setting the tobacco on our slope, and the last four days we had worked on the larger and more fertile patch Mr. Herbert had staked off and Poppie had laid off for us. Now, we had further to carry plants and water, but we had set our half of this patch. We had got our raise, too. Poppie got his check for sixty dollars and Timmie and I got a check for forty-five dollars each.

"I agree with you, your sons ought to have separate checks," Mr. Herbert said.

"That suits me," Timmie said right in the tobacco patch Saturday afternoon when we had quit for the day. "Gee-whilligens! It's great to earn this much in a week!"

"That boy might go places, Gil," Josh Herbert told Poppie.

21 When we walked home proudly with our pay checks, Cousin Bos was there waiting to take us to Cantwell's Super Market.

"Pedike and I got a raise," Timmie shouted.

He showed his check to Cousin Bos and then to Mommie.

"I'll say that's a good wage for an hour," Cousin Bos said. "But you and Pedike are boys who will work. People on Lower Bruin used to have to work or starve. Who was it who said in an early day in our country, them that won't work shan't eat?"

"Captain John Smith," Timmie shouted like he's the only one who had ever known this fact. "He told the settlers this at Jamestown! I've had my history."

Well, Mommie just looked at him. She was plagued with his affliction—that his tongue would cut his throat.

"Now, I've got the grocery lists made out," Mommie said. "Cassie-Belle can go with you and Gil, Bos, to get our groceries for the week-end and next week!"

"Look who's coming!" Bos said.

"Uncle Dick," Poppie said. "I wonder what he wants!"

Uncle Dick parked his car behind Cousin Bos' truck. He got out, came up the walk smoking a big cigar.

"Howdy, Uncle Dick," Poppie said.

"Howdy, Uncle Dick," Mommie said.

Cousin Bos and all of our family standing out in our yard spoke to Uncle Dick.

"Well, I won't be long in stating my business, Gil," he said. "I've made arrangements for you, Sil, to have my doctor in your confinement, which cannot be very far around the corner."

Hearing the word "confinement" to us children, especially the older ones, and the younger ones above the age of accountability—which was twelve years—meant only one thing. Mommie was about to have another Baby Sister or Baby Brother. And for my sisters, Cassie-Belle, Tishie and Maryann, it meant a lot more work. And Mr. Herbert's black- and red-raspberry and strawberry seasons were near, when he'd need berry pickers. All three of my sisters, Cassie-Belle, Tishie and Maryann, wanted to pick berries, but Mommie would have to have one at the house—maybe Cassie-Belle, maybe Tishie or maybe Maryann—to give her more experience with fixing formulas, feeding the Little Ones and diapering the babies. Mommie always had two since I could remember that had to be diapered—and when another one was born the older of the two babies lost his or her diapers.

"Yes, we know her time is getting close," Poppie said.

"I'll take care of all expenses," Uncle Dick said. "I want you to have my doctor, an older man—Dr. Gaylord Zimmerman. He's a good all-around doctor—a good heart doctor and a good baby doctor. He's brought a lot of babies into this world. A lot of men that he's brought into the world in Landsdowne County, Ohio, are named Gaylord for him."

"Well, that is very nice, Uncle Dick," Mommie said.

"You're really too good, Uncle Dick," Poppie said.

"And something else," Uncle Dick said. "I want you to go to Landsdowne County Hospital this time! I want to know— I want word as soon as I can get it—so I can send the ambulance for you. You've not got a phone."

"Hospital!" Mommie said.

I thought Mommie was going to fall over. Cassie-Belle, Tishie, Timmie and I were standing in the yard with them and honest, this scared us. Not one of us had ever been in a hospital. I thought there must be something seriously wrong with Mommie—more than her just going to have a baby.

"All my children but two have been born in the houses

where we lived," Mommie said. "All but two with a midwife. Pedike and Maryann were born in the corn field before
I could get down off the hill to the house!"

"This time you're in Ohio and we want you to go to the
hospital like other women and have your baby," Uncle Dick
said. "Your children are of my flesh and blood and I'd like
to be of some help to you. I'll always be of more help than
you suspect. I've always worked from the front first and if
I can't work this way, I work in from the sides—all the
way around and even behind!"

"But, Uncle Dick, I'm afraid of a hospital," Mommie said.

"It's a-makin' me awful nervous," Poppie said. "When I
think of the hospital, I can't think of life but I think of
death. Back on Lower Bruin when we hauled one out for
the hospital he was a goner. We hauled him back in a
wooden box."

"Well, I won't laugh," Uncle Dick said. "But Lower
Bruin, back years ago, and even now, is not Ohio. Women
go to hospitals to have their babies! To have your baby at
home and have Dr. Zimmerman come to the home is an old-
fashioned idea here. Women have gone to the hospital to
have their babies as long as we've lived here. I'll leave you
now, Sil and Gil, but I want you to think this over!"

I didn't see anything wrong with Mommie's going to
the hospital to have a Little Baby Brother or Baby Sister
and I don't think Cassie-Belle, Tishie and Timmie did—but
what we feared was there must be something wrong with
her other than having a baby. If something happened to her,
what would and could Poppie do without her? What could
her children do without her? Little Mommie was the boss
at our home.

On Sunday, after church services at the Freewill Baptist
Church, Uncle Dick and Aunt Susie talked to Mommie and
Poppie about Mommie going to Landsdowne County Hospital to have her baby. Even the Reverend Cashew Boggs
talked to Mommie and Poppie. I know Uncle Dick and
Aunt Susie had something to do with that. But Mommie
didn't want to go—for she was still scared.

22 Monday morning Poppie began drilling the corn on the North slope while Timmie and I continued to pull tobacco plants from the large tobacco bed and carry them up the hill to the loamy flat where Timmie dropped plants, poured water and I set.

In three days Timmie and I had finished setting the tobacco and we moved up high on this slope to help Mr. Herbert.

"One of these days, Pedike, I'm going to be an Uncle Dick Perkins or a Mr. Joshua Herbert in Ohio," Timmie said. "I'm not going to be working for the other fellow. He's going to be working for me. I'm going to own a big fine farm, a big home and have everything modern in it! You just wait and see! I can work and think right with the Ohioans!"

"You're getting to be an Ohioan mighty fast," I said. "You're as much Ohioan right now as Cousin Bos, Cousin Faith, Uncle Dick and Aunt Susie!"

"I'm glad that I am," he said. "I want to forget Lower Bruin as soon as I can. I want to forget carrying coffee sacks filled with commodities from Blakesburg to Lower Bruin. I'd rather earn my money and buy than to have it given to me."

I'd never heard brother Timmie so fired up.

When we moved up high on this slope to help Mr. Herbert we found he wasn't near finished picking up roots, stumps and poles. And we soon figured out what his trouble was. He was too big and thick to stoop over like we could.

He couldn't move as fast as we could. So he used the ax—for he could strike a powerful blow—just like Poppie.

"You boys are going to make the difference," he said. "You can really move."

His bragging on us when he was close by and watched us work was a lot of help. We liked to be bragged on by a millionaire like Mr. Herbert, who would still get out and work. And he was old enough to be Poppie's father. He was old enough to be our grandfather! So we did the running, picking up and carrying to the piles. We carried cans of kerosene and poured over the piles so we could get a quick burn-up of the heaps and keep ahead of Poppie. Poppie was down under the hill, with Dick and Dutch hitched to the two-mule drill, coming up this slope row by row.

Now, if we could get the roots, skinned poles, stumps and other objects picked up ahead of Poppie—and burned—we would get this slope planted in corn by quitting time on Saturday. Timmie and I knew this was what Mr. Herbert had dreamed—only he had dreamed we would be finished a week later. We'd be a week ahead of his schedule—and this would be early June—late for planting corn in Lower Bruin—but this far north in Ohio the season was later.

It worked out just right. Saturday at four we had helped Mr. Herbert finish his side of the valley. And when we had finished, Poppie drilled his last row of corn.

"I've never seen anything work out like this, Gil," Joshua Herbert said. "We finished at the same time. I've had good working sons—long ago when they were young, and now. But I've never had better helpers than your sons!"

"I learned them to work on Lower Bruin," Poppie said. Timmie jumped two feet high.

"Calm down, Timmie," I said. "Our father is talking."

I knew he wanted to tell Poppie that he'd made a mistake in his English. Well, Poppie made many of these and so did Mommie.

"Well, we've got the tobacco set," Mr. Herbert said. "And we've got this valley planted in corn. My sons have planted the bottom lands that will be plowed, harrowed, fertilized and planted by machinery. Here was the land I wanted to see planted. And I've worked with the right father and sons—man and boys—who knew how to help me do it! We've done it! I can't believe we've done it one week ahead of my schedule!"

"How big a terbacker base do you have, Josh?" Poppie asked.

"Twelve acres," he said. "We've got six acres already set on another farm. I figure we have close to six acres here. So this will be all!"

"Twelve acres?" Poppie said.

He couldn't believe anybody had a twelve-acre tobacco base.

"But, Gil, my God, I've got 18,000 acres of land," he said. "This is not much tobacco base for 18,000 acres of land!"

"No, I don't guess it is," Poppie said.

"The more a man has the more our Government cracks down on him," Mr. Herbert said. "It is the policy of our Government to crack down on him—if he works and tries to accumulate—and put him on a level with the rest who won't work and who don't give a damn! See, about half of us now help support a little less than another half! And the lesser half is growing by leaps and bounds—yes, even in Ohio! And when that times comes, as our President has said, when one half of this country has to help keep the other half, we are goners! We've met our Waterloo as a nation!"

Poppie, Timmie and I didn't say a word. We'd not heard talk like this before. This was one time Timmie didn't pop off. We had been on that other side, but thanks be to God, Mr. Herbert didn't know it. Even for one week, the grub we'd eaten in Ohio we had brought from home—commodities. We'd brought handouts from Greenwood County!

"When I'm no longer here, and maybe you're not either, Gil, you'll remember the words I've said," Mr. Herbert said. "People should be provided work—and the blind, the lame, the halt and them of unsound mind—the old and helpless—should be helped. But never the strong, able, and willing to work."

I'll tell you, Mr. Herbert's words made me tremble. Look how we could work—how willing we had been when we found work and had a chance to work. Look what we had done and what we were doing. Now on this Saturday afternoon, Mr. Herbert was writing a check to Poppie for sixty dollars and one for me and one for Timmie for forty-five dollars. How life had changed for us since we had begun to work! What a state was this Ohio—this land beyond the River!

"Now one more little secret before we part," Mr. Herbert said. "We've finished this valley, Gil. I don't want you to pick berries. You're not a berry picker with your big hands. But you report to me, Monday morning. Bring your ax—I have a man's work for you. But my strawberries by Monday morning should be red on the hillslopes on my farm down the creek. I want your sons and as many of your daughters as I can get. Last year half of my strawberries rotted in the field. I couldn't get berry pickers! People talk about no work but who wants to work? And over half of my red and black raspberries rotted, too. Can you provide the hands, Gil, in your big family to help save my berry crops?"

"Maybe we can if Sil doesn't have her confinement," Poppie said. "And even if she does, we will send you berry pickers."

"Monday morning?" Mr. Herbert asked.

"My sons and as many of our daughters as we can spare," Poppie said. "Maybe three girls! And all are wanting to pick berries to earn money to buy new clothes when they enter Ohio's schools this September."

23 Saturday after our chores were done and we ate supper, this was a great time for our family. Little Pearse's empty plate was always on our table, but it was so full there was really no place for Little Pearse's empty plate. And there was no need, so I thought, for Mommie's and Poppie's continued grief. There were ten of us living—another soon to be born. Poppie was a happy man sitting up at the end of the table with a little one on each side—Mommie at the other end of the table with one on a high chair, one on her lap. And as she said, she believed she was carrying a boy the way he kicked. She said a little girl couldn't kick the way he did. Now this was funny to Poppie. He was never much given to laughter. Many neighbors back on Lower Bruin even considered Poppie as sour as an old-fashioned winter apple that grew on trees so tall that Timmie and I—who were good climbers up branches of trees—could hardly climb them to get the apples that hung on until after frost. But this rumor that Poppie was as sour as a winter apple was not true. Poppie could laugh. And when Mommie told him she thought her next one would be a Baby Brother because he was kicking like a little bull calf, Poppie thought that was one of the funniest things he'd ever heard. And Poppie wasn't just pleased because Mommie said their next would be a boy. He was not partial. Poppie loved his daughters same as his sons.

After each evening meal we spent time in our wallpapered living room listening to news and music on our radio. But

Saturday was before Sunday, a day of worship and rest, Poppie said, because the Lord made the world in six days and he rested after His hard week's work on Sunday. So on Saturday evening all of us except the sleepy little ones Mommie and my sisters put to bed, stayed up to get the eleven o'clock news.

And when we sat up on Saturday evenings, we listened to our parents talk first. We were silent, except Timmie sometimes, when they talked. And when they were silent we talked and laughed with each other and made plans.

Now what we talked about this Saturday evening was berry picking and who would be the berry pickers.

"I have to have either Cassie-Belle or Tishie with me," Mommie said. "Maryann is too young for an emergency. She can pick berries all right!"

"I'll say if there has to be one with you, she ought to be Cassie-Belle," Poppie said.

"It's always 'Cassie-Belle,' " Cassie-Belle said. "I've done and I'm sure doing my part to help raise this family! I want to pick berries and earn money, too! I want new clothes for school here in Ohio!"

Mommie looked plagued at what Cassie-Belle had just said. Poppie looked straight across the room at her but he didn't say anything.

"Cassie-Belle, I can understand that you want to work and earn money same as the rest of us," I said. "It's not fair for the rest of us to work and earn when you have to stay at home. But I have a plan!"

"What is your plan, Pedike?" Mommie asked.

"Why don't Maryann, Tishie, Timmie and I put our wages together and divide it by five and give Cassie-Belle a fifth," I said. "This would be her part."

"I wish I'd have thought of that," Poppie said. "That's good thinking, Pedike!"

Now Cassie-Belle smiled. She was pleased.

"Yes, you will share with us, Cassie-Belle," Tishie said. "You'll be working harder than we who pick the berries."

"But I will be making money same as you so I can buy my clothes for school," she said.

"We're earning the money aren't we, Pedike?" Timmie bragged. "We've even got a raise!"

"Gil, Ohio and earning money are changing our children and we've not been here very long," Mommie said. "What will it be when our children grow up?"

24 Poppie, two of his sons, and two daughters walked down the road together, on our way to Joshua Herbert's big white house. We called it the "big house." All of us had our lunches and Poppie had his ax across his shoulder.

In twenty minutes we were at the "big house" and Mr. Herbert was standing out front as usual, waiting. He didn't wear a hat and his white hair was tousled by a slow-moving morning wind.

"I'm glad to see you," he said. "I'm in a spot with my strawberries. I can't get pickers!"

"You've got four good ones," Poppie said. "They've picked wild strawberries, huckleberries, raspberries, dewberries and blackberries by the gallons on Lower Bruin for their mother to can, preserve and make jelly—and they've picked them in the hollows and on the rough hillslopes of Lower Bruin to buy clothes and school books! But what I want to ask you, Josh, is what I'm going to do with this ax?"

"You're goin' to follow the streams in the valleys and upon the hillslopes and deaden the sycamores, willows and the buckeyes," he said. "You know how to deaden a tree, don't you?"

"Don't insult me, Josh!" Poppie said with a laugh. "I've done this since I've been a boy! But may I ask you why you are having this done?"

"They take sustenance from the soil and they don't contribute anything," he said. "Willows along streams are no good. Their roots choke the streams. Sycamores are not much good—a pretty shade tree is all. And a buckeye!

We've got so many of them. And we Ohioans are called buckeyes. I'd like to know why we're named for a tree which isn't any good for timber, fence posts or even wood to burn. Even half the nut on a buckeye is pizenous—the other half isn't. Only a squirrel knows which side isn't pizen. I want to get rid of worthless trees that draw sustenance from land I own. Can you blame me, Gil?"

"I can't say that I do," Poppie said.

"You're the man with the ax, Gil," Mr. Herbert said. "And you'll be doing this all week!"

"But where is the strawberry patch, Mr. Herbert?" Timmie asked.

"Don't you worry," he replied. "Not far away and I'll lead you there. You follow me. I thought we'd have more berry pickers. More promised but they're not here! They don't want to work."

Poppie went on his way to peel the bark around trees which killed them. And we were on our way, following Mr. Herbert.

When we arrived at the strawberry patch, we found only a green hillsided slope, on a south hill, stretching up to the morning sky. We were the only ones there to pick berries. There were stacks of strawberry crates and quart cups awaiting us. And here were the red strawberries among the green plants—big and middle-sized ripe berries waiting to be plucked by our hands. They were beautiful strawberries.

"I don't know how many you Perkins children can save," Mr. Herbert said. "All I ask you to do is to pick as many as you can. Fill these quart cups and fill the crates. I'd like for you to top the quart cups off with the biggest berries."

We had his orders and we were ready to begin. Mr. Herbert left us with the vast field ahead. We were ready to go. And all of our fingers were nimble and fast. We began picking the strawberries. I do not know who was the fastest. But we knew we had work to do. We had a big strawberry hill ahead of us. So we worked and we carried our quart cups to the crates which were placed in the shade of a huge sycamore tree at the foot of the hill.

Quart by quart we carried them to crates. We didn't look

up. Maybe Maryann, our younger sister, was the fastest strawberry picker among us. Very soon we had crates filled. We were moving up the hill.

I didn't know how many crates of berries we were supposed to pick in one day. But I do know we were filling the crates fast. At noon we took about ten minutes to eat our lunch and then we started picking berries again.

In the afternoon the sun had dried the dew. And here before us were the ripe red berries. We not only picked them but we clutched them from their stems to save them. I plucked these ripe red berries by the handsful. So did my brothers and my sisters. I carried crate after crate to the shade of the sycamore.

At the end of our day we had picked twenty-four crates of strawberries. In each crate there were twenty-four quarts—six gallons. I didn't know about picking strawberries to be sold in markets. I didn't know if we had done it well or not. Each had picked six crates. Mr. Herbert had told us to dress the top of each quart with some larger berries. And when we finished Mr. Herbert drove up in his truck.

"Twenty-four crates!" he said. "I'm pleased! I'll take these to Agrillo right now!"

"You want Pedike and me to help you load them, Mr. Herbert?" Timmie asked.

"It would be a great help," he said.

Timmie got up in the truck and he carried the crates back while Mr. Herbert and I carried them from the sycamore tree shade.

"You boys ride in the back of the truck and let your sisters ride up here with me," Mr. Herbert said. "I'm driving past your house! And remember, I want you here to pick berries in the morning! You're the only pickers I have! I need you! I want to save my berries. The season has come upon us!"

On Tuesday morning when we arrived to pick berries, Mr. Herbert was there walking back and forth under the sycamore tree.

"No new help," he said. "I don't think you four children will be able to pick all my berries!"

"I don't know, Mr. Herbert," Timmie said. "Don't be so sure! We can do about anything!"

Then Timmie gave that wild laugh he always gave after he had spoken. Poppie wasn't around now to chastize him. Mommie wasn't here to make a face.

"I'm sure if we only had Cassie-Belle with us we could do it," Timmie added.

Tishie, Maryann and I were silent. We looked at the big hillslope above us that stretched to the early June's blue morning sky. The morning sun was lifting the dew in so many little white clouds from over the green strawberry field—and this was good. But the dew-wet patch, early in the morning, didn't stop us. We were ready to go.

Last night we counted what we had made, which was thirty dollars. And we divided this by five. This meant Sister Cassie-Belle had earned six dollars. And she was as happy as Timmie and I when we got our first check.

This morning as we picked berries, Timmie said: "Pedike, why can't we go overtime? Why can't we go eleven or twelve hours—berry picking is easy if you don't mind bending over. And we'd really make Mr. Herbert happy! Our picking overtime might save his berries."

"Timmie, if you'd just stop talking," I said. "Why can't you use your little head and do some reasoning? We've got the pigs to feed! They'd be squealing louder than ever because they'd be hungrier! And what about our cows that are in from the pasture standing in the barnlot mooing to us—asking us to feed them in the barn and milk them!"

"I know, Pedike, but twelve hours here for us means nine dollars each," Timmie said. "Poppie makes ten. We'd be right at his heels!"

Sister Tishie, who overheard our talking, started laughing.

"Tell Pedike, if you will—and since you don't like to talk—" Tishie said jokingly, "that the extra hours will buy more clothes for us girls! And we will need new clothes in Ohio. We scarcely have a change of clothes!"

We had some strawberry hillslopes above us where the big ripe strawberries' red eyes looked silently at us. Timmie had said they seemed to be saying: "Come and pick us! We are waiting for you! We want to be eaten! We want to make boys and girls, their poppies and mommies and other people happy!" Before we stopped to eat our lunch, we had picked twelve crates, same as yesterday at noon.

Mr. Herbert drove up in his farm truck just as we sat down under the shade of the sycamore to eat. He counted our crates.

"Wonderful, children," he said. "You know, people in Agrillo are crying for my berries! I could sell all I have and twice as many. If I could only get some more help. Young people don't want to work any more—they don't want to pick berries anyway."

"Why don't they want to pick berries and make money, Mr. Herbert?" Timmie asked.

"Afraid to get up early and go to work," he said. "Afraid of the morning dew. I used to get up before daylight and go to the corn field barefooted. My young friends, times have changed. You're the last of the earth people! They're not earth people here in Landsdowne County, Ohio, any more. They were when I first came here. But not any more!"

"Mr. Herbert, think of all four of us here making seven-fifty a day!" Timmie said. "This is thirty dollars. And you know, because our sister Cassie-Belle can't work with us—she has to stay with Mommie—well, we divide our money earned with Cassie-Belle. She gets a fifth!"

"Ah, that's wonderful, you children work together like that," he said. "That is what's made us have a great country. It's taken work! Never fear work! And you children will work—you're good workers!"

"But you pay us, Mr. Herbert," Timmie said. "We've never earned such wages. We've never seen so much money! Now, we made thirty dollars a day and Poppie makes ten and this is forty dollars a day! The farm wages back on Lower Bruin for Poppie was three dollars a day! Pedike made two dollars. And I made fifty cents!"

I made a face at Timmie this time. My silent sisters did, too. Mommie and Poppie, I thought, were right about him.

"Pedike, quit making snoots at me," Timmie said. "My mind works and I have thoughts!"

"What kind of thoughts, Timmie?" Mr. Herbert asked.

"I've been thinking if Cassie-Belle could run out and feed the pigs for us and turn the cows into the barn for us—and let us milk them later, well, then, we could work longer and help you save your berries. We'd make more money. We'd make more money for you. What would be wrong with this?"

"Not anything, Timmie," he said. "You're a thinkin' boy for a youngster!"

"See, Poppie, with his big body and big hands on this hillslope wouldn't be much of a berry picker," Timmie continued.

"I'm afraid he'd be about like I am, Timmie," Mr. Herbert said. "It takes young people to pick berries!"

Mr. Herbert always carried his lunch in a paper sack. He ate two sandwiches with us. And we brought our lunches in paper sacks, now. So we ate and talked under the pretty sycamore tree—one that Poppie would find and peel a ring around its body to deaden because it had no timber value. Well, at midday in early June in Landsdowne County, Ohio, it had a real shade value.

In the afternoon on the dry strawberry patch with the sun on our backs, we picked berries steadily. Maryann and Tishie picked more than we did, for Timmie and I carried the filled crates down to the sycamore tree and put them in the shade. And at the end of this day when Mr. Herbert came, we had twenty-five crates of berries.

25 While Timmie and I did our evening chores, I wondered why we picked an extra crate of berries this afternoon. I believe it was because Timmie had stopped talking so much. Honest, there were times in the berry patch when I stood up and plugged my ears with my index fingers to muffle the sound of his chatter.

When we fed the hungry pigs he talked. I don't know exactly what he said—I didn't want to listen, for I would have to remember. And when we fed and milked the cows, he talked. When we took care of the milk in the cellar, he talked. Well, I was proud to be earning seven-fifty a day and so were my sisters, but we didn't talk about it all the time.

While we had our supper, Poppie said: "I don't understand why Josh Herbert wants me to deaden all the sycamores, willows and buckeyes. I've been thinking about it. The Word says everything was put on this earth for a purpose. I know the purpose of many things haven't been discovered yet. The willows, sycamore and buckeye must be useful for something!"

"Well, Poppie, I'll tell you that big sycamore at the strawberry patch makes a wonderful shade," Timmie said. "It's a pretty tree. I hope you never deaden that one!"

"I've had a hard day," Poppie said. "How did you get along, Pedike?"

"We picked twenty-five crates today and twenty-four yesterday," I said.

"Two hundred and ninety-four gallons of strawberries," Timmie said.

"Is Mr. Herbert pleased, Pedike?" Poppie asked.

"I never seen a happier man," I said. "He can't get help! He's afraid he's goin' to lose some of his berries! He's selling them in Agrillo as fast we we can pick them!"

"I think we can help him save them," Timmie said.

Mommie looked very straight at Timmie.

"Mommie, we can make more money and Mr. Herbert can make more money," Timmie said, "if Cassie-Belle can feed the pigs and put the cows in the barn and feed them! We'll milk them! So we'll have more time to work over-time on these long days. Berry picking is not hard work. It's not like using an ax. This means more money for Cassie-Belle! It means more money for all of us."

Before Mommie or Poppie could speak, Cassie-Belle said: "I'll do that. It's no job. It won't take long."

"Now, I've been thinking about something else," Timmie said. "I'm almost afraid to mention this one. But Mr. Herbert can't get help and he might lose part of his berries. Why can't we pick berries on Sunday? Let Poppie stay here with Mommie and Cassie-Belle go help us!"

"I'm for that, too," Cassie-Belle said. "Timmie, you talk all the time, but this time you're right!"

Well, Mommie sat at her end of the table with Baby Sister in her arms. I don't know how she held her for Mommie was big and growing. Poppie sat at his end of the table, a proud and happy man, with Baby Brother on his lap. Mommie was plagued the way Cassie-Belle was talking.

"I think it will be all right to work on Sunday and help Mr. Herbert," Poppie said. "The Word says when the ox is in the ditch on the Sabbath to get him out. Now Mr. Herbert has the ox in the ditch—he's trying to get help and can't get it—so, I think it is a good thing to do. When Cousin Bos comes by tell him to tell Jimmie Artner not to bring the Freewill Baptist Church bus for us, but we'll be obeying the Lord on this Sabbath!"

"Then we can tell Mr. Herbert tomorrow," Timmie said. "I think I should get to tell him for I am the one who thought about this!"

26 Wednesday morning when we went to work, Mr. Herbert was already there.

"Mr. Herbert, I've got some good news for you if you still can't find berry pickers," Timmie said.

"Well, I've not been able to find them," he told Timmie.

"We're going to work overtime today," he said. "And we're going to work on Sunday. Sunday five of us will be helping you! Poppie will be home with Mommie, and Cassie-Belle will be here with us. We want to help you save your berries!"

"Will working on Sunday be all right with your parents?"

"Yes, Poppie said The Word said when the ox was in the ditch on the Sabbath it was all right to work to get him out," Timmie said. "And Poppie said your ox was in the ditch with strawberry season on and not enough berry pickers!"

"That's right, Timmie," Mr. Herbert said. "I'm glad Gil looks at it like this."

"Now Mr. Herbert, don't come back until six o'clock," Timmie said. "Then we'll be ready for you!"

Then, Timmie gave his wild laugh.

"I like your spirit, young man," Mr. Herbert said. "I like the way you work. And I like the way your silent brother and your silent sisters work! Say, Pedike, I'll bet you are good in school for I've always heard still waters run deep!"

"No, not as good as Timmie or my sisters," I replied. "I guess Cassie-Belle might be the best among us!"

"Cassie-Belle can set the woods on fire when it comes to books, Mr. Herbert," Timmie said.

"Timmie," I said.

"Well, if I'm not telling the truth let Mommie show Mr. Herbert our report cards when he's up home sometime," Timmie said. "Let him see for himself. And I'm not a slow one. Books come easy to me, too!"

I wanted to put my index fingers in my ears again to muffle the sounds of Timmie's talking. I wanted to tell him what Mommie and Poppie had told him more than once, that "self-bragging was half scandal."

"This is not the time to discuss school, Timmie," I said, getting up from the grass where I'd sat to eat my lunch. "This is the time to pick berries! The big red eyes way up there on the hillside are looking at us. They are saying: 'Come and pick us for the people want to eat us.'"

This time I used Timmie's talk and our sisters laughed loudly.

"Red eyes looking at you and wanting to be picked," Mr. Herbert said.

He clapped his big hands and laughed louder than my sisters.

At four o'clock we had thirteen more crates. This made twenty-five full crates under the shade of the sycamore tree. Now was our overtime! What could and would we do?

"One hundred and fifty gallons," Timmie said. "Can we go three crates more? Let me see!"

He raised up straight and counted.

"One hundred fifty gallons in ten hours, that would be fifteen gallons an hour! Two more hours, thirty gallons. That would be five more crates!"

"Timmie's good in arithmetic," Sister Tishie said.

"Get to picking, Timmie," Maryann said. "We can't get them picked standing up straight in the field and talking."

This coming from Maryann, who worked and never talked, made Tishie and me laugh. But up toward the top of this field the ripe berries were larger and more plentiful.

"I can tell you why the berries are better up here than at the foot of the hill," Timmie said.

"Then, tell us," Tishie said.

"More sunlight," he said. "The morning sun hits here first—and goes down the hill as it rises!"

"Isn't Timmie smart?" Tishie said. "He even told Mr. Herbert he was!"

We laughed again. But all the time we laughed and talked our fingers clutched the big berries gently. And to fill a quart cup didn't take too many berries. Timmie and I carried two crates down to the sycamore. Back up the hill—work was play—it was a game we were playing. Tishie and Maryann were working while we carried the crates down.

Well, they finished their crates before we did and helped us. We had one more crate to go. We were picking faster up here than we had picked below us.

"Wait until we finish the last crate," Tishie said. "Timmie said five crates! So we've got only one more to go!"

Timmie and I carried the crates down to the sycamore shade.

"I can beat you back up the hill," Timmie said.

"Don't step on the berries," I said.

Timmie had a start on me. I didn't push to beat him. A little run was nice after stooping over and picking. We made short time filling the last crate.

"Since you beat me up the hill, Timmie, and since I'm our father's first son, now it is my duty to take this crate down," I said.

I looked at my cheap little wrist watch that I'd worked out at two dollars a day on Lower Bruin and ordered from a catalogue. My little watch had kept good time.

"It's fifteen minutes until six," I said. "We're cheating Mr. Herbert!"

"No, we're not," Timmie said. "We've been helping him load them!"

I'd just put the crate down on the ground when Mr. Herbert drove up. He counted the crates.

"I can't believe it," he said. "You made good use of your overtime!"

"And we'll help you load them," Timmie said.

Now when we got home at six Poppie was already there.

Poppie and Cassie-Belle had not only fed the pigs milk and corn but they had fed and milked the cows.

"Cassie-Belle, we made thirty-six dollars today," Timmie said. "So you get a fifth. Seven dollars and twenty cents for you!"

On Saturday we finished going over this strawberry patch for the first picking. We picked thirty-one crates, too. Now, at the foot of the hill where we had first started picking berries, the strawberries were larger, riper, and better than our first picking. And tomorrow, Cassie-Belle would be with us.

27 When the five of us walked down to the berry patch on Sunday morning, Mr. Herbert was there with his truck, empty crates and stacks of little wooden quart cups as usual.

"The ox is really in the ditch," he said. "Look at the ripe red berries! But don't go overtime today!"

"Then, we'll go twenty-eight crates," Timmie said.

But on this day, Timmie was wrong.

"I'm so glad to get away from work at home, I welcome this work," Cassie-Belle said. It's a fresh wind here. Ripe strawberries are beautiful!"

"Cassie-Belle picks strawberries like she's got four hands, sixteen fingers and no thumbs," Timmie said.

"Smart talk," I said.

It was great to have Cassie-Belle with us. And I liked to work with my sisters, actually, better than I liked to work with Timmie. Timmie was a good worker but his tongue always bothered me.

My sisters' hands were good. They were fast hands and their fingers were nimble. With these better berries, on this second picking, we might set some kind of a record on this Sabbath. We might get two oxen out of the ditch.

And at four o'clock, with five pickers instead of four, we had set a record. We had picked thirty-four crates of berries. If the five of us had picked as the four of us had been picking from six in the morning until four in the afternoon we would have picked only thirty crates.

"Now, I go back home to harder work," Cassie-Belle said

when we'd finished our day. "This has been beautiful and a wonderful Sabbath."

When we got home Poppie was trying to help Mommie with The Babies and the Little Ones.

"I've never missed anyone as much in my life, Cassie-Belle," Mommie said. "Your Poppie can't do the things in this house you can do!"

"I guess I'm too slow," Poppie said.

"Well, I've never had a more enjoyable day," Cassie-Belle said. "That strawberry field is beautiful, filled with fresh berries and a fresh wind blowing that is so good to breathe. No wonder Tishie and Maryann like to work with Timmie and Pedike!"

Mommie didn't say anything.

On this Sabbath evening after we had supper we moved into our living room and turned on the radio. First thing I tuned in on was a church service.

"Keep that on, Pedike," Poppie said. "Let us hear it. We've missed going to church today."

"I've not thought about Church," Timmie said.

"I've been out in God's Church," Cassie-Belle said.

"Cassie-Belle," Mommie said, "what makes you talk like that? You've never talked this way before. Has making money changed you? Or has Ohio changed you?"

"Both, Mommie," she said.

"I've been talking to your mother, children," Poppie said. "Since Uncle Dick and Aunt Susie wanted her to go to the hospital—and have offered to pay her expenses—I think she should go now!"

"I've told you, Gil, I'm not going," Mommie said. "I've never been in a hospital in my life—and to go there and wait for my baby to be born! I say, NO! What will the Babies and the Little Ones do here? I've never been away from them! A good mother never leaves her children! Just because Uncle Dick offered to pay for my going there doesn't mean I should go!"

"But it's near time," Poppie said. "When I go to work in the morning I hate to leave you. I worry about you all day."

"Just don't worry about me, Gil," Mommie said. "How did women have babies, I'd like to know, before there were hospitals? Mary birthed Jesus in a stable. I have no fear. The Word says a mother walks into the Valley of Shadows when she has her baby. And if I die in childbirth according to The Word, there will be a place for me in Heaven!"

I didn't like to hear Mommie talk this way. None of us did. Cassie-Belle got real silent when she heard Mommie's words of courage and faith.

"I might have my twelfth baby in the barn," Mommie said. "Who knows? I do know I'm not going to a hospital and, maybe, have to wait."

28 After Timmie and I had done our chores by lantern light as usual and had eaten our breakfasts, we were ready for work. Today we would be without Cassie-Belle in the berry patch. She'd be with Mommie, Baby Brother and Baby Sister and the Little Ones.

We were working in a pattern now. But this pattern would end for us about the end of this week or early next week. Strawberry season would be over.

Mr. Herbert was waiting for us with twenty-five crates with twenty-four quart cups in each crate. He was judging how many berries we'd pick for the day. And, really, with all he had, I wondered why he worked the way he did. He had all he'd ever need, all his children would need and I wanted to ask him why he kept on working. I couldn't this morning. I might ask him at noon. I had thoughts, too, but I couldn't let the words go like Brother Timmie.

When Mr. Herbert came at noon, we sat down on the grass under the sycamore shade to eat our lunches and as usual Mr. Herbert sat on the grass. I heard his old bones creaking as he sat down. We'd placed ourselves like four wheels on a wagon and he sat between us. Well, we'd just started eating when my question I wanted to ask him came to my mind. I had a little trouble asking him. It was like trying to get a wind to blow.

"Mr. Herbert, what makes you work the way you do?" I said. "You've got plenty. You don't have to do it!"

"Oh, that's a good question coming from you, Pedike,"

he said. "I don't remember your ever asking me a question before! And I'm happy to answer you. Work is habit with me. You see, we form habits by practice! And I've always liked to work. I live to save. I like to have! I like to put my wits up against the other fellow in buying, selling and trading."

"But, Mr. Herbert, after you make a million dollars what do you want then?" Timmie asked.

Then he gave his cackling laugh, which was the sound of a strong wind blowing over old corn stalks, snapping them off at the ground in our old winter corn field.

"If I had one million, I'd want two millions," he said.

"What if you had two millions?" Timmie asked.

"I'd want three," he said. "If I had ten millions, I'd want eleven! As I say, work is a habit. I set a goal and I work for it!"

Well, I'd never heard talk like this. We just sat and looked at Mr. Herbert who had only two sandwiches same as we had. He was dressed in work clothes, no better than Poppie's and not as clean as Poppie's had been on this Monday morning. Mommie saw to it we took a bath a day in the smoke house in a washtub, and we wore clean clothes each morning.

Mr. Herbert left as we went back to the berry patch.

"It's a long way to the top, but, maybe, we'll be up there by Saturday," Timmie said. "We're not leaving much behind us to pick over again. Maybe not worth picking."

When Mr. Herbert arrived promptly at four, we were standing under the sycamore with our crates filled.

"You children beat all," he said.

"Mr. Herbert, I'd rather pick strawberries and earn seven-fifty a day than go to Sunday school or sit in church and hear a sermon," Timmie said.

"I predict one day, Timmie, you might be a millionaire," Mr. Herbert said.

When Mr. Herbert stopped to let us off at home, Tishie got out of the truck and said: "' I hear a new baby crying! Listen!"

I jumped out of the truck with Timmie jumping off behind me.

"It's not Baby Brother or Baby Sister, either," Tishie said, running for the house with Maryann and Timmie behind her.

"Don't go in yet, Mr. Herbert," I said. "Mommie might have a baby and Poppie's not here yet!"

"Didn't she go to the hospital?" Mr. Herbert asked.

"She wouldn't go," I said. "Uncle Dick tried to get her to go! He offered to pay her expenses!"

Timmie got in the house last but he was out first and he yelled: "Mommie has a little Baby."

"Mr. Herbert, can you tell Uncle Dick's Dr. Zimmerman to come?" I said.

Mr. Herbert gunned his truck and I never saw him drive as fast. Now I hurried to the house. When I got there I saw Poppie coming up the road with his ax. I motioned with my hand for him to come. He knew something had happened and he broke out in a run! Poor, old, slow Poppie! He trotted up the road like a big ox.

"I've had it," Cassie-Belle said.

When Poppie came in at the door he heard the new cry.

"A Brother Baby," Tishie said.

"So many boys born now is a sign of war," Poppie said. "When was he born?"

"About an hour ago," Cassie-Belle said. "Tishie, you get Baby Brother and Baby Sister quiet and help me take care of the Little Ones!"

"Baby Brother, my foot," Timmie said. "He's Little Dickie now. He's no longer a Baby Brother! We've got a new one!"

Cassie-Bell was standing in the door of Poppie's and Mommie's room. We'd not gone in to see Mommie in bed with Baby Brother. Only Cassie-Belle had been in.

Poppie walked in with a big smile.

"Let me see the Little Fellar," Poppie said.

He bent over Mommie's bed and looked on. There was a happy smile on his face.

"Eleven living and Little Pearse gone," Poppie said. "How do you feel, Sil?"

"All right, Gil," she said. "I feel very good. I'm glad it's over. Really I feel comfortable now! The load is gone!"

"Poppie, Dr. Zimmerman should be here soon," I said. "I told Mr. Herbert to send Dr. Zimmerman!"

"We don't need him now," Mommie said.

"Yes, we do," Poppie said. "I wonder what Uncle Dick will say. He tried to get you to go to the hositpal."

"Don't mention that now," Mommie said. "I don't care what he says!"

"Mommie, we'd like to come in and see Baby Brother," I said.

"Come in and see him," Mommie said.

Timmie, Maryann and I went in to see him. Well, I couldn't tell much about a young baby. Baby Brother was pink and cried, and had a little hair on his head. He had little hands that moved. He had little eyes half closed. He was like a little young mouse I had seen in the field when Poppie plowed up a nest. We had gathered around the bed looking at Baby Brother when Tishie walked in.

"Oh, he's so pretty," Tishie said.

"Looks a lot like me," Timmie said. "I mean he will look like Mommie and me when he grows up."

"I hope he doesn't have your blab," I said. " I hope he walks before he talks."

Poppie looked straight at me.

"Since I've been away from you, you're gettin' out of control," Poppie said.

"So you think he's a pretty baby, Tishie?" Mommie said.

"Yes, I do, Mommie!"

Well, Little Mommie, lying on the bed with Baby Brother in her arms, smiled a big smile. I'd seen her so often in bed before with a brother or sister.

"Sil, you've had a dozen now," Poppie said.

His face was all smiles as he looked down on her.

"Yes, and Gil, I hope someday it will be two dozen," Mommie said. "It's so easy for me to have my babies. I don't care where—just so I have them—in the corn field or in the house. But never in a hospital."

"Well, I knowed one mountain mother who lived by The Word to have twenty-two," Poppie said. "She had two sets of twins and a set of triplets and she never lost a one of them. She was Lucy Tillman."

"Look, who's coming," Timmie said. "Uncle Dick and Dr. Zimmerman!"

Dr. Zimmerman was a low, heavy, fair-complexioned man, with a red face and a redder nose. He was wearing spectacles, a black hat, dark suit. He looked pliam-blank like Stubby Stevens back on Lower Bruin.

"Sil, I tried to get you to go to the hospital," Uncle Dick said.

"I know you did, Uncle Dick, but I'm afraid of a hospital," Mommie said. "Just as I've told Gil here at my bedside, I've had my babies in the corn field and in the house. And I've not had a hard childbirth yet. Women make too big a fuss over having their babies and their husbands make a still bigger fuss!"

"Had babies in the corn field!" Dr. Zimmerman said.

"Yes, two," Mommie said. "Pedike and Maryann! Here they stand beside you. I was out hoeing corn and couldn't make it to the house. All others were born in houses where we lived. I've never had a doctor either. I've had a midwife!"

"Dr. Zimmerman, I tried to get her to go to the hospital," Uncle Dick said. "Susie and I never could have children. It's been the regret of our lives! We wanted to help our niece and nephew, Sil and Gil Perkins! I've told you about them. Look at this family here! And there's more!"

"Another roomful," Timmie said proudly.

"You've got fine looking children here," Dr. Zimmerman said. "Now, Mrs. Perkins, I would like to examine you. And I'd like privacy in the room. I wonder if you would mind stepping out?"

All of us left the room and went over into the living room. Here, Poppie and Uncle Dick talked while we listened. Dr. Zimmerman wasn't too long in the room examining Mommie. He joined us in the living room. There was a smile on his face.

"I've come to the conclusion in all my years of practice—and I've practiced many years and delivered many babies—that small women have easier births," he said. "Mr. Perkins, how large is your wife?"

"If her clothes are soaking wet, Sil will weigh a hundred pounds," Poppie said in his slow way.

"How much do you weigh?" he asked Poppie.

"In dry clothes I weigh about two hundred and thirty," Poppie said, smiling again. "I love my little wife! But, Doctor, why is it a little wife tells a big husband what to do? Why is it, she's head of the family?"

Now, everybody laughed.

"She had a perfect birth," Dr. Zimmerman said. "And you've got another fine son. A beautiful baby. I weighed him. Eight pounds and three ounces. Twenty inches tall! Now, I'd like to see the rest of your family."

"Come, Dr. Zimmerman, and I'll show you Cassie-Belle, our oldest sister, the Little Ones and the Babies!" Timmie said.

"Just a minute, Timmie," Poppie said. "I'll do that! You hold your horses!"

So Poppie took Dr. Zimmerman and Uncle Dick and we followed into the room where the three Little Ones slept at night. Now there would be four Little Ones in this room in one bed.

Here was Cassie-Belle, who said: "Shh—" meaning to keep quiet for she had them all asleep. And here they spoke in whispers.

"Our oldest daughter, Cassie-Belle," Poppie whispered. "Take a look at our Little Ones."

Dr. Zimmerman and Uncle Dick looked them over.

"This one is Little Dickie, named for Uncle Dick," Poppie whispered pointing to Baby Brother before our last brother was born. "Ain't he a pretty little boy!"

"He sure is," Dr. Zimmerman said in a hoarse whisper. "All are fine looking youngsters. Think of two being born in a corn field—and not one with a doctor! It's hard to believe!"

"Shh—," Cassie-Belle said in a whisper. "You will wake them."

We went back to the living room.

"I never saw nicer looking children, Richard," Dr. Zimmerman said to Uncle Dick. "No wonder you like this family. Eleven children!"

"Twelve," Poppie corrected him. "We lost our oldest son, Little Pearse, back on Lower Bruin."

"But eleven fine children," Dr. Zimmerman said. "You're still lucky parents! What a family! What nice children you really have! Such healthy-looking children! And your oldest daughter is really a little mother!"

"Yes, she's had enough experience," Poppie said. "Dr. Zimmerman, how much do I owe you?"

"I'll take care of this," Uncle Dick said.

"No, you won't, Richard," Dr. Zimmerman said. "This is one of my free calls. Here I've learned something! And I've enjoyed this trip! I won't take a penny from you or anyone! This is absolutely free!"

"Well, I don't know how to thank you," Poppie said.

"I'll see you later, Gil," Uncle Dick said as he left with Dr. Zimmerman.

The excitement at our house today when a Baby Brother was born caused us to be late doing our chores. The hungry pigs had squealed and the anxious cows had mooed. Timmie and I did our chores while Maryann watched over the Little Ones and the Babies and Tishie and Cassie-Belle prepared supper, and Poppie waited on Mommie. He stayed in the room with her and they talked lovey-talk. When she wanted something he got it in a hurry.

After we had finished supper, Poppie went back to Mommie's room. We always left the table to Mommie and our sisters. Tonight our sisters would clear the table, put food away, and wash the dishes. So Timmie and I, with our chores done, were the first in the living room and turned on the radio.

"How will we manage now, Pedike?" Timmie asked me.

"Well, I thought you'd know," I said. "I don't know! We'll have to wait until Poppie, Tishie, Cassie-Belle and Maryann come in!"

Poppie came first. Then, Cassie-Belle and last Tishie, Maryann stayed with Mommie where she could help her and listen for a cry through the open door into the other room.

"We've got to make our plans," Poppie said. "I know you have a Baby Brother, but we've had baby brothers and baby sisters before. Mommie is all right. And she won't be in the bed long!"

"I think I can take care of everything," Cassie-Belle said. "But I really had a time here today! I'll never in my lifetime ahead, so I believe, ever have another day like this! But all is calm now. The house is quiet!"

"You think you can handle everything tomorrow?" Poppie asked her.

"Yes, I am sure I can," she said.

"I thought maybe it might mean Tishie would have to stay too," Poppie said.

"No, let Tishie go on and work," Cassie-Belle told Poppie.

"Then, there won't be any changes," Poppie said. "We'll go back to our work as usual."

29 After our chores Tuesday morning, Timmie and I ate breakfast. And we left home with Poppie, Tishie and Maryann. As soon as we reached the berry patch, we found Mr. Herbert waiting.

"Baby Brother was born just about two hours before we got to the house," Timmie said.

"Didn't your mother go to the hospital?"

"She wouldn't go," Timmie said.

"Who was there with her?"

"Sister Cassie-Belle."

"Well, I never heard of anything like that," Mr. Herbert said. "Did your father go to work this morning?"

"Yes, Poppie went to work," Timmie said.

"Who's with your mother now?"

"Sister Cassie-Belle," Timmie said. "She's the oldest living. She knows and understands! We're going to save your berries!"

"Yes, but your mother comes first."

"But Mommie is fine," Timmie said.

Timmie, as usual, was doing all the talking. Mommie and Poppie could never let him in on a secret. He would blab it.

When Mr. Herbert came at eleven-noon to eat with us, he said, "When I drove past your house awhile ago, I stopped to see how everything was. I was a little uneasy about your mother and all the other small children there with just your oldest sister looking out after them! I found everything all right. I was surprised."

"Cassie-Belle is sure, Mr. Herbert," Timmie said. "She knows how to manage. Mommie has trained her!"

"She knows how to manage all right for a girl," he said. "I wonder how many girls her age could do what she is doing?"

We were anxious to get home on this afternoon. We wanted to see how well Cassie-Belle had done and we wanted to help her.

Poppie must have been anxious to get home, too, for he hurried up the road just a few minutes after we had arrived. And when he came, he set his ax by the porch and rushed into the house and into Mommie's room. Here he found Cassie-Belle, Tishie, Maryann, Timmie and me all around the bed looking at our Baby Brother who was nursing now.

"Well, how are you, Sil?" Poppie asked.

"Just wonderful, Gil," she said. "I feel like getting up from this bed! Dr. Zimmerman told me to stay in bed three days then sit up some. But I feel like sitting up now. I think I'll sit up tomorrow."

"And about the baby," Poppie said.

"Oh, he's fine," Mommie said. "He's like a little pig!"

"Say, Poppie, the way our pigs have grown, shouldn't we call them shoats now?" Timmie said.

Who would have ever thought to have asked such a question now but Timmie?

"Yes, we should," Poppie said.

"Well, I've always heard a shoat was the size between a pig and a hog," Timmie said. "I've never seen anything grow like they have!"

"Timmie, we're talking about Mommie and Baby Brother now," Tishie said. "Why change the subject to pigs and shoats?"

"I just wanted to know," Timmie said. "I like to know things!"

Well, Poppie and Mommie laughed at Timmie and Tishie. We always had fun among us. Poppie said that was because we were a large family and would be still larger. He and Mommie said our family wasn't near through growing. If I ever heard him say this one time, I heard him say once a week it was man, and woman's duty, according to The Word, to marry and replenish the earth. And I had heard him and Mommie, when they sat close on our divan in the rose-papered living room with Baby Brother on Poppie's lap and Baby Sister on Mommie's lap, coo like two pee wees building a nest in spring. Yes, we were a happy family. But Timmie vexed me the way he was always blabbing.

"Today, Sil, you've been on my mind," Poppie said. "Each time I struck a lick with my ax barking a tree, I thought of you!"

"Gil, I've just got along fine today," Mommie said. "Only one time the Babies got fretful and I couldn't get up to help them. The baby had colic and I sent Cassie-Belle to see if she could find catnip to make tea. And she found it in a hurry out there on the creek bank. It grows in Ohio just the same as in Kentucky. She made the tea. It cured his colic. I'd rather give a baby catnip tea for the colic than bounce one! This is the only time we had any trouble and it wasn't for long. Cassie-Belle knows what to do."

Cassie-Belle had to leave us. There was a cry in the Little Ones' room. Maryann and Tishie, who had picked berries all day, went with her to help. There were three mothers, I thought, in our family. Mommie, the real mother, who had her children, and Cassie-Belle and Tishie who had learned how to take care of babies and little children by experience. And Sister Maryann, as young as she was, was learning fast.

"Sil, have you ever thought of a name for our son?" Poppie said.

"Yes, it came to me this afternoon," Mommie said. "And I think I have the right name."

Well, we waited for the name.

"Gil, I'm thinking of Joshua Herbert," Mommie said. "Joshua is a great name in The Word. He fit the Battle of Jericho! And Joshua Herbert has done more for us—has been nicer to us—than any man we've ever known. He's fit our Battle of Jericho for us. Look how nice he is to our family! And look at the wages he is paying us!"

"Gee-whilligens!" Timmie shouted. "It's great news! I'll tell Mr. Herbert first thing in the morning!"

"Easy, Timmie," Poppie said. "Sil, I think Joshua is a great name. I'm glad you thought of it. Joshua, it will be! Joshua Herbert Perkins!"

"Timmie, I think our shoats are calling us," I said. "We'd better get our work done and leave Poppie here with Mommie."

"Pedike, I've been thinking about something," Timmie said as we had fed our shoats.

"What now, Timmie?" I said.

"If we finish the strawberries this week, and if Poppie finishes deadening his trees, Poppie will plow tobacco next week and you and I will be hoeing tobacco," Timmie said. "Mr. Herbert's raspberries are going to be getting ripe and who will pick them?"

"I'm not sure who will," I said. "Maybe he has someone to pick them!"

"I'll bet he hasn't," Timmie said. "And I'll bet his raspberry picking won't be half the work his strawberry picking has been! But you and I can't do it."

"No, we can't," I said. "But he will take care of his raspberries. He'll manage his own affairs."

We got feed for our cows, our milk buckets and we turned our cows into the barn.

"I've got the answer, I think, to save his raspberries," Timmie said.

"All right, Timmie," I said. "What is it this time you've solved?"

"Since Cassie-Belle can take care of Mommie, the Little Ones and Baby Brother and Baby Sister, why can't Tishie and Maryann pick the raspberries and make money? I'll bet sister Cassie-Belle will be for this. See, all four of us will be working and Cassie-Belle will get her fifth!"

"It's good thinking, Timmie," I said. "I'll have to admit it is!"

"I'll ask Mr. Herbert about that tomorrow," Timmie said, "after I tell him Baby Brother has been named Joshua Herbert Perkins!"

30 When we went to work Wednesday morning, just before we reached the strawberry patch, Timmie broke out in a run to get there first. So, we stepped up our pace behind him. We wanted to hear what he told Mr. Herbert.

"Guess what, Mr. Herbert," Timmie shouted, almost out of breath. "Mommie named Baby Brother for you! She named him Joshua Herbert Perkins!"

"That's a great honor," Mr. Herbert said. "Not one of my children named a child for me. Not one of my grandchildren named a child for me. They have thought my name was old-fashioned in Ohio!"

"Mommie said it was from The Word and it was a great name," Timmie said.

We didn't linger to talk with Mr. Herbert. We'd do this the few minutes we had at noon when we ate our lunches together.

Now upon the hillside, in the morning dew, those red strawberry eyes looked at us and we at them. And we put them into quart cups and into crates. This was the same old routine. And I was getting tired of it. I wanted to get this job finished and get to the tobacco field! I would rather hoe tobacco than pick strawberries any old time.

At noon Mr. Herbert came. He was more than pleased because Mommie had named our Baby Brother for him. I was disturbed about his saying not a son or daughter of his —I didn't know how many he had though I had heard seven —and not one of his grandchildren—I didn't know how many married grandchildren he had—had ever named a child for him. As he had told us, his kinfolk thought Joshua was an old-fashioned name in Ohio. It might be an old-fashioned name in Ohio, but it was an old and an important name for us. It was a Bible name. And I thought Josh would be a wonderful name for a brother. I thought it was better than the old name among the Perkins family, Pedike, that my parents had named me.

"Mr. Herbert, I've thought of something," Timmie said as we sat on the grass under the sycamore shade and ate our lunches. "So I think I'd better ask you first!"

"What's that, Timmie?" he asked.

"Do you have anybody to pick your raspberries?" Timmie asked.

"No, I've not," he said. "I don't have one picker. I can't get one. I've tried. So I've given up my raspberries as a loss. I know you boys will be working in the tobacco next week with your father!"

"Since Cassie-Belle can take care of Mommie, the Little Ones and the Babies, why can't my sisters Tishie and Mary-ann try picking them?" Timmie said.

"It's a great idea, Timmie, if they could do it," Mr. Herbert said.

"I think we can," Tishie said.

"We'd be glad to try," Maryann said.

"Cassie-Belle will be for this, too, because, as I told you," Timmie said, "what the four of us earn we divide by five and give Cassie-Belle a share."

"Well, if they can pick the raspberries, I'll come and get them and take them to the patch and take them home," Mr. Herbert said. "You've saved my strawberries! Maybe you girls can save my raspberries I'd figured on losing! See, I must have Pedike and Timmie hoeing tobacco!"

"I think we can, Mr. Herbert," Tishie said. "We'd like to do it!"

On Thursday, when we got home, we got a surprise. Cousin Faith was there. She had been with Mommie and Cassie-Belle all day. If there was ever a good cook on this earth, she was Cousin Faith. After our chores, we sat down at the supper table, with Poppie at his end of the table and Mommie at her end, and I'll say we never had better cooked food. Cousin Faith was like this. She helped us every time she could.

"I'm sorry I couldn't come sooner, Sil," she said. "But preparing meals for Bos and Buster Boy and getting them off to work, I couldn't make it!"

On Saturday, it took thirty crates to finish our strawberry patch. But we worked overtime to finish this job. We had done it! Timmie let out a "Gee-willigens" when we reached the top. Mr. Herbert said: "You've saved my strawberries!"

And I believed we had. Our sisters, Timmie and I had never had a job working together to save a crop. I really felt great that we had done this; I was proud that we had!

With the strawberries picked, and with trees deadened that Mr. Herbert said didn't amount to anything but took sustenance from his ground, we had accomplished our tasks.

"It's great Mommie has been so successful giving birth to Baby Brother, Joshua Herbert Perkins, and we've finished our tasks this week. We need to be in church tomorrow," Poppie said at the supper table. "This is the will of the Lord. He is with us. We couldn't do these things if the Lord wasn't with us! We've had great fortune. And we are making so much money, what will we do with it?"

"Cousin Bos was here to see about us today," Mommie said. "I told him to send the bus for us tomorrow!"

"Are you able to go, Sil?" Poppie asked.

"As able as I will ever be, Gil," she said. "I told you it wasn't as big a problem as so many women let on, having a baby. I feel fine! I want to get back to the Freewill Baptist Church. I want to hear The Word!"

31 On Sunday morning, Timmie and I did our chores early. We had breakfast and my sisters dressed the Little Ones and the Babies. Mommie dressed herself and wrapped Baby Brother in a little blanket. We were dressed in our country clothes we had worn on Lower Bruin, not near as fashionable and modern as the people wore to the Freewill Baptist Church in Ohio. People from the old country had been there long enough to know the new fashions and how to dress. To see Mr. Herbert in his truck on the farm and to see him in a hat, shirt and necktie, Sunday suit and polished shoes, he wasn't the same man. Uncle Dick, Aunt Susie, Cousin Bos and Cousin Faith didn't look the same on Sunday. And Buster Boy, as Poppie and Mommie said, came to church dressed like a Philadelphia lawyer. To look at him in church, dressed the way he was with widow Ollie and her five children, one could not believe his past had been as wild as any young man in Ohio.

Our clothes marked us. No one in our family was more conscious of this than Cassie-Belle. And this was why we were working ten hours a day to make money and buy new clothes. Mommie's dresses and Poppie's Sunday suit were old fashioned and out of date. We sure did have a long way to rise in Ohio to catch up with the other average people.

This morning we were waiting when Jimmie Artner arrived. First thing he did after saying, "Good morning," he walked up to Mommie and said: "Mrs. Perkins, let me see his face."

Mommie opened the blanket enough to let him have a peep at Baby Brother's face.

"Pretty little baby," Jimmie said with a smile. Jimmie wanted to help Mommie onto the bus, but Mommie refused help. Poppie was carrying Little Dickie and Sister Cassie-Belle had Baby Sister Faith. And we loaded into the bus in our regular seats with Poppie and Mommie up front.

When we arrived at the Freewill Baptist Church, about twenty minutes early, Uncle Dick, Aunt Susie, Cousin Bos and Cousin Faith, Buster Boy and Ollie and her children, and Mr. and Mrs. Herbert were on the steps waiting for us. And when we went in a family group up the steps, Cousin Faith rushed up. "Sil, let me see Little Josh again!" Uncle Dick, with his cigars in his front coat pocket, and Aunt Susie came up.

"Josh, we've got namesakes here," Uncle Dick said. He took Little Dickie up in his arms and held him affectionately. "Susie, if we could have had only one boy like this."

"But it wasn't to be, Richard," Aunt Susie said. "All happenings are for a purpose in the eyes of the Lord!"

Then, Mr. and Mrs. Herbert stepped closer and looked at Baby Joshua.

"My first namesake," Mr. Herbert said.

I thought there were tears in his eyes. Mrs. Herbert didn't say anything while Mr. Herbert looked affectionately at his namesake.

"Aren't you getting out awful early after he was born, Sil?" Uncle Dick said.

"No earlier than I always get out after one of my babies is born," Mommie said. "What have I to fear? Our days are numbered in the Lamb's Book of Life—and when I've lived up my days, I'll change worlds. I'll go to a better world than where we moved from and a world better than this wonderful state."

Uncle Dick reached for a cigar then he realized he was on the church steps and put the cigar back in his coat pocket.

On all sides people began to gather. They looked at us as we went into the church house. My sisters took the Little Ones to the nursery, so they could go to their Sunday-school classes. Poppie, with Baby Sister in his arms, went to the Men's Bible Class and Mommie went to the Women's Bible Class holding Baby Brother Josh asleep in her arms.

Later when we assembled for church, they still had them in their arms. Poppie had a bottle for Baby Sister and Mommie nursed Little Josh in church. This was the way it was back on Lower Bruin, but I never saw another mother nursing her baby in this church. Many had young babies, but they gave them bottles. But there was not a baby in this church as young as Baby Joshua. And when I looked over at Tishie and Cassie-Belle, I thought they were a little plagued that Mommie was nursing Baby Josh in church.

We heard Reverend Cashew preach a long powerful sermon. And we heard great singing in our Freewill Baptist Church. After the service, so many people we'd never met before came up and introduced themselves to us. There were so many names I'd never remember half of them. It would take me and members of our family a long time to remember about three hundred faces and names. And all these people were dressed well. When we went toward the church bus, eleven children and two parents, people followed us and talked until we got in the bus. Jimmie was soon on the way. I guess he thought our little brothers and sisters, Mommie and Baby Josh ought to be back home. And our home did look good to all of us—even after we'd just gone to church. I know Mommie was glad to be back.

"One thing about it, Tishie," Cassie-Belle said when we got back in the house. "You, Maryann and I are going to have new clothes. We have to have. Poppie and Mommie need new clothes, too! I certainly realized this awhile ago in church!"

"Yes, Pedike and I need new clothes, too," Timmie said. "But don't you worry. If we keep on working like we have been, we'll have the money to buy clothes before school begins!"

"We need not wait until school begins," Cassie-Belle said. "The time to have new clothes is now! And we can buy more new clothes later!"

Poppie was making enough to buy our groceries now and to hold back a few extra dollars. Mommie was holding our money for clothes.

32 Monday was a new week. Poppie plowed the tobacco and Timmie and I used the hoes. If we knew anything on earth, it was how to grow tobacco from planting a seed bed, through all the summer season to autumn when we harvested, hung the cut tobacco on tier poles—waited for it to cure—then stripped, graded and put the tobacco in hands. And this is why Mr. Herbert had rented this farm to Poppie after Uncle Dick had told him how good we were at growing tobacco, which we called "the money crop" back on Lower Bruin.

It was fun to get hold of a hoe again. We could stand up straight and use a hoe. We didn't have to stoop as much as we did when we picked berries. And Mr. Herbert had come this morning for Tishie and Maryann to pick raspberries. So we were back at different kinds of farm work.

When we stopped at noon, Poppie watered the mule he was plowing single between the tobacco rows, and fed him in a feeder that hung from the mule's neck. And then we sat down to eat our lunches.

"I'd rather plow than deaden trees," Poppie said.

"We'd rather hoe than pick berries, too," Timmie said.

"I wonder how Tishie and Maryann are getting along picking raspberries," Poppie said. "Raspberries are smaller than strawberries. I wouldn't think one could pick half as many raspberries as strawberries in a day. But one good thing, the girls won't have to stoop much if they have to stoop at all to pick them. Raspberry vines are high!"

I'd be anxious to see Tishie and Maryann when we got home to see how they had got along.

"I've just been thinking, boys, the reason Mr. Herbert has done so well. Everything he plants, such as strawberries and raspberries, are money crops. He has white-face cattle for beef. He has a dairy herd. He has a sawmill, and chainsaws to cut paper wood, and bulldozers to clear his land. He has a mill to grind corn into meal and wheat into flour. And he owns thousands and thousands of acres of land. Yes, he's got a big chicken farm one of his sons operates. They sell eggs by the truckload!"

"Yet he had time to sit down under the sycamore shade and eat lunch with us," Timmie said.

"Mr. Herbert told me he went from one farm to another to keep the work moving. See, we have his tobacco and some corn on this new farm he bought! We're really running this one."

We had the old-fashioned farm with no electricity, that he had just bought. No wonder he called our family the last earth people. We were the last earth family in this part of Ohio.

Mr. Herbert had not come to see us this noon as he had before when we picked up the poles, roots and stumps and burned them. I figured he was eating his lunch with Tishie and Maryann at the raspberry patch.

"I'll plow this field, then I'll stop plowing and help you boys finish hoeing this tobacco," Poppie said. "Young terbacker plants are such tender things. Just a clod rolled down against one will kill it. See, I'm not plowing too close to the row of young plants!"

That afternoon Poppie plowed slowly and carefully so as not to damage the plants. Timmie and I did the finishing work with our hoes. This wasn't as fast as hoeing corn would be. We had to take time to hoe tobacco the first time. Second time Poppie plowed, it would be the last. After the second plowing, due to the size of the leaves, we couldn't hoe it. All we could do would be chop a few weeds.

At the close of the day Poppie unhitched the mule from the plow and we laid our hoes in the rows.

"We've made a good showing," he said.

Poppie had to take the mule to Mr. Herbert's barn, remove his harness and turn him loose in the barnlot. Timmie and I walked on home ahead of Poppie. When we got home, Mr. Herbert had brought Maryann and Tishie.

"How'd you get along picking raspberries?" I asked.

"It's hard to pick half as many raspberries as strawberries," she said. "The vines are high and tied to stakes."

"How many crates did you pick?" Timmie asked.

"Six," she replied.

"Not very many," Timmie said.

"But we picked raspberries," Maryann said.

"You know how much Mr. Herbert gets a gallon for raspberries?" Tishie said. "Four dollars a gallon!"

"Gee-whilligens!" Timmie said. "Twenty-four dollars a crate! Six crates, one hundred forty-four dollars! Big money!"

"Mr. Herbert said he got twice as much for raspberries as he did strawberries," Tishie said. "He said he couldn't get raspberry pickers! Said one reason young people refused, they said they were afraid of snakes!"

"Are there snakes up this far in Ohio?" Timmie asked.

"Who has seen one here?" I asked.

Not one of us had seen a snake in Ohio.

"Mr. Herbert said young people here didn't want to pick berries or use axes and hoes," Tishie said. "He said they'd drive trucks and do that sort of thing. He said most of their parents had made enough money that they didn't have to work."

"Can you save his raspberries?" Timmie asked.

"That's a good question," Tishie said. "We don't know. If we had you and Pedike with us we could. And if we had Cassie-Belle, we could."

"But maybe we can do it, Tishie," Maryann said.

"We can't help you now," I said.

"I can't help you either," said Cassie-Belle.

But Timmie and I did get to help them. This was the way it happened. We had worked Monday and Tuesday, and after we came home and did our chores, Poppie, Timmie and I hoed our late potatoes and did some work in the garden as long as we could see. And that night we had a warm rain to fall all night. It was what Poppie called "a growing rain."

"Ground too wet to plow and hoe," Poppie said the next morning. "So you boys can help your sisters pick berries! And I just wonder, since I don't have to do too much stooping, if Josh will let me pick. I don't know what he'll have for me to do. I don't want to lose a day. I'll ask him when he comes for you."

When Mr. Herbert came with his truck, Timmie and I were waiting with our sisters.

"The ground is too wet to plow and hoe, Mr. Herbert. Can you use Pedike and me to pick raspberries today?" Timmie said.

"I was going to ask you to do this," he said. "You bet I can!"

"What about me, too?" Poppie said with a laugh.

"You'll pick about as many as I can, Gil," Mr. Herbert said. "But I don't have anything else for you today. So, come on!"

"One thing I can do well is carry the loaded crates out," Poppie said.

It was so funny to have Poppie going with us to pick raspberries. Poppie was not for light farm work. He was made for heavy farm work. His hands were so big he could hardly milk a cow.

Mr. Herbert drove us to another farm. And here was the strangest raspberry patch I'd ever seen. The clumps of vines were tied to stakes. And the vines had been plowed between and plants had been hoed. They had been cultivated like corn and tobacco. The berries were small but I could stand up and pick most of the berries on a vine.

"Half this field is red and the other half black raspberries," Mr. Herbert said. "This is a twenty-acre flat low hilltop. Berries get the morning sun here. And this land is fertile."

"It's shore a nice place to pick berries," Poppie said. "Maybe I can do right well here even though I'm not a fast picker!"

"I'll have to return with more crates, Gil," Mr. Herbert

said. "I brought quart cups and crates for four pickers. I didn't know I'd have the children's father too!"

Now we began picking berries. And this was tedious—picking berries smaller than strawberries. But it was much easier. We could stand up and pull the black raspberries from the vines. And strange about this kind of berry picking, each one of us took a row. Yesterday, Maryann and Tishie had picked four rows through the field. If we had luck and could help Poppie, we would pick ten more rows today.

Mr. Herbert had brought us twelve crates. And Poppie sure got behind with his row. Since he had the row between Tishie's and mine, we'd walk over from our rows and pick a cluster of vines around a stake in his row. Maryann led in her row and Timmie was next to her. When Mr. Herbert came at noon and brought three crates for Poppie and one extra crate, we had finished five rows through the field. We had picked seven and a half crates of berries standing on soft, water-soaked land.

The ground was so wet we sat in a circle up in the truck-bed and ate our lunches.

"Maybe you'd better not have brought that extra crate, Josh," Poppie teased him. "Tishie and Pedike have helped me with my row. I believe it takes young people to pick these little berries. I know big slow hands and clumsy fingers are not good! I hope the ground will be dry enough so we can get back to plowing and hoeing tomorrow!"

"I'll check the ground this afternoon and let you know when I come for you," he said. "But today is going to be a big push in this raspberry patch. Five pickers instead of two."

"Ten hands, forty fingers and ten thumbs instead of four hands, sixteen fingers and four thumbs," Timmie said.

I wanted to tell him what a smart aleck he was but I remained silent.

"All these hands, fingers and thumbs have to get back to work," Poppie said. "We've got plenty of ripe raspberries to pick!"

So we went back to work. And this afternoon the fun wasn't on Timmie. We had our fun on big, slow Poppie.

"Poppie, are you in sight with your row?" Timmie would ask.

And we would laugh.

"If we were hoeing corn, I'd be ahead in my row," Poppie said.

Then we would laugh some more. It was so much fun to beat big strong Poppie, who could sink his double-butted ax up to the handle each time he struck a green tree. That's how powerful Poppie was. But he couldn't pick half as many raspberries as Maryann. So we had fun all afternoon teasing him.

"Don't think I'll ever pick raspberries again with my fast set," Poppie said with a big smile.

Well, I really felt sorry for him. I went over in his row until I got behind with my row. And Tishie did the same until she got behind in her row. But Timmie and Maryann were younger and they liked to race each other. Maryann finished her row first. She picked more berries than Timmie.

Timmie and Maryann wouldn't help us finish our rows. They began new rows.

"Maryann, you won't beat me this time," Timmie said.

"I will too beat you this time," Maryann told him.

Tishie and I finished our rows which made us two each for the day. And then we helped Poppie. And we began three new rows. When we had finished the fifteenth crate, Poppie looked at his watch.

"Fifteen minutes until four," he said. "I guess Josh was right bringing that extra crate!"

"Yes, he was," Timmie said. "Maryann and I are using it between us!"

"Well, I'll take a few of the extra cups," I said. "Five for me, five for Tishie and two for Poppie!"

When Mr. Herbert came in his truck, Poppie was carrying the last crate out to the oak-tree shade where we left the berries so the sun wouldn't hit them. Maryann and Timmie had really picked berries. Their trying to beat each other had more than made up for Poppie's slowness.

"Sixteen crates!" Mr. Herbert said. "You did fill that extra crate!"

"Yes, we've just finished it," Poppie said. "What about plowing tomorrow?"

"I've checked the ground," Mr. Herbert said. "It will be dry enough!"

"Good," Poppie said with a sigh. "Josh, I'd rather use an ax, plow mules in rooty new ground—I'd as soon do any kind of the hardest work as to try to pick them little berries and have my children beat me!"

This was so funny all four of us had to laugh. We had found a work where we could beat our strong Poppie.

"Gil, I've been thinking about something," Mr. Herbert said as Poppie, Timmie and I helped load the crates onto the truck. "Your children saved my strawberries. Now it looks like they might save these raspberries. They saved my berries when I couldn't get pickers!"

What a smile came over Poppie's face. And I thought I knew Timmie so well that he would blurt out: "Yes, and Mommie named Baby Brother for you—your only namesake." But Timmie didn't. I was glad I missed on him this time.

"I don't know how to thank you, Josh," Poppie said. "You've been so good to us!"

"But you've been so good to me," Mr. Herbert said. "You don't own a car, can't drive one, can't drive farm machinery. But you can use an ax, hoe, plow with mules in root-new grounds. You're the man I need. You can do things—and so can your children do things others can't or won't do! And you've got a big family—a fine family. I've got plenty, Gil, I'm an old man who likes to work—and who has to work or die for I'm in such habit of working. But you are a poor man with a big family!"

"Yes, we are poor people all right," Poppie said. "But because we are poor so many people want to help us. And you've done more for us in the short time we've been on your place than anybody has ever done for us!"

This time Poppie got up in the truck with Mr. Herbert, and Tishie and Maryann squeezed in beside them and we were on our way home. And as I stood up and looked over the truckbed on one side and Timmie on the other, I looked at the fields that belonged to Joshua Herbert. I just couldn't believe that he possessed so much of the world's goods.

When the truck stopped, Timmie was out first and made a run for the house.

"He's going to beat Poppie to Mommie and tell her Mr. Herbert said we saved his strawberries and now we'd save his raspberries," I said in a whisper to Tishie.

Sure enough, when we got to the house, Timmie wasn't in the living room with Mommie. Maybe he'd gone to the Little Ones' room to tell Cassie-Belle. But Mommie said: "I've just heard the good news! It's wonderful, Gil! To think Mr. Herbert has said our children saved his strawberries and will now save his raspberries!"

"It pays to live by The Word, to have a big family as The Word tells us and to be poor," Poppie said. "Look what our children have done!"

Poppie was a happy man.

Mommie was a happy woman with Baby Brother Josh in her arms covered in a little blanket and fast asleep.

After Timmie and I had done our chores, we had supper at the big table Cousin Bos had purchased second-hand for Poppie at a bargain. All could eat at this table—there'd not be any more second sittings. All eleven of us were at the table and Little Pearse's empty plate was there, too.

33 Thursday, Poppie finished plowing the smaller tobacco field in about two hours. He tied the mule at the end of the field to an oak-tree branch. Then, he helped us hoe tobacco until noon. Poppie was no raspberry picker, but when it came to using a hoe, he led Timmie and me in the tobacco rows.

After lunch he began plowing the tobacco patch on the other side of the valley, which was twice the size of where we were working. I knew if Timmie and I had good luck we would finish hoeing this field today. We wanted to get this field finished and get into the other one in the morning. For the corn planted in this valley would soon be big enough to plow and hoe. And plowing and hoeing the corn would be real fast. Timmie and I could almost keep up with Poppie's plowing with our hoes.

Timmie and I did have this good luck. We finished our last four rows after four o'clock quitting time. And now we would have one day, tomorrow, Saturday, hoeing in the field where Poppie was plowing. He would plow far enough ahead so all three could hoe here tomorrow. Poppie knew how to plan this kind of work—with mule and hoe—for he had done it all his life.

In the following week, while we were working in the second patch of tobacco, we had another "growing rain" that made the ground too wet to work. And we helped Maryann and Tishie pick raspberries. With our two days work helping them we knew we had saved Mr. Herbert's black and red raspberries.

This week we finished the second patch of tobacco. The

long green rows of tobacco on these Ohio hillslopes were beautiful in the sun.

Now we were ready to begin plowing and hoeing corn. Poppie plowed the mule between the green rows of corn. He ran a top furrow and a bottom furrow in the corn balk. Timmie and I used our hoes fast. We kept up with Poppie. We were not hoeing tobacco now. This was much easier.

Believe it or not, in six days Poppie had plowed the corn in this field. Timmie and I had hoed the long rows behind him. There were long green rows around the slopes. The tobacco was pretty in shorter green rows. We had come into this valley. We knew what to do and we had done it.

Mr. Herbert had not visited us until Saturday, our last day.

"Gil, you and your boys have really done it," he said. "And Maryann and Tishie have finished with the raspberries. They saved them. This has been a great week on this farm."

In the six weeks we had worked and the four weeks Tishie and Maryann had worked—and on the Sunday when all five of us had worked, and some overtime we had worked—Mommie had collected nine hundred dollars of our money.

"It's the most money that's ever been in this house," Mommie said. "I'm afraid to have this much money in this house! And to think my children have earned this much!"

"We've worked for the money," I said. "Now, I think it is the time all of us get some new clothes!"

"I agree with you, Pedike," Cassie-Belle said. "It is time we change the old clothes we wore on Lower Bruin!"

"With nine hundred dollars, we ought to buy new clothes for all of us," I said. "New dresses and shoes for Mommie. A new suit, shirts and shoes for Poppie! New dresses and slippers for my sisters. New suits, shirts and ties for Timmie and me. We've never had new suits of clothes in our lives!"

"Well, I agree we need new clothes," Poppie said. "We're not as well dressed as the people here in Ohio!"

"We're so poorly dressed when we stand out among all the people who come to the Freewill Baptist Church," Cassie-Belle said. "I'm actually ashamed of the way we're dressed! I'm ashamed of the dresses Mommie wears—her shoes and her two old hats!"

"But we're a poor family," Poppie said.

"But we're earning money now," Cassie-Belle said. "And we don't have to stay poor. And we can buy new clothes and we can go better dressed. And I think it's about time for us to be somebody!"

"Gee-whilligens, we can go back to Lower Bruin some day all dressed up, riding in a fine car," Timmie said. "Drive past that old schoolhouse where we used to live. People wouldn't know us then!"

"That's not it, Timmie," Cassie-Belle said. "I feel for the people there. I know how hard they live. I don't want to show off and put on airs there. I want us to dress decently in Ohio! We're not going back there to live! I'd run away from home before I'd go!"

"Cassie-Belle, do you realize what you're a-sayin'?" Mommie said. "You are turning your back on your own raisin' and your own people! Look how many of our kinfolks live there. Our dead are buried there!"

"I know what I'm saying, Mommie," she said. "I won't turn my back on them. I'll turn my front on them! I know, I'll never go back there! No wonder all the people back there want to cross the River and come North to Ohio. What's back there for the old people or the young people?"

"I'll never go back, either," I said. "I'll stay on in Ohio where I can work and make money! I'll never go back to the mountains! I'll never go back to Appalachia! Look how many people from there have come here and made good!"

"I'm getting some pride," Cassie-Belle said. "I know it's not the pride a lot of people have! But just to live in a wall-papered house for the first time in my life! And to eat food we bought in a store is something better than the old commodities we carried home in sacks in Lower Bruin!"

"I tell you, money is trouble," Poppie said. "Now we don't want arguments amongst us, but look what this nine hundred dollars is causing! I've made the living here so you could save money for your clothes! I know you need them. I'm glad you will be able to buy them. But remember we are poor people and we have been poorer than we are now!"

"Yes, I often think what if something would happen to your father, children, what would we do?" Mommie said. "He's the breadwinner for eleven! I mean if he's to cut a tree and it would fall on him!"

Well, Timmie puckered his face like he was going to laugh, but Mommie sure looked at him. One look stopped Timmie's laughter and whatever he started to say.

"But, Sil, I'm awfully keerful," Poppie said. "I know when parents beget a big family there are big responsibilities. You know, Sil, we've held our family together!"

"But I don't know how much longer we could have done it without all this Ohio money coming in," Mommie said. "Our boys could hardly get a day's work back in Lower Bruin! And when they did Pedike first got a dollar and then two dollars and Timmie got fifty cents. And you got three dollars, Gil!"

"I know, Sil, but all this is behind us," Poppie said as he sat down in his big rocker in our living room with Baby Sister on his lap. "Now, we need clothes! Our children have earned the money. But they've made so much in our short time in Ohio they want to buy more fashionable clothes for you, me, the Little Ones down to the Babies. And I say we let them do it!"

"Cassie-Belle, not given much to affection, ran over and put her arms around Poppie's big bull neck and squeezed it.

"Thank you, Poppie," she said.

"And why don't we get Cousin Faith to tell us the store in Agrillo to buy clothes?" Poppie said. "She will know the place and she might want to go along with us! I think she could help us."

"I'm all for it," Mommie said. "I want peace and happiness among us! And I know our daughters and sons need new clothes! You and I, Gil, can get along in our old clothes. But our children need a change!"

"You need a change, too, Mommie," Cassie-Belle said. "And Poppie needs a change. Look how well Uncle Dick, Aunt Susie, Mr. and Mrs. Herbert, Cousin Bos and Faith and Buster Boy dress on Sunday. You ought to see how shabby you look beside them! What you wear here is all right for Lower Bruin but it's not right for Agrillo, Ohio!"

34 Cousin Bos and Cousin Faith made arrangements with Poppie and Mommie at the Freewill Baptist Church to take us on a Wednesday, first week in July, to Tockabee's Clothing Store in Agrillo.

"You will have to lose a work day anyway," Cousin Faith said. "And Saturday is such a busy day at Tockabee's when the country people come in, you can't stir them with a stick. Wednesday will be a quiet day and you'll get better service."

"Yes, we'll have many outfits, dresses for the girls, suits for the boys, outfits for the Little Ones and a suit for Gil, dresses for me and shoes for everybody," Mommie said. "Cassie-Belle, Tishie and Pedike think we're the most old-fashioned dressed family at the Freewill Baptist Church in Agrillo—maybe in all Landsdowne County."

"Sil, I have to agree with them," Cousin Faith said. "Honest, you wear hats and dresses to church like our grandmothers wore back on Lower Bruin. Gil's still in a double-breasted suit, peg-legged pants, brogan shoes, stiff-celluloid collars, bowties and a plug hat! I've told Bos I'd like to see you get out of the dark ages in the clothes you're a-wearin'! Remember, you're in Ohio—in a progressive county with plenty of wealth. And I'll go with you and help you all I can. I know you've not been in a clothing store in a long time."

"I never was in one," Mommie told her. "We'll be glad to have you help us!"

"Yes, we'll certainly be glad to have you go with us," Cassie-Belle said.

Cassie-Belle had stood by smiling when Cousin Faith told Mommie about hers and Poppie's old-fashioned clothes and that we were in the dark ages the way we dressed.

Now, I felt the same way Cassie-Belle did only I didn't express my thoughts. Cousin Faith and Cassie-Belle had already said what I wanted to say.

35 Poppie was plowing and Pedike and I were hoeing the young corn now. We had given the two tobacco patches a thorough hoeing and plowing. This was Mr. Herbert's late corn on these slopes. If we had not moved to his farm, maybe he would not have got these slopes planted. Not many men in this area of Ohio wanted to plow mules in new ground and use axes. And as Mr. Herbert once told Poppie, people from the old country and from down through Appalachia had taught the Ohioans how to raise tobacco.

So as I hoed along fast in my corn row with Timmie at my heels in his row above me, I thought about who would have set and cultivated this tobacco on these slopes for Mr. Herbert but our family. And who would have saved his strawberries and raspberries but our family. And we couldn't have done this unless we had numbers. On two occasions we had ten hands, forty fingers and ten thumbs picking berries.

Poppie watered the mule at noon in a pond gouged out by the bulldozer in the stream between these slopes. Then we sat down on the dry corn field to eat our lunches, which we pulled down from behind the branches of a tree at the end of the field. Poppie had told us long ago to put them up where a stray dog or a fox couldn't get them. We had just begun to eat when Mr. Herbert came down the slope.

"Mr. Herbert, we got more money in our house than we've ever had in our life," Timmie said. "Tishie, Maryann, Pedike and I have made and saved nine hundred dollars!"

Timmie just had to tell it.

"And we've got our work up and ahead," Poppie said. "We want to go to Tockabee's Wednesday and buy clothes for all of us. Cousin Faith plans to go with us!"

"That's wonderful, Gil," Mr. Herbert said. "I know all of you need clothes."

"It's money the children have worked for and their mother has saved for them. They think we dress too old-fashioned for Ohio! And they're thinking about when they'll start to school. They want new clothes!"

"That's right, Gil," Mr. Herbert said. "Your children are right. So you take Wednesday off and buy clothes. It'll take about a day to get outfits for all in your family."

"And Cousin Faith said go on Wednesday and never on Saturday to Tockabee's. She said Saturday was a busy day there when all the country people came to Agrillo. What do you know about Tockabee's?"

"It's a good family store, all right, Gil, but my wife and I usually go to Columbus to buy our clothes," Mr. Herbert said. "I know Mr. Tockabee very well. He's a fine citizen, an accommodating and good man. I'm sure your Cousin Bos and Faith Auxier, who trade at Tockabee's, can tell you more about the store than I can."

36 Wednesday morning Cousin Bos and Faith drove up in their red truck. They had the truckbed on to break the fresh morning July air from the Little Ones' and the Babies' faces. And they had put plank seats for us back across the truckbed which they used for hauling. After Cousin Bos' and Faith's bragging I wondered why they didn't own a passenger car. Poppie and Mommie thought the reason was Buster Boy might take it over for his own, for he lived with them. But they didn't have a passenger car. They had a fine home and good furniture and every modern convenience I'd ever seen in a home—of course, this was the only modern home with a bathroom and electrical appliances we'd ever been in. So this red truck was the symbol of Cousin Bos and Faith. When we saw it coming up into our drive we knew. And it came often with them to see about us. Every time I saw a red truck on the highway I said: "Cousin Bos and Cousin Faith."

Well, Mommie got up in the front seat with Cousin Bos and Cousin Faith. Poppie with Baby Sister on his lap sat back with us. Our family filled the three seats Cousin Bos had prepared for us. And we were off to Tockabee's to get new clothes for everyone in our family from Mommie and Poppie to Baby Brother Joshua.

Cousin Bos was the little man with the big voice which carried his words back to us. A little man with a lot of brag and a booming voice he couldn't control.

"See, since we're taking all of you to Tockabee's, Faith and I have decided to get clothes, too," he said. "Thirteen of you and two of us. Fifteen of us. We'll be spending money with Fred Tockabee. We ought to get some bargains —maybe, a few extras thrown in free like ties and socks for the men."

Cousin Bos was a practical man. He had said many times he shopped where his dollar went the farthest. Mommie said when he and Cousin Faith lived on Lower Bruin, they weren't as positive and bossy as they were now, and the reason they were this way was they had more of the world's goods and were so sure of themselves! She and Essej Trants had let them run his big farm until they thought they owned it.

But how can we talk about them? I thought. How can we ever say a word about them? They are wonderful to us. Look what they have done to help us. With the exception of Mr. Herbert and Uncle Dick Perkins, they have done more for us than anyone. And Poppie has always said Uncle Dick Perkins was like an old fox—never underrate what he might wangle for us yet. Even back on Lower Bruin Poppie said, the old people remembered Uncle Dick as a young man everybody called a silver-tongued fox. And people were afraid to sell, trade or buy cattle from him.

I had these thoughts while Cousin Bos sped his red truck toward Agrillo. This was one time when Brother Timmie and I sat on our seats and didn't stand up and look out at the countryside, as we had done most every time when we had driven this way. We were contented to sit and ride. Maybe Timmie dreamed of his first long suit of clothes. But don't you think I didn't sit here and dream of the stationwagon I might help Poppie buy or I might some day buy myself to haul all our family. I had my dreams, too. Silent one or not, I had my dreams.

When Cousin Bos pulled up to a sudden stop, I knew we were there. Cousin Bos jumped out of the truck and he shouted: "Roll out! Every last one of you, roll out! We're in Agrillo at Tockabee's!"

While we were rolling out, Cousin Bos was putting a big coin in the parking meter. One quarter for four hours.

"We'll be here longer," he said. "But we'll replenish the meter with another quarter."

Now as a body of fifteen we walked into the store.

"Mr. Tockabee, we're here for outfits of clothes," Cousin Bos said. "We've brought you customers who have cash to pay!"

"All of you?" he asked.

"Every last one of us," Cousin Faith said. "These are our kinfolk from the old country. They want something respectable to wear!"

"We have what you want," Mr. Tockabee said. "From parents to babies."

I thought Fred Tockabee had the ugliest face I'd ever seen. He had a face that looked like a raccoon's. Mr. Tockabee himself didn't wait on customers on Wednesdays. But he had two women and two men clerks in this store. Cousin Bos and the two men clerks stayed with Poppie, Timmie and me.

The clerks showed us suits—suits for Poppie and suits for Timmie and me. They were pretty suits, too, just about all of them—beautiful, more beautiful and most beautiful. But Cousin Bos was interested in helping Poppie get his suit first.

"No more peg-legged pants, Gil," Cousin Bos said. "This is Ohio!"

"But I don't know about a suit like this," Poppie said.

"I do," Cousin Bos said. "Choose your color and get your size."

Well, it was a dark suit and the coat wasn't double-breasted.

Then, before Timmie and I had a chance to buy our suits, Cousin Bos saw to it Poppie had four new shirts, new shoes and socks. And he asked the clerks to give Poppie four neckties, not bow ties, and let Poppie choose his colors.

"We're spending hundreds here today," Cousin Bos said. "So you can be a little generous with neckties and socks!"

"We sure can," said one of the smiling young men waiting on us.

He not only let Poppie select the neckties of his choice but he gave him two extra pairs of socks. Then Cousin Bos helped Poppie select a hat. Cousin Bos was wonderful for Poppie. Poppie depended on him and took his word. While Cousin Bos was helping us, Cousin Faith was helping

Mommie buy a new hat, new dresses and shoes. Cousin Faith, I knew, would see to it Mommie changed her clothes from shoes to hat. All her old-fashioned clothes would have to go.

Now it was mine and Timmie's turn to see new suits shown to us by the young clerks. I guess we were like blind dogs in a meat house when we saw these suits for young men laid out before us. I know I would have liked to have had all of them.

"I just can't choose," Timmie said. "I've never seen anything like this. And to think Mr. Herbert said he went to Columbus, Ohio, to buy his clothes!"

Well, we knew we had to choose only one suit of clothes, a hat, shirts, shoes and socks. We couldn't buy all we wanted to buy. I finally chose an oxford-gray suit. It was a beauty. When I tried it on I saw myself in a mirror and I couldn't believe I was Pedike Perkins. I was a new young man. This suit made the difference.

Timmie chose a lighter suit. And of course he blabbed: "It's the prettiest suit I've ever seen!" This pleased the clerks. And then we selected a half-dozen shirts for each of us—some buttoned down at the collars and some didn't. They were white and blue. And next we bought underwear, shorts and undershirts which we had never possessed in our lives. Then we bought the first hats we had ever owned. Cousin Bos asked that we be given four neckties and four pair of socks after these purchases. And the clerks didn't quibble. They let Timmie and me choose our neckties and they gave us four pairs of socks each.

"Now let's go and see how Faith and the womenfolks are getting along," Cousin Bos said.

When we walked over to the woman's department, Cousin Bos asked: "How are you getting along?"

"We've got Cousin Sil's hat, shoes and dresses and other clothes. And Cassie-Belle, Tishie, Maryann have parts of theirs. But they've more to get! And we've not begun to outfit the children yet!"

"Don't you think we'd better go down to the Corner Restaurant and eat and then come back and finish the job?" Cousin Bos said. "It's mealtime for me. I'm getting hungry!"

"I think this would be a good idea," Cousin Faith said.

So Poppie, Mommie and Cousin Faith carried the Babies and Little Dickie down to the Corner Restaurant. There wasn't anyone in the restaurant until the fifteen of us went in. Talk about the high chairs, they pulled out three! Here, with Cousin Bos' and Faith's help, all of us ate in a restaurant together for the first time. But Cousin Bos, the little boss that he was, ordered the waitresses around. This was Cousin Bos' way. He couldn't help it. He was just that way. After we had finished our meal, Cousin Bos asked one waitress to give him the check, which was for more than seventeen dollars. Cousin Bos paid for our lunch and when we left he tipped the waitress three dollars.

We went back up the street, not a block away, to Tockabee's. In the afternoon, Cousin Bos got a new suit, shoes, hat and shirts for himself. The clerks gave him neckties and socks.

My sisters, who saw so many nice things and were hungry for everything they saw, bought dresses, underclothes, and shoes. Cousin Faith helped him. And Cousin Faith helped Mommie buy suits and dresses for the Little Ones—even booties and dresses for Baby Brother Joshua.

"I wonder about our money for all of this," Poppie said, in a low voice to me. "Do you reckon, Pedike, we'll have enough money to pay for all we've bought?"

Cousin Faith was the last one of all of us to buy dresses, shoes and a hat for herself. She was very choicy going over the dresses Tockabee's had. And she grumbled as she tried on this dress and that one, looking at herself in the mirror. Finally, she made her purchases. Now, we were ready to pay and go.

I stood by the cash register to see how much Cousin Bos paid and how much we paid. Cousin Bos paid just for himself and Cousin Faith two hundred and thirty-nine dollars. I didn't know whether our money would pay for our clothes or not! I was relieved when the clerk said: "Eight hundred and thirty-six dollars, Mr. Perkins."

Well, Mommie carried our money. And Cousin Faith held Baby Brother Josh while Mommie counted eight hundred and thirty-six dollars. How could I have ever believed back on Lower Bruin there would have ever been a time in our lives when we would have spent at one time eight hundred and thirty-six dollars for clothes! When a short time ago, not more than three months, we were carrying commodities home on our backs in sacks five miles from Blakesburg to Lower Bruin.

But I knew we had worked for our clothes.

"Gee-whilligens, there goes nearly all of our work money," Timmie said. "But I'm glad! Look what we've got! We'll be new-looking people! We won't be old-fashioned looking now!"

Then he laughed his wild laugh.

"What will the people think of us at the Freewill Baptist Church and Sunday School Sunday?" Timmie said.

Mommie couldn't square herself around to make a face at him for she was counting out the money to pay.

"Mommie, it would be easier to take out for ourselves sixty-four dollars and give Mr. Tockabee all the rest," Timmie said.

Then Timmie gave another wild cackling laugh which was akin to a young mule colt's trying to bray.

But Mommie got a straight look at him this time, and excited Timmie, proud of all the new clothes we had, cooled off. Mommie counted the money and paid—the biggest bill she'd ever paid in her life. We couldn't carry all the bundles and boxes out to the truck, for Mommie, Cousin Faith, Cassie-Belle and Tishie went with the Babies and Little Ones, now getting fretful and crying. Cousin Bos, Poppie, Timmie and Maryann and I carried all we could to the truck. And the two women and two men clerks helped us. And when we reached the truck Cousin Bos had a ticket on his windshield for not putting more money in the parking meter.

"Come to Agrillo and spend hundreds of dollars and then get a parking ticket," Cousin Bos shouted. "That's the thanks we get for spending money here!"

Cousin Bos, a little man, talked loud. He could be heard three blocks away.

"I'll take care of that ticket, Mr. Auxier," said one of the clerks.

He took the parking ticket from the windshield. Cousin

Bos thanked him. And we loaded into the truck the same way as we had come, plus all our boxes and bundles. We were on our way home. This shopping day we would never forget.

"Gee-whilligens," Timmie chattered away. "Where are we going to put all these new clothes when we get them home?"

"Don't you fret about that," Cassie-Belle said real quickly. "I'll find a place for every piece and parcel."

37 Thursday, Friday and Saturday, Poppie plowed corn and Timmie and I hoed. And Timmie, two years younger than I, tired when we hoed on some of the new-ground bluff parts of the field where Poppie had to plow the steep ground with a mule. This land wasn't as well prepared as where the big bulldozers had pulled the weighted bogharrows and pulverized the new-ground earth.

We fell far behind the plow on Thursday. And when Mr. Herbert came to see how we were getting along and to eat lunch with us, brother Timmie said, "Mr. Herbert, you know something? Pedike and I just can't keep up with Poppie's plowing with our hoes. But we'd like to do it. Look, we've got the other side of the valley to plow and hoe! I know how we can do it!"

"Timmie, you're just full of ideas," Mr. Herbert said.

I really didn't know what Timmie was going to say. But I thought his tongue would cut his throat again. Poppie looked so straight at Timmie that he turned his face from Poppie.

"You know, my sisters, Cassie-Belle and Tishie are good with hoes," Timmie said. "Tishie is as fast or faster than I am with a hoe and Cassie-Belle is faster than Pedike!"

"Your sisters in the corn field with hoes!" Mr. Herbert said.

"Yes," Poppie said, "you know women worked in the old country, Josh, on the steep Kentucky hills with hoes—father, mother, sons and daughters—to make a living. Yes,

Timmie is telling you right. I don't know what made him think of this. I know I didn't think of it."

"It's because we're behind with our hoes, Poppie," Timmie said. "And when you plow that last row of corn I want us to be able to hoe it. And I know Cassie-Belle and Tishie would like to work and make more money! More dollars, Mr. Herbert!"

Then, Timmie gave that laugh like a guinea hen's cackle —that laugh that sometimes made me laugh and sometimes made me so ashamed I wanted to hide my face in my hands.

"It's a wonderful idea if the girls can hoe corn and want to work," Mr. Herbert said. "Do you mind, Gil? What about help at home? Wouldn't your oldest, Cassie-Belle, be needed at home with her mother?"

"I'll see about it when I go home and talk to Sil," Poppie said. "But Sil is up and doing and Maryann is a great help at home now!"

"Poppie, Cassie-Belle wants to get out and work for a change," Timmie said. "I've heard her say so many times! She likes to make money, too!"

And Timmie laughed again. I didn't know why he laughed. What he said wasn't funny. I put my hands over my face. Poppie looked very straight at Timmie.

"Bring the girls tomorrow, Gil, if they want to work," Mr. Herbert said. "If they can use hoes on this new-ground hill and want to work, I'll sure let them do it. If they can hoe like they picked strawberries and raspberries, they're one hundred percent in my book."

"Well, they can use hoes all right, Josh," Poppie spoke in his slow voice. "I think one or both will be here in the morning!"

"It's been so long since I've seen girls or women hoeing corn on a new-ground hillslope. I'll come with hoes for them in the morning," Mr. Herbert said.

Well, after Mr. Herbert left and Poppie was plowing again—getting farther and farther away from us—Timmie turned to me and said: "Pedike, you're my oldest living brother and you should do the talking. You're a shut-mouth! Somebody has to think! Somebody has to talk!"

He leaned on his hoe handle and looked at me. I leaned on my hoe handle and looked at him—we'd always been as close as brothers could be. This was the first time he'd ever called me a "shut-mouth." And I had to admit he was right.

"I talked out of turn," Timmie said. "But you wait and see if Cassie-Belle and Tishie don't come to work in the morning! They'll be glad to come to earn more money. We've not got much of our nine hundred dollars left! And our whole family will have something to show for the money we've already made but spent."

"Timmie, you're always figuring something out," I said. "I'll bet you've got it figured out how many days' work they'll get and how much they'll earn!"

"Friday and Saturday of this week and all six days of next week, if we don't have a rainy day," he said. "Seventy five cents an hour, ten hours a day for eight days will be three hundred twenty dollars! Gee-whilligens! That's money! Four of us and Poppie working, we'll be back to forty dollars a day on this farm! People on Lower Bruin couldn't believe this if we told them! Mommie will be for this, you wait and see!"

Then, Timmie gave his cackling victory laugh.

"I don't like your laugh," I said.

"I can't help how I laugh," he said. "Just so I laugh! I like to laugh! You'd better try laughing."

"We'd better get back to work," I said.

Now Timmie was right again. When we walked in sight of our home, Timmie broke out in a run to get there first so he could break the news to Mommie and my sisters. Poppie and I walked on to the house.

When we got inside, Mommie met us.

"I've just heard the good news, Gil," Mommie said. "Tishie and Cassie-Belle are happy, too!"

"Can you manage with Maryann?" Poppie asked.

"I certainly can, Gil," Mommie said. "I'm all right. I am the children's mother. I can take care of my children with so little help. Let the older ones work and earn while they can in this summer season.

38 Friday morning on a fair day with warm fresh winds and blue skies, Cassie-Belle, Tishie, Timmie and I walked down where Mr. Herbert was waiting. Poppie, who was far up on the slope above us, was hitching his mule to the plow.

"Good morning," Mr. Herbert said. "I have two hoes filed sharp and waiting! I wasn't sure whether or not you girls would be here!"

"Got an extra file, Mr. Herbert?" Timmie asked. "In this kind of hoeing our hoes get dull!"

"Can you file a hoe?" Mr. Herbert asked Timmie.

"Yes, Pedike and I can file hoes when they get dull, can't we, Pedike?" Timmie said.

"Sure we can," I replied.

Mr. Herbert gave Timmie a new file which he put into his overalls hip pocket.

Mr. Herbert stood watching us. He knew about hoeing corn. And maybe he was surprised when he watched Cassie-Belle take the bottom row and I the one above her. Tishie took the third row up and Timmie the fourth. I knew what Cassie-Belle could do with a hoe. To look at her one would never think about her skill with a hoe. She was fast. I didn't want her standing above me, waiting for me to move out with the row below her. She was fast enough to rake the weeds and clods down on me. So, I was glad for her to take the bottom row.

"Mr. Herbert, see all the rows plowed ahead of us?" Timmie said. "Now, we will start gaining on Poppie. At the end of next week, when he plows that last row we'll be hoeing it!"

Mr. Herbert stood there watching us hoe corn. Just as we began our rows I looked up and he was smiling. I knew we were doing our work to suit him. And I knew he was pleased to see the way Cassie-Belle and Tishie were hoeing corn.

Mr. Herbert still didn't know that we had almost quit work for three years. Now, as Cousin Bos and Faith said, since we had started working again we were getting our pride back. We had become somebody again. And if I could talk like Timmie, I could tell anybody we'd never forgot how to work. When we got paid as well as we were paid now—when we could see something in the future—we didn't mind to work.

When we were getting our rows near the far end of the field, Cassie-Belle was out in front. I was second, Tishie was behind me and Timmie was behind her. The spaces between us were about the same. I looked back and Mr. Herbert was still standing there watching us work.

And when we stopped for lunch, we had gained a few rows on Poppie. But we hadn't gained many. We sat on the dry soft ground with Poppie in the middle and we ate our sandwiches and each drank a pint of sweet milk. Each of us had brought a half-gallon fruit jar filled with water. If we drank this, there was more water flowing from a spring from under the hill down in the valley. This was where Poppie watered the mule at noon.

"I'm proud of my sons and daughters," Poppie said. "You know how to do this kind of work. And you will work!"

"But, Poppie, look at the money we get," Timmie said. "And wait until Sunday morning! I can't wait to get into my first real dress-up suit!"

"I can't wait either, Timmie," Cassie-Belle said. "We'll be a different-looking family Sunday, won't we?"

"You can include your mother and me in on that," Poppie said. "The Little Ones and the Babies, too!"

"We won't look like girls who have hoed corn and picked berries on Sunday, will we, Cassie-Belle?" Tishie said.

"I'm the youngest of the four and I've helped every one

of you," Timmie said. "I helped to get you into the strawberry and raspberry picking and I helped get you in the corn field! I'm the youngest and have to take the top row!"

Well, Poppie, Cassie-Belle and Tishie laughed. I didn't laugh because Timmie couldn't take the bottom row but I wanted to say to him: "Maybe we'd better all cry because you can't beat your sisters or me with a hoe." But, being the silent one, I didn't say what went through my mind.

At the end of our thirty-minutes' lunch period, our laughter, talk and a little rest, we went back to our work and Poppie went back to his plowing. By midafternoon, Cassie-Belle had gained one full row on me. I'd gained one full row on Tishie and Tishie had gained a row on Timmie.

"Little Brother, what do you think of my hoeing corn," Tishie said to Timmie.

Then we laughed. This was our joke and our fun hoeing corn on an Ohio hillside in the early July sun.

"I don't feel bad about it. Pedike, you're Poppie's oldest living son and our sister Cassie-Belle is a row up on you," Timmie said. "Not all the joke's on me!" Then Timmie laughed as his hoe went up and down in rhythmic motion. "Besides, I do a lot of your thinking for you. And I'm the youngest among you!"

"No apologies, Timmie," Tishie said. "We know you're 'The Brain' amongst us!"

"I disagree," I said. "I think the fastest with a hoe amongst us and the fastest berry picker, Sister Cassie-Belle, is the brain! One thing I do know, I'm not 'The Brain' amongst us!"

"Well, if Sister Cassie-Belle is 'The Brain,' why doesn't she get the extra day's work for us?" Timmie asked.

Then he gave his laugh that sounded exactly like a guinea hen.

We laughed again. All of this broke the spell of the constant peck-peck of our hoes on the dry ground.

"For a nearly fourteen-year-old boy, Timmie, the youngest of our four, you do mighty well working and thinking," I thought. "But I'm not going to tell you. If I told you, you'd be so happy and worked up, we couldn't hold you in this big corn field."

Poor old Poppie didn't know what was going on below. He kept on plowing. He knew we were below, that we would be gaining on him if and when he stopped long enough to look down the hill. But we had a long way to go to reach him.

At four o'clock each of us was a row and a half ahead of the other. Cassie-Belle was first and Timmie was last. I was second and Tishie was third. Poppie unhitched the mule and came down the hill. We left our hoes in our rows. This day was over for us. We had worked. We had made this hillslope look different. Behind us were the long green rows of corn without a weed in any row, waving in the late afternoon's slow lazy wind.

We walked more slowly toward home than we had walked toward this corn field when we were fresh in the morning. Our clothes were wet with sweat. Even my socks were wet where my feet had sweated. We had done a good day's work for Mr. Herbert.

And Saturday Poppie finished plowing the corn on this side of the valley and he had gone over to the other side and had done some plowing. And we had climbed high on this slope. Could we catch up with Poppie's plowing and when he finished the last row on the other slope, would we be up with him and finish the last row with our hoes when he finished plowing? This was our goal.

39 Sunday morning we were up before daylight. Timmie and I did our chores. Then we ate our breakfasts. This was the morning for all of us to dress in our new clothes.

The first one amongst us to get on his new clothes was Poppie. We looked at him.

"Poppie, you look like a new man," Cassie-Belle said.

"I've never seen you look better in my life," Mommie said.

Well, we gathered around Poppie and looked him over.

"I'm proud of you, Poppie," Tishie said. "You look better than Cousin Bos, Uncle Dick or Mr. Herbert!"

Poppie was a very handsome man dressed in a new suit, shirt, string necktie, shoes and hat. He stood before the mirror and looked at himself.

"Maybe clothes make the man," Poppie said. "I know I look different. I don't look like a man plowing a mule in the corn field on a hillside in Ohio!"

Then my sisters helped our Little Mommie get dressed. Well, I hardly knew my mother in a new dress, new shoes and a new hat. Cousin Faith had certainly helped her select the right clothes. Our Little Mother didn't look like one who had given birth to a dozen children. Right now, she looked as young and pretty as her oldest daughter, Sister Cassie-Belle.

When Timmie took a look at Mommie in her new clothes he jumped up high in our living room and said: "Gee-whilligens, Mommie, you're pretty! You're my pretty Mommie in your new clothes!"

I was really proud of the way my father and mother looked. I'd never seen them look the way they looked this Sunday morning. And now was our time to get dressed. Timmie and I went to our room and we dressed from the skin out. Our underwear, first. We'd only worn long underwear in winter and no underwear in summer. Now we put on shorts and undershirts. When Timmie got into his, he jumped up and down. He talked so much I put my index fingers in my ears to stop the sound. He got noisier as he grew older. He'd got awfully noisy in Ohio.

Maybe Timmie looked better than I did. I'm six feet with my legs slightly bowed. But I looked at myself in the mirrors in our room. I thought I looked pretty good. Then, Timmie got into his pants and his new shirt, and I had to tie his necktie. Well, I'll admit he didn't look like a boy fresh from the corn field and blabbing all the time. He put on his coat and hat, and looked at himself in the mirror.

"I'm not Timmie Perkins," he said. "I'm somebody else. I don't know myself. Gee-whilligens! I'm glad I worked picking up roots, picking berries, setting and hoeing tobacco and hoeing corn! Look at me now. Ohio is a wonderful state! Really, Pedike, I'm an Ohioan! Look at me! Do you know your brother Timmie?"

I looked at him. Really I didn't know my brother. Straight as an arrow and five ten. Timmie was a new boy! He really looked good. And now I got into my new pants and shirt and I tied my necktie before the mirror. Right now I looked different. And when I put my coat on, I knew I didn't look like the Pedike picking up roots and burning brush piles. I was really a new man.

"I don't know you, Brother Pedike," Timmie said. "You're a new brother!"

Timmie laughed. I put my index fingers in my ears.

"What do you say we walk over to the living room?" Timmie said.

We walked over to the living room where Cassie-Belle, Tishie and Maryann were dressed in their new clothes. Really, we didn't know our sisters in their new clothes. Cassie-Belle looked like an angel. She was really pretty. So was sister Tishie. Neither one of my sisters looked like she did yesterday when they left the corn field without a dry thread on their clothes.

"Cassie-Belle, you're beautiful," I said. "I'll say this although you took the lead row in the corn field on me."

"Tishie, you're prettier than Cassie-Belle," Timmie said. "I'll say this for you even if you beat me over a row in the corn field yesterday."

We bragged on Maryann, our twelve-year-old sister. She was beautiful in her new clothes as she walked out and back before us in the living room.

Now, Mommie and our sisters began dressing the Little Ones. And then Cassie-Belle and Tishie helped Mommie dress Little Dickie in a new little boy's suit. Baby-Sister Faith wore a new dress and ruffled panties. And Baby-Brother Josh was dressed in a new gown, booties and a receiving blanket.

When Jimmie Artner drove up with the church bus, he got out and came in. He stood there looking at us. He couldn't believe we were the same family he had hauled last Sunday to the Freewill Baptist Church in Agrillo. He was speechless at first.

"Jimmie, we're ready for church," Poppie said. "Are you ready to take us?"

"Oh, yes, Mr. Perkins," he replied.

Jimmie Artner didn't know how we had worked for Mr. Herbert to buy our new clothes. And of course we were not going to tell him—not unless our Timmie spouted off at the mouth. But this morning Timmie was a new proud brother, dressed as he had never been before. And he wasn't likely to talk. He wanted to be seen.

Yes, we rode in splendor. Timmie and I looked from our windows. We saw the beautiful Ohio countryside as we had seen it before. But we sat in silence and we just looked. This morning we were a new family. And as Poppie had said, clothes made the difference.

When Jimmie stopped at the Freewill Baptist Church, Cousin Faith and Bos were waiting for us. They knew we'd be dressed in our new clothes. They wanted to be first to see how we looked. When we got out of the church bus, Cousin Faith came down the steps to greet us.

"Cousin Sil and Gil, I really don't know you and your nice family. You're really beautiful—I say beautiful! Look what clothes have done for you! You're in Ohio clothes now—no longer Lower Bruin ones."

"I'm proud of you," Cousin Bos said. "You've come a long way! And you've done it by hard work. I think you're on your way!"

Cousin Faith and Bos knew us better than any two people in Ohio. They had done more for us than any two people. Look how they had helped us in this new land. And they had never once told we had been on "relief" in Kentucky.

And there was our Cousin Buster Boy with his Widow Ollie Mayhew and her five children to greet us, too. And, really, I've said this before—there was not a better dressed and a finer looking man in Ohio than Buster Boy. Somehow, I couldn't quite go for him. I didn't know why. I knew he loved children and that he was confused. And I knew Sister Cassie-Belle didn't like him.

Uncle Dick and Aunt Susie came next and met us. They looked us over.

"You look wonderful," Uncle Dick said. "I'm proud of you."

Uncle Dick, with the weak heart, had his cigars in his coat pocket. He also had fountain pens and pencils which he never used, clipped in the same front pocket. Aunt Susie, whom we hardly knew, never said much. Really, I wasn't too fond of Uncle Dick. I had heard him called "the fox" so often I wondered if he was a fox or not.

Next to greet us before we entered the Freewill Baptist Church were Mr. and Mrs. Herbert. He had a great interest in us. But Mrs. Herbert didn't. She really didn't know us. Mr. Herbert's face always looked good to us. We had worked for him. He had paid us the best wages we had ever earned. And he was responsible for our improvement. And when Mr. Herbert came to meet us, his kindly old face smiled. He had been the real friend of our family. He looked us over. He was pleased. He knew how we had worked for our money to buy our clothes. We greeted him affectionately before we went into the church for Sunday School and the sermon.

After our Sunday-school classes where brother Timmie and I were hardly recognized, we assembled for church services. Reverend Cashew Boggs preached a powerful sermon on *The Will to Live*. In this he told how even animals fought to live. He told about his illness, blood cancer, and how he had fought to live and how, by the Grace of God, he had lived. We didn't know he had ever had blood cancer. I would never forget his sermon.

I had the feeling when we left the church we were not as popular as we had been when we were poorly dressed. People didn't throng around us as they had before. Now we had changed. We were slowly becoming somebody. There were not as many out to greet us when we got into the church bus to leave the Agrillo Freewill Baptist Church, as there had been on Sundays before.

"I tell you, it pays to be poor," Poppie said when we reached home. "Now this should be a lesson to you. When we go to church well dressed, people are not as friendly."

And I had to agree with Poppie that this was the truth. People everywhere were friendly to the real poor.

40 Timmie had made a wild guess last Thursday when he told Mr. Herbert that if Cassie-Belle and Tishie joined us, we would catch up with the plow, that when Poppie plowed the last row, we would be behind him hoeing this one. After he had predicted this, we had held this in mind the eight days our sisters helped us.

Now we knew Timmie had made a lucky guess. But there was something more than magic when he predicted for four of us hoeing for eight days right to the last corn row. And Poppie plowed it right on the button—four o'clock quitting time. This was something I'll never forget. Just as Poppie had plowed the upper four rows in the corn balk he dropped his plow down to do the second and last one. And when he dropped to plow the last furrow, Timmie shouted: "Gee-whilligens! How right I was!"

Then he gave his wild laugh. But four hoes went up and down and when Poppie got to the end of the row we were with him.

Timime was jubilant. He dropped his hoe. He jumped up and cracked his brogan workshoes together before he came back to the plowed ground. "See, Poppie, how right I was when I told you and Mr. Herbert!"

We stood there laughing at Timmie. We were all happy and ready to laugh, after getting tobacco and now the corn in this valley cultivated for the first time on both sides. I felt like Timmie only I just couldn't jump up and crack my heels together because this task was finished.

"And Tishie, you and Cassie-Belle have made one hundred twenty dollars, too," Timmie said.

"Don't you think we don't know it," Tishie said.

"Do you think we earned it, Timmie?" Cassie-Belle asked.

"Well, you have," Timmie said. "You've hoed more rows than any of us! But each gets the same pay! Strange, isn't it? Strange I've made as much as you!"

Then Timmie laughed again. And Poppie who stood leaning on his plow, letting his mule rest, laughed too. We had finished the big valley.

Mr. Herbert just got to the field in time to pay us. When he looked at his valley, which now was as clean as a garden, his eyes seemed to get bigger. He had five checks already written for us. Timmie reminded him how his prediction had worked—that when Poppie plowed the last row we had just caught up with him and we had it hoed when Poppie stopped his plow. Timmie was really bragging about this— he would break into a run and leave us before we got to the house to be the first to tell Mommie.

Mommie would have the grocery list made out and Cousin Bos would come with his truck. And Mommie and Maryann would go to Agrillo today to get the groceries. Mommie was a lot like Timmie. She'd have made her plans, her grocery list and be ready.

When we got to the house, Poppie gave Mommie his endorsed check to buy our groceries. We signed our checks for her to cash and to keep our money.

"Come on, Sil, you and Maryann," Cousin Bos said. "We've got to be moving. I'll have work to do after I take you and fetch you!"

This was Cousin Bos. Always in a hurry. Always on the move.

So, Mommie and Maryann got in the red truck. Cousin Bos gunned it down the drive to the lane road. He was off like a red fading ball of sunset over the low Ohio hills.

"Boys, you do the chores as usual," Poppie said. "I'll chop wood for the stove! I'm good with an ax, you know!"

Poppie was powerful with an ax. A stick of stove wood for each stroke with his ax.

"Timmie, I got the radio with my money," I said as we walked toward the pen where the hungry shoats were squealing for their feed. The cows in the barnlot were mooing to us to be turned into the barn, fed and milked. "Some of these days I'm going to buy a car!"

"Gee-whilligens, Pedike," Timmie said. "That's great! What kind will you buy? One of them racers that will go a hundred miles an hour?"

"Don't be silly, Timmie," I said. "I'll buy a second hand stationwagon. One I can pay cash for—one big enough to haul our family. And I'll learn to drive it. Poppie never will. He's an ax man, a mule man. He's really what Mr. Herbert called an earth man! You and I are earth people too! So's our whole family!"

"But we won't be earth people long," Timmie said. "Something's bound to happen for us!"

41 Timmie, Poppie and I worked six days a week, with the exception of rainy days, through July. Poppie had wondered if there would be "slack time" when Mr. Herbert wouldn't have work for us. He plowed the tobacco and the corn a second time but Timmie and I kept up with our hoes.

Then Poppie, Timmie and I went to another farm where young potatoes were plowed from the ground. This must have been a forty-acre bottom. We picked up these potatoes in bushel baskets. They were early potatoes, and they were sold from trucks at the markets. Mr. Herbert made his farms pay. There was never a time he didn't need us. But there was no more farm work for our sisters. And, believe it or not, Mommie saved something each week from Poppie's check. We had bought the family clothes with our money. And now Mommie was saving Cassie-Belle's, Tishie's, Timmie's and my money for us for a later time when she thought it would "come in handy."

"We'd better make money while we can," Poppie said, one noon when we were eating our lunch in the potato field. "Money is a good thing to have on cold, rainy and snowy days when I can't work. Winter is ahead of us and you will be in school. Then I'll be going it alone."

"No, you won't, Poppie," Timmie said. "I've asked Mr. Herbert if Pedike and I could work on Saturdays during this school year. I told him we helped you cut, haul tobacco to the barn and put it in tier poles. I told him Pedike and I could climb over tier poles like squirrels! And I told him

Mommie, Pedike and I had helped you strip, grade and hand tobacco!"

"But your mother doesn't have to work at stripping ter-backer now," Poppie said. "She's got her hands full at the house. She's needed in the house with all of you, especially the Little Ones and the Babies!"

"I didn't try to get Mommie a job," Timmie said. "I was just telling Mr. Herbert about how good our family was with tobacco! And I did get Pedike and me work on Satur-days. He said he'd have something planned for us every Saturday if we wanted to work. And he said we could help you with the tobacco. He said people from the old country—where tobacco was the main money crop—were the best he'd ever seen in tobacco. Said he was going to let Poppie manage the whole thing."

"But Mr. Herbert has never told me this," Poppie said in his slow voice. "Timmie, you really do talk too much. But I'm glad to know this. You're sure he told you this?"

"Oh, yes, Poppie, he really did," Timmie said. "He likes me and he knows I like him. You think I talk too much but Mr. Herbert likes to talk with me!"

"Then we'll have work on Saturdays," I said. "This is good. Timmie, I'm glad you found it out. We can make our school money!"

Since Mr. Herbert wouldn't use spray on his tobacco, for he said spray that would kill a worm might hurt a man who chewed or smoked tobacco, we had to go through the fields, take worms off with our hands, pull suckers from behind the leaves and later top the stalks. Timmie was the best at finding the worms that had eaten into the green tobacco leaves. We had to pull them in two and they were filled with green tobacco juice. This work I didn't like. I hated tobacco worms. If we didn't pull them in two, but just threw them on the ground, they'd climb back up the tobacco stalks and start eating tobacco leaves again.

"It's strange that only this worm and man will chew tobacco," I thought.

I knew I'd never chew it. I'd worked in too much to-bacco. I didn't smoke it either. Only Poppie in our family used tobacco. But we could really grow tobacco. I had often thought of a name that would fit Cousin Bos—Tobacco Worm. But I couldn't call him this name for he'd been too good to us. But after his breakfast early in the morning until early in the evening when he went to bed, he went holding a chew of tobacco in his jaw as big as a hen's egg. He had to swallow some of the spittle, for his mouth was so full at times he had trouble speaking. I've seen him run out of our house to keep from spitting amber spittle, color of sorghum molasses, on the floor. I've seen it run from the corners of his mouth down his chin when he'd have too much in his mouth to spit. Then he'd clean his chin with a big bandanna he carried to wipe sweat from his face. If he wasn't a tobacco worm, I'd never seen one. Just like so many of the old men on Lower Bruin that I remembered.

Working in green tobacco ruined our clothes. There was a glue that came from touching the broad green tobacco that made Poppie's, Timmie's and my overalls so stiff they'd stand alone. It made our shirts stiff, too. When we came home on afternoons we changed out of our "tobacco clothes." And when we went back to work in the morning we put them on again. In August when we had finished with the tobacco, we burned our "tobacco clothes." Poppie said all the people he knew in the old country as far back as he could remember had done this.

Now as August was coming to a close with September near, Cousins Faith and Bos took us to Tockabee's Clothing Store to get our school clothes. He hauled us there in his red truck. And this time it would not be clothes for all our family but only those among us who went to school.

This year there would be seven of us in school. Cassie-Belle, Tishie, Timmie and I would be in Landsdowne County Central High School at Agrillo. Cassie-Belle was a senior. I was a junior, Tishie was a sophomore and Timmie would be a freshman. Maryann would be in Agrillo Junior High School. Martha and Little Eddie would be in Agrillo Elementary. Three different school buses would stop where our drive was intersected with our lane road to pick us up.

Landsdowne County was very similar to Greenwood County back in the old country. I got a map of Ohio at the filling station. This map had Ohio counties and county seats and towns. There were three big high schools in Greenwood County—West Greenwood High School, Wonder High School and Greenwood County High School. And there were eight consolidated elementary schools.

In Landsdowne County, there was East Landsdowne County High School, West Landsdowne County High School and Landsdowne County Central High School at Agrillo. There were eight elementary schools same as in Greenwood County. And the roads in Landsdowne County all led to Agrillo except two state roads and one national four-lane highway. I checked up on the population of Landsdowne County and it had nearly twice as many people as Greenwood County. So I knew the schools had to be bigger.

Of course, the biggest change for us would be better school clothes in Ohio. When we went to Tockabee's Clothing Store, new clothes were in. There were plenty of dresses from which my sisters could choose, with Cousin Faith's help. Mommie wasn't much help.

Cousin Bos helped Timmie and me. We bought extra trousers, socks, shoes, shirts, neckties and sweaters. Well, Cousin Bos asked them to throw in the socks and neckties. Timmie and I bought our first raincoats and rainhats. Cousin Bos asked for reversible coats we could wear either for rain or for cold weather. He said it was colder in winter here than on Lower Bruin. He said we'd know when the winter winds blew over Ohio's flatlands and low hills unchecked and snow sometimes drifted up to four feet deep. Cousin Bos scared us about the Ohio weather. We even bought gloves for our hands which we didn't wear to Wonder High School in Greenwood County. Timmie wanted red and yellow shirts—the louder the colors, the more he liked them.

"I wouldn't be caught dead in them colors," Cousin Bos said.

"But you'd look terrible in them," Timmie said. "You're older. I'm younger!"

Poppie wasn't with us. He was home taking care of the Babies. Poppie could do this. He was kind and gentle with the Little Ones and the Babies. He could diaper and fix bottles. All the girls, including Maryann, could do this. Timmie and I were the only ones who couldn't. I never had a hankering for this sort of thing, myself. But I'd seen it done so much I could have done it if I'd had to.

On this Wednesday, last week in August, before school began next Monday morning, first week in September, we had over five hundred dollars to spend. Mommie didn't plan to spend all. She planned to hold some back for us. Timmie and I had earned all of this but one hundred twenty dollars. Had there been more work my sisters could have done, we would have had eight or nine hundred. Timmie probably had already figured it.

When we left Tockabee's Clothing Store, Mommie was upset. We'd paid with cash and she had only ten dollars left. My sisters, Cassie-Belle, Tishie, Maryann and even Martha, were the ones who wanted clothes and more clothes. Mommie knew that it would never pay to turn Cassie-Belle and Tishie loose in a store without Cousin Faith and her to guide them. They were so hungry for nice clothes they didn't know when to stop buying.

"Timmie and I have clothed our family," I thought. "But our sisters worked all they could. All of us have worked for this! Maybe we'll go as well dressed as the others. We will soon know."

42 The first bus to stop was the elementary bus. This was the first time Martha had ridden on an elementary bus without Timmie. She was in the third grade. This was the first time Little Eddie had ever ridden a school bus. He had ridden the church bus with our family. And he'd ridden in Cousin Bos' red truck.

"Take care of Eddie," Cassie-Belle told Martha.

They were seated together on the bus. Martha had her report card from Wonder Elementary. They were dressed well. Eddie wore his little suit, knee pants, sandals and half socks. Martha wore a pretty blue dress, black slippers and half stockings. She wore ribbons on her blonde pigtails.

Next bus was for Agrillo Junior High and Maryann got on alone.

"I hate to see Maryann go alone on a school bus," Poppie had said before he went to work. "I like for you children to stay together as much as you can!"

In Greenwood County there were only two separate buses. One hauled elementary pupils from the first to and including eighth grade. The second bus hauled ninth-, tenth-, eleventh- and twelfth-grade pupils.

Just as the junior–high-school bus pulled out, our bus pulled in. Timmie was the first on, then our sisters, and I was last. There were several on the bus but not nearly all the seats were filled. Those on the bus looked at us. They knew we were new. And we looked them over. Those on the right-hand side of the bus glanced through the bus windows at the house we'd come from. Maybe they knew this place. They certainly didn't see any telephone wire or electric wires leading to our home.

We were given assigned seats with numbers. Timmie and I had twin seats on the right side of the aisle and Cassie-Belle and Tishie had the twin seats before us. And now we were on our way. No wonder we left home at seven-thirty. It was a good thing Timmie and I had gotten up early, same as when we went to work, and had done our chores. Cassie-Belle and Tishie were up early, too, to help Mommie.

Our bus stopped all along the way. We made a circuitous route to Landsdowne County Central High School. Students talking on the bus referred to it as "Landsdowne Central."

When we arrived, the bus driver, an older man with a serious face, had us leave the bus by twos, going from the front first, all the way back to the rear. We had to march up the walk and school steps by twos. I noticed all other students on the bus were carrying books and school supplies. We were taking only our report cards.

When we entered, students went to their lockers.

"What's going on here?" Cassie-Belle whispered.

Then a teacher who was on Corridor Duty came over to us and said: "Are you new?"

"Yes, we are," Cassie-Belle replied.

"Were you here Monday of last week when we had pre-registration?" she asked.

"We didn't know anything about it," Timmie blurted. "Never heard of it!"

"Had we known we would have been here," Cassie-Belle said.

"Come with me and I'll take you to the principal's office," she said.

Now, looking over these many Ohio students in the long corridor on the first floor, I thought we were as well dressed as the Ohio students. Our clothes would not be our worry.

When she led us into the principal's office, she said: "Mr. Armstrong, four new ones who were not here on pre-registration day."

Mr. Armstrong, about forty and six feet tall, dressed

in a dark suit, white shirt and black tie, first looked us over. He had two women helpers in his office. They stopped using their typewriters to look us over.

"What's your name?" he asked me.

"Pedike Perkins," I said.

A smile came over his face when I said "Pedike."

"And yours?"

"Cassie-Belle Perkins!"

"Yours?"

"Tishie Perkins."

"Mine is Timmie Perkins," Timmie said before he could ask him. "This must be a big school!"

"Yes, fourteen hundred and over," Mr. Armstrong said.

"Gee-whilligens," Timmie remarked.

Mr. Armstrong and the women in his office laughed.

"I'll bet I can guess where you're from," Mr. Armstrong said. "South of the Ohio River. Appalachia?"

"Yes, old country," Timmie said.

"What's the old country?"

"We're from the hills of Kentucky," I said. I wanted to stop Timmie. He wasn't in the field working with us now. "Yes, we're from Appalachia!"

"I get students from there—not exactly students—poorly trained in the schools down there, each school year," he said. "Have you got your report cards?"

"Yes, we have," Cassie-Belle said.

"Wonder High School! All A's! Right?"

"Yes, Sir," she said.

"Wonder High School," he said. "Strange name. Maybe it is a wonder high school."

And he laughed loudly.

"Yours," he said to Tishie.

"Only one B," he said. "Unusual."

Timmie handed him his report card.

"All A's in the eighth grade?" he said.

"Yes, and I'll make them here," Timmie bragged. "Wait and see if I don't!"

"Now don't be too sure," Mr. Armstrong warned. "You're in an Ohio school. I've had many from Appalachia enroll here, so poorly trained they barely struggled through. So many we put in vocational education!"

"What's that?" Timmie asked. "I never heard tell of it!"

Mr. Armstrong and his two helpers laughed loudly.

"Teaching youth to do with their hands as well as their heads," he said. "Electric, plumbing, welding, carpentering, car-body work, working on automobile engines!"

"All that sounds wonderful," Timmie said. "Pedike and I can work with our hands. Our sisters can, too. Try us in books first! Mommie's been so proud of our grades, she thumbtacks our report cards on our living-room wall for people to see!"

"You must have a fine mother," said one of the women at a typewriter.

"Four in high school," Mr. Armstrong said. "You must be from a big family."

"Eleven living and one dead," Timmie said. "Seven in school."

"What does your father do?"

"Works on a farm for Mr. Herbert," Timmie said. "Pedike and I have worked part of the spring and all summer for him, too. Cassie-Belle, Tishie and Maryann helped him pick his strawberries and raspberries. Yes, even hoe corn!"

Cassie-Belle made a face at Timmie. We were ashamed of his talking. It was hard to get him stopped when he got started.

Outside, a school bell rang and the big school got very quiet.

"Mrs. Hart, will you get them registered?" Mr. Armstrong said. "Say, I've not seen your report card. You've been standing here so quietly!"

I gave him my report card.

"What, only a few A's?" he said. "And you've got C's—yes, here's a D!"

"I'm not as good in books as they are," I said.

"We'll soon be finding out about all of you, Pedike," Mr. Armstrong said. "We'll see how you measure up in this school. Our top ten percent of graduates here can do college and university work in the best schools in America. We send them to Harvard, Yale, Western Reserve, Ohio State, Ohio University."

Mrs. Hart, who was very kind, helped us make out our schedules. Then she took us to the "Book Room" where a man gave us our free textbooks. She explained there were three sittings, thirty minutes each in the cafeteria, and that lunches cost us fifty cents each, if we were able to pay.

"We're able to pay," Timmie told her. "We've got school money we earned this summer. Mommie saved it for us."

I knew we didn't have much left after buying clothes for our family and ourselves. But I knew on Saturdays, thanks to Timmie this time, we would be making fifteen dollars. Meals here would cost the four of us ten dollars each week. We could help Maryann and one of the Little Ones. Poppie would only have to buy one lunch for two and a half a week. We could make it. I figured this before Timmie. He was already so excited over this big school, he thought he owned it.

Mrs. Hart took us to our lockers on the second floor. Timmie and I shared a locker and Tishie and Cassie-Belle shared one. We were late registering and our lockers were on the end of a long line of lockers on either side and at the ends of the corridor. This was really a big school—twice-and-a-half again as large as Wonder High School. Here was a place one could get lost until he knew his way around.

First class period was over. I didn't have a first-period class. And we watched students coming from classrooms, just as they had done at Wonder High—but there were so many more of them here. There was five minutes for changing classes just the same as at Wonder High. Students ran to their lockers same as they did at Wonder High. They ran to beat the bell and get back to their classes.

"Mrs. Hart, I missed a first-period class," Timmie said. "But I'll tell my teacher what happened. I'll make it up."

"I didn't miss one," I said. "I've got a second-period class!"

"Same here," Cassie-Bell said.

"Mine is second period, too," Tishie said.

Mrs. Hart was nice enough to take each of us to our second-period class and Timmie on to the Study Hall.

"You reckon Timmie will make it all right?" I whispered to Cassie-Belle before leaving her for my classroom.

"Never worry about him," she spoke in a low voice. "He'll get there and find out every thing if any freshman in this school does."

We attended two classes one after the other before cafeteria. I followed in line, did what the others did. I sat at a table for ten, all strangers to me. While they laughed and talked, I listened. We'd never get to know all the students in this school like we had at Wonder High School. And I had to wonder how well we'd do in this big school.

I made the rounds on my first day, four classes, went to the cafeteria and had Study Hall, my last period. I'd have Study Hall first period in the morning too.

When the last bell rang for dismissal, Timmie and I met at our locker. In the locker next to ours, there were two boys older than Timmie, but about my age.

"Say, are you briars?" one asked me. "From Kentucky? We call you briars up here!"

"Don't you call me a briar," I said.

I went over and I collared him. I'd not done any fighting. But I had him by the neck with both hands and I used my knee on his belly when I backed him against the locker.

"I'll bash your damned head in," I said, "if you call me that again."

"You want me to get his locker mate?" Timmie asked.

When Timmie said this the other boy ran.

"I don't like briars," I said. "I've cut too many of them on the Kentucky hills—and now on the Ohio hills in the corn fields and tobacco fields."

"And besides they grow on our dead brother's grave back on Lower Bruin," Timmie said. "I've not been called a 'briar' but I've been called "pop-off" by some smart-aleck girl!"

"Let me go," said the boy I had backed up. He was shaking. "Let me go!"

Other students came up and stood and a man teacher ran up.

"What's going on here?" he asked.

"Looks like a fight," a boy said.

"He called me a 'briar,' " I said, "and I won't take it. I'd rather be called a son-of-a-bitch."

"Break it up," said the teacher.

I let him go.

"That's what we call Kentuckians from the mountains up here," said an older boy, much larger than I.

"Well, I won't be called that," I said. "I don't like briars. I've cut too many with a hoe."

All the students gathered around us began to laugh.

"I don't want these new students called briars," said the teacher. "And young man, I don't want profanity! You realize what you said here?"

" 'Profanity,' a new word," said Timmie.

"I'm sorry, Sir," I said. "First time I ever used the word in my life. But I'd not done nothing to him. He started it. I've never had a fight in my life but I can have one."

"Fighting is not condoned here," said the teacher.

" 'Condoned,' another new word," said Timmie.

The boy I'd backed up against his locker got his books and left in a hurry. Well, I, the silent one, had never had an experience like this one on my first day at Landsdowne County Central High School. We got our books, paper and pencils and hurried to our bus. It was a long line of buses holding up buses behind. We were the last ones in our seats. I heard "briars" whispered among students behind us on the bus. Our way home was about an hour and fifteen minutes.

When we got home at four-fifteen, Maryann, Martha and Little Eddie were already there. But, Timmie, as usual, ran ahead of us to be first to tell Mommie we were dressed about as nice as anybody in school, but we had been singled out as new students from Kentucky and we'd been called "briars"—Cassie-Belle and Tishie and I. Timmie hadn't been called a "briar" but he'd been called "pop-off" by a girl student. Timmie could talk fast. He'd even told the story we should have gone last week one day when they had pre-registration.

"I'm sorry, Pedike, about your trouble," Mommie said. "And I'm sorry you missed going that day last week."

"What I'm sorry about, Mommie, is we don't take a

newspaper," Cassie-Belle said. "I found out that this was announced in The Landsdowne County News. The paper comes once a week. It gives the news of this county. It doesn't cost but three-fifty a year and we need it."

"You know something," Timmie said. "Not one in Mr. Armstrong's office asked us if we didn't read about pre-registration in the paper!"

"I'll give Cousin Bos the money and tell him to subscribe for us," Mommie said.

"I could have told Mr. Armstrong, if he had asked us, we had never taken a newspaper," Timmie said.

"Why make it worse, Timmie?" Cassie-Belle said angrily. "We're backward enough and we're trying to be some-body. We want to dress and act like the others."

"Not like some of them who don't mind their own business," I said.

"I know, but telling the principal we've never taken a newspaper, we don't have a bathroom, a television—that all we have is a battery-set radio to get news. And we don't get real local news. Why tell all of this?"

"Cassie-Belle is right," Mommie said.

At four thirty Poppie came in. And before we changed our school clothes for work clothes to do our chores, we gathered in the living room to tell Mommie and Poppie about our first day in Ohio schools. Martha, who was in the third grade, said she got along all right. Little Eddie said it was a strange place but he liked to play. Maryann had a lot to say about Agrillo Junior High School, how big it was and she didn't know anybody—that she missed us but said she got along all right.

But we had to let Timmie tell our story. He was all excited about Landsdowne County Central High School. He told what he had said, what Mr. Armstrong, the principal, had said and what Mrs. Hart did and said. Then he told about my trouble at the locker over somebody calling me a "briar."

"We do have a lot of briars down there in the Kentucky hills," Poppie said. "But we've got a lot of briars up here in Ohio, too! Look how you boys and girls cut them in the tobacco and corn. I jist never liked a briar very much and, Pedike, I can't blame you for not wanting to be called one."

"What did they think of your report cards?" Mommie asked.

"Mr. Armstrong let us know he didn't think Timmie, Tishie, Pedike and I would make as good a grades in Landsdowne Central as we'd made in Wonder High," Cassie-Belle said. "But I want to show them!"

"He smiled at my cards and asked me why I wasn't as good in books as my brother and sisters," I said.

"Did you tell him about Maryann?" Mommie said. "She's made all A's."

"No, Mommie, I didn't," Cassie-Belle said. "Why speak of her now? If we live here, she'll go to this school and she can speak for herself as we're going to have to speak for ourselves this year."

"I told them, Mommie, in Mr. Armstrong's office, that you liked our report cards so well you thumbtacked them on our living-room wall," Timmie said.

"Well, Timmie, you would," Mommie said. "I'm afraid your tongue is going to get you into trouble. You talk more than Pedike, Cassie-Belle, Tishie and Maryann put together."

43 Our lives changed now. Five days in school each week, working Saturdays for Mr. Herbert, and to church on Sunday. And Cousin Bos subscribed to the Landsdowne County News for us. All of us, Cassie-Belle, Tishie, Maryann, Timmie and I, read about every word in the paper. Even Poppie and Mommie read some things in it. When we got through with the paper it was as worn out as an old dish cloth.

Our first week in school was the hardest. We had to get adjusted to classes, new teachers, new students. And we learned other students from South of the Ohio River were called "briars." What was so strange to me, students who had moved up from South of the border when they were in the elementary school only a few years ago, had become such Ohioans that they too called the new ones like us fresh up from the old country "briars."

I could never walk in the corridor before the first bell in the morning, or any time when we exchanged classes or any time after the last bell, that I didn't hear the word "briar" many times.

On my second day in school, after I challenged the boy whose locker was next to mine, I was invited by Coach Harding Creech to come out for football. I told him I couldn't, for I worked when I went home and would be working each Saturday for Mr. Herbert all the school year.

Now, how we learned to find out what was going on in school was to read the bulletin boards on the lower and upper corridors. Each of us read these every day. But many students didn't. They passed their bulletin boards by.

We read on Monday on the bulletin board where the whole school would be given the Ohio Scholarship Achievement Tests. We would take these in our home rooms. This test would last the first two periods. We would resume our regular classes with the third period. And on that day we took two pencils each, so if we broke the lead in one, we'd have a spare.

I thought the Ohio Scholarship Achievement Test was hard. There were many things on it, on a great number of subjects that I couldn't answer. I thought one of these might be as hard as I had heard college was. And I certainly wondered about how well Timmie, Cassie-Belle and Tishie would do on this even with A's on their report cards. After all, our schooling had been in schools in Greenwood County, which Mr. Armstrong had warned us were inferior to Ohio schools.

After this long two-hour test, we went to our classes. I was tired in the head, more than I had ever been in body when I worked with my hands. I was a little shaken up. The students around my table in the cafeteria talked about this test while I listened. Tomorrow morning it would be announced the first ten places in order among Seniors, Juniors, Sophomores and Freshmen. It would be announced over the school's intercom (this was a new word for me) system and posted on the bulletin boards.

I heard students talking about how teachers and office help would remain after school grading our papers and would have keys to grade them by. I asked what a key was. I was told it contained the right answers. Well, I wondered if some of the teachers could have answered these questions. There were seventy teachers, a principal and two assistant principals, one on each floor, and two secretaries in Mr. Armstrong's office. Each assistant principal had a secretary. All seventy-seven would be working. They did things in a hurry in Ohio—even in their schools. There was none of the old slow, easy-goingness that we had known in Wonder High School.

"How do you think you did on the test?" I asked Cassie-Belle when we were seated on the bus.

"I don't know," she said. "It was a hard one all right!"

"It was a tough one," Tishie said. "There were some I know I didn't get."

"I'm surprised how many of the questions I knew," Timmie said. "I put answers down for all whether I knew 'em or not. I broke the lead in one pencil. But my spare came in handy."

Timmie talked loud to listening students on our bus. Well, there was laughter all over the bus.

When we got off the school bus I said to Timmie: "I wish you'd keep your mouth shut on the school bus. Since you won't do this—since you have to talk and brag—why don't you whisper?"

"I'll beat you on the test, Pedike," he bragged again.

When we returned to school next morning, we looked on the bulletin boards upstairs and down, but the results were not posted. When we were at our lockers Mrs. Hart came and said: "Mr. Armstrong wants to see you four in his office."

"But we've not done anything, Mrs. Hart," Timmie said.

She didn't say another word but smiled and went away.

"Wonder why he wants to see us!" I said.

"We'll just have to go and see," Cassie-Belle said.

When we went into the office, Mr. Armstrong said: "This is Dr. Wayne Laudermilk, Superintendent of the Landsdowne County Schools."

Mr. Armstrong introduced each of us by name to Superintendent Laudermilk. He shook our hands. Here was a Superintendent about six-four and two hundred forty pounds. He reminded me of an oak sapling growing in a valley where it had never been bent by the winds. He wore a dark suit, white shirt and black tie. His legs were very straight and looked long for his body.

"Sit down, all of you," Mr. Armstrong said.

We sat down in the chairs and I wasn't comfortable. Cassie-Belle and Tishie weren't either. Timmie was the calmest one among us.

"Something very strange has happened here," Mr. Armstrong said.

"But we've not done anything," Timmie said.

Superintendent Laudermilk laughed. Mr. Armstrong smiled. By now, even Timmie was getting real nervous.

"But you have done something," Mr. Armstrong said. "You've done something no other family has done in Central in ten years I've been principal here. What you've done hasn't been announced yet. It won't be announced and posted on the bulletin boards until second period. We want to talk to you first."

We sat in silence.

"Cassie-Belle Perkins, you made first in the Ohio Scholarship Achievement Tests in the Senior category."

"A new word 'category,' " Timmie said. Timmie carried a little notebook now in which to write down new words.

"Tishie Perkins, you lost tieing for first place by one point in the Sophomore category," he said.

"I made that high here in Ohio?" she said. She couldn't believe it.

"Timmie Perkins, you were first in the Freshman category with points to spare."

He didn't finish writing his new word down. Timmie jumped high from his chair, cracked his heels together.

"Gee-whilligens," he shouted. "Boy, won't Mommie be pleased!"

"Sit down, Timmie," I said.

"Now I want to talk to you about your parents," Mr. Armstrong said.

"But what did I do, Mr. Armstrong?" I asked. "Why am I here?"

"You're down there about the middle," he said. "I wanted to see all of you and to talk with you."

"I told you, Pedike, I'd beat you," Timmie shouted.

I looked hard at Timmie. But I knew he was happy and excited.

"About your parents' education," Mr. Armstrong repeated while Dr. Laudermilk sat silently looking at us.

"I think Mommie went to the fourth grade in Lower Bruin's school. Poppie went to school there, too. I think he went to the fourth grade," Cassie-Belle said.

"Any schoolteachers, doctors among your people?"

"None that I know," she replied. "Mommie's father was a farmer and Freewill-Baptist preacher."

"Your father works on a farm for Mr. Herbert, doesn't he?"

"Yes, Sir."

"Do you have television?"

"No."

"We've never lived in a house with electricity," Timmie blurted. "But since we've come to Ohio, Pedike bought us a battery radio. Our first one and we get music and news —and now we take a newspaper, our first one—The Landsdowne County News—and we wear it out reading it!"

Superintendent Laudermilk shook his head.

"Unbelievable," he said.

"I didn't know any houses near here didn't have electricity," Mr. Armstrong said.

"Ours don't but Mr. Herbert promised to wire it next year. Then we can have a bathroom, television, sweeper, electric iron," Timmie said. "But we've got a water pump in the kitchen. Mr. Armstrong, it's so much better than Lower Bruin where we came from."

"Timmie, you've said enough," I told him.

I was really ashamed I'd ever come into this office.

"I like to hear him talk," Superintendent Laudermilk said. "And there are eleven in your family?"

"Yes," Cassie-Belle said.

"Our oldest brother, Little Pearse, is dead—dead at six— and doesn't know what he's missed," Timmie said. "Mommie's had a dozen. Pearse would have been eighteen if he'd lived."

"I don't know how hard life has been for you," Mr. Armstrong said. "But what I've read and observed, so many young people in poverty get into mischief—ever had any trouble in your family?"

"I nearly had my first fight here the first day when a boy called me 'briar,'" I said. "I didn't like that name. I don't like briars. I've cut too many on the Kentucky hills and this summer on the Ohio hills with my hoe. But none of our family, Poppie's or Mommie's families, were ever in jail. Being poor doesn't make you bad. If that was true, we'd all be in jail."

"Mommie tells us we are the best," Timmie said. "And I believe Mommie! We try to be the best!"

"That's a new thought," Superintendent Laudermilk said. "There is truth in that statement. I believe you have good parents."

"Poppie and Mommie try to follow The Word and they want us to," Tishie said.

" 'The Word.' I don't exactly know what you mean," Mr. Armstrong said.

"The Word in the Bible," she replied.

"Oh, I see," he said. "Where do you go to church?"

"Sunday school and Church every Sunday in the Freewill Baptist Church," Tishie said.

"Do you own a car?" he asked.

"We've never owned one," Timmie said. "Jimmie Artner brings the church bus and gets us and takes us back. And our family fills that little church bus."

"Let them talk some more," Superintendent Laudermilk said. "I'll tell you—you can't beat this good homelife for children! These are solid land people. They're unspoiled! And look at the results here! I'm glad, Mr. Armstrong, you invited me in this morning to meet them."

"Miss Cassie-Belle Perkins, I doubted your all A's from Wonder High School at first, but I don't doubt them now," Mr. Armstrong said. "This goes for all of your grades! If you continue here as you did there, you will finish here with great honors. And we'll recommend you to Ohio State University!"

"But I can't go," Cassie-Belle said. "Poppie can't pay my way."

"No, we have to work and help Poppie," Timmie said. "We've worked all late spring and summer, and Cassie-Belle, Tishie and Maryann—she's in Agrillo Junior High School and she has all A's too—well, they worked all they could picking strawberries and raspberries, and they helped us hoe the big valley of new-ground corn. We've made money to buy our Sunday clothes and school clothes. Our old Lower

Bruin clothes didn't look right in Ohio. Bought clothes for Poppie, Mommie, the Little Ones and even the Babies."

"Shut up, Timmie," I said.

I stood up. I walked around my chair then sat back down.

"Well, is he telling lies or the truth?" Mr. Armstrong asked.

"The truth," Cassie-Belle said. "But sometimes we don't want him to talk. Some things don't need to be said."

"About your going to Ohio State," Mr. Armstrong said. "That's why I wanted to interview you about your family. We might be able to get all your expenses paid and pay you fifty dollars a month while you go to the University. Allow you medical expenses and buy your clothes!"

"I can't believe that," Cassie-Belle said.

"Pedike, we can't do this for you," Mr. Armstrong said.

"I don't expect it," I said. "I know what I want. I want to finish high school. Then I want a good job. I want to use these!" and I raised my hands. "Poppie has often said hands are the best tools in the world."

"But for you, Tishie, you and Timmie, if you keep up your school work, and graduate here, there will be something for you later. Now, don't any of you mind being called a 'briar'!"

"After today when the winners of this test are announced and posted on the bulletin boards, they'll all want to be called 'briar,' " Superintendent Laudermilk said with a big smile. "This will change things here for you."

"The interview is over and second-period classes will soon begin and the announcement of the top ten will be announced over the intercom and posted on the bulletin boards," Mr. Armstrong said.

"Mr. Armstrong, I missed my first class, Algebra, first day I came and I've missed it today," Timmie said.

"I've already sent an excuse to your teacher, Mrs. Brooks, so don't worry," he said. "You've been marked present in class."

"I can't understand it," Timmie said. "I wasn't there. How could Mrs. Brooks see my absent face?"

But there was the bell to change classes and we hurried

from Mr. Armstrong's office to our second-period classes.

We were no more than in our classrooms and seated when we heard over the loudspeaker from Mr. Armstrong in his office: "Stand by for important announcement—Results in Ohio Scholarship Achievement Tests—Senior Category. First: Cassie-Belle Perkins," and then he read nine other names down to and including tenth place. When Cassie-Belle's name was called I felt like Timmie did when Mr. Armstrong told him in the office he was first, only I couldn't jump up and do what he did with his heels and say what he said.

Jack Holmes, who was first in the junior category, sat beside me in class. He was a happy young man. Nine other names were called; three of these I knew, but not well.

In the sophomore category, Beatrice Benz was announced winner, but the second name Tishie Perkins. And I was really happy again.

"Announcing this fourth category, Freshman Class," Mr. Armstrong said. "The winner has points to spare and, in relation to the other first-place winners, for a Freshman he is the highest in this contest. He is Timmie Perkins." Then he went on to read the following nine names. I didn't know them. But I knew Timmie, wherever he was in Study Hall or class, must have jumped up from his chair, cracked his heels together and shouted: "Gee-whilligens!" He would be something when we got home tonight. Well, all of us would be something. All of us would go to the rose-wallpapered living room to discuss this. We would be a happy family. Mommie and Poppie would be happy.

"What about them 'briars' from Kentucky?" Paul Gray said over on the far row of seats. "They got two firsts and a second. All in one family. Can you beat that?"

Yes, briars, I thought, remembering what Dr. Wayne Laudermilk had said in Principal Armstrong's office—that all would be wanting to be called briars.

When second-class period was over, students gathered around the second-corridor bulletin board. They were reading the names. For the very first time, this bulletin board was crowded. This test meant something in Landsdowne County Central High School.

"Well, the Perkinses got it," a student said. I didn't know him. "And they're briars from Kentucky."

"I'd say not 'briar' but 'brains,'" said a nice-looking girl student. "Think, two firsts and a close second from one family."

"There are four of them," said another boy I didn't know. "Why didn't he rate?"

I was there looking at the bulletin board, but I didn't speak up. Yes, why didn't I rate? I just didn't take to books like my sisters and brother Timmie. I heard students talking of how important this test was. And the first ten would get scholarships to colleges and universities. The first, second and third ones would get better scholarships. And we had been interviewed in Mr. Armstrong's office with Superintendent Laudermilk because three of the four of us were winners.

Before this day was over sister Cassie-Belle's name of "briar" had been changed to "brain." She was called "Brain One," Tishie was called "Brain Two" and Timmie was called "Little Brain." But I was still called "briar" in whispers but not openly to my face.

44 When this school day ended and we were seated on the bus, students took a different look at us. They were much nicer. And this time, Timmie whispered to me: "I can't wait to get home to tell Mommie and Poppie."

When our school bus got within a hundred yards of our house, Timmie went up and said to the driver: "Stop the bus and let me off."

The driver, Mr. Maxwell, stopped the bus in a hurry.

"Are you sick?" he asked Timmie when he opened the bus door.

"No," Timmie said.

Timmie made a wild leap. He hit the road running. Before Mr. Maxwell could start the bus and pick up slow speed, Timmie was running up our drive.

"I don't understand," the driver said.

Well, Tishie, Cassie-Belle and I understood. When we got off the bus, we hurried to the house.

"My children," Mommie greeted us. She hugged and kissed us. And this was something she hadn't often done. "I'm so proud of you. I can hardly believe this. Never has anything greater happened to our family."

Maryann's and Little Eddie's and Martha's buses left Agrillo Junior High and Elementary Schools earlier than our bus. They always arrived home sooner than we. And Poppie came home about fifteen minutes after we arrived.

"The greatest thing ever has happened to our children in Landsdowne County Central High School, Gil," Mommie said. "I'll let them tell you about it."

"Timmie, let Cassie-Belle talk," I said. "You've told Mommie! She's the oldest. She's a Senior."

Then Cassie-Belle, in her quiet way, told how we had taken the test with all fourteen hundred and fifty others. How Dr. Wayne Laudermilk, Superintendent of Landsdowne County Schools told us we had won two first places and a close second out of four categories, and this had never been achieved by one family before. And she told what they planned to do for her at Ohio State University—all expenses, medical care, books, clothes and fifty dollars a month.

"It's great," Poppie said.

"Now they don't call us 'briars,' " Timmie said. "They call Cassie-Belle 'Brain One,' Tishie 'Brain Two' and me 'Little Brain.' But they still whisper Pedike is a 'briar.' "

And Timmie laughed.

Out of our school clothes into our work clothes, we did our chores. Timmie was so high in the air he hardly knew he was feeding the shoats corn and pouring milk in their troughs.

"I'm up in the air as high as a star, Pedike," Timmie said to me.

After supper, we gathered in the living room to hear the news and music and to talk. When the news came on, which must have been a radio station close by, Cassie-Belle's, Tishie's and Timmie's names were mentioned as winners of the Landsdowne Central's Ohio Scholarship Achievement Tests.

"Gee-whilligens," Timmie shouted. "Our names over the radio. Maybe Cousin Bos and Faith, Uncle Dick and Aunt Susie and Mr. and Mrs. Herbert will hear this!"

And after the news we listened to low, soft music. Poppie and Mommie were never prouder of us in their lives.

"It pays to live by The Word," Poppie said. "And I think it is better to be poor than rich. I think of Josh Herbert, many times a millionaire and still working like he didn't have a cent. I wonder if his children and grandchildren have ever done what our children have done."

The morning after we'd won honors at Landsdowne Central, we were on the bus going to school when the same girl on the right side of the bus who had been paying so much attention to our house said to Cassie-Belle: "Your house doesn't have any electricity—or a telephone!"

Cassie-Belle didn't answer her. But there was laughter behind us on the bus.

"You can't have radios, TV, bathroom, refrigeration?" she said.

"We do have a radio," Timmie blurted, breaking our close silence to such questions. "We've got a battery set. And besides," Timmie continued, turning his head and looking back on the bus, "Mr. Herbert will wire our house next spring, and put us in a bathroom. Then, we'll have the things other people have."

"How d'ya take a bath?"

"In the smokehouse in a washing tub," Timmie said. "We've got a partition, two tubs, boys on one side, girls on the other! And we bathe every day."

"Timmie, shut your damn mouth," I said. "And I mean it."

But there was such a roar of laughter that no one except Timmie, our sisters up front and maybe the two behind us heard me.

The girl whose name I didn't know and didn't care to know, who had first asked about the wires to our house, said, "I've always said Ohio was a backward state!"

"Like hell Ohio is a backward state," I said. "You don't know what backward is!"

The bus driver and everyone on the bus heard me for the laughter had subsided. Mr. Maxwell slowed the bus, looked back quickly and said: "Young man, watch your English back there. I'll have no profanity on this bus."

"There's that new word again—'profanity,'" Timmie said. "That's cussing in our mother tongue."

And the students laughed again.

When we got off the school bus, I whispered to Timmie as we marched up the walk to the school: "Please, Timmie, keep your mouth shut. They're only making fun of us."

Today the photographer came from the Landsdowne County News—and he took pictures of first, second and third winners of each category in the Ohio Scholarship Achievement Tests for this week's paper that would be delivered to our mailbox on Friday. Timmie, Tishie and

Cassie-Belle and nine others had to be called from classes and study halls into the principals' office for their pictures.

"When Cousin Bos comes to get Mommie on Friday, I'm going to give him three dollars of my money to go to the newspaper office and buy papers," Timmie whispered to me at the locker. "Cousin Bos will get there first before they're all gone!"

"You want thirty papers?" I said.

"Thirty papers won't be enough," he said. "First time Tishie's, Cassie-Belle's and my picture has ever been in a newspaper. Fifty papers won't be enough! Send some of them back to our relatives on Lower Bruin. And Mommie will want to keep several!"

When we returned from school, Timmie was first off the bus to run and tell Mommie. And after thinking this over when we talked in the living room I added the other two dollars to get fifty papers.

Friday afternoon when our bus stopped, Timmie was off first, running toward the house to see his picture in the paper. My sisters hurried, too. They knew Mommie had watched the mailbox for this paper. And when we got inside the house, Mommie and Timmie were looking at the front page together. But I think Timmie was just looking at his own picture.

"Your picture's in the paper," Mommie said. "Wait until Cousin Bos and Gil get here to see these! I'm so proud! Yes, we'll want the extra copies. This paper will be worn out this evening. We want to save copies to help you later on to get in college!"

It was something to see three of our family on the front page of The Landsdowne County News.

"Circulation thirty-seven hundred," Timmie said. "Look at the people who'll be seeing this!"

Mommie, so much like brother Timmie, always jumping ahead, had her grocery list made out. She was waiting.

"Cassie-Belle, you go with me to Cantwell's today and help me with the groceries," Mommie said. "Cousin Bos, who is always a great help, will be going to the newspaper office to get the papers."

Cousin Bos drove up the drive. Poppie walked inside the

house at about the same time. He rushed over to look at the paper. Cousin Bos came up.

"Got mine, and Faith and I have seen it," Cousin Bos said. "I'm proud of you. It's great. I wish Buster Boy could have done it. But he didn't take to books very good. So he took vocational classes instead to educate his hands."

"Hurry on, Mommie, you, Cassie-Belle and Cousin Bos," Timmie said. "If you don't get the papers first they might be all gone."

And this how we got fifty copies of the Landsdowne County News. Mommie did send some papers back to Lower Bruin. I sent one back to Wonder High School and Timmie sent a copy back to Wonder Junior High School. Timmie, Cassie-Belle and Tishie each kept ten copies and Mommie put away all copies left.

45 Now we could tell our Little Mommie was pregnant again. I'd been thinking it for some time. But I was silent about this. I'd seen Mommie pregnant so many times. And as Poppie always said after we older children knew, "Your mother is going to give us another heir."

I knew Cassie-Belle and Tishie were greatly disturbed. They knew many of the responsibilities of caring for another baby fell on them—as well as caring for the other Babies and the Little Ones. If this one was born alive, there would be four babies in four years, five babies in six years.

"Yes, I'll be glad to go to Ohio State," Cassie-Belle told Tishie, Timmie and me one morning when we waited for the school bus. "I'll not be diapering, feeding and dressing Babies and the Little Ones at home. I'll have privacy there. And I don't care what The Word says about marrying and replenishing the earth. I don't believe it. I know, after all I've been through, I'll never do it."

Not one of us said anything. Not even Timmie.

On Saturdays Timmie and I had work with Mr. Herbert. Poppie continued working six days a week. With our good garden and our potato crop—with all Mommie had canned and preserved and with the jellies she had made—this cut down on our grocery bill.

And butchering six hogs, we had hams, shoulders, middlings, headcheese and lard galore in our smokehouse. We had more food than we had ever had in our lives. As Poppie had said: "We worked up our hogs, all but the squeals." Mommie even pickled the feet.

On the sixty dollars a week Poppie had earned, Mommie had managed to save three hundred dollars. The fifteen dollars a week Timmie and I earned had bought all our lunches at schools. With special jobs, such as stripping, grading and handing tobacco, we had worked evenings in a lighted barn. We had earned extra dollars. It wasn't any problem for us to make money in Ohio. But we always had a place to spend it.

Since we first began going to the Freewill Baptist Church, we had not missed but one Sunday—the Sunday we stayed at home to pick strawberries. Jimmie Artner came with the church bus and we went to church.

And Cousin Bos never failed to come on Friday with his red truck to take Mommie to Cantwell's to get our groceries and haul them home for us. Cousin Bos, the little bragging, tobacco-chewing, hard-working, ever-on-the-move cousin— best worker I'd ever seen—would stop his work to help a friend or relative. And he wouldn't take a penny from Poppie for all his help. When Poppie wanted him to take five or ten dollars, held the bill up, begging him to take it just to buy some gasoline, Cousin Bos would laugh and say: "Gil, you need that money more than Faith and me. You need your dollars. We're so proud of our kinfolks. You and your family. You're doing so well, you make us proud."

46 September, October, November, December with Christmas, came and went and at the end of first semester in January, Cassie-Belle, Timmie, Tishie and Maryann had done it in the Ohio schools. They'd made A's. And I kept up with my few A's, several B's and C's. Martha had done well in the third grade.

Our second semester on until May was much the same routine. Mr. Herbert needed us all the time. He had days of work for us. During a week's spring vacation, we helped Poppie burn and sow tobacco-seed beds. On afternoons after our chores were done we helped Poppie plant potatoes, corn and the garden. This second semester was a busy time for us. And it was a busy time for Sister Cassie-Belle, who was still called "Brain One." But I was no longer called "briar." I thought that was because I was becoming more like the young Ohioans. Sister Cassie-Belle was often called out of class to take some kind of test. "I'll tell you, they've really tested me," she said. "About sixteen times. It's about my going to Ohio State University. And I really do want to go!"

There were other straight-A students in our school. But three were from our family. Cousin Bos and Faith stayed at our home on the night of May 22nd so Poppie, Mommie, Tishie, Timmie, Maryann and I could go to the graduation to hear Cassie-Belle give the Valedictory Address.

I'll tell you, Mr. Armstrong had seen to it our family had special seats up front. And we were dressed in our best clothes—all but Mommie who was heavy with child. It could happen any time—even here on Commencement Night. This time Uncle Dick had made arrangements for her to go to the hospital—and Mommie had agreed. She was no longer as afraid of a hospital as she had been in Lower Bruin. A hospital wasn't the place of death in Ohio as much as it was on Lower Bruin.

On this evening a class of three hundred and ninety graduating seniors was up front in the basketball gymnasium —Central's auditorium wouldn't hold the graduates, their parents and friends. Up on the platform sat Cassie-Belle with John Sloan, who was Salutatorian. They were seated behind a table where there was a microphone, along with Mr. Armstrong, Principal of Landsdowne County Central High School, Dr. Laudermilk, County Superintendent, and the five members of the Landsdowne County School Board. There was the minister of the Methodist Church of Agrillo and the commencement speaker, Dr. Howes from Ohio University.

First there was a prayer and we stood. Second, still standing, we said the Pledge of Allegiance and saluted the large American flag hanging over the platform. Then, Mr. Armstrong introduced Dr. Laudermilk who stood, took a bow and sat down. Next he introduced the five board members.

"Now it is my pleasure to introduce our Valedictorian, Miss Cassie-Belle Perkins," he said. "I'd like to make a few remarks about this young lady. When she came to us last September she was called a briar. Now, she is called 'Brain One.'"

There was a ripple of laughter back among, maybe, two thousand seated in the gym.

"And something happened, I might add, that never happened at Central in the ten years I've been principal here— and there is no record of its happening before. There are four members of the Perkins family in this school. One in each year of high school. And in the four categories of our Ohio Scholarship Achievement Tests, three of this family were winners. Miss Cassie-Belle Perkins has won our Scholastic Certificate of Honor, and first place scholarship with all expenses paid to Ohio State University!"

There was more applause.

"Her sister, Miss Tishie Perkins, was one point behind the first-place winner in the Sophomore Category. Mr.

Timmie Perkins was far out in front in the Freshman Category—actually in ratio, the highest in school!"

Timmie started to jump up from his chair. Poppie grabbed him by the coat tail and sat him down.

"Mr. and Mrs. Gilbert Perkins are seated down here with four of their children—one is here on the stage—and I understand there are six more at home with two baby-sitters!"

A sigh went up over the auditorium.

"I'd like for this remarkable family to stand!"

Well, we stood up, but Mommie sat back down quickly.

"And there'll soon be another one," I heard a woman say across the aisle. "Looks like any time!"

I was glad to stand with my family. I was proud of my sisters. And don't get me wrong, I'm not jealous because I rated average among the Juniors. There has to be one. And I was proud of Timmie. When we sat down Mr. Armstrong said:

"Miss Cassie-Belle Perkins!"

I'd never seen Cassie-Belle prettier and better dressed than when she stepped in front of the microphone. And everyone seated in the gym became very quiet. She never used a paper or a note. She'd worked on her speech. She'd written it herself. "You Amount to Something."

In her speech she said just about anyone in America, and especially Ohio, with reasonable intelligence but with the will to work, plus ambition, could do what he or she wanted to do. She said everyone should prepare with head or with hands, or with both, for the future.

I'd heard her speech at home. It was better now than ever. And I thought about her cooking, dressing, diapering and feeding babies, and her quick hands in the berry fields and her good hands in the corn fields with a hoe; also how quickly she and Tishie learned to milk a cow, and I thought of their bathing in a washtub in the smokehouse. And here she was first in her class in this big school in Ohio. Her speech was her life and it was right. When she had finished, everyone in that gym clapped and cheered Cassie-Bell. This was surely a great night for our family.

Now John Sloan read his salutatory address. He got a

fair applause. Then, Superintendent Laudermilk introduced the Commencement speaker, Dr. Kenneth Howes, who, in his beginning remarks, mentioned our family and said his family had come from the Appalachian hills of Virginia to Ohio for better opportunities to make a living and to educate their children. His speech, which was in the same vein as Cassie-Belle's, was well received. And this made me wonder how many people back in the audience had come to Ohio from long ago to the present time. And they were still coming.

Now the Chairman of the Landsdowne County School Board, Dr. Tom Abrams—he was a medical doctor—gave out the diplomas. The graduates arose in an orderly line with Dr. Abrams calling each name as he gave each graduate his or her diploma. This was something to see. I knew if I lived, honors or no honors, I'd be in this line next year.

47 Jimmie Artner had brought us in the church bus. And he was in the audience waiting for us to take us home.

"Well, Mr. and Mrs. Perkins, your family has done well," he said. "This is an honor to you and our church!"

"Cassie-Belle is the first high school graduate in her mother's or my people," Poppie said.

"But there will be more," Timmie said. "I know there'll be one more!"

"I think there'll be eleven, maybe, twelve," I said. "You're not the only one, Timmie!"

Then Mr. Herbert walked up to us.

"This is wonderful, Gil and Mrs. Perkins," he said. "My wife wasn't feeling too well and couldn't come! But I'd be here if I had to crawl, after knowing how your children will work! And to think they can do this! I'm really proud of you—and in about three weeks we'll start wiring your house and put you in a bathroom!"

"Gee-whilligens," Timmie said.

"Thank you, Josh," Poppie said.

"Maybe I'll see you tomorrow," Mr. Herbert said as he turned to walk away.

"Mr. Herbert doesn't look too well," Mommie said.

"That man works like a brute," Poppie said. "Hardest worker I've ever seen in my born days."

I wondered why Uncle Dick and Aunt Susie hadn't come. They took the Landsdowne County News. They had known that this was our big night with our first high school graduate.

Each of us riding home in the church bus took a look at Cassie-Belle's diploma.

"That will be framed and hung on the living-room wall," Mommie said. "Wouldn't it be wonderful if your father and I could live long enough to see twelve high school diplomas framed and hung on the living-room wall!"

"Maybe fourteen or fifteen," Cassie-Belle said in an unfriendly voice.

"Cassie-Belle," Mommie said. "I'm surprised! This has been your great night!"

Jimmie Artner got us home and Poppie thanked him for taking us there and bringing us home.

And as we went into the house, Poppie said: "I'll tell you, we're moving up in the world."

"But we've got a long way to go yet," Cassie-Belle said.

When we got home it was eleven. Cousins Bos and Faith had the Little Ones and the Babies in bed and asleep. They were in our living room playing the radio.

"It's been a long time since we've played a radio," Cousin Bos said. "Faith and I have enjoyed it!"

"Well, I know this has been a big night for you," Cousin Faith said.

"Yes, it's been a great night," Mommie said.

Timmie wanted to tell what had happened but Mommie put her hand on his shoulder.

"Now I want to thank you and Bos for making this night possible," Mommie said. "This house is so quiet!"

"It's been a great night for you and a wonderful day for us," Cousin Faith said. "The wonderful day for us is I've made Buster Boy turn his checks over to me for more than a year—I've given him all I think he needs to spend. Today I paid the last one of his debts. Now he's out of debt."

"And he's settling down since he met Widow Ollie and her children," Cousin Bos said. "I've never seen such a change in our son."

"Will they marry, Bos?" Poppie asked.

"I hope so," Cousin Bos said.

"I don't like the situation the way it is," Cousin Faith said. "He just about stays at her home after his day's work is done."

"Yes, but he spends his nights with us," Cousin Bos said.

"I'm turning his checks over to him now," Cousin Faith said. "I don't know what he'll do!"

"But, Bos, a man needs children and plenty of them," Poppie said. "Remember The Word. Remember the faith of our fathers. Remember to be fruitful and multiply and replenish the earth."

Poppie and Mommie thanked Cousin Faith and Bos again for their helping us as they left our living room.

48 I'll never forget this day in my life! It was May 23rd, when Timmie and I went back to work full time for Mr. Herbert. Poppie, Timmie and I went to the tobacco bed to pull plants to set for Mr. Herbert. He'd planned to reset in tobacco the same two fields he had had in tobacco last year. And he planned to plow and plant the same fields in this valley in corn again this year. He said he had done so well on his tobacco and that Poppie had made the difference knowing how to grow tobacco, cut, hang it to cure, strip, hand and grade it. His tobacco had brought the top price from bidders on the Agrillo Tobacco Warehouse Market.

We were pulling the nice plants from the tobacco-seed bed which Poppie had prepared in late March. These were nicer plants than we'd had last year when Poppie hadn't prepared the seed bed. We had lifted the canvas which kept out the sun from over the bed. Poppie was pulling plants on the end of the bed and Timmie was pulling plants from one side and I from the other.

All of a sudden Poppie fell backward like he'd been shot between the eyes.

"My God," he screamed. "A copperhead got me! I'm a dead man!"

I was nearly as fast as a shot out of a gun.

"You god-damned son-of-a-bitch," I shouted. "You can't fang my Poppie and get by with it! Forgive me, God," I said, "first time I ever took your name in vain!"

I grabbed a tobacco stick and almost as quick as a flash

of lightning, I came down over that big rust-colored copperhead that was coiling to strike again—this time at
Poppie's leg. And Timmie ran up with a hoe. But with
my one hundred and sixty five pounds, my six feet of
height—when I struck him, I knew he'd never strike again.
And Timmie started cutting him up with a hoe.

"I didn't know there were copperheads in Ohio," Timmie said.

"Oh, my hand," Poppie said, holding his bitten hand
with his good hand and laying flat on his back on the
plowed ground.

"Your knife?" I said.

"In my left overalls pocket," Poppie groaned.

In the old country on Lower Bruin where there were
so many copperheads that lived among the rockcliffs,
all our people had been trained on what to do when one
was bitten by a copperhead. I got Poppie's knife out of
his pocket in a hurry and I cut quickly a cross, over the
two red dots, where the snake's fangs had pierced the
skin. Now the blood oozed. But I put my mouth over
the place, sucked blood and spit it out.

You talk about something awful. It is to suck your
father's warm blood from his hand and spit it out. This
almost made me sick at my stomach.

"I cut him in two in seven places," Timmie said. "He'll
never bite again."

"Copperheads are always together," Poppie said. "Be
keerful, Timmie!"

Timmie knew what to do, too. He twisted his big
bandanna into a small rope.

"Suck out all the pizen you can, Pedike," Poppie said.
"I'm a sick man. I'm a ruint man. I've lost one of the best
tools a man ever has. I may lose my whole hand."

"Maybe not, Poppie," I said.

I drew the twisted bandanna rope tighter and tighter
around Poppie's wrist to cut off the circulation of the
blood from his hand.

"Ride the mule. Find Mr. Herbert," I said. "If you
don't find Mr. Herbert at home get Mrs. Herbert to phone
Uncle Dick, get Cousin Bos. Have one come as soon as

he can and take Poppie to the doctor. Timmie, don't tell Mommie yet."

Timmie unhitched the mule from the plow where Poppie had planned to lay off tobacco rows. He leaped on the mule's back and the mule was off in a gallop up the up-hill road.

"Feelin' better, Poppie?" I asked.

"I'm as sick as a pizened suck-egg hound," he said almost in a whisper. He was still on the ground flat on his back just the way he fell. "If I hadn't just smoked that cigarette, I'd have smelled him in that terbacker bed. A copperhead smells like a cucumber on a hot day."

A copperhead is one of the most dangerous snakes on the face of the earth, I thought. We might even lose Poppie.

I looked at my father lying so helpless on the ground.

"What on earth will we do in this strange beautiful land if we lose Poppie?" I thought.

Sweat popped out like raindrops over Poppie's sun-and-wind-tanned face. He was really sick. But it didn't take Timmie but a jiffy. He worked fast on the mule. He returned running the mule downhill.

"Couldn't get Mr. Herbert," he said. "He was off somewhere on one of the farms. But Mrs. Herbert called Uncle Dick and he's goin' to try to find Cousin Bos!"

He found Cousin Bos, all right. There was no time to lose and Uncle Dick knew it. When a man got a copperhead bite something had to be done for him in a hurry. Back on Lower Bruin where there were no doctors, yarbs and yarb root poultices were used to reduce the swelling; spicewood, boneset and Queen-of-the-Meadow and slippery-elm bark were all boiled together for a tea to cleanse the body of poison and to regain life. Another medicine given was corn whiskey, distilled from the pure corn until the patient had passed out senseless into another world.

I'll tell you, when Cousin Bos came over the hill in his red truck with Uncle Dick beside him, he was flying. When he put on the brakes the tires smoked on the ground.

Bos jumped out and came over to Poppie.

"A copperhead bite is a dangerous thing," Cousin Bos said. "Did you kill the son-of-a-bitch?"

"He's in seven pieces there in the tobacco bed," Timmie said.

Uncle Dick got out of the truck slowly with a cigar in his mouth. He looked at Poppie there on the ground.

"Uncle Dick, I'm hurt," Poppie said. "What will my family do if I lose my hand? I'll be out of work a long time—and, maybe, end up with one hand!"

"Now, don't worry, Gil," Uncle Dick said. "You'll have my Dr. Gaylord Zimmerman—and you're going straight to the Landsdowne County Hospital. We'd have come in an ambulance for you—but an ambulance can't get down into this valley—only trucks, mules and people come here."

"Faith and I didn't have time to put a mattress in the back of this truck," Bos said. "But we spread quilts and put a pillow in there for your head."

Poppie tried to rise up under his own power.

"Dizzy," he said. "I may faint! I'm sick!"

He laid back down.

"Get him by one shoulder, Pedike, I'll take the other," Cousin Bos said. "Timmie, get between his legs and lift his feet. Dick, you let the tailgate down."

Poppie was like a dead weight to lift but we lifted him up into the truck. We got quilts under him and one over him and the pillow under his head.

"Ride the mule back to the barn, Timmie," I said. "Jerk his harness off—turn him loose in the barnlot and join us by the road."

Again Timmie mounted, was off in a gallop. Cousin Bos had a time turning the truck. He finally made it. Uncle Dick was with Cousin Bos. I was back in the truck beside Poppie. His hand, where I had tightened and tied the twisted bandanna around his wrist, had turned black.

Cousin Bos climbed the hill in low gear. But down the other side was easy sailing. When he got to Mr. Herbert's barn, Timmie was beside the road waiting to join us. Cousin Bos slowed, Timmie came running, climbed over the tailgate into the truck. Now, Cousin Bos gunned it—all his truck would do—up the lane road, past our house onto the highway and to Agrillo and Landsdowne County Hospital.

Aunt Susie had called Dr. Zimmerman. He was standing by when we arrived. Poppie was taken out of the truck by four men in white coats, put on a cot and wheeled into the hospital. Uncle Dick had a room there for Poppie. He had Aunt Susie phone in and make all the arrangements. I didn't know if one didn't have a thing called Medicare or some other kind of Medical Insurance that he had to pay fifty dollars to enter the hospital. But I found this out. Our family didn't know about this.

Timmie and I followed Dr. Zimmerman, Poppie and Bos into the room.

"Snake bite, huh," Dr. Zimmerman said.

"But my hand," Poppie groaned. "Doc, will I lose my hand?"

"I've doctored a few copperhead bites on the hand," Dr. Zimmerman said. "Yes, on the foot and leg, too. Not one of my patients ever lost a hand, foot or leg!"

"Plez Gray lost his hand back on Lower Bruin," Poppie said. "Flesh rotted and the bones showed and he had to have the hand taken off at the wrist. He went around with a hook on his arm the rest of his days."

"Who doctored him?" Dr. Zimmerman asked.

"They used poultices on his hand and give him yarb teas!" Poppie said in a low, slow voice.

"No wonder he lost his hand," Dr. Zimmerman said.

Well, the four men left the room quietly after putting Poppie upon the bed. And a woman came in dressed in white.

"Now, we've got a few things to do here," Dr. Zimmerman said. "I would like for all except the nurse to leave the room. Go out to the waiting room—Dick, Bos and the boys."

When we went out of the door toward the waiting room, Uncle Dick muttered, "Rehabilitation."

"A new word, Uncle Dick," Timmie said. "I never heard it before. It's a big word, too."

"Oh, it doesn't mean much but I was just thinking about Gil, your father, my hard-working nephew!" Uncle Dick said. "Dr. Zimmerman was right about saving his hand. But he won't be able to work again for some time. That hand is going to be stiff. As Gil has often said, man's hands are the greatest tools in the world. When he loses one or one gets too stiff to use, man is at a loss. Gil can't be at a loss with eleven young mouths to feed and another one due. Gil has such powerful strong hands just like all the Perkins men all the way down the line. You'll have his hands, Pedike—Timmie's got hands like his mother's people—smaller, and less powerful."

"But I can use 'em," Timmie said.

"I know, I know, but don't vex me right now," Uncle Dick said. "I'm thinking. Wasn't last night the last full moon? Doesn't it change tonight?"

"Yes," Cousin Bos said.

We had reached the waiting room.

"Bos, I'm sending an ambulance for Sil," Uncle Dick said. "Will you go with the driver—go get Faith. Sil's baby will be born tonight as sure as we're here. That's a sign that hardly fails. Ask the doctors. And our people back on Lower Bruin went by that sign."

"Poppie in the hospital," I said. "First time one of us was ever there! Now Mommie? First time Timmie and I have ever been in one!"

"Well, get used to one," Uncle Dick said. "A hospital is a modern thing—a place to get you well and not a place of death!"

"But Poppie and Mommie," Timmie said. "Both in the hospital. Home won't be home!"

"Now don't you worry," Uncle Dick said. "You children can manage!"

"Yes, I'll come and get you and take you to see them," Cousin Bos said. "Everything will be all right. Faith and I will come and spend the night with you!"

"Rehabilitation," Uncle Dick said as he walked the floor and smoked his cigar. "I'll talk to others! I'll talk to my Lawyer Leonard Nichols. No Social Security. Good!"

Uncle Dick always stood back a little from the crowd

and smoked his cigars. He was always thinking and conjuring up ideas. No wonder he had been called an old fox with a silver tongue.

"You boys stay here with me," Uncle Dick said. "If you'd go home, Sil would know something is wrong. Don't tell her Gil is here, that he's been bitten by a copperhead."

"You know me, Dick," Cousin Bos said. "I'll go get Faith. I'll go with the ambulance to fetch her."

"We'll wait out here in the corridor," Uncle Dick said. "It's about time for Dr. Zimmerman to be out and we'll learn about Gil!"

Uncle Dick walked the floor and smoked. He acted like a man in a dream.

"Your Poppie was in World War II, wasn't he?" Uncle Dick asked.

"But he didn't go overseas and do any fighting. He was too nervous." I said. "He was at Fort Benjamin Harrison in Indiana all the time. I've heard him talk about K.P. duty. Then, he got to be a cook."

"And I believe his nervousness started in the Army," Uncle Dick said. "I'm sure it did."

This was the worst time right now that I could ever remember since I was born. My Great-uncle Richard Perkins, I thought, was a very different and unusual man. This didn't excite him. Right now he had other things on his mind. And now, Dr. Zimmerman came walking up the corridor.

"Well, Dick," he said. "Your Nephew Gil has been given the proper medication! I removed the tourniquet."

"A new word," Timmie said. "It means to bind and cut off circulation of the blood."

"Smart boy," Dr. Zimmerman said.

I wanted to say smart aleck in a time like this with Poppie in the hospital and, Mommie maybe coming. But brother Timmie had to be Timmie no matter where he was.

"Now, I've finished," Dr. Zimmerman said. "Maybe his sons' knowing what to do really saved his hand. But his hand had turned black. I had to get that tourniquet off—in

fact had to cut it off. Had it been on much longer without circulation of blood to his hand he would have lost
it. I gave his hand proper medication. And I gave him a
shot to put him to sleep!"

"Poppie asleep in daytime?" Timmie blurted.

"Shut up, Dr. Zimmerman is talking," I said.

"About that hand, Doc?" Uncle Dick asked.

"It will be some time before he can use it," Dr. Zimmerman said. "I think his hand can be saved but he won't
be able to use it. Maybe up until the middle of the summer."

"A hard-working man with eleven young mouths to
feed—maybe a twelfth one after tonight," Uncle Dick said.
"See, I've sent Bos and Faith Auxier after my niece Sil to
fetch her to the hospital. She's expecting any minute.
You're her doctor."

"Yes, Dick, I know," Dr. Zimmerman said.

"But, Doc, I'm worried," Uncle Dick said. "I've got
things I want to talk to you about. After all, I pay more
than forty thousand in taxes every year!"

"Forty thousand dollars!" Timmie said. "Gee-whilligens!"

"I match you, Dick," Dr. Zimmerman said. "And like
you, Susie Beth and I don't have any children!"

Well, I never dreamed a doctor paid such taxes!

"You and I, Doc, help finance Government spending on
the liars, cheats and the no-goods," Uncle Dick said. "Yes,
between us, over eighty thousand. Some few of our dollars
go for good purposes. But I want to talk to you—I've got
ideas. You know, we work to support the Government
while others work for the Government to support them."

"I'll work with you, Dick," Dr. Zimmerman said.

"Uncle Dick, you pay over forty thousand dollars in
taxes?" Timmie said.

"Yes, I do, Son," he said, puffing his cigar.

"Well, I've heard Poppie say he never paid a dollar
taxes in his life," Timmie said.

"Your Poppie has never made enough to pay taxes,"
Uncle Dick said. "A man with an ax, and plowing a mule,
with eleven children—working for farm wages—won't pay
any taxes! Your Poppie and Mommie are deserving of

some of my tax money that I have to pay this Government. Your Aunt Susie and I have been taxed to death for years!"

I didn't know what was going on. But I thought a copperhead bite on Poppie's hand might be changing our way of life. I certainly couldn't believe it would bring us riches and fortune. I never could believe Poppie's words that it paid to be poor. I knew Ohio was one of the greatest states of all fifty in America. I had heard so many times over our radio that America was the richest country in the world. So if Ohio was fourth in money, as I had heard over the radio and read in the Landsdowne County News, maybe Poppie was right that it paid to be poor in Ohio and in America.

"It might be close to the time for your mother to arrive," Uncle Dick said. "I want you boys to go over there in the waiting room and just wait until your Cousin Bos comes to take you home. I don't want her to see you. I don't want her to know Gil is here, either. And, Doc, I want you to wait with me here until she arrives. Maybe she won't—but I think Faith and Bos will fetch her. And I want to talk more to you!"

Brother Timmie and I went to the waiting room where we sat among old people and strangers. Here we waited. We were near the front door and corridor where patients were wheeled in. We could look through the door of the waiting room to see people coming and going. Each time a cot was wheeled in with a patient, Timmie ran over by the door, peeped around to see if it might be Mommie. At last he saw her.

"Mommie," he said in a loud whisper and stood behind the door. "Cousin Bos and Faith, Uncle Dick and Dr. Zimmerman are with her."

Why wheel her in? I thought.

But this is what they did. And she never saw us. I wondered how scared Mommie was to enter a hospital for her first time. Timme and I shed tears. Now Mommie and Poppie were both in this hospital.

Timmie and I were waiting for Cousin Bos and Faith to come out and to take us home. It was more than a half hour before they came. And when they came, Cousin Bos came to us and asked us to go with them to Poppie's room. Uncle Dick and Dr. Zimmerman were with Mommie.

"Now don't you boys worry about your mother," Cousin Faith said. "I told Cassie-Belle and Tishie not to worry. We didn't tell them about Gil. This would have upset all the family so much—I told them Bos and I would be over to see them after supper when our chores were done. I told them I'd stay with them but they said they didn't need me. Said they'd get along all right."

Poppie's room was a turn to the right from the entrance corridor, four rooms down on the first corridor. When Bos opened the door, Poppie was wide awake lying there, dressed in a gown. He had thrown the sheet and blanket from over him. And he had a white bandage over his hand where the copperhead had fanged him.

"So glad to see you again," Poppie said. "A hospital is a funny place! Look what they've dressed me in just because of a snake bite. I was just alayin' here athinkin' whoever on Lower Bruin went to a hospital for a snake bite?"

"Well, whoever on Lower Bruin ever went to a hospital unless they were carried out on bed springs nine miles to the road where a car could take them on their last trip to die?" Cousin Faith said.

"And look how many people lost fingers, hands, feet—yes, a few children killed by their bites," Cousin Bos said. "You're lucky to be here under Dr. Zimmerman's care and in this hospital."

"Oh, that awful pain and sickness," Poppie said. "My hand is numb now! All that throbbing up my arm to my shoulder! It's eased now after this sleep! You've not told Sil, have you?"

"No, we've not told her," Cousin Faith said. "We'll break the news to her easy when we take the boys home."

"She's so afraid of a hospital," Poppie said. "I've been alayin' here aworrin'," Poppie said, "about her. You know, she's overdue for our baby!"

"We'll watch over her, Gil," Cousin Faith said.

"She ought to know Poppie is here," Timmie said.

"No, never, Timmie," Cousin Faith said. "Your mother doesn't need to know now. I think you'll have another brother or sister before morning."

"Gee-whilligens," Timmie said. "So don't tell her anything."

"Look out for her, Cousin Bos and Faith," Poppie said.

"Don't you worry, we'll see that everything is all right," Cousin Faith said. "We'll take the boys home."

So Cousins Faith and Bos left Poppie's room and we left with them. It would be up to me and Timmie to tell our sisters. And when we left Cousin Bos' truck, Timmie didn't run to the house to be first to break the news, for Mommie wasn't there. We walked in the house together.

"Cassie-Belle, I know Mommie is in the hospital," I said. Tishie and Maryann were listening. "Timmie and I were there. We didn't let Mommie see us when they took her in!"

"For goodness sakes, what's happened to Poppie?" Cassie-Belle asked.

"Now don't worry," I said. "A copperhead fanged his hand in the tobacco bed this morning. And we got him there. Cousin Bos took him!"

"Is he all right?" Tishie asked. "Will he lose his hand?"

Our sisters knew what a copperhead bite was. We had known all our lives back on Lower Bruin to fear the dreaded copperhead that never warned before biting. We knew this deadly snake would coil quickly and strike again. That it wouldn't move from a forest fire, that it would coil and strike at the fire until it was burned to death and left a gray line of ashes.

"No, he won't lose his hand. Dr. Zimmerman said. Uncle Dick and Dr. Zimmerman were in the hospital when we left."

"Mommie doesn't know Poppie is there and he doesn't know she's there," Timmie said.

"Well, Pedike, we'll just have to manage while they're gone," Cassie-Belle said. "We children can't let Mommie and Poppie down. It's no time to cry now!"

Cassie-Belle, Tishie and Maryann took care of the Little Ones and the Babies and prepared supper for us while Timmie and I did our chores and I cut more stove wood and Timmie carried the wood onto the kitchen porch.

This evening at our table was the first time Poppie hadn't been at one end of the table and Mommie at the other. And it was certainly lonesome without them. Something big went out of our house when they went. Cassie-Belle and I had to take over.

When Cousin Bos and Faith came at about eight, my sisters had the Babies asleep and the Little Ones in bed. Maryann, Tishie and Cassie-Belle, Timmie and I were listening to the radio. We were so glad to see them.

"Children, don't worry," Cousin Faith said. "Your father is resting well and your mother is all right. She's better off in the hospital than she is here. The time for Cousin Sil to have her babies at home is over! No more of that!"

"I agree with you, Cousin Faith," Sister Cassie-Belle said. "I know what her last childbirth was when Baby Brother Joshua was born!"

"But I'm worried, Cousin Bos," I said. "What will we do now that Poppie can't work?"

"Oh, there is always a way," Cousin Bos said. "Something will happen. I've heard a lot of talk today between Dr. Zimmerman and your Uncle Dick. Who'd ever think either of them paid forty thousand a year in taxes?"

"Rich men," Timmie said.

"I say they're rich," Cousin Bos said.

"Forty thousand in taxes?" Cassie-Belle said.

"Yes," Cousin Bos replied.

"And we've never paid any taxes," Timmie said. "I've heard Poppie say this."

"Well, we've paid taxes haven't we, Faith?" Cousin Bos said. "Not as much as they have. But we've paid taxes—our Buster Boy has paid taxes. And I'd like to know just how much taxes Essej Trants pays! But he doesn't make all his money on the farm!"

"Children, these taxes have got to be something awful," Cousin Faith said. "I wonder sometimes if we work for the Government and the State of Ohio or for ourselves! And I often wonder why we work at all! Work just to pay taxes! It's getting worse and worse each year!"

"We can't stay any longer," Cousin Bos said. "We've got to go home and get our rest. We've got to be up at four in the morning! But we'll go to the hospital in the morning after our work is done. And we'll come to tell you about your parents."

"Yes, we'll take you to see them," Cousin Faith said.

Then they left us. They were the last link of travel between Poppie and Mommie in the hospital and us. Life hung on a slender thread for us. I thought the thread was as fine as one in a spider's web. I'd seen spider webs so often in the tobacco patch or on blades of corn. I liked to watch spiders make their web to trap flies. And sometimes they caught a tobacco worm.

Cassie-Belle and Tishie slept in Mommie's and Poppie's bed with Baby Brother Josh and Baby Sister Faith. Maryann slept with Little Dickie, and Martha, Little Eddie and Susie slept in the same bed with their room door open so Cassie-Belle and Tishie could hear them if they cried. We knew by teachings of our parents and the closeness of our family ties to hold our family together even if Poppie and Mommie were not with us.

"Wonder why Mr. Herbert didn't come to the hospital today to see Poppie?" Timmie asked when we went to our room. "Do you reckon he was too busy?"

"I don't know," I said. "But I've been wondering, too! He thought so much of Poppie and all our family. After you had Mrs. Herbert phone Uncle Dick and Cousin Bos, I know he knows Poppie was bitten by a copperhead and had to be hauled out of the tobacco patch!"

"Wonder why he didn't stop by the house to see if we'd help him tomorrow," Timmie asked me. "I don't like to miss seven fifty a day!"

Timmie gave his cackling laugh.

"It's not a laughing matter," I said. "Let's get to bed."

We changed from our clean work clothes and got into our pajamas. On Lower Bruin we slept in our shirttails. In Ohio, now we bought our clothes and we slept in pajamas. We had not done any work on this day except our morning and evening chores.

"What are we going to do now without Poppie, and Mommie going to have another baby?" Timmie asked.

"I don't know," I said. "You and I will have to keep our family! We'll have to be the breadwinners without Poppie! Berry picking time again, and Tishie and Maryann can pick and Cassie-Belle will have to help Mommie."

Timmie and I often talked things over when we worked in the fields, or did our chores, or after we went to our room for sleep. For the first time in our lives we were home without both parents. And Mr. Herbert, who had done so much for us, had not been to the hospital to see Poppie or at our home to ask about him. Mommie was in the hospital for the first time in her life to have a baby and Poppie was in the hospital for the first time in his life. This situation had me worried.

49 When the alarm clock sounded at four in the morning, Timmie and I were up, dressed and went to do our chores—to feed six pigs, put milk into their troughs—feed and milk two cows by lantern light. We'd done this so many times now that it had become routine.

When we returned, Cassie-Belle and Tishie had breakfast ready. And now the Little Ones were getting up and the Babies were crying. Maryann knew how to fix Baby Brother Josh's formula and Baby Sister Faith's bottle. She worked with them. Then Tishie had to help Little Dickie with his bottle. Susie, Little Eddie and Martha came to the table to eat with us. Martha, at eight, could very well take care of herself.

Now we had eaten our breakfasts. If Mr. Herbert came for us and asked us to work, we were ready. We knew Cousins Faith and Bos and Uncle Dick would help us now. They were the connecting links between our family and our parents. Mr. Herbert had his truck and his cars. If he wanted us, he'd be after us. And if he wanted to know about Poppie, he could go to the hospital or he could stop here.

"Do you suppose we'd better go to Mr. Herbert's home?" Timmie said. "He might need us!"

"If he needs us, he'll come," I said. "Let's wait for Cousins Bos and Faith to tell us about Poppie and Mommie! They'll be here to see us this morning."

It was after eight when Cousin Bos drove his red truck into our driveway. Cousin Faith was there beside him. They got out and walked over in the yard where my sisters, Timmie and I gathered around them.

"What about Poppie?" I asked.

"He had a good night," Cousin Bos said. "Doc Zimmerman had to give him more shots for pain. His arm is swollen and his hand is swollen and numb. But don't you worry, he is going to be all right! It just takes time. Your Uncle Dick is with him!"

"Now for the good news," Cousin Faith said. "You've got a new Baby Brother!"

"Gee-whilligens!" Timmie shouted. "Thirteen for Mommie! A dozen of us living now!"

"Born at midnight," Cousin Faith said.

"Mommie didn't get there too soon," Cassie-Belle said. "And I'm glad she had this Baby Brother in the hospital! I know I never want to deliver a baby like I did Josh for any woman again, especially my own mother!"

"A dozen living!" Timmie repeated with a big smile. "Little Mommie's had 'em!"

And in front of Cousins Bos and Faith he jumped up and cracked his heels together twice this time. This was something he'd been practicing in the fields with me. Said he would someday crack his heels three times and wondered when he came down how far the earth would have rotated from under him. And I had enough practical sense to remind him of a thing called gravity. I'd read about Sir Isaac Newton's wondering why an apple didn't fall up from the tree instead of down and therefore he discovered gravity. It was this simple. I wondered what Timmie might discover. Not any boy ever had a better-to-work, a much smarter-in-books, and one who-could-never-stop-talking brother than I had. My brother Timmie! And I'd fight for him any time he needed me. I doubted he would fight for himself. He did cut the copperhead into seven pieces after it fanged Poppie's hand. But I had him killed already with one powerful blow with a tobacco stick.

Cousin Faith and Cousin Bos thought Timmie was real funny. They laughed at his antics. They kept hanging around with us. They didn't ask us to go to the hospital to see Poppie and Mommie. Not right now. They'd have to take part of my sisters at a time. Part of them would have to stay with the Babies and the Little Ones.

"You tell them the rest of the news, Bos," Cousin Faith said.

"It's sad news," Cousin Bos said. "I hate to tell you but you will know it!"

"Is our new Baby Brother alive?" Timmie asked quickly.

"Yes, very much alive and crying," Cousin Faith said. "I saw him a few minutes ago."

"Mr. Herbert died last night," Cousin Bos said.

"Oh, no," Timmie screamed.

"What will we do now?" Cassie-Belle said. "What's going to happen to us in this strange land?"

"We loved him," Tishie said.

Maryann turned and walked away from our circle. She was crying. He had been so nice to us—nicest man ever to help us like a father or grandfather. We openly cried—all of us in front of Cousin Bos and Cousin Faith.

I remembered how he gave us the best wages we had ever received. Mr. Herbert had furnished us a house rent free, bought wallpaper of Mommie's and my sisters' choosing, gave us free garden and truck patches, plowed them for us, furnished us free seed. He gave six pigs and free feed to feed them. He loaned us two of his best cows from his dairy herd to furnish us milk and butter. He furnished us feed for our cows.

Last spring and summer he'd come to the tobacco patch, the corn field, and the berry fields and eaten his lunch at noon with us and we talked. He loved us. We loved him. Now, he was gone. And what about our house? He wasn't here to wire it! And what about our bathroom? Things would change here. Maybe we'd be out of a home. What would we do? I knew Timmie and our sisters were think-ing the same thing.

"We've talked to Mrs. Herbert," Cousin Bos said. "Faith and I saw her at Stafford's Morgue in Agrillo this morning. She's making arrangements. You can't see the body until this evening at seven."

"I don't want to see him dead," I said. "I won't be there or at the funeral either!"

"I won't either," Tishie said.

"Nor me," said weeping Timmie. "Why did he have to die?"

"He was seventy-two years old and he worked himself to death is why," Cousin Bos said. "Yesterday morning he managed to drive his truck home from the field and told his wife he had indigestion. She gave him two Alka-Seltzers and he said he felt better—that he'd take the day off at home, for he still didn't feel well—that at times he was dizzy. Mrs. Herbert wanted to call Dr. Zimmerman but he wouldn't let her. He said he'd go to bed and sleep it off. He watched a TV program with Mrs. Herbert. They went to bed. This morning she couldn't wake him. He was dead in bed beside her."

Poppie and Mommie couldn't be at the funeral and we children wouldn't be. No wonder he hadn't come to see Poppie at the hospital! I'll tell you we were hurt! The roof of our new and better world had fallen in on us.

"Does Poppie know Mommie is in the hospital? Does she know he's there?" Cassie-Belle asked.

"Oh, yes," Cousin Faith said. "He knows about his new son, too! And Gil's a happy man! Your Uncle Dick is there walking between the rooms with a trail of smoke following him! He told your mother about the copperhead biting Gil—but not until this morning. He waited until after your brother was born! All is well, children, at the hospital! Now, we'll take Pedike and Timmie and two of you girls—Cassie-Belle, we'd better leave you and take Tishie and Maryann. We could take Martha, too, and let her see her new Baby Brother! Later, when we bring your sisters home, we'll come for you!"

I knew what Cousin Faith was thinking. She thought it took our other three sisters to do what Cassie-Belle could do with the Little Ones and the Babies in our family. Cassie-Belle was a top student but she was also a second mother in our family. Tishie was a coming-on third mother.

Cousin Bos had seats across his truckbed for us—except little Martha who rode up front with them. At the hospital we followed a nurse to Mommie's room. Cousin Faith went with us. Cousin Bos went to Poppie's room.

"Here's a fine-looking family here to see their Baby Brother," said the nurse.

"There are more left at home than here," Mommie said with a smile.

She had wee Baby Brother on her arm. We crowded around to see him as we'd always done when Baby Sister or Baby Brother was born.

"Things have happened to us," Mommie said. "Look at your father! And Mr. Herbert! New life here! Death there!"

Not one of us said anything. I thought Timmie would. I looked at Mommie's face and Timmie's face. Anybody could tell Timmie was Mommie's son. I wondered if Mommie could tell by looking at our eyes all had been crying but Little Martha. We were scared and bewildered. We were frightened children.

"Uncle Dick comes in here every few minutes and tells us not to worry," Mommie said. "He says everything is going to be all right."

Now the nurse left Mommie's room. She rushed off to other duties at the sound of a bell.

"Is everything all right at home?" Mommie asked.

"Everything is wonderful, Mommie," Tishie said.

"I miss all of you," Mommie said. "First night I've been away from you!"

"We miss you, too, Mommie," Timmie said. "I dreamed about you last night. I dreamed we moved again and you put a new list of our names on the kitchen wall!"

"If we move again, I'll do that, Timmie," she said. "Twelve names now to remember."

Now there were smiles on all our faces. We knew Mommie was funning with Timmie.

"We want to see Poppie, too," Tishie said.

"I'll lead you to his room," Timmie said as if he knew his way around in this two-story hospital. "Follow me!"

When Timmie opened the door to Poppie's room, Uncle Dick, Dr. Zimmerman, Cousin Bos and a strange man were in his room.

"Sign right here," said the strange man.

"It's better that copperhead bit me on the left hand," Poppie said. "But I'm so nervous I can hardly write my name."

Poppie signed his name.

"Your children?" said the stranger.

"Less than half of them," Poppie said.

"Nice-looking children," he said and was off in a hurry.

"I'm so happy to see you," Poppie said. "I'd like to be home!"

"Not yet, Gil," Dr. Zimmerman said. "You'll be here several days yet."

"But this is expensive," Poppie said.

"Not to you, Gil, and not for Sil," Uncle Dick said. "I'll pay now. You will be able to pay next time!"

"How'll I be able to pay?" Poppie said.

"Leave this to me," Uncle Dick said as he walked the floor.

"With Josh Herbert gone, I wonder," Poppie said. "He was so good to us!"

"Leave that to me, too," Uncle Dick said. "I think I've got this solved, too! I've worked fast, Gil!"

"I think his family will take back the cows he lets us milk," Poppie said.

"I don't doubt that," Uncle Dick said. "I know the Herberts. I know there will be a family fight over his vast holdings and his wealth. But let them take back the cows and pigs, too. Let them not wire the house. We'll have something better for you and your family. The deal is in the making."

Cousin Bos looked strangely at Uncle Dick. So did we. We didn't know what he was doing or what he was up to.

"At least four more days in this bed," Dr. Zimmerman said. "Stay here while your wife is here. She'll be here four days!"

"But, Doc, I need to be home with the children," Poppie said. "Sil and I both need to be there. We've never been a night away from them before."

"Your over-worked nice little childbearing wife needs a few days rest away from the children here in this hospital," Dr. Zimmerman said. "And I want to save your hand, Gil! You don't want to go through the rest of your days with only one hand, do you?"

"Oh, no, Doc," Poppie said. "What would I do a one-handed farm laborer with fourteen mouths to feed?"

"Then listen to me," Dr. Zimmerman said.

"Yes, stay here at least four days," Uncle Dick said. "It's no expense to you. Your children can do the chores and keep the house going."

"We certainly can," I said.

"Dr. Zimmerman is right," Uncle Dick said. "There are a few more things I want to do. And my word in Agrillo and Landsdowne County, Ohio, will get them done in a hurry. There's no time to lose! Gil, do you have money to buy groceries this coming Friday?"

"Yes, more than enough," Poppie said. "We can go a couple of months on what Sil has saved for us!"

"I just wanted to be sure," Uncle Dick said.

Timmie, Cousin Faith and I stayed on at the hospital, while Cousin Bos took Tishie, Maryann and Martha back home. Cousin Faith was with Mommie.

"It's best, Doc, for Bos Auxier to be out when we talk," Uncle Dick said. "He doesn't pay the real big taxes but his landlord, Essej Trants, pays them. We don't want him to get ideas!"

"Right," Dr. Zimmerman said.

"Pedike, you can plow a two-acre tobacco field with a good span of mules, can't you?" Uncle Dick asked me.

"Sure, why?" I asked.

"Could you and Timmie set the tobacco and farm it?" Uncle Dick said. "Your father won't be able to work this season!"

"Sure we can," Timmie said. "We can plow, hoe, worm and sucker it, too! And with Poppie's guidance we can strip, hand and grade it."

"They can do that all right, Uncle Dick," Poppie said. "But won't my hand be so I can use it? Am I going to lose my hand? Have you been deceiving me?"

"No, you won't lose your hand," Dr. Zimmerman said. "But we don't want you working!"

"You can walk over the pastures, Gil, and look over the white-face cattle," Uncle Dick said. "Count them. See they have salt. I've found you a better farm, a better landlord than Josh Herbert. I hate to say this with poor old Josh over at the morgue. Poor old Josh was my friend. Right now he's being embalmed to prepare him for his last resting place! We've found a twelve-room house—almost a mansion —with two bathrooms."

"Does it have electricity?" Timmie interrupted.

"What a silly question," Uncle Dick said. "You know it does if it has two bathrooms! Stetson Koniker is Division Plant Manager of Ohio Steel Corporation. He has just fired his bearded fake tobacco grower—who didn't know fiddles about growing the stuff. A fancy farmer, he rented under false pretenses! He sat on the porch all the time and stroked his beard. Never lived on a farm before. He strummed his guitar and, as Stetson said, he was 'way-out.' And the whole house will be re-wallpapered for you before you move in!"

"But can't I help with the terbacker?" Poppie asked.

"You can't work, Gil," Uncle Dick said. "Yet you will get half of the tobacco! Give this to the boys, for you won't be needing it! You're heading for a better life. You are heading for plenty of money. That set-up that Bos and Faith have with Essej Trants is not half you will have with Stetson Koniker. Stet just runs his farm for joy and a show. He likes to walk among his white-face cattle and watch them graze. This is part of his recreation when he's home. His farm never pays. He charges off loss on his farm to tax deductions. He has no children—no exemption but his wife, Arabella, who sings in the choir in the Presbyterian Church each Sunday morning. I know the Konikers well. When I had a better heart, I played golf with him at Agrillo Golf Club."

Now I knew Uncle Dick was more than a silver-haired, silver-tongued fox. I knew he was a wealthy old Uncle. And I knew he got around. I knew he had connections and he could get things done.

"Say, Doc, that 'way out' bearded no-farmer Stet rented to, Homer Glick I believe the fellow's name was, even went to the Konikers' dump and checked the Scotch bottles, wine bottles and beer cans and spread the news about the number he counted, all over Agrillo," Uncle Dick said.

"He must have been a nut," Dr. Zimmerman said. "Everybody knows how Presbyterians drink. I'm one myself. It has been said of our more saintly Presbyterians we stagger up to the polls to vote dry!"

"I don't go for this drinking," Poppie said. "Freewill Baptists don't."

Uncle Dick, who almost built our big church, had to turn from Poppie to hold his laughter.

50 For the first time in over a year, Timmie and I were not working on the farm or going to school. First time we had only our chores to do. And we cut a little stove wood. And when we fed the pigs and milked the cows, we knew we wouldn't be doing this much longer. Not if Uncle Dick had told us the truth.

When we told Cassie-Belle, Tishie and Maryann about the new twelve-room house, that it had electricity and two bathrooms, that it would be re-wallpapered for us before we moved there, maybe two weeks from now, and that it would be rent free, they couldn't believe Timmie or me. We told them Poppie wouldn't be able to work and that Timmie and I would farm only two acres of tobacco and Poppie would count the white-faced cattle.

"A mansion," Timmie said. "Gee-whilligens!"

He jumped up and cracked his heels together, three times, the first time he'd been able to do this.

"Cousin Bos and Faith never returned in the red truck to take us back to the Landsdowne County Hospital," I said to Cassie-Belle. "I know something is wrong. And I know what it is!"

"What is it, Pedike?" Cassie-Belle asked, while Tishie and Timmie listened.

"They're mad at us," I said.

"Why would they get mad at us?" Cassie-Belle wondered. "They've been so wonderful to us. Who among our relatives have ever been better except Uncle Dick?"

"See, Bos smelled a mouse at the hospital," I said. "He

wouldn't stay out of Poppie's room when Uncle Dick was walking the floor and talking about rehabilitation and asking Poppie if he didn't serve in the Army in World War II. He heard Uncle Dick and Dr. Zimmerman talking about the taxes they paid. He heard Uncle Dick talking about 'benefits' and about his nephew with a fine family. He heard Uncle Dick tell Poppie not to worry. Bos is a good worker and he's nosey and he's smart."

"But still, why didn't Cousins Bos and Faith come?" Tishie asked. "Surely this wouldn't have caused them to break with us."

"Don't you ever doubt it," I said. "As long as we lived in a house without a bathroom and electricity and worked the way we have, they tried to help us. They did help us. But now they know we're moving to the Koniker mansion and farm—much better than they have, with everything free—they're jealous."

"Just as Poppie said when we wore our fine clothes to the Freewill Baptist Church, people were not as friendly as they'd been when we wore our old-fashioned clothes we'd worn in the old country," Timmie said. "Remember Poppie said it paid to be poor? The higher up we get in the world, the fewer friends we'll have. Poppie was right. Look at our good Cousins Bos and Faith."

"I'll bet if Uncle Dick went to the Ohio Public Assistance office in our behalf, Cousin Bos has watched him with his hawk eyes. He's nosey, as I've said, and he's smart. And you know how Cousins Bos and Faith, workers that they are, hate food stamps and public assistance. They're of the old school—like Captain John Smith at Jamestown, Virginia—those who won't work can't eat!"

"Surely not," Tishie said.

"I can't believe it," said Cassie-Belle.

"But I can," I said. "I saw Cousin Bos listening to everything Dr. Zimmerman and Uncle Dick said in Poppie's hospital room. He was really getting an earful. And he's watched every move Uncle Dick has made. He knows it all."

"I hope you're wrong, Pedike," Tishie said.

"I'd like to be wrong," I said, "but I don't think I am.

You know when Cousin Bos told us he'd be here, he has always been. There's some big reason why he hasn't been. And I believe this is the reason why.

"We'd almost be their next-door neighbors when we moved to the Stetson Koniker farm. Uncle Dick said there would be only two houses between us, the Koniker Mansion and the Essej Trants near-mansion, and the highway that separates the Trants and Koniker farms. Our kinfolks don't like that."

On Friday Uncle Dick came in the ambulance with Mommie and Poppie. Uncle Dick and Poppie rode up with the driver. Mommie rode in a bed with Baby Brother in her arms. Oh, we really ran out to the drive—all the Little Ones, too—all but Cassie-Belle who stayed with the Babies. We welcomed Mommie and Poppie home. Poppie with a clean bandage on his hand.

"So wonderful to be home with you," Mommie said. "I've missed you so. Is everything all right?"

Little Mommie was crying. Big Poppie was shedding tears.

Uncle Dick paid the ambulance driver. He backed out of our drive and was on his way. We walked into the living room together.

"Has Bos been here?" Poppie asked.

"No," I said.

"I told you, Gil," Uncle Dick said. "He's eavesdropped in your hospital room. He heard me and Dr. Zimmerman talking and planning. I was so afraid of that. He and Faith will be so jealous of you they'll just about die!

"Don't you worry," Uncle Dick talked on. "Someone will be here in my car to take you to Cantwell's Super Market. You'll bring home enough supplies they can afford to haul them here for you! My tax money I think will be well spent on my well-deserving relatives. When I walked into the Ohio Public Assistance Office, they knew who I was—my first time ever there—I stated my business. When they talked about investigation, I told them both parents were in the hospital. Eleven children at home and the twelfth in his mother's arms. Well, that was it. I did more explaining— how you worked, Gil, until that snake got your hand. And

I took with me Dr. Zimmerman's report. So I got three hundred dollars worth of food stamps for ten dollars. I could have done it for five under the circumstances I presented, but I thought it best to give them ten dollars. So you can bring home three hundred dollars worth of groceries tomorrow!"

"How can we eat that much, Uncle Dick?" Mommie said.

"Feed them better," Uncle Dick said. "Use up my tax money. Money I'll never see again or get benefits from. I'm sick of taxation. Most of this stuff is a cheat—a wrong—so we'll ride it into the ground if we can and force a change! One has to come."

Uncle Dick smoked his cigar. He talked and we listened.

"You're going to a better house than I live in, rent free," Uncle Dick said. "You'll need an electric stove, vacuum cleaner, iron, refrigerator and a television, and a lot of new furniture. And you can get these on credit. I'll stand behind you."

"But the money?" Poppie said. "We've not saved enough!"

"Keep your saved dollars," Uncle Dick said. "But keep them in a stocking or throw them up and let the wind blow them away. You know how the wind carries autumn leaves! In a land—my country—where they pay you not to farm. Our system needs overhauling all the way down the line— from the President to the street loafer."

"But the money?" Poppie said.

I'd never heard Uncle Dick talk so crazy. Throw paper money up for the wind to blow away! Now if anything was "way out" this had to be. This was farther out than the beardy young man who rented the Koniker farm to raise tobacco and sat on the porch and strummed his guitar and stroked his beard.

"Gil, you'll get a check each month from the State of Ohio Public Assistance for three hundred forty-four dollars," Uncle Dick said. "You'll get another check and still another. I'm not sure what either will be! Not yet."

"Gee-whilligens, we're rich," Timmie shouted. "Poppie, you'll be making more than all three of us did working for Mr. Herbert!"

"And there's food, over three hundred dollars a month for ten dollars," Uncle Dick said. "No cost for medicine. No cost at the hospital. All free! You'll get free lunch at school and maybe free breakfasts. No, Gil, remember you can't work. If you do, there will be trouble!"

We sat in silence. We couldn't believe it.

"Now," Uncle Dick said, "in the State of Ohio Public Assistance program, if this house wasn't rent free, you'd get the extra benefits of your rent being paid. This is known in fancy words as 'shelter cost.' So much allowed for each room in your domicile."

"A new word," Timmie shouted, interrupting Uncle Dick. He took his notebook from his hip pocket, his pencil from his shirt pocket. "Domicile—it means a house where people live."

"If you're through, young man, I'll continue," Uncle Dick said. "You see, Stetson Koniker wants to rent it free. He doesn't want these dollars. So we skipped over this. But here's a benefit I latched onto. You're allowed a maximum of twenty-seven dollars a month for utilities, gas, water and electricity. Since water is free, and the house is heated by an oil furnace, all you'll have to buy is oil and electricity. You'll almost get enough to pay for these!"

"No wood to chop," I said.

"This will be high living," Poppie said. "Just like Cousin Bos and Cousin Faith have!"

"Higher than they have," Uncle Dick said. "They work for theirs. And Uncle Sam, your real rich uncle, will be keeping you."

"Turn the cows back to the Herbert heirs," Uncle Dick continued. "And give them back the truck patches you've planted and your garden. You won't need them! You're really going to live a good life!"

"Speaking of Mr. Herbert," Poppie said in his slow voice. "I'm sorry none of us could go to his funeral! Poor man killed himself working."

"I came close to it myself," Uncle Dick said, "but there's a new way of life in this country. People are getting on the bandwagon. And it had just as well be you. You can really qualify on all counts! Oh, yes, you'll get free dental work and free clothing. There are so many fringe benefits that come with this. I don't know all yet, but I'll help you find out."

"I've said it pays to be poor," Poppie said. "But this is more than I expected. All these good things and benefits for not working."

"Gil, you and Sil are in for some good living," Uncle Dick said. "Now, you've got a few rules to follow. And don't be too foolish not to follow the rules! This is a new day in your lives! Not one of your checks can be taxed. Everything is tax free."

Right when Poppie got snake bit, Mommie had her thirteenth child and Mr. Herbert died, all in twenty-four hours, when I thought the roof of the world had fallen in on us, we were heading for a new life, better living and even riches. All over a copperhead's biting Poppie's hand. And because we had a silver-haired and silver-tongued foxy old Uncle Dick who knew how to get things done in a hurry.

"I wouldn't advise young people to work and save," Uncle Dick said. "If you earn, live it up. Money will be worthless. Live today and enjoy it."

Just then a car pulled into our drive.

"That's my car," Uncle Dick said. "I phoned Susie and told her to tell Leonard to come for me here at about four. I've got a chauffeur to drive me now!"

"A new word," Timmie said.

Timmie put the word down in his little notebook.

"Someday I'll speak in a language of big words," Timmie said.

Uncle Dick just looked strangely at Timmie as he got up from Poppie's big chair to leave.

"I'll be in touch with you," Uncle Dick said. "I expect to come with Leonard to take you to the market tomorrow. I will be here at nine in the morning."

When Uncle Dick got in his car he took the back seat. Leonard, a middle-aged man, sat up front and drove the car. The car was a big, expensive one.

"Poppie, wonder how much all the checks will come to?" Timmie said. "Food stamps, three hundred, minus ten, equals two hundred ninety, plus three hundred and forty-four make six hundred and thirty-four and two more checks to come! Free mansion, medicine, hospital, dentist, free lunches, free everything! And no taxes!"

"It does pay to be poor," Poppie said. "I've heard our country was the richest country in the world and Ohio is one of the best states in America. Now I can believe what I've heard. A great country and a great state! No wonder people come here from South of the Border! If they keep on a-comin' I believe they'll all be here. I'm proud to be called an Ohioan!"

"I am too, Poppie, when I think back on Lower Bruin," I said. "I don't have good memories of the place."

"But our dead are buried there," Poppie said. "Our oldest son, Little Pearse, sleeps there!"

51 After we had done our chores, Timmie and I and Sisters Cassie-Belle, Tishie and Maryann got together with Mommie and Poppie in the living room. I had turned the radio on to soft music while we talked.

"How wonderful to be home with you children," Poppie said. "That hospital, even with a good doctor and good treatment, was no fun. I was never in bed in my life that long."

"But your hand, Poppie, that great tool!" I said.

"But now I'm told I can't use it," Poppie said. "I don't know what I'll do! I'm so used to working, it's going to be hard to try not to."

"Like farmers paid not to farm, you'll be paid not to work," I said. "Remember what Uncle Dick said. That his nephew and niece and great nephews and nieces would benefit from his tax money."

"I am caught between big money, free food, free everything and a bare living working with my hands," Poppie said. "Right now I can't work, so I'll have to follow Uncle Dick's advice."

"Bathrooms," Cassie-Belle said. "Electrical appliances like other people have. A nice home. Television! Get colored television, Poppie. I heard my classmates say it was the thing! I can't blame you, Poppie. We know what it is to work and sweat. If Ohio and the United States Government have it to give away, why not take it? Others take it."

"Well, I've go something to tell you," Mommie said. "No one has asked me what I've named this Baby Brother. I thought of the name there on my hospital bed, Gil in the hospital, Mr. Herbert dead. I didn't know what we'd do. I gave his name then, Daniel. I thought of Daniel in the Lion's Den. We've been there, too. But we believe the Word. Gil, we're out now."

"What a pretty name," Poppie said.

"He will be Baby Brother Dan," Tishie said. "And he'll be called later Little Dan or Little Danny!"

"Or Danny Boy," Timmie said. "I've heard that song over the radio!"

I wondered why they'd called me Pedike and my brother Timmie. But these were family names.

"Now, I want you, Cassie-Belle and Tishie, to help me make out a grocery list for tomorrow," Mommie said. "This will be a different one. Uncle Dick told me before I left the hospital this could be for anything we ate in the store but foreign imports such as Norway sardines and Danish hams. But we've never had these. He said we could order broasted chickens. He said we could order T-bone steaks. He said we'd have to eat a lot of fancy grub to spend our food stamps."

So Mommie and my sisters got to work on our food list which included steaks and "broasted chickens." We'd not had steaks since we'd eaten with Cousin Faith and Cousin Bos. Now we'd be getting our own T-bone steaks and with food stamps. And as Uncle Dick had told us, when these stamps were spent, we could get more, ten dollars for three hundred dollars worth of food in the store.

When Uncle Dick came, with his chauffeur Leonard driving, Saturday morning at nine, Mommie had a three-page food list. Uncle Dick asked for Cassie-Belle, Tishie, Timmie and me to go to Cantwell's Super Market and help wheel out the groceries.

"You stay here, Gil, you and Sil," he said. "You're not able. I'll go with the children and help this morning. You can do this later."

Timmie sat up front with Leonard and three of us sat in the back sat with Uncle Dick. Uncle Dick carried our food stamps.

"All you have to do, Cassie-Belle, is to give these to the

clerk who checks you out," Uncle Dick said. "You've been there before and paid cash. Not any more. Food is almost free for you! I'll be in the store. I'll see that food stamps go well for you!"

It used to be Cousin Bos and Cousin Faith, two hard-working cousins to Poppie and Mommie, helped us. Now, they were no longer with us. And we missed the red truck. But Uncle Dick, who had stayed in the background, had taken over for us. And he acted like a man happy to do this because he wasn't happy about his taxes.

When we got to Agrillo, Uncle Dick walked into Cantwell's with us as if we were his children. He asked each of us to take a grocery carriage. So we had four. And each of us took a fourth of Mommie's list and we began to fill from the shelves what she had listed. If one of us couldn't find something, we went to Uncle Dick and he asked for a clerk to help us.

"At least eight broasted chickens and eight T-bones," Uncle Dick told me. "Your parents and you older children have appetites for these new foods and you'll eat them."

Uncle Dick helped me select the T-bones. And he was choosy about the steaks. He helped me select the broasted chickens. But he was less choosy about these.

"A broasted chicken is a broasted chicken," he said. "See why you can't get anything of foreign imports? Food stamps for the poor is to help the American farmers who are paid not to farm. Can't you see how much sense this makes to an old-timer like your Uncle Dick—about ready to depart this world and leave what I have to the United States Government to squander the way it pleases! I'll do all I can to get even before I leave this world. I'm sick of all this god-damned stuff!"

He swore—used the Lord's name in vain and he was a member of our church.

Well, we got the eight chickens and eight T-bone steaks. And we bought bacon, milk and butter, which we didn't need. But Uncle Dick said buy it. We bought three kinds of soft drinks. Uncle Dick said we should get used to the different kinds of pops. Our four grocery carriages were loaded high with as many items as they could hold. We even had twelve loaves of bread. But all we had purchased came to less than two hundred sixty-three dollars in our food stamps. This was the biggest grocery list we had ever purchased in our lives. But our Government was paying about ninety-six percent of it.

There were four checkout points. We'd really taken over one. People behind us with fewer groceries shifted to the other three lines. Uncle Dick was behind us with the food stamps. This was something new we would soon be used to doing by ourselves. When I, the last of us, got my fourth grocery carriage checked through, Uncle Dick said: "Here are the stamps."

"Stamps are the same as money to us," said the lady clerk at the cash register. "Government money is as good as what the people spend."

When the Cantwell customers saw us giving food stamps to pay for our groceries while others were paying cash, people looked at us with mean eyes. They mumbled things we could not hear.

"With an order like this one, I want you to haul this load to Gil Perkins' home on the Josh Herbert farm," Uncle Dick said.

"Yes, we know where the Perkinses live," said the clerk. "With a two hundred sixty-three dollar order, we can take them there!"

People in the store knew Uncle Dick. And they knew us, too. Always before we'd paid our cash for groceries. I figured in my head quickly. Poppie would have had to have worked four weeks, six days a week and two days and three hours for the groceries that had cost less than ten dollars. Should our pride, which we had regained by working for a living in Ohio, after we had been on hand-out commodities back on Lower Bruin, stand in our way? Or should we forget pride and accept like the others who were getting on the bandwagon? This was the question. Pride and work and lesser food in our bellies, or swallowing our pride for fancy foods, foods we'd never had, such as broasted chickens and T-bone steaks, juices for breakfast never made by Mommie, bakery bread and no more cornbread and butter-milk. Should we fill our bellies on fancy foods, not work, grow fat and lazy on the Government bandwagon? We'd not exactly made the decision. Uncle Dick had made it for us. And to look at the groceries we had, to know of the rent-free mansion we were moving to and to know of the checks that would be coming Poppie's way, we were now on that bandwagon.

The truck got home with our groceries—ten paper boxes canned vegetables had come in, that the clerks kept to pack people's groceries. And our ten boxes were loaded.

"Uncle Dick," Poppie said as the Cantwell helpers unloaded and Timmie and I started carrying in, "how can we eat all of this?"

"There'll be more groceries if you want them," Uncle Dick said.

When Mommie looked into a box and counted eight broasted chickens, I thought she'd faint. In another box there were eight T-bone steaks. Uncle Dick was in the kitchen beside Mommie. "I've not got a place to keep part of the steaks," Mommie said.

"Cook all this afternoon and have a big steak supper," Uncle Dick said. "If you can't eat all eight—and I believe you can—after they're cooked they'll keep. Start on your broasted chickens for Sunday dinner after church!"

"And all this milk and butter and we've got milk and butter," Mommie said.

"Let the boys take the cows back to Herberts this afternoon," Uncle Dick said. "Or tell them to come and get the cows. You won't need them! You've got bacon, spareribs, and porkchops here! I helped Pedike select them. I helped him with the steaks and broasted chickens. We added to that grocery list you made out. That grocery list was one for a working man who pays with cash. This is one paid for with stamps!"

Then Uncle Dick laughed a forced laugh. "Ha! Ha! Ha!"

He put his cigar back into his mouth and puffed a cloud of smoke. He blew a smoke ring up against the kitchen ceiling.

"Well, you won't be using this kitchen pump much longer, Sil," Uncle Dick said. "You'll be turning faucets for hot or cold water! You'll have modern gadgets for the first time in your life!"

When Uncle Dick left our house, Cassie-Belle went about putting groceries away—any where and place she could find to put them. And brother Timmie set the table for her. Poppie sat in his big chair in the living room and smoked a cigarette. I worked helping Cassie-Belle put groceries away and put food on the table.

"We don't have time to cook steaks now," Cassie-Belle said. "But we'll have broasted chicken. It's already prepared!"

When my sisters and Mommie got the Babies asleep, they came to a table filled with food. We had milk for everybody for we were trying to use it. We had enough food for two families. We ate broasted chicken and it was as tasty as Cousin Faith's cooking. We had besides broasted chicken other food-stamp benefits that went with it. As Poppie said, "We've really got a full table. Fullest table that has ever been in our house."

"I think we're all a-goin' to eat too much," Poppie said. "I'll tell you, the grub in the hospital was awful—and not enough of it. I nearly starved to death there! It will take me a spell to get my body replenished but a meal like this will help do it!"

"I'm almost too full to get up from the table," Timmie said. "I'm full up to my ears!"

"Mind your manners, Timmie," Mommie told him.

Well, I thought Timmie had a point in what he was saying. I know I had eaten too much.

"With all this milk we got with food stamps, you boys had better take the cows down to Josh Herbert's barnlot and turn them in," Poppie said. "Go to the pasture and get them. Ropes out in the barn you can tie in their halters and lead them. They're so gentle they'll nearly follow you."

52 Timmie and I went to the pasture and found the cows. When they saw us coming they mooed to us. They stood still and waited.

"They're surprised to see us," Timmie said. "Good old gentle cows! How many times we've fed and milked them! They're our friends!"

"Friends have to part," I said.

We put ropes in their halters and led them from the pasture. When we got to the barn they wanted to turn in for feed and to be milked, but we took them through the gate and led them down the lane road.

When we got to Mr. Herbert's big barn leading the cows home, Mr. Herbert's sons, Jim and Al were there.

"So, you're bringing the cows home," Jim said. "We've heard the news. You won't be needing them any longer."

"Typical briars," Al said. "Our father gave you a good chance but you've taken the easy way out!"

"We're no more briars than the Herberts," I said. "We know where you came from—South of the Border—we're Ohioans same as you. I want to be called an Ohioan and not a briar."

"Yes, we've cut too many briars for Mr. Herbert," Timmie said. "We don't like briars!"

"But these god-damned food stamps and welfare is ruining this country," Jim Herbert said. "And people like the Herberts are paying for it! Dad said you Perkins children were the best workers he'd ever seen."

"And we loved Mr. Herbert," I said. "Just like he was our grandfather!"

"But welfare with all its food stamps and benefits has stopped a good family from working," Jim Herbert said.

"Poppie couldn't help a copperhead's biting him," Timmie said. Timmie was about to cry. "He might even lose his hand yet!"

"That was a costly snake bite for us," Al said. "We're sorry about that. Now we know you're going to move to the Stetson Koniker farm. He's a rich gentleman farmer!"

"But we're not goin' until the house is wallpapered," Timmie said. "Who is setting your tobacco?"

"We're trying to set it," Jim Herbert said.

"Pedike and I can drop plants and set tobacco fast as any two men you can get," Timmie said. "Can't we, Pedike? And, Mr. Herbert, we loved your father. He did so much for us. You pay us what you like. If you don't want to pay us, we'll do it free."

"We will be with you Monday morning," I said. "But remember, we're Ohioans and not briars. We'll help you set your tobacco. Harness the mule for me. I can lay off the rows!"

"It's not your fault," Jim Herbert said. "It's our Government's fault—making cheats, liars and lazy people out of good working people. I don't know where we're heading when half the people have to keep the other half."

"We'll give you our garden and truck patches," I said. "We'll have to plant these on the other farm."

I broke the news to him as gentle as I could. We didn't need a garden. We wouldn't have one on the Stetson Koniker farm. But Jim and Al Herbert, large, powerful men, bigger than Poppie, were pleased—yes, tickled—to get Timmie and me back to set their tobacco. I was happy, too, that Timmie had talked this time. We couldn't stay at the house and not do anything.

Timmie and I went home and told Poppie and Mommie about our promise to start pulling plants and setting tobacco for the Herberts Monday morning.

"Watch for copperheads in that tobacco-plant bed,"

Poppie said. "Just to see a stick on the ground now makes me nervous."

"Don't you worry, Poppie," Timmie said. "We'll go over the tobacco-plant bed before we pull a plant."

"I wish I could help you," Cassie-Belle said.

"So do I," Tishie said.

"It's an idea," Timmie said. "Poppie will be here with Mommie! Maybe, we can get both fields set for the Herberts while we wait two weeks for our new home!"

Cassie-Belle and Tishie knew how to drop plants and set tobacco. Any girl, boy, father or mother from Lower Bruin knew how to do this.

Poppie and Mommie thought this would be all right for us since we didn't have anything to do—for two weeks— not even pigs to feed and cows to milk. All we had to do was cut more stove wood. And Tishie and Cassie-Belle were excited about helping us. The four of us would be working together again.

That afternoon Jim and Al Herbert came with the truck to take back the feed their father had left with us for the cows. Poppie didn't go out with his bandaged hands to see them. But Timmie and I went out to help them.

"Cassie-Belle is the best worker among us," Timmie told them. "Tishie can beat me in a corn row. They can drop and set tobacco. They've done it before! If they can help us, maybe we can get both tobacco fields set before we leave your place!"

"Great! Great," Al Herbert said. "Bring them!"

53 Sunday when Jimmie Artner took us to church, Cousin Bos, Faith, Buster Boy and Widow Ollie were not outside to meet us. Very few of our friends came up to see our new Baby Brother Danny Boy. More than a year ago when we came to this church in the church bus, half the congregation would be outside when we arrived and when we departed.

I figured the word spread that we were on welfare and that we bought so many groceries yesterday that we held up a line of grocery carts trying to get to a cash register. When it came to gossip spreading like winds over the spring plowed fields, Ohio was the same as the old country. A copperhead could fang in an Ohio tobacco-seed bed the same as one could in a tobacco-seed bed on Lower Bruin. Some few came up to Poppie and asked him about his hand.

"Dr. Zimmerman says I won't lose it but my hand's not got much feeling in it," was Poppie's answer. "I don't know when I'll be able to use my hand again."

Some woman, whose name I didn't know—but I'd seen her here at church every Sunday—came up and said to Mommie: "I hear you folks are moving to the Stetson Koniker mansion."

She didn't ask Mommie to see her new baby. Mommie walked on up the steps and paid her no mind. Cousins Bos and Faith were in the church house but didn't come around and speak.

When we took the Little Ones to the nursery room, Buster Boy and Widow Ollie were there but didn't speak.

After Sunday school was over our family sat grouped together to hear Reverend Cashew Boggs preach a sermon on The Power of Sin. He made it plain in his sermon how Old Beelzebub, the source of all evil, made evil tongues wag against the people who were trying to live according to The Word.

When the sermon was over and we loaded into the church bus, there were only Uncle Dick and Aunt Susie around to see us off. Jimmie Artner, our church bus driver, was still friendly. First thing he said when he came after us: "Mrs. Perkins, I want to see that wee thing in your arms!" And Mommie smiling, opened the blanket. He bragged, saying he was such a pretty baby. Well, we knew better. Little babies as young as Baby Brother Danny Boy were like little young mice. They looked very much alike.

When we left the church bus, we thanked Jimmie. He backed out of our drive where the daffodils in a double row on either side were blooming.

"Well, Gil, what do you think of the way Bos and Faith acted?" Mommie said. "You noticed their strange actions, didn't you?"

"Yes, you and me just out of the hospital and people seemed cold to us," Poppie said. "Our gettin' into a higher-up world, I believe, is the reason. We won't be poor people any longer. We're getting into big money and easy living. The news is out and I'll bet Bos, Faith and that Buster Boy helped spread it."

"It hurts our kinfolks more than it does strangers to see us get ahead," Mommie said. "As long as we were poor they helped us—we never had better friends. Now when we get to the place we have as much or more than them, they get as cold as ice and won't speak to us in God's House. What kind of religion do they have?"

"One thing for certain," I said as we entered the living room. "I'm getting tired of somebody having to take us every place we go. The next thing I plan to buy is a car to haul our family!"

"How can you, Pedike?" Timmie asked. "And who'll drive it?"

"I'll learn to drive it," I said. "I've got good hands, good eyes, and I'm old enough."

"But the cost," Poppie said.

"Second-hand stationwagon, Poppie," I said. "There's a Freewill Baptist car dealer in Agrillo: Fred Williams. I'm going to him one of these days and talk about a good used stationwagon—owning a second-hand car now isn't anything big. We need one."

54 Not any chores to do now but stove wood to chop—no pigs to feed, no cows to feed or milk to prepare in the cellar—and on Monday morning we got up at five instead of four. Cassie-Belle, Tishie, Timmie and I were at the tobacco bed at six and Al Herbert was there with the mule in harness, and feed for him at noon. Today, I would start doing the work Poppie had done.

"I got here thirty minutes ago and I checked the tobacco-plant bed for snakes," Al said. "It's as clean of snakes as a hound dog's tooth. It's safe for you to pull plants there now!"

"Only ten rows of tobacco set here," Timmie blabbed. "If that snake had not bitten Poppie's hand, we'd have about had both fields set!"

Timmie raised up on his brogan shoe toes, stretched and looked first up the slope above the tobacco bed where ten rows of tobacco had been set. Then he spun around on his toes and looked at the other slope. Poppie had plowed all this land before the copperhead had bitten him.

"This week and next," Timmie said. "We'll have it done!"

"Oh, no," Al Herbert said.

"Wait and see," Timmie told him.

"We've not had the time, and after losing our father I'd about given up the idea of raising this tobacco until you said you could help us," Al said. "Just how much can you help us this spring, summer and fall? One of us will come to get you and bring you home."

"We don't want to try to keep from working, Mr. Herbert," I said to Al. "Trying to keep from working is the hardest work I've ever tried to do."

"You've never before had the experience of wanting to work and couldn't, have you?" he said.

"Yes, I have. Back on Lower Bruin," I told him, "we'd farm our crops, tobacco, corn and truck, and then we'd have extra days when we wanted to work for other people but couldn't get the work."

I didn't tell Al Herbert about our slowing down when we got the commodities and carried them home five miles in coffee sacks like pack mules. I didn't tell him all the story. Now, I wondered if Cousins Bos and Faith would go around telling this. If they did, they'd hurt us more than we were already hurt.

I noticed we'd have many plants to reset in the ten rows Jim and Al Herbert had set. And Timmie discovered some dead plants in the rows.

"We won't lose as many plants as you, either," Timmie said. "Tamp the ground with the ball of your hand until you can't pull the plant up by its leaf!"

"What did you say?" Al Herbert said. "Show me!"

Timmie pulled a plant and set it without water just to show him. No wonder they'd lost so many plants! Our sisters, who talked little, smiled because two men, maybe in their middle forties, didn't know how to set tobacco, grow and care for it. Yet, they were trying to grow tobacco on their farm.

I went ten rows up the hill laying off tobacco rows. Here, I hitched the mule to the laying-off plow. I noticed, too, the rows of tobacco they'd laid off with the mule were not very straight rows. They didn't follow the curves of the slope. But Al and Jim Herbert used bulldozers well. They drove trucks. They farmed bottom land with machinery. They were not mule, hillside-plow and earth men. They'd never farmed like the people had farmed on Lower Bruin.

Al Herbert walked up the slope to see my row. He waited until I returned with another row.

"A good eye and steady hands," he said. "It looks like two tractor plows made them!"

He left me and went down to the tobacco-plant bed. He was doing the same thing his father had done. His father knew us, talked to us, laughed with us. His father was like a grandfather to us. But Al Herbert, as old if not older than Poppie, would never be like a father to us. And we let Al Herbert set the wages he wanted to pay us. He raised our wages to one dollar an hour and would pay us in cash, so we would not have to declare our earnings and, maybe, pay a little tax.

Al Herbert remained until the tobacco plants were pulled, which Timmie carried on a burlap sack fastened at each end with a strap that went over his shoulder. He could drop plants with his left hand from this and he carried a bucket of water in his right hand. He walked between the rows. Cassie-Belle and Tishie each took a row. Timmie poured but little water, for the ground was very moist.

"We never used water," Al Herbert said.

"That's where you missed it," I heard Timmie tell him.

"Well, you children know how to do it," he said, leaving the field.

"Sure we know how to do it," I thought. "We've known how to do this since we were Little Ones. Both boys and girls in our family know how to do it."

We were helping Poppie and Mommie in the fields long before we ever got on commodities. Even when we got on commodities, we worked for people everywhere we could get work if people would pay us in cash. We'd heard our commodities would be taken away if we worked. I remember how Poppie wanted to work in some deep hollow or in the woods where he wouldn't be seen.

At the end of this day I had finished laying off the rows in this field. Cassie-Belle, Tishie and Timmie had climbed up on the slope. Tomorrow, I'd help them pull plants and set. When we were ready to leave at four, Al Herbert came. He was as excited about what we'd done as his father had been this time last year.

This week we finished setting this slope, had replaced the dead plants in the ten rows the Herberts had set, and had done one full day's work on the other slope. I had laid off rows in half of the field.

"I told you we'd do this in two weeks," Timmie said.

Timmie was always proud of his calculations—that is, if we didn't miss one too far. If we did, Timmie never mentioned it.

Al and Jim Herbert got a surprise when we had finished the second field by Friday at four. We were one day ahead of Timmie's prediction. Both came to the field in a little farm truck to see how we were getting along. They'd not visited us this second week.

"You could work for us all the time," Al Herbert said. "But we know Cassie-Belle is going to Ohio State with all her expenses paid. And we know about the new place where you'll move."

"We're going to move Tuesday," Timmie said. "The house will be ready and we'll move in!"

"And farm two acres of tobacco for that Gentleman Farmer," Al said quickly. "And you boys can do this easily. And you'll get half the tobacco crop—about a thousand dollars which you will divide. This will be put in your name and not your father's."

"How did you know all of this?" Timmie asked him.

"I know your father's Uncle Dick," he said. "I know how his mind works. We know he's called the silver-haired, silver-tongued Fox. And he's earned his name. It fits him like a glove fits the hand."

"We know your father is now on welfare with plenty of food stamps," Jim Herbert said. "We know he can't receive other checks he earns by working. In other words—he can't work. But you children can. And we need help so much this summer with strawberries and raspberries soon to be ripe, tobacco to plow and hoe on these slopes also, corn to plow and hoe for the last time in this valley before we sow grass here for pasture land. We need you so much. If you can help us this spring and summer, we'll come and get you, take you home, pay you in cash and we won't talk. Mum will be the word. But I'm telling you, you children are going to grow up and be wage earners and pay taxes. You'll understand some day what a joke this welfare is! It's made liars and cheats of nearly a fourth of this country. To think such a program has been sponsored and condoned by our government. I tell you I'm sick—sick as any man can be—sick enough to vomit when I think of the low down parasites getting a good living from the sweats of wage-earning taxpayers' brows. I had my say. I had to get this off my chest! I'm sorry!"

55 Last night I could hardly sleep for thinking about what Al and Jim Herbert had said about welfare, how part of the hardworking taxpayers were keeping so many who were able bodied and didn't want to work. Work didn't bother me, my brothers, sisters and parents. We liked to work.

But, honest, I was beginning to wonder. I was beginning to think. What was going to happen to us? My mind was troubled. I'd been as hard hit in my thinking as that copperhead hit Poppie in the tobacco bed when he fanged him on the hand. I was troubled in mind and spirit. Now, I knew, Uncle Dick was doing something more for Poppie. And Uncle Dick had the power to do it.

Saturday was a strange day for me. I didn't know that public offices were opened any more on Saturday. But one was. Uncle Dick had finally made arrangements. He said we had to be in a hurry. So, Leonard came with Uncle Dick's car. Uncle Dick was riding in the back seat alone when Leonard drove up. He left Leonard in the car, came in the house. And he said to me: "Pedike, we're on our way to Columbus, Ohio, to the Veterans' Administration. And when we go in you are to be leading your father. See, Pedike, your father is suffering from loss of memory. He's in a bad way. I've got papers from Doc Zimmerman regarding his health. And I know how long, when and where he was in the Army in World War II. That's where a lot of his trouble started. The very thoughts of war made him nervous! So, I'll do the talking. You just lead your father in the V.A. Building when we get to Columbus. I don't want to talk in front of Leonard. I don't pay him as much as he could get on welfare and food stamps. And I want to keep him."

When we walked toward Uncle Dick's car, I was leading Poppie.

"More trouble from the snakebite?" Leonard asked.

"Complications, yes," Uncle Dick said. "And more than that. My nephew is suffering from nervousness he got out of World War II. We're taking him to the Veterans' Administration in Columbus, Ohio!"

From Agrillo to Columbus, a distance of about one hundred miles slightly northwest, we passed over some of the prettiest farming country I'd never seen. It was even prettier than in Landsdowne County. Men were everywhere plowing, disking and planting with tractors. In one vast field I saw six men on tractors.

Uncle Dick knew where the Veterans' Building was.

"I know Columbus as well as I know my ABC's and multiplication tables," Uncle Dick said. "Here is a place I visit often. I have to come to see my friends—to pay visits to 'the boys.'"

When Leonard parked the car, Uncle Dick told him to do what he pleased, for we wouldn't be back until after lunch. And when we left the car, I was leading Poppie. Uncle Dick was beside us smoking a ten-inch cigar. When we went in, Uncle Dick directed us to the head office.

"Always see the top man," Uncle Dick said. "Never fool with the underlings."

"Mr. Carlin, I've called you about my nephew," Uncle Dick said. "Here is Gilbert Perkins and his son Pedike. And here are Dr. Zimmerman's reports!"

"Yes, you told me about his snakebite, too," Mr. Carlin said. Mr. Carlin was a small, well-dressed, pale-faced man with a long sharp nose, who wore glasses and sat behind a big desk. "I see you still are wearing a bandage on that hand."

"Yes," Poppie said.

"I think his hand will be saved but he can't work for a long time to come," Uncle Dick said.

"How many children do you have, Mr. Perkins?"

"Thirteen, I believe," Poppie said. "One, our oldest boy is dead but he's still with us!"

Mr. Carlin looked strangely at Poppie as if he might be off in the head. He stopped to read the letter and report from Dr. Zimmerman.

"Oh, I see, loss of memory," he said. "Can you give me your children's names?"

"No, but I might be able to write them down for you if you'll give me my time and let me think," Poppie said. "I write slow for I'm so nervous! And I don't think fast! Give me my time, will you? Get me paper and pencil!"

Mr. Carlin gave Poppie a pencil and writing pad.

"Let me see, Little Pearse," Poppie said. "He comes first. Dead and buried on Lower Bruin in the old country. Briars grow on his grave. They've called my children briars in the high school—"

Then, Uncle Dick handed Mr. Carlin the clippings from the Landsdowne County News about Cassie-Belle, Tishie and Timmie's grades on the Ohio Scholarship Achievement Tests, while Poppie wrote the names of us children. Poppie fumbled, sighed and rested. He put his elbow on the desk, put his chin in his hand and stared into space. Then he'd scribble another name.

"Some school records for your children, Mr. Perkins," Mr. Carlin said. "What about you, Pedike?"

"I'm average," I said. "I'm like Poppie. I like to work with my hands!"

"Four children in high school this year," Uncle Dick said. "Two in elementary and one in junior high. Four at home and one born just after school was out. This man can't work and he needs help! I thought about calling my personal friend, the Governor of Ohio!"

"What?" Mr. Carlin said.

"I thought about calling the Governor, then I thought it best to go through the regular channel."

"Are you Catholic, Mr. Perkins?" Mr. Carlin asked. "I know this is a personal question."

"No, Freewill Baptist," Poppie said. "But we don't believe in birth control! We follow The Word—marry and replenish the earth!"

"Very religious people," Uncle Dick said. "In the old country, The Word means the word in the Bible!"

"How many names do you have, Mr. Perkins?" Mr. Carlin asked.

"Not all of them yet," he said. "Let me count!"

Poppie counted slowly, calling out the numbers. He'd stop, rest, and count again. He counted to eight.

Now Poppie began writing our names again. And while he thought and wrote Mr. Carlin went over his medical reports again. We didn't finish in the V.A. office until two o'clock.

"There won't be any trouble of doing something for your nephew even if he didn't see any service fighting overseas," Mr. Carlin said. "With his trouble and twelve living children, he needs help! I am convinced of this. My word will go far recommending him a pension."

"As soon as you can get a check through to him, do it," Uncle Dick said.

When we left the office, Poppie thanked Mr. Carlin. I took Poppie by the hand and led him from the office. He'd been about three hours thinking of our names and writing them down. Mr. Carlin had asked Uncle Dick if he could keep the school records of Cassie-Belle, Tishie and Timmie. Uncle Dick let him keep these.

"I've got plenty of copies of the Landsdowne County News with your children's records in school," Uncle Dick said. "I thought these might come in handy. I work in many ways!"

When we got to the car, Leonard was waiting. He'd had his lunch. We hadn't, but we were less than two hours from home. Uncle Dick told Leonard to take us home. And when we got home, Poppie thanked Uncle Dick. I led Poppie in the house. This was the last time I ever had to lead him for loss of memory.

56 Monday the moving van came to haul our belongings to our new home. This time, Uncle Dick didn't bring one of his large trucks with Cousin Bos driving to move us. Uncle Dick, with Leonard driving, followed the moving van. Our moving this time was done in style. There were three men with the van. Cassie-Belle, Tishie, Timmie and I had helped Mommie pack. Really we didn't have many things to pack except clothes. When we'd moved from the old country, Mommie packed one week's supply of commodities. This time she packed as good food as money could buy. We'd got this food with stamps. The give-away program had changed from hand-out commodities in the old country to food stamps in Ohio. It had changed from a few foods to about anything and the best in the store.

"Sil," Uncle Dick told Mommie, "You're going to get a surprise. Part of your furniture is already there! New wallpaper on the rooms is really something! Of course, I've seen the house more than one time. I've been there to see to it. See, Stetson Koniker might be there! And his wife might be with him. I hope she is! I want her to see this family!"

Even on moving day, Mommie had us dress in our good clothes. All of us from Cassie-Belle down to Baby Danny Boy, including Mommie and Poppie, were dressed in Sunday clothes. Uncle Dick was pleased with our looks.

Now, when the loaders loaded the moving van, Timmie and I didn't have to help.

"I'm paying for this," Uncle Dick told Poppie. "So let

them do the work! But I'm going to tell you, if you had all in the new home, plus what you have here, it would take two vans to hold the furniture!"

When the van was ready to go, Uncle Dick said he thought his car was big enough to take us—that is, if six of us held the Babies and Little Ones. There was a back seat and two folding seats in the rear and the big seat up front—we were crowded but we were all in Uncle's Dick's big car.

"First time sixteen people ever rode in this car," Leonard said.

"Drive carefully, Leonard," Uncle Dick warned him. "We have precious cargo here!"

"I always drive carefully," he said.

He quickly caught up with the slow moving van and then followed behind it.

"I'll do without my cigar until we reach your new home," Uncle Dick said. "Cigar smoke might make the children sick. And we don't want a sick family to get out of this car when all of you see for the first time your new rent-free mansion."

We drove five miles to Agrillo. Then we drove five miles on the other side up a green pleasant valley between the Essej Trants and the Stetson Koniker farms, where the State Republican Administration of Ohio had built the broad highway. Here was as pretty a land as I'd seen in Landsdowne County. This valley looked like a park. Then we came to a lane road uphill that was paved and the moving van made a left turn and we followed.

But just at the place where we made a left turn I looked to my right where I saw a little house, really one that looked like many of the homes on Lower Bruin. This was on Essej Trant's farm. I saw an old man sitting out in a chair that was leaned up against the wall by his front door. Since Leonard was driving slowly, I could see the old man looked like he was enjoying the morning sun. He might have been asleep. I couldn't tell. But I knew our mansion was up on this hill not more than a hundred yards away and he'd be our neighbor. After seeing all the other big homes along this valley road, I wondered why there was a shack like this one along the road and who the old man was.

Up this steep hill we followed the creeping moving van to where it stopped. I couldn't believe this house would be our new home. When we passed the big brick home down in the valley, Uncle Dick had said: "The Koniker home." Well, it was a mansion. But I would choose this house, up on this high hill overloking Pleasant Valley below, to the Koniker mansion. Stetson Koniker had two mansions on his farm. No wonder he was called a "gentleman farmer."

Two people walked out of the house—a well-dressed couple. And they walked up to Uncle Dick's car. And when we started getting out there were smiles on their faces.

"I'm Stetson Koniker and this is my wife, Clarissa Jo," he said. "We want to meet the new family coming to our farm, Mr. and Mrs. Perkins! Your Uncle Dick has told us all about you. Yes, he gave us the splendid records of your children in school!"

Mr. Koniker didn't look like a farmer. He was well dressed with a nice suit, collar and tie and a hat. He looked like a banker or businessman in Agrillo. And Mrs. Koniker was a well-dressed woman, with a nice smile and a pleasant voice.

"What a nice-looking family you have," she said to Mommie. "I've never seen nicer-looking children! And so many of them! How happy you and your husband must be with this family!"

Now, all of us started walking across the yard to the big house. When we entered this house, I will never forget.

"Where is mine and Tishie's room?" Cassie-Belle asked.

"You will have separate rooms here if you want them," Clarissa Jo Koniker said. "You'll have plenty of rooms."

Cassie-Belle and Tishie's faces were all smiles. They looked at the wallpaper on the living room. I guess Uncle Dick had told them how Poppie and Mommie loved roses —how they had courted in their youth back on Lower Bruin going to find patches of wild roses. Mommie and Poppie's eyes were moist with tears when they saw this room. Instead of my battery radio there was a television.

"Is it color or black-and-white?" Timmie asked Uncle Dick.

"Color," he replied. "And the best!"

Uncle Dick was now smoking his ten-inch cigar. And the smoke smelled good.

In Poppie's and Mommie's bedroom was a new bed. It was papered in rose wallpaper. I'd never seen anything like this. I wondered if I was asleep and dreaming. I pinched myself to see if I was awake. I was.

"To think this is a rent-free house for us," I thought. "Maybe Poppie is right when he says it pays to be poor, to have a big family and replenish the earth."

I walked with our family and Mr. and Mrs. Stetson Koniker through this house. Cassie-Belle and Tishie each had a room of her own with a new bed, mirror and a chest. And Mr. Koniker pointed out a clothes press in each room for our clothes. In Timmie's room, too, there was a bed, chest and mirror.

"I can't believe it," Timmie said. "I'll be separated from Pedike first time since I can remember!"

And he jumped up and cracked his heels together three times, which made Mr. and Mrs. Koniker turn and watch him in amazement. They didn't know where we had come from and how we had lived. Had I told them—which I wouldn't have—they couldn't and wouldn't have believed it. From a schoolhouse papered with newspapers and pages of free catalogues, to this mansion in just a little over one year!

And now to the dining room and the kitchen. The dining room was big with a large table where we could be seated and not crowded. We'd even have plenty of space for Little Pearse's empty plate. And there were four high chairs in the dining room.

But the kitchen was something else—an electric stove which we didn't know how to use. And there was a large refrigerator to hold our food-stamp steaks and pork. Here was a vacuum cleaner on the floor which we didn't know how to use.

"Is there a telephone in this house?" Timmie asked.

Leave the questions to Timmie.

"To be sure there is," Mr. Koniker said. "Didn't you have one where you lived?"

"We've never had one," Timmie said.

Mommie, with Baby Danny Boy in her arms, made a face at Timmie. Poppie with Little Josh in his arms acted like a man in a dream. Cassie-Belle, Tishie and Maryann were so excited they were beside themselves. They didn't look or act natural. I wondered if they'd ever work in the tobacco and corn fields again for the Herberts.

"Of course, a bathroom is so commonplace," said Clarissa Jo Koniker, "but we want to show you how we've papered, and renovated—"

"A new word," Timmie said excitedly.

He pulled his notebook from his pocket, his pencil from his shirt pocket. "Renovated," he said, "it means 'worked-over,'" and he wrote the word down.

"Don't pay any attention to my brother," I said. "He plans to write a new dictionary some day and title it 'The Timmie Perkins Dictionary.'"

Well, Mr. and Mrs. Koniker laughed.

"After what I've read about him in the clipping from the Landsdowne County News, which your Uncle Dick gave us, he might just do that," Mr. Koniker said. "I wish we had a son like him."

"Too unfortunate not to have children," Mrs. Koniker said. "I wish we could have! Just to look at this fine family. Your parents are lucky!"

This made me think of Uncle Dick and Aunt Susie and Cousin Bos' and Faith's Buster Boy. Maybe Little Mommie and Big Poppie were lucky to have a dozen living children. Everybody had tried to help us. Just about everything had been free. Poppie had never paid taxes in his life. I'd heard him say this many times.

"Bathrooms upstairs and downstairs," Mrs. Koniker said. "We'll look at this one upstairs and then we'll go back to the first floor where we by-passed the bathroom."

When we went into the upstairs bathroom, which was on the floor where Timmie, Cassie-Belle, Tishie and I would be sleeping, we stood in silence. First time in our lives we'd ever had a bathroom. Here it was—a sink and two faucets, one for hot and one for cold water, a commode and a bathtub with curtains.

Koniker took us to the bathroom on the first floor.

"This one is more elaborate," Clarissa Jo Koniker said.

"Another new word," Timmie said, getting his notebook and pencil. " 'Elaborate' which means in my mother tongue, 'much better.' And it really is nicer than the one upstairs!"

Now we walked back to the living room.

"See, there's the telephone over there," Mr. Koniker said. He pointed to it. "Timmie, you asked if there was one in this house. It also has a garage under the house for two cars and a wine cellar!"

"We don't drink," Poppie said. "But this house is great. It's the finest one we will have ever lived in!"

"I hope you enjoy living with us," Clarissa Jo Koniker said to Mommie.

"Oh, I think we will," Mommie said. "But we'll have to get used to this big house and all the conveniences!"

"I'll tell you more about what you are to do," Mr. Koniker said. "I have the best span of mules in Landsdowne County—and the finest herd of white-faced cattle. You won't have much to do but I'll show you later."

Then the Konikers departed.

Uncle Dick went out to tell the movers to start bringing our furniture in. He didn't want the Konikers to see it. Of course, Uncle Dick paid them extra for waiting. They brought our furniture in. Mommie, Cassie-Belle and Tishie showed them which rooms to put it in. Our house plunder looked terrible beside the new furniture which Uncle Dick and Aunt Susie had selected for us. And we had wondered why Uncle Dick and Aunt Susie were not at Cassie-Belle's graduation. And now they were the people helping us. Uncle Dick had even purchased extra copies of the Landsdowne County News, with the articles about us and he was using these to help us.

When the furniture was moved in and after Poppie and Mommie had thanked Uncle Dick over and over for what he'd done, we went about setting up our furniture. Some pieces—the beds—we stored in the attic. Now we began to use our new appliances. Mommie stored her perishables in the refrigerator. Then she discovered a deep freezer in our basement. Uncle Dick hadn't told us about this. I knew I would have to have a car.

57 Now in our mansion, we had to get used to this new way of life. We had to get used to the bathrooms. We had to learn how to use the telephone—how to dial it for local numbers. We would never dial long distance—whom did we know to call?

We had to learn how to use the refrigerator and the deep freezer. If one had never had these appliances for better and easier living, one had to learn. Now fooling with the gadgets on television, it didn't take long to learn. Timmie figured this out before any of us. And when we gathered in our new living room on the first evening in our new home, Timmie got our first programs—and people came into our living room on the TV screen we'd never seen before. And around the dial we could get six stations. We could see the color of people's faces and their clothes. This was the first time we had seen color television. All the programs we had ever seen had been black-and-white films shown at school. But Poppie and Mommie had never seen even these. This was their first time seeing television. We had moved my old battery-set radio here. But we no longer needed it. If we had radio here, it wouldn't be a battery set, for we had electricity. We didn't need lamps now. Pull a switch and the lights were on.

I wondered what Mommie would do with her old kerosene lamps. And here we no longer needed an ax to cut wood. Here we no longer needed our washtubs in which we had bathed so many times. We no longer needed our smoothing irons we had heated on the stove to iron and press clothes. Our way of life had really changed. We no longer needed our brooms for sweeping. We no longer needed our old dust mops. We now had an electric sweeper. Our new appliances were all electric. To think in our rent-free home, our rich and great Uncle Sam had provided us with twenty-seven dollars a month to pay our electric bill.

"It pays to be poor and to have kinsmen like Uncle Dick," Poppie said. "It pays, maybe, to work the country instead of working for the country. This is what Uncle Dick once said. And I believe him now. Look what has happened to us!"

"But all of these new pieces of household plunder cost money," Mommie said. "We've got to pay for these!"

"But I think we'll have plenty of free money, Sil, to pay for these," Poppie said. "Uncle Dick won't be wrong!"

After a late evening at the color television, we went to sleep in our new beds. I went to sleep dreaming I was awake and all of this was a dream.

58 Tuesday morning Mr. Koniker drove up to our house. He asked Poppie, Timmie and me to go with him to show us the barn, the mules, harness and plow. He wanted to show us his wagons and tools. Well, the barn on this farm was prettier than many houses. It was a white barn with a red roof.

"I keep ninety to one hundred white faces in here during the winter," Mr. Koniker said. "I buy my feed for these cattle, store hay in the barn loft, keep feed in the bins."

Well, this was something to see.

"Now I want to show you my span of bay Tennessee mules," he said. "Four years old! They're spirited, blocky Tennessee mules! See the harness with red tassels on the bridles here in the barn. It's the best money can buy."

Poppie, Timmie and I had never seen such a decorative harness for mules before.

Then Mr. Koniker took us to his tool shed where he kept plows and farming tools. Here I discovered everything Timmie and I would need.

"I believe in the old-fashioned way of farming," Mr. Koniker said.

"This is good," Poppie said. "We're used to this more than the farm machinery! We can't drive a truck, automobile or a tractor!"

"I know that," Mr. Koniker said. "And this pleases me. You're earth people! There are very few earth people left. Your Uncle Dick has explained all this to me! Now, I want to show you where the tobacco field is that I want plowed, harrowed, laid off and set in tobacco. The plant bed is overflowing with plants that need to be set. And I want to take you to the mule pasture and show you my mules, Doc and Bess."

"Funny about a mare mule," Poppie said. "She can't breed!"

"No, she's a hybrid," Mr. Koniker said. "A jack, male mule, has to be bred to a mare—a female horse—to beget a mule."

Now we came to the tobacco plant bed. Here was as fine tobacco plants as I'd ever seen. And these plants needed to be pulled and set. Next he showed us the two-acre tobacco field. I looked it over. It would take me two days to plow and harrow this field.

Next we went to the mule pasture.

"See, I have two pastures," Mr. Koniker said. "Thirty acres for my mules but four hundred acres for my hundred head of white-faced cattle."

When we walked to the mule pasture and Doc and Bess saw Mr. Koniker, they came walking up to him. They stood for him to rub their noses. Then Timmie, Poppie and I rubbed their noses. We liked mules. And here were pet mules.

"In the morning, Mr. Koniker, we will begin work," I said. "At the end of this week this tobacco patch will be plowed, harrowed, laid off and set!"

"What?" he said.

"If we don't have rain," I said, "this will be done!"

"Yes, we know how to raise terbacker," Poppie said.

"Your Uncle Dick told me you did," Mr. Koniker said.

Now we had seen and we knew what to do.

Tuesday morning Timmie and I went to the mule pasture, got Doc and Bess and hitched them to a hillside turning plow. The land I was to plow had been plowed many times. And it was a very gentle slope.

This was real easy plowing. And Doc and Bess must have regarded pulling this plow along as play. I know guiding the plow and following them was play for me.

Starting early in the morning, in old ground with a brick-stepping span of mules and a turning plow, a man should plow two acres of ground in a day. Timmie stood by watching me. Then he wanted to take the team over and plow a few rounds. I let him, because on this day Timmie didn't have much to do.

This was the day when most of the work would be done by Mommie and my sisters in the house. They had much figuring to do on how to use the new electrical appliances and so many gadgets and switches on the electric stove. But the big thing was to follow instructions on a coffee percolator. There were four parts but Cassie-Belle worked it out. No more boiled coffee in a pot on a wood stove. At the breakfast table Poppie and Mommie both said they liked their coffee percolated better than boiled. They thought the taste was better and it was not as strong. I didn't know, for I didn't drink coffee, though now with this new-fangled percolator and Mommie's and Poppie's bragging on it, I might take to it.

My first day's work on the Stetson Koniker farm with Doc and Bess, I easily plowed the two-acre tobacco base. And before noon, Wednesday, I had harrowed it with one of the most old-fashioned harrows I'd ever seen—one I could use to help the mules turn at the corners of the field. It was very strange. The Konikers were rich people. They could own tractors and trucks. But there wasn't a truck or a tractor on the place. Not any farm machinery except mule-drawn plows, a jolt wagon, express wagon—even a buggy and a hug-me-tight. There was a mule-drawn mowing machine, hay rake, cultivator, corn planter, fertilizer drill and seed drill.

While I was harrowing the ground, Timmie, who didn't have anything to do, went out exploring the Koniker farm. And while I harrowed ground, a tame crow flew in and alighted on Bess' shoulder. I wondered if he didn't belong to the Konikers. Later he flew down from Bess' shoulder and followed the harrow. I'd never had a crow this close to me before. I liked to watch him picking up cutworms, redworms and grubworms. I was amazed how much the craw of a crow could hold.

Just as I finished harrowing the two acres, Timmie came running stiff legged down the slope.

"I found it, Pedike," he said.

"Found what?"

"The Koniker's dump place on their farm," he said excitedly. "That man who used to live here was right. You go take a look at the whiskey bottles and beer cans. They drink scotch whiskey: White Label, Red Label and Black Label. Gee, how Presbyterians drink! And Mrs. Koniker sings in the Presbyterian choir in Agrillo every Sunday morning!"

"Timmie, listen," I said. "You stay away from their garbage dump; you quite spying, going there, counting bottles and cans! They have no children. If they drink, it's their business! Look what a house they're furnishing us! We're living in a rent-free mansion. We've never had it so good! And look how little we have to do here to get it."

"But, Pedike, I like to know about people," Timmie said. "Remember, I heard Dr. Zimmerman and Uncle Dick talking about the bearded fake farmer who used to live here. Uncle Dick said he found the garbage dump and counted the Koniker's whiskey bottles. I never forgot that. I just wanted to see if it was true."

"Timmie, talk about something else," I told him.

"All right, all right," Timmie said, changing the subject. "Poppie will be in the money and you and I will be in the money—Cassie-Belle and Tishie can be too if they want to work," Timmie said. "And I think they want to work and make big farm wages while they can. Herberts won't farm that valley next year. We know they plan to sow that land in grass for pasture. Yes, make cash wages, no records and no taxes!"

On Wednesday afternoon, Poppie went with us to the tobacco-plant bed. He used a tobacco stick with his good right hand, for his left hand was still bandaged. He searched the tobacco plants for snakes before he would let us pull the plants.

And while I laid off plant rows with Doc hitched to a single shovel plow, Poppie helped Tishie, Cassie-Belle and Timmie pull plants. I knew Poppie, with one good hand, would be restless no matter if he did live in a mansion. He could take only a little of the confinement of a house.

He had to be out with animals, mules, plows, hoes and axes.

I wondered what Poppie would do on this farm. All farming tools were mule-drawn. This was an ideal place for Poppie. Stetson Koniker's old-fashioned way of farming—the way Poppie knew back on Lower Bruin—just suited Poppie. He could handle all the mule-drawn tools on this farm. But Mr. Koniker just had a little farming done. He really didn't have enough for Poppie and his family. And now we didn't have to farm or to work. Everything was free for us—just about everything.

With Poppie's helping us pull plants, with Cassie-Belle's and Tishie's helping us set the ground I'd plowed, harrowed and laid off in rows, we finished setting the plants late Thursday evening. We had two work days left, Friday and Saturday of this week. Yes, Timmie and I had our tobacco set in the ground. This would be the first we had ever grown on the shares. Poppie couldn't have checks in his name other than those that came to him tax free.

When we returned to the house, Mommie said: "Gil, we got our first phone call. And it was from Cousin Faith! It's a sight what she said to me about us over the phone!"

"What's a matter with her?" Poppie said.

"She said we were low on the ground as a snake's belly and a lot of other things like that. Finally, I hung up the phone. I wouldn't listen to her!"

"Well, we could tell something has been wrong with them at church," Poppie said. "That's no way to act in the Lord's House! And they've never come around to speak to us!"

"Remember how Cousin Bos bragged to us when he came in Uncle Dick's truck to move us to Ohio," I said. "I never heard such bragging! So, maybe, they're just jealous of us! We live in a nicer house now! And we can buy T-bone steaks, broasted chickens, bacon—all kinds of food with stamps! We don't have to raise beef cattle, keep hogs and cows! Not any more!"

"Never call Bos and Faith until they cool down and speak to us at church," Poppie said.

"Cassie-Belle, you and Tishie want to work tomorrow?" Timmie asked.

"Why do you think we helped you set your tobacco here?" Cassie-Belle asked. "Sure, we want that cash money. Money speaks a wonderful language. The best American tongue is spoken by the dollar."

"I'll be putting in the first phone call from this house," Timmie said. "I want to call Al Herbert and see if he needs four work hands tomorrow!"

"Timmie do you know how to use the phone?" Poppie asked him.

"If I don't, I can soon learn," Timmie replied. "This telephone directory will tell you!"

"For a local call," Timmie read in the directory, "dial the first number of the first three digits. Then, dial the last four. Now, here I go!"

Timmie dialed the five digits.

"Mr. Herbert, this is Timmie Perkins," Timmie said. "We've got our tobacco ground plowed, harrowed and set here and we've got tomorrow and Saturday if you need us!"

We were silent while Timmie made the phone call.

"You want our sisters too and you say you could use ten if you had them, you're so far behind? Gee-whilligens! Be here for four at fifteen until six—and save the rest of that work you have for six more. Save it for us! We can do it. . . . Thank you, Mr. Herbert, we'll be ready!"

Timmie hung up the telephone receiver. "Forty dollars a day," His eyes sparkled. He was excited. "Poppie, you're not going to get all the money! Forty dollars and six days a week: two hundred forty dollars! Where'll you put it, Mommie?"

"Never mind, Timmie, I'll find a place," she said.

Now, Timmie and I took baths in our bathroom upstairs. Think of this! We stood in the tub under the shower together. Cassie-Belle and Tishie went to their rooms to bathe and change clothes for supper. All Poppie had to do was wash and dry his hands in the wash basin! What a handy home this was. What a mansion this was to live in.

Mommie and Maryann prepared our supper out of as good a food as food stamps could buy. We didn't have Danish ham, but we had good old Ohio ham. Talk about food, we were having it now. And since we no longer had wood to cut, pigs to feed, cows to feed and milk, and milk to strain and put in vessels Mommie had prepared, we had plenty of time after we had eaten to go to our new, big, spacious living room and turn on our color television. Every change we had ever made from Lower Bruin to the Josh Herbert farm—and now to the Stetson Koniker farm—we had fallen into a plan of living and we had adjusted well. Right now, we were having our biggest adjustment to make. For we were rising in our Ohio world.

59 When Al Herbert came in his farm truck, we were dressed in our work clothes waiting for him.

"It's some house," he said as we walked up to the truck. "You know, I admire you young people who will get out, hoe and plow and live in a house like this. Many young folks, especially girls, would be too stuck-up to do this. I hate to see this country lose its finest youth!"

Cassie-Belle and Tishie got up on the truck seat with Al Herbert, and Timmie and I climbed in back. We stood up and held to the cab. We looked at the Stetson Koniker mansion. We looked up the valley at the Essej Trants home. Had it not been for trees, we could have looked farther up the valley where we could have seen the Bos and Faith Auxier home. They were about as high on a hill as we were. If it were not for a high cone-shaped hill between our hill-top and theirs, we could look across the two miles distance at each other's homes.

When we arrived in this valley Timmie and I knew so well, for we had worked over every foot of it, Jim Herbert was there with the mule and double-shovel plow for me. I was to plow twice in each tobacco balk, and since a double shovel has two plows on it that make four furrows, this made it easier and faster for Cassie-Belle, who took the bottom row, Tishie, the second row and Timmie, the third row. In this valley where the tobacco had not had a plow stuck in a balk, and where the corn was high enough to cultivate, not one thing had been done since we had been gone. No wonder Al Herbert had told Timmie he could use ten work hands—another mule and plow, too.

"Here it is," Al Herbert said. "How much of it can you do besides what you have to do on the Koniker farm?"

"I think we can save it," Timmie said.

"You wouldn't consider working on Sunday again, would you?" Al asked us.

"I would, but Poppie and Mommie have to decide this," Timmie said. "I'd rather be here working than go to the Freewill Baptist Church. Cousins Bos and Faith won't even speak to us since Poppie had to go on welfare!"

"Is that so?" Jim Herbert said.

"Timmie, Poppie's not here and let me warn you now to stop talking about our family troubles!" I said.

Then I turned to Jim Herbert. "We'll let you know tomorrow whether we can work Sunday or not!"

So, when I began plowing tobacco, the Herberts got in the truck and left us.

"Maybe we can save them," Timmie said. "I like to make money while I'm doing it!"

After this ground had been plowed and farmed last year it was much easier to plow and hoe this second summer. All day I plowed while Cassie-Belle, Tishie and Timmie hoed. At four, after ten hours, we were tired but we had really made a showing.

Saturday I told Al Herbert we'd work on Sunday and all the next week. And I told him maybe we'd work the following Sunday and week. His father had been so good to us when we needed him we couldn't turn them down now. Cassie-Belle, Tishie and I agreed we'd rather work in the fields and stay away from church where we had kinfolks in the congregation who wouldn't speak to us and others among friends we had made there that were cool to us since we'd gone on welfare and had moved to Stetson Koniker's mansion.

Yes, we worked Sunday while Jimmie Artner came with the church bus and took the rest of the family to church. Again Cousin Bos, Faith, Buster Boy and his widow Ollie avoided Poppie and Mommie. Of course, they would avoid them after Cousin Faith had slurred Little Mommie over the telephone. Only Uncle Dick and Aunt Susie asked about us. Poppie told him the Herberts had their ox in the ditch and we were trying to help them get him out. Poppie said Uncle Dick and Aunt Susie were well pleased that we would work on Sunday to help the sons of Josh Herbert—a man who had helped us.

"It shows great appreciation and loyalty," Uncle Dick told Poppie and Mommie.

Since we got home at four-fifteen, I hitched up Doc and plowed evenings on our tobacco. Although tired, Cassie-Belle, Tishie and Maryann helped us. If Maryann and Poppie stayed with the Babies, Mommie would come out and hoe a couple of rows for us.

"I like to get hold of a hoe again," she said. "It's a break away from the children and the house."

So while we worked for the Herberts, with all the help from home, Timmie and I were getting our tobacco worked soon after we'd set it.

60 On Saturday while we were working, two checks came for Poppie. One was his relief check of three hundred forty-four dollars. And his Veteran's Pension check came for two hundred twenty-two dollars.

"Biggest checks I ever got in my life," Poppie said. "Thanks to our Uncle Dick."

Sunday the Herbert brothers were in the field at quitting time. We had each worked ten days. And each of us received a hundred-dollar bill. These were the first hundred-dollar bills we'd ever seen.

When we got home we showed these bills to Poppie and Mommie.

"Money is really rolling in here," Mommie said.

"Poppie's got five hundred sixty-six and we've got four hundred," Timmie said. "Nine hundred sixty-six dollars in two days!"

"No taxes on our money, either," Timmie said.

One month, if we got every day's work, our cash take-home pay was nine hundred sixty dollars. We made nearly as much, the four of us, working six days a week, ten hours a day, as Poppie, who was now hiding out when he counted the cattle. Poppie thought if anybody—especially Cousin Bos and Faith—caught him counting cattle or salting them, they might turn Poppie in to "the authorities" and he'd lose his checks and food stamps.

But Poppie was a problem. When he saw us working he wanted to be with us. After Dr. Zimmerman took the bandage off Poppie's hand, he had Poppie go around carrying his hand in a sling. But when Poppie went to the barn and got inside, he took his snakebite hand out of the sling and he could handle fifty- and twenty-five-pound salt blocks as well as I could. Mr. Koniker had stakes all over the pasture and we set the hole in each salt block down onto a stake. When I drove Doc and Bess hitched to the express wagon down a winding wagon road into the valley below —where hills closed in and people couldn't see—Poppie took a sledge hammer and drove stakes, replacing the old ones. He used both hands. He was his old self. And it was harder on him now trying to keep from work than it was when he worked. But if he was to remain a man in the money, he could not receive a taxable check and he could not be seen working. And Poppie was well aware of this. Uncle Dick had warned him many times. Poppie wasn't permitted to work and certainly not to earn money if he wanted to keep his welfare.

When once-poor people move into a mansion with all modern conveniences and with luxuries yet to come, and with the money to buy them—over fifteen hundred per month when we worked—well, when this kind of money comes in, a family changes. From being poor to being rich, or to thinking it's rich, a family changes. From what you can do for your community, county, state and country to what you can do them for, makes a lot of difference.

One of the changes in our home was Mommie and Poppie no longer set a plate for Little Pearse at our table—a practice they had had back as far as I could remember.

"I wish Little Pearse could have lived so he could have enjoyed this good life," Poppie said one evening at the supper table.

There was silence around our table. I thought: "Brother Pearse is gone. In the years to come, like so many others sleeping in country cemeteries such as the Perkins Family Cemetery on Lower Bruin, who will remember them when their ancestors scatter over Ohio—over the United States and to all parts of the world? Ours is not ancestor worship."

With plenty of money coming into our home we did not live as strict with The Word as we had when we needed something to lean on. Instead of leaning on Faith in The

Word, we had shifted to leaning on money. We could have and hold money or we could spend it. Money, we had learned, had power. Now we had money and we needed more of life's luxuries that our neighbors possessed.

61 Since Cousin Bos and Faith never visited us or even spoke to us at church, Cousin Bos never came with the red truck any more to help us. But we didn't need him now. Uncle Dick took Mommie, Cassie-Belle and Tishie on Saturdays after five to Cantwell's Super Market to fill her grocery list and to add other goodies so they could spend the food stamps. And Mommie said the clerks were nicer than ever to us since we were spending over twice as much for food now as we did when we lived on Josh Herbert's farm and bought groceries with cash. She said they really did business on "Food Stamp Day."

Poppie said Agrillo didn't have a place to park a car on this day. He said all on food stamps couldn't be people born South of the Border—plenty of them had to be born in Ohio.

One evening at seven-thirty, Uncle Dick and Aunt Susie paid us an unexpected visit. We'd eaten our evening meal and were out in chairs in front of our color TV. We were like a class in school and up in front of us was our teacher, our entertainer—the TV set.

"Uncle Dick, come and take my big rocker," Poppie said. "Pedike, get Aunt Susie a more comfortable chair."

"How does it feel to be in the money, to live in a mansion, have all you can eat and all the comforts of a real home?" Uncle Dick asked.

"We can't believe it yet," Mommie said. "Not with all this money coming in."

"Gil, when you get your checks cashed take them to

two different banks in Agrillo," Uncle Dick told him. "You're getting too much to cash at one bank. I'll take you around to show you how to do it. Remember to cash the same check at the same bank every time!"

"I've got to pay for all the new things in this house," Poppie said. "Then, Uncle Dick, I don't know what I'm going to do with all this money!"

"It pays to be poor, to have a big family, and a saphead uncle like Uncle Sam!" Uncle Dick said. "Old Uncle Sam is very old and he's what I'd call the soft touch. Yes, the real soft touch!"

"But is all this we're doing all right, Uncle Dick?" Poppie asked. "We're really getting more than food stamps and money. We are getting free dental work. We get free medicine. Free hospital. Our children get free lunches this year at school!"

"And free breakfasts this year, if the family is on welfare —and if they're from minority groups," Cassie-Belle said. "We are from the Briars. This is a minority group. I've been reading up on all this stuff. I thought I was something special to go to Ohio State with all my expenses paid, plus an allowance for clothes, plus other benefits and an allowance of fifty dollars a month spending money. But just about anybody can get a free education. There are different levels!"

"Is there one for Pedike?" Timmie asked.

"There certainly is," Cassie-Belle replied. "If he wants to go to college!"

"I want a job with a good company where I can work up," I said. "I don't want to go to college. I want to work with my hands."

"See, Gil, you and Sil," Uncle Dick said, "with a big family you are most fortunate. Your Aunt Susie and Uncle Dick, who are without children, we're taxed to death for all this nonsense that makes hoodlums out of many of the young. I feel like you're getting some of the tax money we're paying. So don't you feel you're stealing all you're getting. Never feel you're not deserving. You are. I say for you to get more. I say for you to get everything you can get. I want you to ride all this stuff into the ground.

Go into Agrillo and see the people—believe me, we know them—and what they've got! They drive their big cars into town, get their food stamps and go home loaded. In this country there's no discipline and no foundation all the way down the line."

"Uncle Dick, I had a dream when we lived on the Herbert place," I said. "I wanted a radio. Cousin Bos helped me get it. Since there was no electricity in our house, I got a battery set. It was great to all of us! It was so great, I'm keeping it upstairs in my room. Now, I have another dream. I want to save what I'm making this summer—maybe Timmie and Tishie will help me if it takes more than I have —to buy a good used stationwagon and learn to drive it so I can take our family to church, to Agrillo and other places!"

"What a noble idea you have, my Grandnephew," Uncle Dick said. "Since you don't know much about used cars— but I know the people who have the cars—I'll see you get the best for the least money. Let me know when you're ready. And I'll have Leonard teach you to drive so you'll pass a driver's test and get your license. You're over sixteen?"

"Yes, of course," I said.

"Yes, at this big home and for this family a stationwagon is the right car," Uncle Dick said.

"But Uncle Dick, after I pay my bills what am I going to do with all this money?" Poppie said. "Everything is free. And I can't pay taxes even if I'd want to!"

"We'll work out things as we come to them," Uncle Dick said. He got up from his chair and lighted the cigar he'd been holding in his mouth. "Susie and I must be on our way and let you get back to your programs. Enjoy yourselves while you can and there is time. Enjoy our Uncle Sam's gifts and his benefits."

62 One afternoon just about suppertime Cousins Bos and Faith pulled up our hill lane road, turned the truck back toward home. Bos came to a stop and blew the horn. Poppie opened the door and went out and Mommie followed him. Of course, Timmie had to rush out with Cassie-Belle, Tishie and me behind.

"You really do live in a mansion up here, don't you?" Cousin Faith said. "Since I didn't want to make a scene at church and since I couldn't talk to my kinfolks over the telephone, since, Sil, you hung up on me, I asked Bos to drive up here. I just want to tell you that you've ruined our name coming over here and getting on welfare and food stamps!"

"Now if you've come for a quarrel, Faith, you and Bos, just drive on toward home," Poppie said in his slow, soft voice. "We don't want to quarrel with you, for you helped us when we couldn't help ourselves. We remember and appreciate it!"

"But you don't need help now," Cousin Faith said. She opened the truck door where she could see Poppie and Mommie better. Cousin Bos sat there with a chew of tobacco in his mouth, with the window down, spitting amber spittle into the road. He wasn't saying anything. Cousin Faith was doing the talking. "You're sure gettin' above your raisin' on all this free stuff!" Cousin Faith was mad. "People, before I'd lose my pride and take that stuff, I'd put a pistol to my temple and pull the trigger!"

"Look out, Mommie," Timmie said. "Cousin Faith has

her big pocketbook in there beside her. She has the one in which she carried a sawed-off iron pipe."

"All right, what about your Buster Boy?" Mommie asked. "Why hasn't he married Widow Ollie Mahew? Because Buster Boy is working for the State and Widow Ollie is on welfare and stamps!"

"Not so!" Cousin Faith said. "And if you repeat that, I'm coming out of this truck to get you!"

"You won't get far, Cousin Faith," Cassie-Belle said. "We live here. This is our new home!"

"I'll say this before we leave," Cousin Faith said. "The only people who are lower are the men who have big families, who divorce their wives so they can get welfare and commodities down there and come up here and make big money—and then go back home to their divorced wives and beget a youngin every year! Don't you beget a youngin a year? Come on, Bos, let's get out of this den of iniquity!"

"Begone and stay begone," Poppie said as Cousin Bos gunned the red truck. "And don't ever come back!"

"They're jealous, Mommie," Cassie-Belle said. "We're getting up higher in our Ohio world than they are!"

"I know but I'm so nervous I'm shaking all over," Mommie said. "I could tell at church our cousins had changed!"

"Gee-whilligens, what if they knew how much money Poppie was getting now," Timmie said. "How much we were getting paid cash. And no taxes! They would blow up!"

"Don't you ever tell anything, Timmie," Mommie said. "They'd report us!"

"The trouble with Bos, Faith and Buster Boy is they don't have an Uncle Dick Perkins," Poppie said.

We went back into the house to eat our evening meal. We were all shook up. Cousin Faith and Bos had ruined our evening meal when we had pork chops and instant mashed potatoes for our main course and a lot of other goodies on our big table. We hadn't really quieted down when we went to our living room to watch one of our favorite TV programs. Think of our kinfolks coming up in our own driveway and talking to us like this!

63 In early August when Timmie, Cassie-Belle, Tishie, and I were going over our white burley tobacco for the last time, Mr. and Mrs. Stetson Koniker came walking up. Here we were, Cassie-Belle and Tishie in broad-brimmed straw hats, Timmie and I bareheaded and sun tanned, pulling last suckers and worms from the tobacco. Of course, they'd visited us, but only briefly, several times before. And several times Mr. Koniker came up and Poppie harnessed and hitched the mules to the wagon, the red tassels on their harness floating on the wind, and they had ridden over the farm together looking at the grass, salt blocks and white-faced cattle.

This was the first time Mr. and Mrs. Koniker had ever seen the four of us working together in a tobacco patch. And the white burley was over our heads—with leaves a foot broad.

"What a wonderful scene to see you here working, brothers and sisters," Clarissa Jo Koniker said.

"And the best tobacco we've ever had grown on this farm," Stetson Koniker said. "It's rare when a young woman who'll be going to Ohio State next month will get out and work like this!"

"Stet, the camera is in the car," Mrs. Koniker said. "Go back and get it. Let's get a picture. We'll not find another picture on our farm like this one!"

"We're so glad to have a nice big family on this farm," Mrs. Koniker said while her husband went to get the camera. "You're always so clean. And since Stet and I were only children in our families and since we have no children of our own, we're fascinated by big families!"

I knew Timmie was thinking about something. He was thinking about the garbage dump with bottle and cans. But I thought Mrs. Koniker was such a pretty woman with a soft, nice voice and Cassie-Belle thought she had such a pretty name, Clarissa Jo.

"Stand right where you are and just the way you are," said Mr. Koniker. "I want a picture of you four!"

He took a picture of us. Then he asked for us to stand where we were for another picture and still another. Taking pictures on his farm of his mules, wagons, cattle, houses, barn, salt blocks, was part of his hobby and his recreation. Now, he took pictures of the tobacco patch from both sides and both ends. He had us stand where the tobacco was over our heads and each hold a hand up through the tobacco leaves like people going down in deep water, holding up a hand.

The Konikers didn't try to make their farm make a profit like the Herberts. They wanted to keep their farm and let it lose some money for them. Uncle Dick had explained this to us. How they didn't have children and if he made seventy-five or a hundred thousand year, over half of it went for taxes. Maybe he was like Uncle Dick, too, trying to help poor people like we had been. Maybe he didn't know what Poppie was getting now on welfare, stamps and other special benefits. "Benefits" had become a familiar word in our vocabulary—all the way down to Maryann. And it was a most important word, too, in our every-day conversation. There were the words "benefits," and "special benefits."

64 When Leonard chauffeured Uncle Dick over home on an evening in early August, Uncle Dick brought Leonard in with him this time. We were getting ready to watch a TV program, all except Cassie-Belle who was in her room reviewing her last year's textbooks and preparing for Ohio State University. Mommie and Maryann were out putting the Little Ones to bed. The Babies were asleep.

"Since the Little Ones and the Babies aren't in this room, I'll light my cigar," Uncle Dick said.

Uncle Dick was at home in our house. We had more big comfortable chairs in our living room now, so he sat down in one.

Leonard was a little shy to come into a home like ours. I don't know why but he chose one of the smaller chairs. Maybe he felt inferior.

"What's on your mind, Uncle Dick?" Poppie asked him slowly with a smile on his round-as-a-plate face.

"I've come to tell Pedike I've found a good used stationwagon for him for seven hundred dollars," Uncle Dick said. "I know the careful drivers who turned it in! It's a real good buy. You can't beat it. Have you got the cash, Pedike?"

"Yes, I have," I said.

"Are you working tomorrow?" Uncle Dick asked.

"Yes, but I'll take off," I said.

I wanted that stationwagon. I knew Uncle Dick had found a bargain. I'd certainly take his word. And now was my time to get it.

"And I've the real driver in this room, Leonard Williams, to teach you how to drive," Uncle Dick said. "I can send him over any time during the day you want him!"

"Send him over at four thirty," I said. "We've got more work to help the Herberts before school begins. It's money I earned working for them I'm spending for this car."

"You have a lot of roads on Stet Koniker's farm here, don't you?" Uncle Dick asked. "Farm roads where you use muleteam and wagon?"

"Yes, we do," Poppie replied.

"All right, we'll be here at eight in the morning," Uncle Dick said. "We'll have the stationwagon here at nine! In the afternoon, Leonard will be here—say two o'clock—and give you your first lesson."

"It's all very simple," Leonard said. "Not anything hard about it. You'll soon know how to drive and pass your driver's test! First we'll practice on these farm roads. Then we'll drive on the highway. Then, we'll drive in Agrillo and get used to the stop lights!"

The next morning, Cassie-Belle, Tishie and Timmie went to work with Al Herbert. I stayed home and waited for Uncle Dick to help me get what I thought we now needed most—a car—a way of travel for our family.

At eight Uncle Dick came with Leonard driving. Uncle Dick rode in the back seat where he said he could stretch his long legs better. I had cash money to pay for the car in an envelope.

Leonard drove us to Agrillo and to Vaughn's Used Car Lot. When we drove in, a man came from a small building on the lot.

"All right, Mr. Perkins, we've lubricated the wagon, filled it with gas and it's ready to go," he said.

"Sam, this young man, Pedike Perkins, will pay you with cash he's earned hoeing and plowing corn and tobacco," Uncle Dick said. "Remember your guarantee on this car. He has the cash to pay you."

"It's a great buy, Mr. Perkins," Sam Vaugh said. "You've befriended me and my father. You're the only man I'd let have this stationwagon for seven hundred."

"Now, paying you in cash, I'd like for you to follow us with the stationwagon. Leonard and I can drive you back to town. I don't like to drive and my grandnephew can't drive."

"All right, Mr. Perkins."

I went with Sam Vaugh to the stationwagon. What a pretty car it was all shined up and waiting to be driven! It looked larger than Uncle Dick's car. Now, I paid Mr. Vaughn the cash. He counted the fifty- and twenty-dollar bills.

"Okay—correct," he said. "Say, it's seldom ever we're paid cash for a car!"

"Uncle Dick, would you mind if I rode back with Mr. Vaughn?" I said.

"Not at all," he told me.

Then I got into my car, front seat of course, to watch Sam Vaughn's hands and feet and to get the feelings of the first car I owned and the first one I would be driving.

When we got home and parked the stationwagon on the end of the drive, Poppie and Mommie came out to take a look. I thought this stationwagon belonged to this big house.

"What a pretty car," Poppie said with a smile. "Pedike, you earned the money that bought it with plow and hoe."

"This is what you and Sil need here," Uncle Dick said to Poppie and Mommie.

Now Sam Vaughn got in Uncle Dick's car for Leonard to drive him back to Agrillo. And Poppie, Mommie and I stood looking at the stationwagon in silence. This was the first car we had ever owned. It was hard for me to believe less than a year and a half ago we were living on Lower Bruin in an old schoolhouse. Who, I wondered, had ever come up in the world faster than we? Part of this we had worked for—as I'd worked for this car. Most of what we were getting now was given to us! And we would have more special benefits coming when Landsdowne Central High School began next month.

In the afternoon at two, Leonard was back and since Uncle Dick didn't come with him, he drove over in a pick-up truck. And when he came I got in the stationwagon, under the wheel and he beside me, and he showed me how to start the car. Since it was automatic shift he showed me how to push the lever into drive or park or reverse. That was all there was to it.

So I started the engine, took off the brake, put it in drive, stepped on the gas and away we went. Leonard was close beside me so if I made a mistake, he could correct me. I felt power at my fingertips. To be behind the wheel and drive a car of my own was a great sensation. No wonder this was a world on wheels instead of the mule-and-plow and horse-and-buggy age. My family was still in the horse-and-buggy age but we were getting ready to leave it—all but Poppie. He'd never learn to drive a car. He'd be afraid to try.

Out in a pasture field I practiced stopping, putting the car in reverse and backing. All of this was so wonderful and so beautiful, I knew now why high school boys from average to well-to-do families owned their own cars and liked to drive them.

Leonard stayed with me out on the farm roads until it was time for Cassie-Belle, Tishie and Timmie to be home. When we drove toward the house, I blew the horn. They came running out of the house. Poppie and Mommie were with them. I drove up in the car and stopped and they gathered around. I know this wouldn't have been anything to another family but it meant a lot to people who had bummed rides and carried loads on their backs. Here I parked the car and Leonard got in Uncle Dick's pick-up truck and went home.

65 After Leonard had taught me to drive the stationwagon and I had passed my driver's test, I had to have the car insured. And insurance cost me almost a fortune because of my age. I had to pay two hundred forty dollars a year!

"I don't know what's going to happen to our family," Poppie said. "It might get out of control with all this money and with this living high on the hog. Maybe we'd have better not come to Ohio."

"I'll take Ohio," I said. "I'd take anything before I'd ever go back to Lower Bruin."

"Amen," Cassie-Belle said.

Timmie and Tishie agreed with me, too.

"You would rather work on Sunday than to go hear Brother Cashew Boggs preach The Word at the Agrillo Freewill Baptist Church," Poppie said.

"I've been thinking I might be a Presbyterian," Cassie-Belle said.

"You stole my thoughts, Cassie-Belle," I said. "When kinfolks won't speak to us, people turn cool toward us, I think it's time to change. Wait until I drive our family to the Freewill Baptist Church in a stationwagon! Then see how they act! Cousins Faith and Bos will about faint! They never owned as fine a family car as that stationwagon in their lives. They go places in a farm truck! And no other couple I know work harder than they do!"

"I've listened to all you've said, Cassie-Belle and Pedike —that you want to be Presbyterians," Poppie said. "I can't understand it!"

"Well, don't you think Mr. and Mrs. Koniker are about as fine a people as you've ever met?" Cassie-Belle asked Poppie. "What's wrong with them?"

"Drinking that Scotch whiskey," Timmie said.

"Who can be more narrow than the people in our church?" I said. "Some have to be hypocrites to stay in it. We've got 'em who drink, too! And they're our relatives! Think twice! What's so wrong with a social drink?"

They knew I was referring to Uncle Dick and Aunt Susie who had liquor in their home, and Uncle Dick carried a flask. I'd seen him nip in the car. I wondered why Uncle Dick and Aunt Susie hadn't switched to the Presbyterian Church where they'd have been much happier.

"My children," Poppie sighed. "High school and Ohio has changed you so much, I wonder what college will do for you!"

I could have said more to Poppie but I didn't. I never said very many things to which my father disagreed. But the thing that had changed us most was free food and free money—that we no longer had to work for it. I knew that I wasn't going to live like he was living now—a man who liked to work and wanted to work and who was working harder than he had ever worked in his life by trying to keep from working.

People didn't have to work when there was a way to make a living without work. The choice was an easy one to make—not to work and pay taxes to the State and Federal governments but let the State and Federal governments pay to keep the people. We were cheating. We were not declaring what we had made, for if we had, we'd have had to pay taxes. If we had received checks and paid taxes, we would have ruined Poppie—he couldn't have drawn his checks and lived on welfare and food stamps. Who wouldn't want three-hundred dollars worth of food each month that cost only ten or twenty dollars! It didn't matter. It was what you told them you had, to pay for the stamps. They'd believe you. Yes, people like Uncle Dick, Stetson Koniker, the Herberts, Cousins Bos and Faith, and others down to small wage earners, were taxed to pay for Uncle

Sam's free gifts, benefits and special benefits our rich and old Uncle Sam parceled out to his kinsmen.

Mommie had a small trunk where she kept our money. Poppie's cash money was kept in the larger division of this trunk. Cassie-Belle, Tishie, Timmie and I each had smaller divisions. But Mommie had a few thousand in this trunk. We were afraid to put our money in the banks and let it draw interest. We were afraid to have a checking account and write checks.

When payments were due on our new household appliances, Leonard brought Uncle Dick over to take Poppie or Mommie or both of them to Agrillo to make these payments. These were made in cash. Poppie could have everything paid for by the end of August. He was afraid someone would get suspicious and there might be talk and even an investigation of his affairs, although we had not heard of one investigation, for merchants were too happy to have food stamps or cash payment no matter how the customer came by the stamps or money.

66 Before Cassie-Belle left home for Ohio State University, she'd looked in catalogues and magazines which she'd purchased from the newsstand in Agrillo to see what the fashions would be for young women in college. Of the conservative things she liked the most, she purchased certain items. "Extreme" or "way out" clothing Cassie-Belle didn't buy.

She packed a new trunk and two new suitcases—Cassie-Belle had bought her clothes, trunk and suitcases with her own money. And she was ready for Uncle Dick and Leonard to come for her on a Sunday morning to take her to Ohio State University in Columbus, Ohio.

It was almost like a funeral when Leonard and I carried her trunk, and, with the help of Poppie, put it in the baggage rack on top of Uncle Dick's car. Leonard got on top of the car and roped it down. Then we put the suitcases into the trunk of the car. She carried a large purse and a small bag. She'd had her hair done at the beauty parlor for the first time. Mommie and my sisters had done each other's hair before this.

Mommie cried and Poppie shed tears.

"Be good, Cassie-Belle, and write often to us," Mommie said. "Write every day so we'll know about you!"

Timmie, Tishie, Maryann and I cried to see her go. What a sister she was. Mommie would miss her. We'd miss going to school with her. Now, Tishie would have to take her place as second mother. And Maryann would have to take Tishie's place. And next to move up would be Martha. The Little Ones and even the Babies would miss Cassie-Belle.

But she got in the back seat beside Uncle Dick—and when she waved to us, she was crying. This was the first time one of our family had gone away from home to stay nine months with only visits back home. After the car sped down the hill, we walked silently into the living room. We'd phoned Jimmie Artner not to bring the church bus for us on this Sunday. We wouldn't be going. This was a day of mourning for us!

Can Cassie-Belle make the grades at Ohio State? I wondered.

I was glad Cassie-Belle had gone to Ohio State before she learned Mommie was pregnant again.

"I know she would have been upset if she'd a-knowed this," Mommie said. "I didn't want her upset before she went to Ohio State."

This time it was Tishie who walked the floor and didn't say anything. In the last four years Mommie had had four. In the last six years Mommie had had five. If this one came in May she would have had five in five years.

67 This September when Timmie, a sophomore, Tishie, a junior, and I, a senior, went back to Landsdowne Central High School, we were on free lunches. Maryann in the eighth grade in Agrillo Junior High got free lunch. And Martha, now in the fourth, and Little Dickie in the second got free lunches in the Agrillo Elementary. All of us could have free breakfasts if we wanted them.

Now that we were on welfare the County Health Nurse, Mrs. Gertrude Holmes, visited us. She came often to our home because people who had just got on welfare got special service. When she examined us, she found we'd not taken good care of our teeth. Each one in school had to have dental work done. But this was free. I was now driving our stationwagon and Mrs. Holmes set up appointments for us on late afternoons and on Saturdays. And soon all of us had good teeth, from Poppie and Mommie down to Little Dickie. I ought to know. I'd almost run a taxi service getting them to the dentist, Dr. Clyde Orphanton, in Agrillo. The Government paid our dental bill, which must have been a whopper. In order to save some of Poppie's and Mommie's teeth Dr. Orphanton crowned them in gold. And gold crowns in Poppie's and Mommie's mouths looked odd to us. They shone in society every time they opened their mouths.

Mrs. Holmes was from the Landsdowne County Health Department. She visited homes of people on welfare, poor people of minority groups. We were the Briar minority group.

But when Mrs. Holmes first came she thought we were

Catholic. She told Mommie that she was Catholic and that she had fallen in love with our big family. She said everyone of us would get special attention from her. She told Mommie the regret of her life was she couldn't have children. Mrs. Holmes was like a mother to all of us.

We got free medicine. Our doctors, if we needed them, were free. If one of us had to go to the hospital, this was free! And now I had to agree there was never a life like this. No wonder more and more people would be seeking this new way of life. Was there a country in the world with a way of life like this?

Mommie wrote Cassie-Belle about all of this. But Cassie-Belle didn't need this kind of letter. Officials at Ohio State knew she was from a poor family, minority group, and her family was on welfare. They knew she got everything paid and fifty dollars a month spending money. Cassie-Belle knew poor people were an obsession in America. If anybody's philosophy had ever held good—it was Poppie's: "It pays to be poor!"

Now, we knew, since six of us could get a free breakfast at school, there was no need for Mommie to work and prepare it with the help of Tishie and Maryann. Since we didn't have chores to do at home, we could do without breakfast until we got to school.

All Timmie and I had to do at home, and with the help of Poppie, was cut, haul and hang our tobacco on tier poles in the Koniker barn, which was a show barn—better than most houses in Ohio.

68 It was really something one evening when Al and Jim Herbert came to our house in their pick-up farm truck.

"Mr. Perkins, we can't save our tobacco without your help," Al said. "You and your boys, if we can only get them on the weekend!"

"Yes, Saturdays and Sundays," Timmie said.

"Just a minute, Timmie," Poppie said. "This is your father's business."

"Our tobacco this year is better than last year," Jim Herbert said as he looked over the big furniture in our living room, with new chairs and a TV. "We know you're on welfare—we'll pay you cash—and no one will see you working. You'll be over in the valley where no one except us ever goes—and you'll be hidden in our barn! Yes, one-fifty an hour. Same for the boys if they can come! Our ox is really in the ditch. We don't know how to handle tobacco! You do. We can't get anyone else to do this. We need you! Save us!"

"Your father, Josh Herbert, saved us," Poppie said. "I'll try to help save you." Then Poppie added in his slow soft voice, "Don't tell anybody—not even Uncle Dick Perkins about this. But it will do me as much good to work again, not that I need the money now, as it will do you to save your tobacco. A man is in jail when he can't work. I want to use my muscles again. They're getting soft. I'll work for you for nothing if you can't or don't want to pay me. I really would like to work. I want something to do."

"We'll pay you," Jim Herbert said. "We don't want you

to work for nothing even if my father did help save you and your family. You can help us now. We won't tell anybody you're working and we'll give you cash so there won't be any records of our payments to you."

The Herberts told Poppie one of them would be there at six in the morning for him. They hurried away home. They were busy men.

So Poppie went back to work, hiding out, to help the Herberts. Timmie and I worked with him on Saturdays and Sundays. There was no church for us now. And I didn't care. I knew when we went again we'd all file into the stationwagon and go.

When Poppie got into the tobacco, here was a man who knew his trade. He could cut more sticks of tobacco in a day than any man I'd ever known. He'd had a long rest and he was ready to work again.

We cut tobacco and the Herberts hauled it to the barn. This was all they did. We got it cut and hauled to the barn before frost. Then, Poppie, who was great with a corn knife, cut and shucked their corn. And the Herberts were too pleased to have us ever to go back on their word. No one saw us working. And they paid us with cash.

Of course, all autumn we had been taking care of our own two acres of tobacco too. In early December Timmie's and my tobacco from the Koniker farm sold at the Agrillo Warehouse and averaged eighty-four cents a pound. We had thirty-two hundred pounds. Our crop brought twenty-six hundred eighty-eight dollars. Half of this went to Stetson Koniker. Half went to Timmie and me. This would make six hundred seventy-two dollars each. A single individual who made over six hundred dollars had to fill out a tax report. There was no way we could be paid cash for this. We got real checks. This worried Poppie.

We had hoped we wouldn't make over five hundred each. But we had the best tobacco on the market. The Herberts had over twelve thousand pounds and it averaged eighty cents per pound. This was second best on the market. And we'd really grown their tobacco. After they'd paid us they'd made good money. But they would have to pay more. They had to pay taxes.

"I'll tell you, Gil, with all this food coming in—more than we can eat since the children are eating two meals, five days a week at school, and Cassie-Belle is away from home, I don't know what we'll do with the food stamps," Mommie said. "Food is piling up on us. Refrigerator full and the deep freeze is full."

"Yes, we've got plenty for a rainy day," Poppie said. "But they expect us to buy for the family of fourteen. They expect us to take three-hundred-dollars worth of food stamps."

"And about this cash money piling up," Mommie said. "It's got me worried. I'm getting afraid to stay in this house with all this money."

"I've thought about taking it back to the old country and putting it in two or three different banks so people won't be suspicy," Poppie said.

"Why take it down there?" Mommie said. "We've made it in Ohio. Let's keep it in Ohio. I know we can't begin to spend all of it with just about everything free!"

"Uncle Dick will find a way to help us," Poppie said. "Maybe we can go beyond Landsdowne County to three different counties where we are not known and they don't know how we got it and put so much in a bank in each county. I think it ought to be out of the house, too!"

69 Cassie-Belle had asked Uncle Dick and Leonard to come and get her when she came home for Christmas holidays. She ran from Uncle Dick's car to the house. She was happy to be home.

"Mommie, pregnant again," she said. "Oh, Mommie, why?"

"What about your hair, Cassie-Belle?" Mommie said. "It's changed."

"Not my real hair, Mommie," she said. "I'm wearing a wig—a wig of natural hair—not this artificial stuff!"

"But you have pretty hair, Cassie-Belle, prettier than that wig," Mommie told her.

Well, we gathered around Cassie-Belle—wig or no wig— didn't matter. We were glad to have her home.

"Mommie, it's the fashion to wear wigs," Cassie-Belle said. "Some girls have a half dozen. They change the color of their hair as often as they change their clothes!"

"I didn't know college would be like that," Mommie said. "You've changed."

"I hope I have," Cassie-Belle said. "Something else I've done, too! I've changed my name. I'm no longer Cassie-Belle—I'm now Clarissa Jo!"

"Mrs. Koniker's name," Timmie said.

"How could you do that?" Poppie said. "We give you that name!"

"What, to go through my life with such a name!" she said. "My name is legal. It's on Ohio State University records. Clarissa Jo Perkins."

"I never liked my name either," Tishie said. "I'm the

only Tishie I know. Where on earth, Mommie, did you ever get such a name?"

"Off a tombstone back on Lower Bruin," Poppie said.

"Oh, you took it from the dead," Tishie said.

Mommie went in one direction and Tishie went in the other. Poppie stood as if in a half sleep and he shook his head sadly.

Now we'd not been going to church all autumn. Poppie, Timmie and I had worked on Saturdays and Sundays. And no one had come from our church to inquire why we were not coming.

"All of us need to get back to the House of the Lord together," Poppie said. "We must hold together as a family. We cannot fall apart."

So, on Sunday before Christmas, we dressed in our best and we filled the stationwagon together. The stationwagon was not big enough for fourteen but we squeezed in a little one or a baby on somebody's lap, except mine, for I was the driver. I had to have plenty of room and drive carefully with my precious cargo—all of us—but my eyes were good and my hands were used to the plow and hoe.

When we arrived at the Freewill Baptist Church, dressed as well, if not better, than any family there—yes, in our own car, not the church bus any more—Uncle Dick, who always stood outside and smoked until the minute he had to go in, was there. Aunt Susie was with him. What a pair! They came down the steps to greet us.

Cousin Faith and Bos and that son of theirs, Buster Boy and his common-law wife, Widow Ollie Mayhew, and their five were there and had been talking to Uncle Dick and Aunt Susie on the steps until we arrived. They turned and went into the church. They didn't have manners enough, through their jealousies, since we were up in the world and ahead of them now, to come down and speak to sister Clarissa Jo—not Cassie-Belle any more—and believe you me, we had to call her her new name. Yes, Clarissa Jo home from Ohio State! And were we proud of her! Dressed in the newest fashions, wearing a wig. And I must say this now! Clarissa Jo was a good looker. She was small, wiry, built like Mommie. She was the type men would look at the second time. She'd never have trouble if and when she ever had babies nursing them! And Sister Tishie was built the same way.

"What a fine, prosperous-looking family," Uncle Dick said.

"Oh, and you're back, Cassie-Belle, from Ohio State," Aunt Susie said. "You're so pretty!"

"Aunt Susie, I've had my name changed to Clarissa Jo," my sister said.

"Honey, I don't blame you a bit for changing that old Appalachian name, Cassie-Belle, to Clarissa Jo!" Aunt Susie said, smiling. "This really shows how smart you are. Why go through life with a name you don't like? You're an Ohio State co-ed. You're no longer in a Kentucky or an Ohio tobacco patch with a hoe!"

Aunt Susie was really pleased my sister had changed her name which helped lessen Poppie's and Mommie's embarrassment. I would hate for Cousin Faith to find this out. I was glad she hadn't come around. She was bad to gossip. She'd have got on her telephone and called all her neighbors and our neighbors about Clarissa Jo.

Members of the Freewill Baptist Church, people we knew —people who came around before we got up in the world— were cool and standoffish. But this was our church same as theirs. And even if we didn't pay to support it, our Uncle Dick did. Our religion came in a free package too. So I know I walked in—and so did the family—with Uncle Dick and with Aunt Susie with our heads high. Again our Little Mommie, heavy with child, and my sisters took the Babies to the church nursery and the Little Ones to their Sunday-school classes. I'd never cared much for one of these classes and now I cared less. Somehow I felt above and beyond this church since we'd come to Ohio. I thought all the time about the Presbyterian church—a place I'd never been.

Our family reassembled for Brother Cashew Boggs' sermon on the humble birth of Jesus Christ—that he was born in a barn and wrapped in a swaddling cloth. And believe me, all in our family was all too familiar with a barn and a swaddling cloth, which we had used after we had curried and brushed the mules. But even a birth like our Saviour's in a stable was a better place than the corn field in Kentucky where Mommie had birthed two of us.

"Church ain't the same as it used to be," Poppie admitted when we got back in the stationwagon. "When money comes in at the front door, religion goes out at the back door. I didn't dream we'd ever have so much money and live in a mansion. And I never dreamed money would be so much trouble!"

I did know—and thoughts flashed through my mind as I drove my family toward home—that last week, Uncle Dick came with Leonard and Poppie went off with them. Poppie carried a small valise. I knew what was in it, too: folding money. They must have gone to a bank in three different counties to deposit money. I know Mommie was scared to death with all the money we had in the house.

I'd heard them talking about always keeping so much of Poppie's money—should they ever need it for emergencies. And Mommie still had Tishie's, Timmie's, Clarissa Jo's and my money in separate stacks, locked in the trunk. Money we'd earned! But how could we spend it all when everything was free!

Sunday evening Clarissa Jo told us about Ohio State University. How she'd seen football games that were free. And in addition to these games her way had been paid one time to Cleveland to see the Cleveland Browns play the Baltimore Colts. She said she liked football, but to see one professional game spoiled her watching Ohio State University games in "The Big Ten." Not one of us had ever seen a college-football game. We didn't know what she was talking about. She spoke of Federal Funding for this and that— and how young people from poor homes were getting to do and see more than their friends from middle-class and wealthy homes.

And then she told us how she had learned to dance at Ohio State.

"Dancing is a sin," Poppie said.

"Don't be so old fashioned, Poppie," she said. "The way I've worked, I'd get fat and lazy unless I did something for exercise. And I'm telling you, the exercise that will take off the extra pounds is rock and roll!"

"Tell me more about it, Cassie—I mean Clarissa Jo," Timmie said. "I'd like to learn to dance! Could you teach me?"

"Yes, if we had a stereo and the records," she said.

"Let's get one," Timmie said. "I've got the money!"

"Stereo?" Poppie said. "What is it?"

"Remember the old Victrolas people had back on Lower Bruin?" Clarissa Jo said. "Well, you don't wind one. It's electric, takes records off and puts them on! Timmie, you can get one for about four-hundred dollars!"

"I thought it would cost more," Timmie said. "Maybe a thousand dollars."

"The big ones like the one we have in our dorm at Ohio State do cost that much," Clarissa Jo said. "But you can buy a good one for four or five hundred!"

"Pedike, take me to Agrillo tomorrow," Timmie said.

"I'll take you," I said.

Mommie and Poppie really looked plagued. They sat in silence. They knew this was our money—money not given to us—money we'd earned by hard work. They couldn't and they didn't say anything.

70 On the day before Christmas I never saw such crowds in Agrillo. Money flowed in Agrillo like a river. People were buying, buying, buying.

And in the music store where I had once gone to buy a battery-set radio, when Timmie asked to see a stereo, three clerks came running. And Clarissa Jo was right. Prices ranged from three hundred to a thousand.

"Boy, oh boy, what a Christmas present—buying it for myself, too," Timmie said when he looked at a five-hundred-dollar stereo. "Gee-whilligens!"

Timmie went up in the air in his jubilation and cracked his heels together three times.

"This is the one," he said.

Clarissa Jo, Tishie and I thought he'd made the wise choice.

Now, I thought of how poor old Cousin Bos used to ask the merchant for extra socks for us when we bought shoes. Only a poor man would do this. A man who had to work hard for everything and then have to pay taxes out of what he earned! Poor old Cousin Bos who had pretended that night on Lower Bruin when he came to move us to Ohio that he had so much! After Timmie bought the stereo and paid cash, not one of us asked for a free recording to go with the stereo. "People who have money don't do this," I thought.

Clarissa Jo knew the rock-and-roll recordings. She found five of her favorites. Each record had many tunes. And then she found five others—songs and music by popular

singers of today. These records were five dollars each.
Tishie paid for the recordings. We asked to have our stereo
sent now to our home. We took the recordings with us.

The stereo was home by the time we were. I helped the
music clerk carry it in. He plugged it in in Tishie's room.
And he didn't have to show us how to use it. Clarissa Jo
already knew. No sooner was the cord plugged in than
Clarissa Jo put on a dance record. She had to turn a knob.
The music was as loud as thunder and as fast as lightning.
Timmie and I pulled the rug back so we could dance on the
hardwood floor.

Clarissa Jo stepped out and did a dance by herself. I never
saw such action. Then she asked me to try. Well, it was
awkward at first—but I got the swing of this rock-and-roll
music—fast dancing and only for the young. While Clarissa
Jo helped Timmie, I helped Tishie all I could. We weren't
picking berries, hoeing corn and tobacco now. But we were
working harder. We were not exactly good at it, but we
were so willing to learn it wouldn't be long before we could
tap to the music on this hardwood floor. Mommie and
Poppie wouldn't come into the room.

When we had danced until we were tired, we put the
rug back over the floor and went out into the living room
with Poppie and Mommie and the Little Ones. While we
were there we heard a knock on our door.

Poppie got up and went to the door.

"Mr. and Mrs. Koniker," Poppie said. "Come in, get
yourselves chairs and sit a spell with us!"

"Call us Stet and Clarissa Jo," Mr. Koniker said.

"Oh, what a nice scene," Mrs. Koniker said. "And not all
of you are here?"

"No, the Babies are asleep," Mommie said. Mommie didn't
get up from her chair. Maybe, she didn't want to show
Mrs. Koniker she was pregnant again. "See, the Babies nap
each afternoon. There are four in there in one bed in a
quiet room!"

"Mr. Koniker, I've just bought a stereo with my tobacco
money," Timmie said. "We've never had one before and
we've been dancing!"

"Oh, how wonderful," Mrs. Koniker said. "Stet and I

danced when we were young. And we still go to dances. But we dance the slow dances now. We used to kick up our heels."

"Your Presbyterian church is not against dancing?" I said.

"Oh, no, what church is against dancing?" she asked me.

"I just asked you," I said. "I think some churches are against dancing!"

"I never heard of one," she said. "We dance in the Recreation Room of our Presbyterian church. Young people come and dance!"

This was enough for me. I knew I was getting closer to the Presbyterians all the time. Poppie and Mommie understood something, too. They didn't speak up. After all, we lived in the Koniker's second mansion and it was rent free! What a house! And why shouldn't we learn to dance! What was wrong with dancing? Anyone who called it sinful—any church that condemned dancing—had to be old fashioned and far removed from modern times in Ohio.

"Mrs. Koniker, when I heard your name, I thought it was so beautiful that I have had my name legally changed from Cassie-Belle—a name I never liked—to Clarissa Jo! I'm now Clarissa Jo Perkins!"

Clarissa Jo hadn't more than said these words until Mrs. Koniker sprang up from her chair, embraced Clarissa Jo, hugged and kissed her!

"My first namesake," she said. "A beautiful co-ed from Ohio State University! I must really get you a Christmas present. I'll give you cash and let you buy it! How wonderful you like my name so well!"

Mr. Koniker took his checkbook from his pocket, his face all smiles and began to write a check.

Really, I'd been afraid Mrs. Koniker might not like it when Clarissa Jo borrowed her name. But beautiful Mrs. Koniker, who believed in dancing, was overjoyed! How we loved the Konikers.

"Now we thought we'd come up and see if we couldn't go to Agrillo and get Christmas candy for your children," Mr. Koniker said to Poppie as he gave Mrs. Koniker a check. And Mrs. Koniker looked at it, then reached over and gave the check to Clarissa Jo.

"Not this much for a present," Clarissa Jo said.

"Sure, it's really not enough," she said.

"Thank you, thank you," Clarissa Jo said.

"It's for my namesake," she said.

"About the Christmas candy, Stet," Poppie said. "We have three-hundred dollars of December food stamps we have to spend. We thought we'd go to Agrillo this afternoon and get the candy with these."

"Oh, Gil," he said. "Can you buy candy with food stamps?"

"Anything but soap, washing powders, cigarettes, tobacco and foreign products, such as Danish hams and Norwegian sardines," Poppie said. "Not any imported foods!"

And I will say Mr. Koniker looked plagued when Poppie told him this. Uncle Dick had never let Mr. Koniker know Poppie was in the money—not like Mr. Koniker—but Mr. Koniker had to pay taxes and to pay for everything he purchased. Not anything came free to men like him, Uncle Dick and Dr. Gaylord Zimmerman.

Poppie didn't draw the biggest salary in the world, but he didn't have anything to buy. He didn't have any taxes. Everything, everything was free! How could Poppie spend now? All he could do was bank free money—hide it out in different banks!

Mommie did have to get up from her chair before the Konikers left, for Baby Danny Boy was crying to be fed and she had to excuse herself and go. And when she arose Mrs. Koniker could see she was heavy with child. And I wondered how a barren woman felt when she saw a houseful of children and the mother pregnant again. Mommie now had twelve-and-a-half living children and one dead.

The Konikers, a handsome, well-dressed couple, maybe a little older than Poppie and Mommie, smiled and said their friendly good-bys to us and went back to their large car—largest in the valley.

"They have everything in wealth and worldly possessions

but they're like Buster Boy," Poppie said. "They're lost when they don't replenish."

"Poppie," Clarissa Jo interrupted him, "don't say it!"

"Clarissa Jo, how much is your present?" Timmie asked. She gave Timmie her check to look at.

"Two hundred dollars," Timmie said. "Gee-whilligens! Maybe I'd better change my name to Stetson. But I like Timmie better! I don't want to be called Stet."

While sister Clarissa Jo was home we had a great Christmas. Timmie had bought himself his finest gift which was for all the family, too. And Tishie had bought ten records which we played, both sides, over and over again. And believe me, we danced and danced until we could almost dance as well as Clarissa Jo. "Rock around the Clock" and "Rock Away from Here" I thought we'd wear threadbare.

71 We had a neighbor, the old man who lived in the little shack at the foot of the hill on the other side of the hard-surfaced Republican road, as it was called, that divided the big farms of the Konikers and the Trants. He'd never once come up the hill to the mansion where we lived. Not one of us had ever gone down to the shack where he lived. His name was on his mailbox beside the road: Fox Underwood. But who was Fox Underwood?

Often when we waited for the school bus, we'd seen the old man out sawing wood with a little gasoline-engine saw. This was on a rack and he held a pole of wood up before it. The little circle saw finally ate its way through with sawdust flying in the wind.

Then on warm sunny afternoons during the autumn and early winter when our bus brought us home from school, we'd seen him sitting in his chair, which was leaned against his cabin wall, fast asleep with his mouth open.

And I'd never passed his place that I hadn't seen at least a half-dozen hounds in the yard. They were very well-fed hounds, with their tails arched over their backs, growling, snapping and biting at each other.

I'd heard him scold them often, call their names—Fleet, Jack, Sharp, Big Boy, Daddles and Old Doc—to make them behave. They were all males and they fussed among themselves.

Saturday, Clarissa Jo went back to Ohio State and since Timmie and I didn't have anything to do now, I thought it would be a good time for a visit to our neighbor that evening when a soft January wind was blowing. When we opened the gate, we were met by six happy hounds. I'd heard their names many times but I didn't know which one was which. They were friendly, well fed and curious. Each one came up friendly-like and whiffed the scent of Timmie and me. Satisfied, each hound walked away. We walked over to the door and Timmie knocked. There was an electric light above the door of his little shack.

When the door opened there stood old Fox with a cigar in his toothless mouth.

"We're the Perkins boys from the house upon the hill," I said. "I'm Pedike and this is my brother Timmie!"

"I never thought anybody living in that big house upon the top of the hill would visit me living in this shack at the foot of the hill," he said. "Only rich people live in houses like that!"

"But why can't rich people visit poor people?" Timmie asked. "It's wrong if they don't. People ought to know one another!"

"I agree," old Fox said. "Come in—sit on the side of the bed!"

Well, here was a color TV and old Fox had a program on —one of Poppie's favorites. He had a front room—living room—with his bed, TV and a big chair in which he sat. Then he had a little kitchen with a table, wood stove and a refrigerator—old clothes were piled everywhere. It was the dirtiest house I'd ever been in.

Old Fox, about six feet tall, had uncontrolled hair that was salt-and-pepper colored. He had a face like a terrapin with his upper lip hanging over. He didn't have any teeth. His eyes were blue and his nose long and thin.

"You've got some nice dogs," Timmie said. "Gee-whilligens, they're so friendly they tried to talk to us when we walked across the yard!"

"Yes, they're like children," old Fox said. "They can talk to me. I talk to them. We understand one another. Fleet told me awhile ago they wanted to go possum hunting tonight!"

"Possum hunting?" Timmie said.

"Yes, you boys want to go possum hunting with me?"

"I wouldn't mind," Timmie spoke up first, as usual.

"Yes, my hounds are good possum hounds and they're good fox hounds, too," old Fox said. "See, I've fox hunted a lot. That's how I got the name Fox. When I got older, I was called old Fox. My real name is Henry. A lot of my friends in the old country—where I used to live and cut timber—called me Hank!"

"Where are you from in the old country?" I asked.

"Menifee County," he said.

"We're from the old country, too, Greenwood County," Timmie said.

"And you never possum hunted?"

"No, Poppie was never a hunter," I said.

"How did you ever get up here?" Timmie asked.

Leave it to Timmie to ask the questions.

"Oh, this land beyond the river," he said, raising up from his chair with his unlit cigar in his hand, looking at the ceiling. "This wonderful Ohio! I wish I'd a-been born here. I wish I'd a-come as a young man."

Then he dropped back into his big well-worn leather-backed chair that was coming apart at the seams. He brought a lighter from his pocket and relit his cigar.

"Then you like it here as well as we do," Timmie said.

"I like it better, I'm sure," he said. "Why wouldn't I like it? I nearly killed myself cutting timber and fighting rattlesnakes and copperheads. You ever been bitten by a copperhead?"

"No, but Poppie was," Timmie said. "He was fanged on the hand. But it was an Ohio copperhead!"

"Well, a Kentucky copperhead bit me on the leg and I thought I'd lose my leg," old Fox said. "I was on crutches a year. I couldn't work. And I nearly starved. And when I could work again, the timber had all played out in Menifee County. So I heard about work in Ohio—I came to Ohio seeking farm work. I had parted with my family. I'll tell you more about this as we possum hunt. It's time to go if you want to go possum hunting."

"We do," I said.

"Then just a minute," he said. "You boys like a hooter?"

"What is a hooter?" I asked.

"A drink," he said. "I always take one for a bracer before I go."

"No, we don't drink," I said. "Not if it's whiskey!"

"Old Granddad," he said. "It's better than the moonshine white lightning in Menifee County. Now that I'm able to buy it I have what I think is the best!"

He went over to a box, pulled out a pint, uncorked it, held it up and drank it to the last drop.

"It gives me a lift," he said. "It's wonderful for a man!"

Then he got his electric lantern and a coffee sack in which to put the possums. Outside, he went to a little lean-to built against his cabin wall and got his ax. And his hounds seemed to know. They barked, growled and dug up the dirt with their hind feet. They were happy to be going hunting.

"I feed them well," he said. "See, I'm on welfare and I get one hundred dollars worth of food stamps a month. I can't eat that much. And I want to hold on to a hundred a month for groceries. So I feed it to my hounds!"

What an idea, I thought. Having dogs would solve our problem of too much food! Why hadn't one of us thought of this? I'd learned something tonight! We could solve our problem.

"Are you on a pension, too?" Timmie asked.

"Sure I am," he said. "I'm on the old-age pension in Ohio! If I'd a stayed on in Kentucky I'd be drawing seventy dollars a month. Here I draw two hundred seventeen dollars a month. I hear there is one state better than Ohio—Californiee—but it's too fur away!"

Now, we had walked around the hillslope into the Essej Trants forest. We'd followed a dim path. We'd walked in the moonlight. Old Fox hadn't switched on his lantern light. Here we walked under the barren white oaks, black oaks, black gum, beech, elm and sycamore trees. The hounds had gone ahead of us. When one barked, Old Fox stopped. "That old Daddles," Old Fox said. "He's struck a cold trail. In a minute it will be a hot trail. And you'll hear the sweet music of my barking hounds!"

And Old Fox was right. Soon so many hounds were barking I couldn't tell their barks apart.

"Back in Menifee County I used to eat possum," Old Fox

said. "But now I don't. I eat steaks. Since I don't have false teeth and never want them, I have to gum my grub. So I get a tender, softer steak. I don't eat just any kind, since the Government pays for it. I get filet mignon. Boy, one is sure good! Better than possum!"

"What do you do with possums?" I asked.

"Leave them in the trees," he said. "If they catch one on the ground and don't hurt it too much, I put it in the sack— later, I slip away from the hounds and turn it loose. I hunt for the fun of it. Hunting is something to do to pass the time. If Essej Trants wants me to cut a ditch or cut wood, I'll do it for him. But I don't like the man he's got on his place, Bos Auxier. I won't work with him. He wants me to work all the time. And he wants to boss me. I've been on Essej Trants farm nineteen years. I enjoyed working for him before he got Bos Auxier here! Essej Trants is a fine man. He says my shack is my home as long as I live."

"Oh, we know Bos Auxier," Timmie spoke quickly. "His wife, Faith, is Mommie's cousin."

"Well, I like his wife, Faith, who has cooked me many good meals when I worked for Essej on this farm, but I can't stand that Bos."

"We feel now the same way you do about Bos," I said. "He's one overbearing, smart-alecky, bossy little man. And he's nosey. They're from Lower Bruin, Greenwood County, same place we came from."

"If you boys feel that way toward him, you're my friends and you'll be my friends forever," Old Fox said.

Now the dogs came to a halt. And their barking changed.

"Treed," Old Fox said.

He went running in the moonlight over the brown leaves on the ground under the tall timber. When we reached the tree, all six hounds were around it, looking up and barking. High in a white oak tree was a little possum, holding on to the tree for its life. It didn't look as large as a small house cat.

"Come on, my boys, we'll leave him to grow and re-plenish in our possum world," Old Fox said. "Let's go for bigger game!"

His hounds seemed to understand. They stopped barking,

left the tree and took off, scattering among the moonlit woods ahead of us. They were hunting again.

"Are you married?" Timmie asked.

"Yes, I have a wife," Old Fox said. "If I'd take her back, as she wants me to do, I'd get one hundred eight dollars more on the month! This would make three-hundred-twenty-five dollars for us. But I wouldn't have her with me for a thousand dollars a month. See, my wife served in the penitentiary for stealing. I warned and warned her about her stealing but she couldn't keep her hands off things in the stores! She's on her food stamps and welfare in Indiana! And she can stay on them!"

"How many children do you have?" I asked.

Old Fox didn't answer. We were walking under the barren timber where the bright moonlight filtered through the barren trees that left long shadows in a light almost as bright as day.

Then there was a long bark.

"Old Fleet," Old Fox said. "He's on a cold trail of a fox. I'm afraid our possum hunt has ended! You'll hear more hounds join the chase! We'll have a real fox chase going in a few minutes! We'd better get up the hilltop where we can listen!"

How Old Fox knew they were trailing a fox, I didn't understand. But we started climbing up the hill. And before we reached the top, all of Old Fox Underwood's hounds were barking in a red-hot chase.

"Ain't that pretty music?" Old Fox said.

When we reached the hilltop, after half-running, we were almost out of breath. The night was beautiful. A few stars shone dimly in the sky. The moon was big and beautiful. The winds sang among the barren branches of the trees. I'd never known a night so beautiful and so interesting.

Now we stood on the summit of a round cone-shaped hill. We were up closer to the moon and stars—up where the blowing wind hit us. And here we heard the hounds chasing the fox below us.

"You asked me about my children," Old Fox said. "We had five. But two didn't belong to me. One that didn't belong to me is with her mother. Some man begat her after my wife left the pen. She's not married. All the others are married. I don't know where they live and I don't care—I have now the life I love—in my shack on Essej Trants' farm with my pension, my food stamps and my hounds."

I knew right now, I wanted some hounds. And I wanted to hunt like this. And I thought the time might come when I'd take my hounds and join Old Fox with his hounds and we'd possum hunt and fox hunt together.

This would be my last year in high school. Now, what was I going to do after school but farm two acres of tobacco? This wouldn't take much time. The Herberts wouldn't be growing more corn and tobacco on their hillsides. They wouldn't be growing berries. Farming had changed there since Jim and Al Herbert had lost their father. I knew I couldn't get work there. And I couldn't get a job at public works until I was eighteen, in November.

"The only way in this life is to live to the fullest and enjoy one's self," Old Fox said. "Man doesn't have to work. I live better since I've nearly quit work. Why work when I don't have to? I live better without work!"

The hounds were really making music going round and round the hill below us.

"Do you like this, Timmie?" I asked.

"I love it," he replied.

Then, all of a sudden the hounds stopped barking.

"My hounds crowded him too close," Old Fox said. "He's gone into his den among the Artner rock cliffs! The chase is over and we'd better go in!"

"Yes, Poppie and Mommie don't know where we are," Timmie said.

"Do you have to let them know?" Old Fox said.

"We'd better let them know," I said. "They'll be up waiting for us when we get home!"

We left the hilltop walking down.

"You people must be rich living in that big mansion," Old Fox said.

"If we're not rich, we're well-to-do," Timmie said. "But we're on welfare and food stamps, too!"

"Not you?" Old Fox said, stopping in his tracks. "Not you living in that big house!"

"People on welfare live in both shacks and mansions," I said.

Now we started walking on down the old wagon road toward Old Fox's shack.

"B'dogged if I'd ever thought you's on welfare living in that big house," Old Fox said.

Now Old Fox laughed wildly.

"Ohio is a great state and this is a great country," he said. "When a man in a shack and in a mansion can both be equal and share the same welfare."

We had reached his shack and we thanked Old Fox for a wonderful evening. As we did his hounds came in one by one panting with their tongues out.

72 One, two, three, four, five! Saturday and Sunday! One, two, three, four, five! Saturday and Sunday! This is the way the days in January came with always some new expectation. And this is the way they flowed like the great Ohio River, that river that separated two worlds. One! Two! Three! Four! Five! School days! Saturdays, we went to Cantwell's Super Market in Agrillo—where they were glad to see us spend our stamps. Sundays, the Freewill Baptist Church. This was becoming the most dreaded day in the week for me! I was positive that I would leave this church someday—I knew Clarissa Jo, Tishie and Timmie would. And I knew that Tishie had told me when she finished at Landsdowne County Central and followed Clarissa Jo to Ohio State with all expenses paid and fifty dollars a month spending money —that she would no longer be Tishie—but she'd be Mary Beth. She had chosen the name she wanted.

I knew we needed another car and another driver in our family. We had a double garage, too. At first I liked to drive the stationwagon. But it got wearisome driving to Agrillo just about each afternoon after I got back from school to take members of my family for a medical or dental checkup —yes, taking Mommie now, in her pregnancy, for the first time in her life, to be checked weekly by Dr. Gaylord Zimmerman.

Mommie and my sisters used to help each other with their hair. First, they washed and waved it. Later, they used rollers to wave it. But now I had to take Mommie, Tishie and Maryann to the beauty parlor. Each one went at a different time each week. Then I drove us to church on Sunday. I just didn't like to be in the stationwagon all the time driving it like a taxi.

"Poppie, I want to give my stationwagon to you and get me a smaller car of my own," I told him one January afternoon when we were feeding the mules.

"Pedike, I won't let you do that," he said. "I've got money and I'll buy you a second-hand car and pay as much for it as you paid for the stationwagon. It looks better for people on welfare to drive a second-hand car!"

No sooner said than done. Poppie had learned to dial the phone but he had never liked it. It was a new-fangled gadget he never used unless he had to. He called Uncle Dick. Uncle Dick had the connections. And he found for me a popular-make, medium-sized car one of the Agrillo Elementary women teachers had traded in for a new and more expensive car. This car only had seven thousand miles on it. And Uncle Dick, a most amazing man, got it for seven hundred—just what I'd paid for the stationwagon. I had another car to drive now—smaller and more convenient to park in crowded Agrillo when people drove in to get their stamps. The food stamp list was growing by leaps and bounds! I went early on stamp days to get a parking place!

Since the routine of life was becoming monotonous for Poppie, Timmie and me, we often quarreled over who would feed the mules and feed the white-face cattle. Everything was so handy in the Koniker barn, a show place, that feeding was simple and fast.

And often after supper, if the January night was fair, Timmie and I went down to the shack to see our friend Old Fox Underwood who was a lonely old man living with and talking to his hounds. He had his problems, same as we had, trying to use up his food stamps and to spend his pension money.

I knew how Old Fox spent part of his money. Sitting on the side of his bed one evening, I looked under his bed where I'd seen him throw a pint bottle after he'd downed his hooter straight—his bracer always before the hunt—and the empty pint bottles were stacked up nearly to his bed.

I also saw some old clothes he'd worn and got wet and he'd thrown back under the bed. I saw a fishing worm crawling up through these old clothes.

The smell in Old Fox's shack almost gagged Timmie and me. It was the dirtiest place I ever had entered in my life. Our home, even on Lower Bruin when we had so little, was always cleaner than any house I ever entered. Even the County Health Nurse, Mrs. Holmes, had reported that Mommie, with the help of my sisters, kept the cleanest house and had the cleanest dressed children of any home she visited in Landsdowne County, Ohio.

But possum hunting with Old Fox in January, Timmie and I learned about hounds and hunting. And Old Fox was so fond of us, he agreed to help locate hunting hounds for us at a modest sum. We bought two in January: Scissors for twenty-five dollars and Rags for forty-five dollars. Before Old Fox would let us buy these hounds, he took them with his hounds to try them and see if they would tree possums and chase foxes.

At the end of January we had to quit possum hunting. Mother possums would soon be having little possums. And in February we climbed to the summit of the hill on the Essej Trants farm, where we built ourselves a big outdoor fire. Old Fox's hounds and my hounds knew they were to chase the fox when we did this. Now, Timmie and I learned the barks of each hound. And it was the sweetest music— even more than the recordings on our stereo or the TV programs—to hear these hounds chasing the fox around the slopes beneath the hill. No wonder Old Fox enjoyed his hounds and hunting. And in February Timmie bought two more hounds, Drive and Drum, for forty dollars each.

Now, our having four hounds helped us with our surplus food supply. And when we gave them T-bone steak bones, with a little meat left on them, this was a delicacy for our hounds. Timmie and I would stand and watch them eat greedily but stop long enough to growl at one another. We had to feed them at safe distances apart to prevent fights. But when they were not eating they were friendly with each other.

"You know, it's strange how fast things have happened to us in Ohio," Poppie said. "We never knew what a T-bone steak tasted like until we come to Ohio. Now, we feed the bones with a lot of meat left on 'em to hound dogs!"

73 January, February and March, Timmie and I kept up our fox hunting with Old Fox on the cold clear nights, under moon and stars, sitting up close to a big fire and listening to the music of ten hounds, all well-fed by food stamps paid for by Uncle Sam.

Now I was taking Mommie more often to see Dr. Zimmerman who said he believed Mommie was going to have twins. He had also warned Mommie if she came through this childbirth, she shouldn't have any more.

"I don't believe in what you're saying, Dr. Zimmerman," Mommie told him in the office.

"Well, do you want to die and leave your children?" he asked Mommie. "I'm really uneasy about you this time. You've had too many too fast. And now, I can be wrong but I honestly believe you're going to have twins!"

This really cooled Mommie off. And when I took her back home she told Poppie what Dr. Zimmerman had told her.

"Woman walks in the shadows of the valley of death every time she has a baby," Poppie said. "This is in The Word. Even if it means your life, Sil. But if it's twins and if they live—won't that be wonderful! Fourteen to replenish the earth! We've done our part!"

"And on food stamps and getting money without work," I thought. I could have said this but I held my tongue. My mother was an incubator!

But when I thought of my brothers and sisters there was not one of them I would subtract from our family. Each had different looks. Each was sound in body and mind. Each was a normal child. And Mommie and Poppie had produced some smart ones too: Clarissa Jo, Tishie, Timmie, Maryann —and others coming on. I was, so far, the only average one —Mommie a little wisp of a woman—Poppie a huge, bull of a man with strong muscles and great strength but always awkward and sometimes very nervous!

74 In late February and early March, Poppie had taken his ax into the deep hollow on the Koniker farm, a place hidden from the eyes of man and here he chopped dead trees with his mighty ax in the green forest, carried them to a spot he'd selected for the tobacco bed. Poppie didn't ask for any help from Timmie and me. He wanted to use his muscles. He was restless. He wanted to work. Hidden in the forest, he made the tobacco bed, burned and sowed it with the little tobacco seeds and spread a white canvas over it. Timmie and I would have plants now for our two-acre tobacco base on the Koniker farm.

Timmie and I were as restless as Poppie. We didn't have enough to do. So we fox hunted with Old Fox in the Essej Trants' forest, going to the summit on clear nights and listening to our hounds chase the fox. And in early April, still with a surplus of food, for we didn't want to lessen our food stamps' buying power, Old Fox helped us to get two more hounds—Bullwhip from Perry Hayes for sixty dollars, and Cannonball, a young fox hound, for twenty dollars from Jerry Davis. Old Fox knew the hound-dog dealers. And he knew how to bargain. Now, we had six hounds and Old Fox had six and with twelve hounds we could really have a chase. Often we sat before our woodfire where the high winds bent the flames back and forth and we listened to the sweetest music in the world until midnight.

And after we came home from school, Timmie and I took long walks into the Koniker woods. This was good exercise for us after riding school buses and sitting in the school room all day. We were well fed at home and with two free meals, breakfast and lunch, at Landsdowne County Central High. When we took these long walks in the woods, we were greatly disturbed at the possums we found dead. Our well-fed hounds, which Old Fox and we didn't keep in kennels or keep tied, were free to roam. And being well fed, and in happy moods, with their tails arched over their backs, they had excessive energies, too. They got out and hunted alone. They roamed the woods without their masters. And they killed wild game.

What hurt Timmie and me and made us cry was when we found a mother possum and four young possums dead— with their tails wrapped around their mother's tail. We found possums dead everywhere in the Koniker woods. And to see a dead possum with the hair slipping from its body—a dead possum in the rain—made us sick. This was their country. And food was not plentiful for them as it was for us and our hounds. I wished we could have put the possums on food stamps, too. We read in the Landsdowne County News how people were hungry in East Pakistan and India. How they were starving to death. We couldn't believe anybody in the world was hungry. "It is too bad," I thought, "they can't be in good old America—especially Ohio on food stamps."

75 In April, with blotches of green coming to the Ohio pastures and meadows, with plows making furrows again, turning up the dark farm soil in the best farm land in America and in the world—Timmie and I were more restless. And it made Poppie so restless that he walked among the trees to hide himself on the Stetson Koniker farm.

It was in April that Clarissa Jo said she would be home for her spring vacation. And she said, in a letter to Mommie and Poppie, that she was bringing her boy friend home with her. When Poppie and Mommie got her letter, Poppie said: "A boy friend! I thought she was going to Ohio State to learn!"

But Timmie, Tishie and I knew that when Clarissa Jo returned home with her boy friend, Tony Bartelli, a strange name to us, that she would be wanting to dance. So Tishie and I, Timmie and Maryann practiced with our rock-and-roll records. We pulled the rug back so our shoes and slippers struck sparks on the hardwood floor.

And this time Clarissa Jo didn't ask for Uncle Dick and Leonard to come and get her and her boy friend Tony Bartelli. When they came home, they were in Tony's go-go car.

Well, there was a word for Tony. I'd heard of this word. Candy-ankle. He couldn't have picked berries or hoed corn and tobacco with my sister Clarissa Jo! He was a well-dressed college student—not like any of us. When sister Clarissa Jo brought him in and introduced him to us, he was really not among his kind.

Mommie, in her condition, was a little plagued when she was introduced to Tony. But when Tony told her he was one of ten children this made Mommie feel better. She didn't ask him if he was a Baptist, either. But the name Bartelli was foreign to Mommie and Poppie. It wasn't a name we'd ever heard of on Lower Bruin. Tony, a tall, black-haired, black-eyed, well-dressed boy was really nice. His name could have well been Perkins, Herbert or Auxier.

But, I'll tell you one thing, when Tony saw the six fine-looking hounds in our yard that came up barking to greet him and whiffing the scent of him—all six, well-fed, happy hounds with their tails arched over their backs—he began to take notice. And one paid him a hound's compliment of trying to use his leg for a toilet. Timmie scolded old Scissors just in time.

And when he looked at our home, he got a surprise. When he looked around inside he got another surprise—pretty, papered living room, new TV, new chairs, carpet on the floor and nice lacy window curtains.

"Say, what does your father do?" Tony asked me.

"He's in semi-retirement," I said quickly.

This stopped Timmie from telling the truth. I thought of another answer for Tony's question but I didn't say it: "Our Poppie does everything he can for a living."

"Tony, in here is where we'll dance tonight," Clarissa Jo said.

She took him into her old room, now occupied by Tishie and Maryann. In this room we had the stereo, we pulled the carpet back off the pretty hardwood floor, and in this spacious room we danced.

"Pedike, Steve Koniker, nephew to Stetson Koniker, will be here with his drums this evening," Clarissa Jo said. "He's the best drummer at Ohio State! He'll put so much bang into the rock-and-roll music we'll have to close the doors and pull the windows tight!"

"Have you told Poppie and Mommie he's coming?" I said.

"No," she replied.

"I'll tell 'em," Timmie said. "We're going to dance!"

So Timmie ran for the living room.

"Tishie, is our extra bedroom all right?" Clarissa Jo asked. "Tony and Steve will be staying with us tonight."

"Yes, it's prepared," Tishie said.

We had the extra bedroom with one big double bed. But we'd never had a guest in it. We'd never had a guest to spend a night with us since we'd lived in Ohio.

Now, Clarissa Jo, Timmie and I took Tony for a walk to show him the barn, the cattle and the mules. And we showed him the old-fashioned mule-drawn farming tools and wagons Mr. Koniker had on this farm. He was impressed with everything we'd shown him, especially the herd of white-faced cattle, cows with their suckling calves and the big one-ton bull, Old Pap, more gentle than any hound in our yard. We kept Tony out with us while Tishie and Maryann, under Mommie's supervision, prepared the evening meal.

When we returned, our evening meal was on the table. And Mommie and Poppie had us all at the table—the Little Ones and the Babies too. When Tony saw our family at the table he said: "What a nice big family!"

Not one of us said anything when he bragged on us. We'd been bragged on many times before. This wasn't anything unusual.

There were T-bone steaks for all of us except the Little Ones and the Babies. We had slaw, sliced tomatoes, green beans, peas and early roasting ears that had been shipped in from Florida or California.

"Just one thing I'd like to ask you and I don't mean to be inquisitive," Tony said. "Are you people Catholic?"

"No, we're not," Poppie replied in his slow, soft voice. "We're Baptist. We don't know very much about the Catholic religion. There were none where we come from back in the old country on Lower Bruin!"

"We met our first ones in Landsdowne County Central High School," Timmie said. "We've got several in school! I know because they eat fish on Fridays."

Tony Bartelli's face spread in a smile. Then he burst out laughing.

"Well, I grew up Catholic," he said. "But I don't go to church any more!"

"You ought to go back to your church," Poppie warned him. "That was your people's faith!"

Now Clarissa Jo smiled.

"Poppie, I've been going to the Presbyterian Church and I like it," Clarissa Jo said. "I'll never go back to the Freewill Baptist Church!"

Mommie didn't say anything. But she and Poppie looked at each other with little quick glances.

"Tony's on O.S.U.'s baseball team," Clarissa Jo said. "He's a good baseball player!"

Well, we knew very little about baseball.

"What position do you play?" I asked him.

"I've pitched and I play center field," he said. "And I'm not bad with a bat if I do have to say it!"

We ate our T-bones. We put away the food. And the way Tony Bartelli could eat, I felt sure he'd not been used to a full table. And I wondered how he'd be able to rock-and-roll to our fast music!

After we'd left the table, Timmie and I gathered up the steak bones, plus a few loaves of bread, and we took Tony out in the yard with us to show him how we fed our hounds. This would give my sisters time to clear the table, put food away and get the sleepy babies down in their bed for naps.

Tony was interested in the way we had to separate our greedy hounds so they wouldn't fight over their food. Timmie took old Scissors down to the corner of the yard and gave him his steak bones and a half-loaf of bread. I took old Rags to the other side of the yard and gave him his bones and bread. Each stood above his food and growled at the other hounds. Then we hurried and fed the other four their bones and bread. When each had his food, all began eating greedily but growled as they ate.

Actually, Tony Bartelli clapped his hands and laughed as he watched our hounds eat! We could tell that he was not only fond of Clarissa Jo but he liked our family. I wondered if he wouldn't like to be my brother-in-law some day!

About seven another go-go pulled up and Tony and

Clarissa Jo ran out to welcome Steve Koniker. And when Poppie and Mommie knew that Stetson and Clarissa Jo Koniker's nephew was coming with the drums they never said a word against our dance. They were really against our dancing in their home, but this was Stetson Koniker's mansion.

Steve Koniker was six feet tall, red-headed, slender, wearing loud-colored striped pants, bright green shirt, with a yellow scarf tucked down at the neck. His hair was a little long and he wore sideburns. We helped him carry the big bass drum, which he pedaled with his foot, and his snare drums into the room. How one man could operate all these drums, I couldn't understand. Well, we carried the drums in and then we introduced him to Poppie and Mommie, who had never seen a young man dressed like him. I thought they might as well know and get used to it. This was Ohio State University. This was modern Ohio and America. This wasn't Lower Bruin.

Now, Steve Koniker was ready to get with the rock-and-roll recordings on our stereo. And he didn't have any trouble following these recordings. As he went through an exercise his body rocked and rolled. He shook all over and he would shout: "Get hot! Let's go!"

And so we went! Tony and Clarissa Jo! Tishie and I! Timmie and Maryann! Now you talk about dancing! I'd say there was never dancing like we did in that room with the doors shut and the windows down! Poppie and Mommie never came in to watch us.

Tony told me he'd never seen anybody with the stamina to endure the fury of this dance like we could. He didn't know how much endurance we'd had plowing and hoeing on the Kentucky and Ohio hills. And he didn't know how we'd practiced these dances! I thought Tony, the baseball player of Ohio State, was the weakling. Steve Koniker could get all over his drums! He could make them talk! He was our drummer boy, all right! And when Tony and Clarissa Jo said he was the best at Ohio State, I was sure they were telling the truth.

Occasionally, Steve rested from his drums. He stopped and danced with Clarissa Jo, while the rock-and-roll records played on our stereo. Steve, Tony and Clarissa Jo knew each other well at Ohio State. And Tony and Clarissa Jo had danced many times while Steve had played the drums with an Ohio State University band.

Our dance ended at two in the morning. There'd never been anything like this in our home! Steve left his drums in Tishie's and Clarissa Jo's room. We rolled the carpet back over the floor. And then, Timmie and I took Steve and Tony to their bedroom and showed them the upstairs bathroom. They must have been very tired. I knew Timmie and I were ready for bed and a few hours sleep.

Eight o'clock was a late hour for us to arise. But when I awakened Tony and Steve they thought they were getting up early at eight o'clock. Poppie and Mommie had eaten their breakfasts and had fed the Babies and the Little Ones. So, on this morning, we had a second breakfast—Steve and Tony, Clarissa Jo, Tishie, Maryann, Timmie and I. We ate bacon, eggs, jelly, toast—we drank our juices—and we drank plenty of black coffee to awaken us for the day.

After breakfast, we carried Steve's drums to his go-go. He wanted to stop first at his Uncle Stet's and Aunt Clarissa Jo's before driving back to Columbus where his parents lived. He thanked us for a great time. He was on his way.

Next to go was Tony. He packed his belongings in a suitcase and he thanked my parents and all of us for one of the greatest evenings and nights he'd had in his life. And again, he spoke of our wonderful family and our half-dozen hound dogs.

Right now, I knew with Clarissa Jo's contacts at Ohio State we had moved into a new society. We'd never known anything like this on Lower Bruin in the old country South of the Border—and we'd not known anything like this in Ohio at Landsdowne County Central High, the Freewill Baptist Church or in Agrillo. We were on our way! I didn't know where we were going! But we were going somewhere!

Money and free living had made the difference. Money we couldn't spend! Money where there was no taxes! Money now in three banks! Living in a mansion rent free! No wonder people had said America was the greatest country in the world! No wonder Ohioans had said Ohio was the greatest state in the union. I could agree to this! But I couldn't understand how people were starving in other parts of the world! Why didn't they have food stamps and welfare?

How could all the reports we read in our paper be true about the poor people starving in Appalachia when they now had food stamps and welfare—not as much, maybe, as we had—but as Poppie had said they should be living "high on the hog." Food stamps and welfare was a good living in America. Who would want better? Of course, Poppie had a few extra-special benefits thanks to Uncle Dick Perkins, who had the right contacts and knew how to get these.

If Poppie wasn't a rich man—and he thought he was—give him enough years the way he was going and he would be a rich man. Uncle Dick was now telling him how to invest his money instead of taking the small six percent on certificates of deposit. Uncle Dick was encouraging Poppie to make a change and to be "in the big money." But Poppie was afraid—afraid of losing what he was getting. He was as afraid of this new adventure in finance as he was of being seen working.

76 This was the first time I had ever really quarreled with Poppie. We quarreled over who was going to plow the two acres of tobacco ground.

"Poppie, Timmie and I have rented that tobacco ground from Mr. Koniker," I said. "I'm supposed to plow it!"

"But, Pedike, my muscles are getting soft," Poppie said. "Come spring without anything to do—not even sacks of grub to carry five miles on my back—I get nervous. A real he-man is like an animal. He has to work. It's hard just to do light little jobs like taking the mules and wagon and hauling a few salt blocks to the pasture. I like to follow mules between the handles of a plow and see the green sod turn over!"

So I let Poppie plow the tobacco ground. He was a restless, worried man. And he never plowed except on a couple of Saturdays when my sisters were in the house with Mommie. Mommie could hardly rise up from her chair after she'd sat down and when she sat down, she dropped down fast.

School was much the same, except I was a senior and this would be my last year ever to go to school. When the Ohio Scholarship Achievement Tests were given again this year, I was average in my class. This time Tishie was first in her junior class by six points to spare. And brother Timmie was off and gone in his sophomore class. He led our high school. Tishie and Timmie were in the upper-one-percent bracket in the State of Ohio. We were no longer called "briars" but Timmie was called "Brain Number One" and Tishie was called "Brain Number Two." They were sure candidates when they finished high school for getting a free college education with all expenses paid plus fifty dollars a month spending money. Timmie had confided to me his ambition was to be, someday, Republican Governor of Ohio. I told him he'd come nearer of reaching his ambition if he'd been born in Ohio and not on Lower Bruin in the old country. And I wasn't so sure that our living a free, easy life on welfare and food stamps would help him.

When school ended and I graduated, there was no ado over my graduation as there had been when Clarissa Jo graduated. I wasn't a top honor student. But Poppie, Timmie and Maryann were there; Tishie stayed at home that night with Mommie. We'd been expecting her to go to the hospital any day or night for two weeks. I was the first male among my father's or mother's people ever to get a high-school diploma. Clarissa Jo was the first from either side ever to graduate from high school.

77 We had been very lucky. The morning after I graduated from high school, Sister Tishie called the ambulance to come in a hurry to take Mommie to the hospital. She called Uncle Dick. And she called Dr. Zimmerman that Mommie would be in the hospital as soon as the ambulance could come and take her. Poppie had never got used to a telephone. He would have fit in Ohio better in the days when pioneers were clearing patches of wilderness and fighting Indians. Now, due to circumstances mostly beyond his control— circumstances our Federal, State and local governments had created for poor people—Poppie was in a very good way of life, living as free and easy as the wind he breathed. He was getting rich but he wasn't happy.

When we were in the yard watching for the ambulance, our six friendly hounds gathered around him, whiffing his scent, barking, growling and pawing the dirt. I heard him curse for the first time in my life.

"Get away from me, you damn sons-of-bitches," he said. "You worthless bastards are better fed than a lot of people back in the old country!"

These words had never been in Poppie's language before! And when he gave our hounds the back of his hand, they knew he meant it. They scattered in a half-dozen directions.

When the ambulance pulled up, two men rushed in the house and put Mommie on a cot and hurried back with her to the ambulance. She was moaning, groaning and in a heap of misery. Poppie got into the ambulance beside Mommie and was holding her hand when they left the hill. All of us but the Babies and the Little Ones were out to see her off.

Now, Timmie, my sisters and I were in charge of our home. Mommie wasn't in any shape to worry. But she wouldn't worry with sisters Tishie and Maryann at home. And Poppie knew Timmie and I would be masters of the house and look over all. We had been trained to do this.

While Mommie was at the hospital, Timmie and I were restless. We walked in the yard. Sisters Tishie and Maryann took care of the Little Ones and the Babies in the house. And they listened for a phone call.

As I walked the yard, thoughts came to my mind. Uncle Dick, our elderly rich uncle, was always with us in a time of need. He accepted our family as if all of us, including Poppie and Mommie, belonged to him and Aunt Susie.

Now, there was all this bad blood between Poppie, Mommie, Cousins Faith and Bos and even to Buster Boy and his common-law wife, Widow Ollie Mayhew. We were still not on speaking terms. Mommie and Poppie had picked up here and there at church and in Agrillo the slurring remarks they'd made about us. Tishie, Timmie, Maryann and I had picked these up from students in school.

Buster Boy had a good job with the Ohio Highways Department, yet his common-law wife, Widow Ollie was on welfare and food stamps for herself, her five children, and naturally for Buster Boy, for he ate with them and saved his money. Just as Poppie had told us: "People who lived in glass houses shouldn't throw stones!"

So what right had Cousin Faith and Bos not to speak to us—and to go around Agrillo, at the Freewill Baptist Church, to people at the Stock Market and tobacco warehouse, talking about our new riches obtained through a welfare check, food stamps, and free everything for us when we didn't pay taxes and they worked and paid taxes to support us?

Sister Tishie and Maryann prepared our lunch just as if Mommie and Poppie were home. They fed the Babies and the Little Ones. And we'd eaten our lunches and Timmie and I had fed our hounds before the phone call came— Tishie called Timmie and me from the yard into the house.

"Guess what—boy or girl?" Tishie said excitedly.

"Boy," I said.

"Girl," Timmie said.

"Both right," Tishie replied in great excitement. "Can you believe it? Mommie does have twins. First in our family! Dr. Zimmerman was right in his prediction!"

We were excited. Mommie now had fourteen living and one gone. Our Little Mommie was thirty-six. I wondered what big Poppie was thinking now. He must have been a very happy man. We were happy at our home. We rejoiced with all the brothers and sisters in our family. Now to think Little Mommie had twins.

"More food stamps," Timmie said.

"Shut up," I said. "We can't eat all we get now with the food stamps we have. We have to feed our food to six hounds. And we need from two to four more hounds to take care of our surplus."

"But it's because we have too many Little Ones and Babies," Timmie said. "Wait until they grow up! We'll have to have four hundred dollars instead of three hundred dollars worth of groceries a month! You wait and see! I've been right most of the time!"

Leonard and Uncle Dick brought Poppie home at about five in the afternoon, for Poppie wanted to see how we were getting along. Poppie and Maryann stayed at the house while Timmie, Tishie and I went to the hospital. I took them in my car to see Little Mommie and our twin brother and sister. I took them in a hurry to Landsdowne County Hospital.

"Two at a time, Mommie," Timmie said. "Think of it! This is great!"

I thought it was great, too, to see a little boy and girl like little pink mice without hair I'd seen in the fields so many times when I'd plowed the fields—little mice Poppie, Timmie and I had protected and had never killed although considered destructive by farmers.

We'd not been in the room with our Little Mommie very long until in walked Uncle Dick with an unlighted cigar in his hand.

"Sil, I have the names of your twins," he said. "I've been thinking since these can be the last you ever have. I've talked to Dr. Zimmerman—never any more children. If another one, it will be Sil's life—and we don't want to lose her. And now for the names—not Sylvia and Gilbert—these are not twin names. But Gil and Sil are twin names and most appropriate for your last two!"

"Gil and Sil, wonderful," Timmie shouted. He, in his excitement, jumped up and cracked his heels together three times. "For Poppie and Mommie!"

"Right," Uncle Dick said. "Gil and Sil, wonderful names for twins. Let us pray they're healthy and they'll live!"

So they were named Gil and Sil for Poppie and Mommie. Each baby was over seven pounds. No wonder Dr. Zimmerman predicted Little Mommie would have twins. She carried almost fifteen pounds of sister and brother. And in one week Mommie was home from Landsdowne County Hospital. And you talk about a household of Little Ones and the Babies, we had them.

Martha was now nine. Could you believe we had Little Eddie, Susie, Little Dickie, Faith, Little Josh, Baby Brother Little Dan and now Baby Brother Gil and Baby Sister Sil—eight more since Martha in a time of nine years? Well, we had. Talk about work, Mommie, Sisters Tishie and Maryann—and now even Martha—had work to do. And since big, muscular Poppie wasn't working—couldn't work—he helped in the home with the Little Ones and the Babies.

78 I couldn't tell you sister Clarissa Jo's reaction when Tishie phoned her at Ohio State that Mommie had had twins, Gil and Sil. Tishie wouldn't tell what Clarissa Jo had said. But I'm sure she wasn't very happy about it. And if I could guess her attitude, she told Tishie: "Thank God, I'm no longer there to be a babysitter, a nurse, a second mother! I'm free at Ohio State University." Actually Tishie confided to me Sister Clarissa Jo had said this. She didn't want to come home. She was happy to remain at Ohio State for the summer and continue her work there.

Sister Clarissa Jo now away from home, dancing, making her usual top grades, had deliberately refrained from coming home to help our family. And who could blame her? I couldn't! Sister Clarissa Jo was free at last. She had decided her religious faith, too. She'd be a Presbyterian—the faith of the Konikers—and from Mrs. Koniker she'd borrowed her name!

Now, I thought about how she had worked in the corn and tobacco fields—how she had picked berries—how she'd worked to improve herself. And how free food, free money and free gifts had helped my sister. Yet, all of this had separated her from us. Free money which we couldn't spend, free food, all of which we couldn't eat but had to feed to our hounds, was making our family soft. We were falling apart as Poppie thought we would do.

To think of birth was something mysterious to me. After conception of a baby between my father and mother, how a baby could grow and form, be a living child to make one of us of different personalities and different looks—all of this was mysterious to me. And when I heard my mother's tubes had been severed and tied—that she could never be pregnant again—the dream had died! I'd never dreamed of marrying and replenishing the earth. I didn't follow the Bible. I didn't believe this sort of thing—but Mommie and Poppie did—even at the public's expense. Poppie could have never made a living for all of us in this modern world when he wasn't a modern man. He couldn't have made a living for us by his days laboring on a farm with his ax, behind the handles of the plow following a muleteam, or with his hoe. An earth man in this modern day and time in the progressive state of Ohio, in America—most progressive country in the world—couldn't live by the primitive labor of his ancestors on Lower Bruin.

Despite Mommie's and Poppie's producing children, smartest in Ohio along with average children like me, this had to come to an end. Maybe Mommie could have gone on to nineteen—I don't know. Now, our family, fourteen living children and one deceased, had ended before Little Mommie had reached her thirty-seventh birthday. But, there were so many things against us—we were a public charge. The people's tax money was keeping us. And I had the feeling deep in my mind and heart this was not right.

Even back on Lower Bruin, I had observed the black starling birds and their brown wives that we had called "cow birds." These birds were the worst pillagers I'd ever seen in the world of birds. And these brown cow birds laid their eggs in other birds' nests for mother birds to hatch and to raise. They were real parasites! What did they contribute? Were we not the blackbirds and cow birds? I began to think we were.

79 Through the summer, Brother Timmie and I farmed our two acres of tobacco, and we had so much leisure time on our hands. We were like our father. We didn't know what to do with ourselves. I could manage a tractor and I mowed over Stetson Koniker's pasture fields to mow sprouts, Scottish thistle and obnoxious weeds.

But Poppie drove the muleteam, put salt blocks in place and kept an account of the white-faced cattle. He did his obligations on the Stetson Koniker farm.

In June we had to buy two more hounds, which Old Fox Underwood helped us purchase—to care for our surplus food. We purchased Birchfield for one-hundred dollars and Boss for fifty-five. We now had eight hounds. And all summer long we fox hunted with Old Fox. What else was there to do?

But in August Timmie and I bought shotguns and we squirrel hunted with Old Fox. We'd never squirrel hunted before. But Old Fox taught us how. We killed the little creatures and gave them to Old Fox. We didn't need them, wouldn't eat them—not when we could get the best steaks, broasted chicken, fish and the choice of pork cuts.

Sister Clarissa Jo was not interested enough until the end of the summer term at Ohio State to come home to see her twin sister and brother. In August she returned to spend a week with us. But she was restless and anxious to get back to Ohio State. And in September, Timmie, Tishie, Maryann, Martha and Little Eddie went back to school. And Little Susie entered her first year. But I was out of school. I didn't have work. I had to wait until November when I would be eighteen before I could begin work at "public works."

Now with my brothers and sisters in school, Ohio State University, Landsdowne County High School and Agrillo Junior High and Elementary—and Poppie and Mommie at home with the Little Ones and the Babies, I had only— and with the help of Poppie—to take care of Mr. Koniker's tobacco, and this was play work.

I spent much of my time in September and October with my friend, Old Fox Underwood, possum hunting with our hounds and later fox hunting on the summit. There wasn't anything else for me to do now except drive members of my family to the dentist and doctor and to Agrillo to get food stamps—and to Cantwell's Super Market to buy our food with food stamps.

Uncle Dick took Poppie to get his checks and to the three banks in three counties to deposit his money. And this was the routine of our lives at this time. We were a rich and well-to-do family. We no longer belonged to Lower Bruin in the old country. We were genuine citizens of a world North of the border. And we would never return to Appalachia, that land South of the border.

Uncle Dick had promised me that when I finished high school and when I was eighteen, he would see to it I would have one of the best jobs in Ohio for a man laboring with his hands. And, after all Uncle Dick had done for us, we hadn't any reason to believe he would not be right. He had, so far, been right on everything for us. And I know that the thoughts of my leaving home, driving back and forth to my work in my car, worried Mommie, for who would drive the stationwagon for them when I was gone? Timmie wasn't quite old enough and he might be a poor risk, for he was terribly excitable. Tishie said she didn't have any desire to learn with her last year of high school coming up—she wanted the number one spot, valedictorian, and planned to get it.

But Mommie solved this problem while Poppie, Tishie and Maryann took care of the Little Ones and the Babies. Mommie employed John Bess, an older man from the Driver

Education School in Agrillo, to teach her to drive the stationwagon. She paid him eight dollars and fifty cents an hour to teach her.

"What if I do pay this much an hour?" Mommie said. "We'll save the money we don't need in the long run on car insurance. Being my age and a parent, I can get car insurance for much less than Pedike, who safe as he is, has to pay two-hundred-forty dollars a year, due to his age."

And Mommie was right. Teenagers had to pay a high insurance because of their speeding. But it would certainly seem strange to see Little Mommie driving the stationwagon with our family to the Freewill Baptist Church. Strange to see her driving to Agrillo to the Market and stores and other places with Poppie inside, helping my sisters take care of the Twins, the Babies and the Little Ones. But Mommie soon learned to drive the stationwagon. So when I left the hill with my car, there would be another driver at our home.

80 On November 26th, the day I was eighteen, Leonard and Uncle Dick came in Uncle Dick's car to get me and to relieve me from my boredom—Poppie and Mommie were out to see me get into the car. They were happy to see me off to attempt to get the first real position with industries and to be a real wage earner.

"Pedike, I hope you make it," Poppie said. "You're a good worker. You've always liked to work!"

"You're my oldest living son," Mommie said. "I wish for you the best!"

Now we were off to Agrillo where Leonard stopped at Dr. Zimmerman's office. And here Dr. Zimmerman gave me a physical checkup. I stripped, was weighed and examined from head to toe, before Uncle Dick took me to the DuPont Chemical Plant eighteen miles west of Agrillo.

"I wish I had your body," Dr. Zimmerman said. "You're a healthy young man—sounder than a silver dollar!"

And now we were on our way to the plant.

"It's all set up for you, Pedike," Uncle Dick said. "Since you want to work with your hands I want you to have the best-paying job in these parts."

Uncle Dick and I sat on the back seat. Uncle Dick smoked one of his ten-inch cigars. Leonard, all alone up front did the driving. And he also did the listening.

"Now, you'll find out what Dr. Zimmerman and I told you about taxes," Uncle Dick said. "I've asked the bossman, Carlo Henri, to explain to you the difference in what you make and your take-home pay."

We arrived at the plant, parked on the lot and Leonard, as usual, waited for us. We walked over to the main office.

"Mr. Henri, here's my nephew, Pedike Perkins," Uncle Dick said. "There's not a young man in Ohio better to work than he is! Here is his medical report—sound as a silver dollar from head to toe, so Dr. Zimmerman said, and he's just examined him."

"I'm glad to meet you, Pedike," Mr. Henri said as he took my hand with a good squeeze. "Your Uncle Dick Perkins here has told me a lot about you, how your family —a big one—has worked and struggled!"

I didn't know what Uncle Dick had told him. But I knew Uncle Dick had been smooth in recommending me.

"Yes, I'm one of fourteen children," I said.

"You're smart children, too," Mr. Henri said. "Good in school.

"I'm the average one," I said. "I like to do with my hands, I believe, more than with my head."

"Well, you're hired here," he said. "You can come and start work tomorrow."

Mr. Henri was short, broad shouldered, clean shaven, dressed in a gray business suit with pale blue shirt and blue necktie. He looked very much like a school teacher. Only he had very quick actions. I could tell he was a man who got things done. I was sure he was a native Ohioan.

"You see, Pedike, your Uncle Dick Perkins came here in person and explained everything to me and this is the reason you're one of six being hired to work here," Mr. Henri said. "All the young people of this area want to work here! Look over there stacked on the desk by the window at the applications! There are over twelve hundred. And we're hiring only six men now! You're one of the six! Later, maybe, about April of next year, we'll hire twenty or more men!"

I couldn't believe I was one of six hired from all that stack of applications.

"Many of the applicants are college graduates," he said. "There are scores of excellent men among those hundreds of applications! We are privileged to choose the best!"

"Show my great-nephew, Mr. Henri, the difference in earned pay and take-home pay," Uncle Dick said. "This will show him something of the taxes he'll have to pay!"

"Here's a copy of a young beginner's pay check," Mr. Henri said. "See, you start at four dollars an hour. Sounds like big money. Eight hours a day, five days a week—paid each two weeks. See, straight time and no overtime he earned three hundred twenty in two weeks—six hundred forty a month! Not bad wages! But look at his take-home pay after taxes and other deductions!"

When I looked at this take-home pay for two weeks, I was shocked.

"Over a fourth goes out," I said. "But I want this job. It certainly beats hoeing corn and plowing mules on a hillside for a dollar an hour!"

And I did want this job. And I was lucky to get it. Thanks to Uncle Dick, I'd 've taken this job if I'd had to have paid half my salary in taxes. I knew I couldn't go on living like I was living at home—hunting with hounds—not doing anything. Feeding our hounds free food to absorb what we couldn't eat! It wasn't right.

I thanked Mr. Henri. I told him I'd report in the morning. This time I gladly squeezed Mr. Henri's hand with the strength I had in my good hands. I had hands like Poppie's.

When we stepped outside the office, I thanked Uncle Dick. I squeezed his big soft hand. I was a happy young man when we went to Uncle Dick's big car. I opened his car door for him. He thanked me. I closed the door behind him and walked around to my side. I guess this was the best manners I'd ever shown toward him.

"Well, you got your job," Uncle Dick said. "I like to see a young man who wants to work in these times. And I like to see him happy when he gets a job!"

Now, as Leonard drove Uncle Dick's car back to our home, I was in a dream. I wondered about ever eating food-stamp food again. The purpose of food stamps to help the real poor who couldn't help themselves was all right. But now everybody was cheating on it. What had happened and was happening to the people in Appalachia, Ohio and all over America? And what would be our destiny as a nation if we continued? As a young man, I knew I'd work. I'd never be connected with food stamps.

Uncle Dick had said the system was wrong and the only way to defeat it was for everybody who could to jump on the bandwagon and ride it into the ground. I knew in our home where we didn't have any place to spend our money because everything was free for us, if Poppie kept on banking his money in three banks—if time didn't run out on him—he might even someday have a Dun and Bradstreet rating.

But now I remembered a word Cousin Faith used: "Pride." Cousin Faith and Cousin Bos had worked and paid taxes. But they could have qualified for welfare, food stamps, and this richer American life.

I began to feel a new pride swell up in me before Uncle Dick's big automobile reached our home. It was a good feeling, too. I knew when I got married I would not marry to replenish the earth. I wouldn't be like the starlings and their brown cowbird wives that laid their eggs in other birds' nests for them to hatch and raise their young. My wife and I, if I married, wouldn't have more children than we could feed and educate. And like sister Clarissa Jo, I might even be a Presbyterian.